TO SLEEP NO MORE

In the fourteenth century, Oriel de Sharndene, the beautiful daughter of a Sussex landowner, is married off to the retarded brother of the Archbishop of Canterbury; three centuries later, Jenna Mist, wife of the village carpenter, is hanged for witchcraft; in the eighteenth century, a highwayman captures the love of the delightful Henrietta Trevor – three apparently unconnected events, or are they? This panoramic novel skilfully interweaves past and present, fact and fiction, exploring the enigma of reincarnation through the ages.

'A chilling, compulsive read, vividly brought to life and guaranteed to keep you turning the pages.'

Prima

'Accurate historical detail is linked to fiction in an entertaining novel.'

Yorkshire Evening Post

About the author

Dinah Lampitt was born in Essex but spent her formative years in a haunted cottage in Chiswick. She started to write at the age of five but burned all her early novels as they were 'awful'. Later she worked in Fleet Street for *Woman*, *The Times* and the old *Evening News*, who published her short stories and gave her her first chance. Known for her skilful blending of fact and fiction she has written three novels, *Sutton Place*, *The Silver Swan*, and *Fortune's Soldier*. She has a daughter and son and lives in Sussex in the valley of Bivelham, just outside Mayfield, the setting for this book.

'In this fine historical romance, love defies time, with souls in torment, reincarnations and all that. A good mixture of fact and fiction, fascination and fate.'
Woman's World

To Sleep No More

Dinah Lampitt

CORONET BOOKS
Hodder and Stoughton

First published in Great Britain
in 1987 by Michael Joseph Ltd.

Coronet edition 1988

British Library C.I.P.

Lampitt, Dinah
  To sleep no more.
  I. Title
  823'.914   PR6062.A485
  ISBN 0-340-42541-5

Printed and bound in Great Britain
for Hodder and Stoughton
Paperbacks, a division of Hodder
and Stoughton Ltd., Mill Road,
Dunton Green, Sevenoaks, Kent
TN13 2YA (Editorial Office: 47
Bedford Square, London WC1B
3DP) by Richard Clay Ltd.,
Bungay, Suffolk.

CONTENTS

ACKNOWLEDGEMENTS

I should like to thank all the people of Mayfield who went to such enormous trouble to help me with this book by opening their houses, showing me their cellars, climbing into tunnels, walking smugglers' roads and poring over maps. They are the unsung heroes. Particular thanks must go, however, to Viscount Hampden of Glynde, Gillian Bramley of Great Bainden, Isabel Pike of the Baker family and Deborah Richardson-Hill for the enthusiasm they showed in assisting my research.

                              To die: to sleep;
No more; and, by a sleep to say we end
The heart-ache and the thousand natural shocks
That flesh is heir to, 'tis a consummation
Devoutly to be wished.

                              Hamlet

PROLOGUE

The Legend

A sealskin twilight and nothing moving in the stark winter valley but a solitary figure, grey-clad, making its way barefoot across the snow. Nothing breathing, nothing stirring, the only signs of life the blood trickling from the woman's feet and a curling wisp of smoke hanging above a low dark building set at the forest's edge. Yet, though dusk outside, through the open door of the place came a glow red as the drops falling like rubies on ice, and the shadow of a blacksmith bending over his furnace was that of a giant, thrown on to the winter landscape by the light behind him.

In the brightness the smith did not see the woman come to stand in the doorway and watch him, nor did he see her fall like a broken flower to the forge's harsh earth floor; but he turned as she called out, 'If you do not help me I shall die,' and hurried to raise the fragile body in his arms.

Her hood fell back as he moved her and he found that he was looking into the face of beauty, and both gasped and shuddered. He who had risen so high in God's service and had ruthlessly trampled down the longings and needs which beset all mortal men, was frightened to be in such proximity.

'Help me,' she cried again and he raised a pitcher of water to her lips and watched her drink.

He felt life return to her, saw her sit up and say, 'What place is this?'

The smith hesitated for he did not want her to know his secret. 'This is my forge in the forest of Byvelham, Lady.'

'And you are a blacksmith? Just that? Nothing more?'

'I am also a servant of God.'

'And your name?'

'Is Dunstan, Lady.'

She smiled at that and the smith saw black lashes and mistletoe skin and eyes clear and pure as fresh water. Dark memories stirred within him; of forbidden love when he had been a noviciate, of his role as kingmaker rather than churchman, of

3

strange thoughts and dreams and desires which had tormented him all his adult life.

Staring at the darkness outside, Dunstan felt a bleak mood come upon him. He seemed to see his life as adviser to the Saxon kings as one of self-gratification not service; believed that the son of Edmund the Magnificent had been right when he had labelled Dunstan magician and sorcerer; felt that the boy King Edgar had been misdirected to disagree and reward Dunstan of Glastonbury with the See of Canterbury itself.

Beside him the woman groaned and the smith, who was in truth archbishop of all England, saw that a pool of blood had formed at her feet. Going outside to fetch more water he realised that it had started to snow again, the flakes coming down so fast that he and the stranger seemed cut off from the world in the hidden forge on the edge of Sussex's great forest.

At that Dunstan was more afraid than he had ever been in his life. For the woman who lay on the earth floor – so fragile, so harmless – was utterly dangerous to him. As the archbishop began to bathe her tattered feet he knew that he must not look at her, must not cast his eyes on that perfect face if he were to stay sane.

She knew it, of course, because she said, 'Why do you avert your glance? Gaze at me, Dunstan.'

It was a command, said darkly so that he must obey. He looked up and saw that her eyes were cool, clear lakes in the depths of which a snake had suddenly uncoiled and raised its head. He no longer had free will, the archbishop was a boy to be initiated. He bent forward and kissed her and tasted passion; sweet as blood, red as wine.

'I am yours,' he said. 'Do with me what you will.'

She laughed and his eyes feasted on the curve of her snowdrop throat.

'Then I claim you as mine for ever.'

As he bent his lips to hers again, Dunstan looked down and just for a second saw clearly. Gone were the woman's poor torn feet and in their place he glimpsed scales, horn, unspeakable nails. He knew then that he was in the presence of the darkest power of all.

A moment of madness came. A moment in which he wanted to fling himself down and love her and give her his body and his soul in one vast ecstasy that would make damnation something

4

to be eternally longed for. And then it was over and the archbishop was once again God's pawn, a man who must act out his destiny.

Reaching behind him, Dunstan's hand closed upon his iron tongs, lying red-hot in the depths of the furnace. He pulled them out and thrust them hard and furiously into that exquisite face. He smelt burning skin and heard a scream turn to a shriek as Satan lurched to her feet in agony.

'Be damned to you,' she said. 'I will fight you and your kind till the end of time. You can corrupt my beauty but never my power.'

Too afraid to look at the destruction of such a perfect thing, Dunstan collapsed into a corner, his hands covering his eyes, and did not move until quietness throbbed in his ears like the roll of waves. The forge was empty. Where the woman had been there was now nothing but a single unmelting snowflake.

Moving very slowly, like a man come suddenly to old age, Dunstan began to pack up his things. The fire was doused, the tongs that had disfigured the Devil were plunged, hissing, into a wooden bucket. Then, fearfully, the smith stepped out into the darkness, mounted his horse and rode off solitary into the silent white world which lay before him. And all the time one question repeated itself again and again in his thoughts, 'Why should I have been the one to violate perfection? Is such a reward not a punishment?'

Knowing that the answer would never be revealed, the Archbishop of Canterbury headed through the valley of Byvelham to the hamlet of Magavelda, where lay his church and hall, and where he might, on his knees, ask God for guidance in the savage hours beyond midnight.

PART ONE

The Stone Palace

ONE

That evening the sun set like blood, turning the waters of the moat into wine, and tinting the cob and pen who dwelt thereon to birds of fantasy, pink of wing and purple of eye. To the west the sky took on a rich and royal glow, reflecting the mighty blaze of crimson as it vanished beneath a sweep of indigo. The bitter winter day of 1333 was ending in triumph.

'Tomorrow will be fine again,' said John Waleis from the window.

The figure which sat hunched over the chess-board, its chin cupped in its hand, did not reply.

'Fine and bright – a day for hunting the winter fox. Will you come with me, Robert?'

In the dusk of the hall the chess-player smiled and drew nearer to the hearth which glowed in the middle of the chamber, his dark green robe brushing the floor as he moved. His shoes of soft brown leather, a design like a wheel upon the front, were held up towards the fire as he said, 'No, not I. I'll stay here and rest my bones. You may challenge the elements, John. I would rather keep myself warm.'

Still without turning his companion answered, 'You are getting soft. There was a time when you would hunt and carouse all night and think nothing of it.'

'Time passes, my friend. Remember I have become a king's man since then. Old wild ways are best left for you.'

'I never thought to hear Robert of Sharndene speak defeatist words.'

'No? Why? It is your name not mine that is linked with boldness. Wicked Waleis! You had earned that nickname before you were fifteen.'

John turned with a laugh, his silhouette looming dark behind him.

'Mad blood, Robert. That is my heritage.'

'So you say – often! Now sit down. I am anxious to finish this game. My thoughts are already on tomorrow and I am bored with chess-play.'

'Tomorrow?'

'Don't blank your face at me, Waleis. You know perfectly well what I mean. The archbishop's arrival and banquet.'

There was a pause during which the two men stared at one another appraisingly. Just for a second they looked very alike although they were, in fact, dissimilar to an amazing degree, John Waleis being dark and well made – a barrel-chested man with quick, bright eyes the colour of ale, and black hair which rippled to his shoulders, and Robert of Sharndene being small and light, brown of hair and skin, yet with eyes grey as a frosty October. They spoke Norman-French, as did all those born to high degree, but now they lapsed into the language of the race conquered by their forebears.

In English John said, 'Christ's body, Robert, but you're growing pompous. It is too much high office. Bailiff of the Liberty of the Archbishop, Steward of Battle Abbey. If you're not careful you will end up black-tongued from licking boots – and other things not as low.'

Robert smiled, the left hand side of his mouth twitching up, the rest of it remaining still.

'Quite probably. But if you take my advice – for all the fact your family has cocked a snoot at Canterbury these many years past – you will watch your tread with the new archbishop. He's no lily boy in a pretty robe.'

'No.' John Waleis's face was dark, unreadable, as he watched his host throw another log, still specked with traces of snow, on to the spluttering fire. 'No, I believe you're right. I hear he models himself on Becket.'

'He feels an affinity with him, yes.'

John's great white teeth flashed in a smile and his gusty laugh, booming as a bear's, rang out.

'Then I hope for his sake that he does not end the same way.'

'That remains to be seen. But don't underestimate John of Stratford. He is a kingmaker. Edward will always owe his crown to him.'

They sat in silence, staring into the fire, but seeing instead the long-haired warrior king – the third in England after the Conquest to bear the name Edward – and the terrible events, in which Stratford had played a leading part, and which had led the forceful boy to ascend the throne at fourteen years of age.

Eventually John said, 'The King has finally rewarded his liege man with the primacy. Perhaps now he feels he has paid him back in full measure.'

Robert of Sharndene smiled his crooked smile. 'The King inherited in guilt. He will never forget that as long as he lives.'

'Rubbish,' said John roundly. 'He has forgotten already.'

Robert would have retorted, loving these arguments. All his adult life he and his rumbustious neighbour – younger than he but as clever – had been debating with skill and wit the topics of the day. But now he was not to be indulged, for a voice from the back of the hall said, 'Sirs, we are summoned to dine,' and Alice Waleis stepped forward into the light of the fire.

Small in stature with a slanting elflike face, Alice was in every way a match for her boisterous husband who expansively called 'Coming wild heart,' picking up Alice's fingers and brushing them with his lips. At the same time as he did this, his free hand shot out and fondled her buttocks, but she, her face expressionless, merely slapped him away as if he were an offending fly. She addressed herself to Robert.

'You will not think it rude if we depart immediately after dining? The truth is I dread these bleak nights. And tomorrow when I attend the archbishop I would like a fair face.'

Her host smiled, leaning back in his chair. He had always had more than a sneaking regard for Alice, liking the way her nose turned up at the end and her lips curled easily into a smile.

'You are always fair of face,' he said.

'If only that were so.'

Still without a flicker she knocked John's hand away again and then turned to the far end of the hall, where a great table stood on a raised dais. There, watching the bustling servants stood Margaret of Sharndene, frowning a little, and beckoning her husband to come and take his place at the head. Alice turned back to her host.

'You have spent too long at chess. I think Margaret is annoyed.'

He stood up, giving a comical sigh.

'She is never otherwise these days. She is poised between middle age and old, and has all the ills and heats and tempers to go with it.'

And truly as Alice drew nearer she could see that the face of her neighbour and closest woman friend was flushed and red, her mouth drawn down at the corners in a testy way. John, swarming up behind like a spring breeze would have none of it. He cheerfully raised Margaret's hand to his lips, allowing his tongue to wander in and out of her fingers.

'You are Eve's serpent, Margaret,' he said. 'When you are furious your eyes shine and you look twenty again.'

She glared at him but then relented. John Waleis, for all he was forty and gaining weight, held an irresistible charm for the opposite sex. Cajoled, she sat down as Alice did likewise, and it was then, with her husband and her guest in their places, that Margaret's daughter and son, Oriel and Piers, came hurrying in to dine.

As always, when she looked at them, Margaret felt torn between warring emotions. She knew that she should be grateful for their very lives – for had not seven of the ten children she had borne Robert died at birth or in infancy? But, still, her true affection was for the only other survivor: her first-born, Hamon. Even now, even here, sitting at her dining table amongst her guests, she could remember the sweet sensation of suckling him at her breast. Jesu, but she loved him so much! Great grown man and knight of King Edward that he was.

'... forgive us, Mother?'

Piers was speaking in that strange, fluting voice of his. She sometimes wondered about him; what he was thinking, who his friends truly were. Often he would take to his horse and be away for several days, returning with an odd look behind his eyes and no explanation for his disappearance. The fact that Robert berated him for such misdemeanours did not seem to worry him at all.

But it was the sight of Oriel that really caused Margaret's heart to plummet. It was not easy for a woman who had been considered plain from the cradle to give birth to beauty. But she, ugly Margaret of Sharndene, had done just that. Of course, Margaret had always made the best of her appearance, painting her lips and eyes and tinting her face as Queen Eleanor had once taught women to do and they had emulated ever since. And, also, by wearing clothes of fine stuffs and colours and moving her thighs at the sway and trailing her robe, she had done well enough and married Robert of Sharndene – heir to a fine moated manor house – when she had just turned fifteen.

But Oriel needed to contrive nothing. For some reason – for Robert was merely small and clever and of no particularly handsome feature – Margaret's daughter had been bestowed with all natural gifts. Hair the colour of silver gilt hung to the waist of a small firm body. Yet if Oriel had been as misshapen as poor Benjamin Button, who ran through Maghefeld with a hump on his back, she would still have turned heads. For she had a lovely face, with eyes bright as forest bluebells, lips the colour of rowan berries, and lashes dark as nightshade.

Trying to hide the jealousy that caused her such pain, Margaret controlled her face and said, 'Where have you been? Did you not hear me call?'

'In the solar, looking at the sunset. Oh Mother, did you see it? The moat turned red for a moment or two.'

'No,' said Margaret huffily. 'No, I did not. I had other things to do.'

In the tiny silence that followed John said, 'I saw it. It was like fire and wine and blood.'

Oriel nodded and gave him a smile and, much to his horror, John felt his heart begin to thump beneath his tunic. He turned his gaze away only to find himself having to steal another glance. This was the first time he had realised the daughter of his friend was not only beautiful but desirable.

To hide his embarrassment he said, abruptly almost, 'High time you had a husband, Oriel.'

Everyone stared. It was not at all the thing to discuss, least of all over the dining table. Marriages were things of dower, land and political gain and of considerable concern to fathers from the moment of a daughter's birth. In fact it was known that Oriel had been pre-contracted for years already.

'I agree,' Margaret put in surprisingly. 'I was married at Oriel's age and pleased to be so. And a year after that Hamon followed.'

'Yes,' murmured Piers in the background. 'Let us not forget dear Hamon.'

His mother turned a hostile face to him but, seeing the servants approaching through the screened arches at the far end of the hall, bearing wooden platters of food, decided to let the matter go. Piers, on the other hand, was in a mood to be witty

13

and pursued his line, despite a sharp kick from somebody's remonstrating foot.

'My brother is a brave knight,' he went on to no one in particular. 'He has seen action in Scotland and now serves the king at Court. He is a lion of a man in every way. But then, of course, he is very much older than Oriel and myself, being Mother's first-born son.'

Alice, detecting at once the underlying tone in Piers's voice, looked at him sharply from beneath her pointed brows.

'And will you emulate him?' she asked. 'Will you fight in Scotland as well?'

A hand, rather white and wearing an over-large ring, fluttered in her direction, and Piers was about to hold forth when Robert said, 'No more talk of war, please. Let us enjoy our food,' and everyone fell silent. Various meats, already cut into slices that they might be better eaten by hand, were served together with a huge pigeon pie – the feet sticking up through the pastry to denote its content. Strips of winter deer, closely packed about with red jelly, were also set down as well as a huge jug of hares.

By way of changing the subject Robert turned to Alice. 'Have you met the new archbishop?'

Her pixie face creased into a smile.

'Robert, do not tease me. How could I when I spend all my life hidden away? Why, I am such a bumpkin that a journey to London is a major event.'

Robert smiled and said, 'I think you will like him. He is very – powerful.'

'And godly?'

'Who knows with an archbishop!'

They laughed and John said, 'Stop playing court to my wife. Oriel is watching.'

The girl's cheeks brightened at his words and Alice Waleis wondered yet again how poor Margaret – with her thick pig nose and heavy lidded eyes – could have borne this nymph. If John had not told her of seeing the new-born babe for himself and tickling it with a bony finger, then she would have taken Oriel to be a changeling.

As the girl blushed again every head in the hall turned to look at her. In the sudden silence the voice of a rosewood gittern played by a servant suddenly struck up a plaintive tune. Other than that there was no sound at all in the moated manor house of Sharndene.

Just as the winter sun reached its highest point in the heavens, the party escorting the Archbishop of Canterbury left the close confines of a wood and began to climb the steep slope that lay before them.

First to leave the shadow of the trees were the mounted knights in jangling chain mail, ready to defend the primate with swords, while behind them followed a medley of tonsured monks dressed in plain brown habits and looking like a moving field of stubble. In the press of all those horsemen it was not easy to see the man whom they sought to protect, yet he rode there quite solitary in the midst of the cavalcade. For John of Stratford – the most powerful man in England, save only the king – was coming to his palace at Maghefeld.

Clad in a mantle of crimson, his glittering eyes, the colour of rock crystal, seemed to shine in stark contrast, while within the depths of his hood his grey hair, cut short and closely cropped around his head, looked like a silver halo. At fifty-four years old the archbishop was a handsome man, strong-featured, with the hands of an angel and the body of a whip. Yet there could be no doubt that behind his quiet expression seethed a complex being. For Stratford had a wild, dark history which did not bear too close an examination.

The riders reached the top of the hill and stopped, the escort leader – a massive knight with a scar across both cheeks and the bridge of his nose – trotting back to the archbishop's side.

'There, my Lord,' he said. 'There. That's the palace of Maghefeld.'

He pointed a gauntleted hand and Stratford followed the line of his finger. From the high scrub-covered plateau on which they found themselves – as bare and bleak as the roof of the world – they could see for miles, everything stretching out beyond them in a great pattern of woodland, fields, and shining rivers.

'There? To the right?'

'Yes, my Lord.'

'It looks very grand. And this wooded valley on our left is, I take it, Byvelham?'

'Aye, my Lord, that's it. John Waleis's domain.'

15

Stratford remained impassive.

'It has a magic air,' he said.

Without changing expression he stared down into a beautiful dale, rich with the colour of woodland and field. The escort leader, watching him, wondered what he was thinking, this crimson-cloaked figure who some said was Thomas à Becket born again. But there was no hint as to what went on behind the light, unblinking eyes and after a while the knight broke the silence.

'If you have seen enough we should be moving on, my Lord. I would like you safely within the palace in the hour.'

'Just one more moment.'

The primate's gaze flickered over the valley of Byvelham once again. 'It is said that somewhere down there St Dunstan had a forge and indulged his hobby of metalwork. Do you know its location?'

'No, my Lord, that has vanished long since.'

'Ah well. There will be little chance of finding it I suppose?'

'I'm afraid so, my Lord.'

The leader crossed the short distance to the front and, raising a hand high above his head, shouted, 'Forward,' as the archbishop's retinue moved off, skirting the valley to their left and plunging downhill and into the woods before they emerged at the village of Maghefeld.

It had never been quite clear to the See of Canterbury why Dunstan of Glastonbury, the Saxon archbishop and statesman, had chosen to build himself a church, a home and a forge in this most remote of spots. But the fact remained that he had done so. Yet now, nearly three hundred and fifty years after the death of the saint, nothing of the original wooden buildings was left. It had been Archbishop Boniface who had started to build a palace of stone and this effort had been continued by his successors, and completed by Archbishop Reynolds, who, nine years before, in 1324, had overseen the raising of a magnificent great hall. The Archbishop's Palace had been complete.

So it was with some excitement that Stratford clattered his horse over the cobblestones and dismounted, swinging himself out of the saddle with a wiryness that only a spare frame could allow.

The palace soared to a considerable height, the tower at the west end of the hall rising some sixty feet, whilst at the east end

16

the main buildings stood three storeys high. He had an overwhelming impression of Sussex sandstone buttresses, fine windows and delicate arches, feeling a sense of jubilation at the magnificence of the building. And it was in this mood that Stratford first strode into the palace, his heart lifting and his crimson mantle billowing in the late afternoon wind.

As soon as he was through the door the servants dropped to their knees and the great ring of Canterbury, worn outside the primate's gloved hand, flashed in the gloom as it was raised to lip after lip.

'God's blessing upon you all,' he said, making an extravagant sign of the cross.

'And on you, my Lord.'

Stratford bowed his head and turned to make his way up a broad stone staircase, his flock of monks labouring beneath his baggage. At the top his steward, deferentially leading the way, took him through two rooms, each growing in magnificence, until they reached the most beautiful of them all. Stratford found himself in a great chamber, running from west to east and occupying one entire side of the courtyard round which the palace was built. Through the magnificent west window the sun glowed in a scarlet ball, turning the interior into a blazing paradise.

John of Stratford could think only of one thing. 'Did Becket sleep here?' he asked.

The steward hesitated.

'It is thought, my Lord, that the room is not quite the same . . . But certainly the north wall containing the small chapel and the garderobe is over a hundred years old. It is believed they were there in the time of St Thomas, yes.'

The archbishop did not reply, a curious frozen quality coming over his face. The servant wondered for a moment if the primate was deaf.

'Will that be all, my Lord?'

Stratford answered at once. 'Yes, all for the time being. But wevere . . .'

'Yes, my Lord?'

'Tonight, after dark, when the banquet is at its height, a man will be brought to the kitchen door and given into your care.'

The steward stared blankly.

'A man, my Lord?'

17

'Yes.' The archbishop turned away, throwing his gloves and cloak onto the great bed that stood adjacent to the fireplace. With his back turned to the servant, he added, 'I want you to take care of him and give him his own room in which to sleep. It need only be a small place but it must be for him alone.'

Wevere coughed into his hand.

'Would it be presumptuous, my Lord, to ask who he is?'

'Yes.' Stratford wheeled round, his eyes hard as stone. 'It would. Just treat him with the love and respect you give me. Is that understood?'

'Yes, my Lord.'

The steward bowed before the primate, his mind already full of gossip for the scullions.

'And Wevere ...'

'Yes, my Lord?'

'I do not want this to be mentioned to anyone else. Keep your own counsel and you will not go unrewarded.'

'Certainly my Lord. Will you wish to be informed when the gentleman arrives?'

'Very quietly, yes.'

The last view the steward had of the archbishop was that of a gaunt figure standing motionless, staring out to where the sun fell below the forest in a mass of black ribbons and ochre fronds. But later that night Stratford was in an entirely different mood when he saw the preparations which had been made for his banquet in the great hall, the food and wine for which had been brought to the palace earlier that day by his tenants, as ancient custom decreed.

The central brazier was aglow with a mass of wood brought from the forest, the smoke wisping up to the great roof, made of timber and supported by three giant arches, and out through the louvre above. Every twig that burgeoned could be smelt in that wonderful blaze. So much so that the entering guests, used to choking on smoke wherever they went, stopped in the entrance and sniffed the sweet smell of burning logs before they progressed on their way to the dais at the end of the hall where sat the new archbishop, his crimson robe sweeping the floor and the hand bearing his great ring outstretched for all to kiss.

All this warmth seemed to gleam in the wine already laid upon the table in pitchers of clay, the dull dark glow of liquid picking up the reflection of rush lights and fire, and this, together with the sandstone of the hall, the merry carved figures upon the pillars and the sumptuous gleam of the archbishop's plate, all combined to make a welcoming scene on that cold and cheerless February afternoon.

The very first to arrive at the feast and bow his knee was Robert of Sharndene. Clad in a cotehardie of moleskin with hose of evergreen, he presented a slight but formal figure, while behind him ugly Margaret had painted so well that for a moment Stratford thought her handsome. Immediately after them came Piers and Oriel, the former very fine with pendant flaps upon his elbow, and she rather sombre in deep blue. The archbishop thought her an arresting beauty for such a remote and unremarkable Sussex village. There must be something about the place which produced characters, he concluded, for big Sir John Waleis of Glynde and his elfin wife were no exception, kneeling before him and murmuring apologies for old Sir Godfrey – John's father – who had grown infirm and never ventured forth these days, not even for an archbishop.

No sooner had they taken their places at the table on the dais than another extraordinary figure minced towards Stratford to pay her respects. Quite tall and extremely gawky, the woman was dressed in a long-trained kirtle of quite the finest stuffs, and her fret, holding her hair like a net beneath her barbette, was of goldsmithry. The archbishop took her at once to be a wealthy widow.

As she came closer he could see that it was not only her figure that was strange. For beneath pale, short-sighted eyes, the widow's mouth stuck out like an archer's bow, fighting to close over a very large protruding tooth. But despite all this Juliana de Mouleshale obviously considered herself fair and attempted a simpering smile as she sunk on both knees before the primate.

'My Lord,' she cooed.

Stratford hastily withdrew his fingers and found them taken immediately by an unprepossessing boy.

'My son James,' breathed Juliana.

Like his mother in looks, the poor youth laboured with the additional handicap of a forestation of spots and pustules. Stratford muttered something inaudible and passed on to the next arrival.

Within half an hour all the wealthy inhabitants of Maghefeld and Byvelham had arrived and taken their seats round the

19

tables. On the dais with the archbishop sat Sir John and Alice Waleis, together with Robert and Margaret Sharndene. On the lower tables were settled the archbishop's more important tenants: the families of Petuon, Cade, atte Combe and de Cumden, as well as Agnes de Watere, Peter Guliot, Adam de Rysdene, Nicholas le Mist, Thomas atte Red and Laurence de Wanebourn. But two latecomers, Isabel de Bayndenn and her husband, were found places near the dais.

'It must be witchcraft,' Stratford heard Juliana de Mouleshale murmur to her son, as she stared penetratingly at the woman who had just taken her seat. 'No one of sixty could look so young without casting a spell.'

Unperturbed, the archbishop stood up, clasped his hands together and began formal benediction, being unable to resist, however, the opportunity of looking his company over while their eyes were closed. He noticed little things. That John Waleis had a sprinkling of silver starting in his dark mane; that Oriel's eyelids shone; that Piers Sharndene, who was sitting next to James Mouleshale, had his fingers on the table and that one of them was keeping up an unrelenting pressure on James's hand. A question mark formed in Stratford's mind but his voice droned the Latin phrases without falter.

Down the body of the hall he saw Nicholas le Mist slip out quietly, presumably to relieve himself, for he returned a few minutes later grinning and tugging at the skirts of his gipon, only to be given a reproving look by Agnes atte Watere. Nicholas leered and made an obscene gesture to which, surprisingly, she reciprocated in kind.

The archbishop cleared his throat and brought the prayers to an end. Then he raised his wine cup and said, 'May the blessing of God be with you – all of you.' Just for a second his eye flickered over Nicholas, who looked unrepentant.

Then Stratford drank deeply, both beautiful hands supporting the jewelled vessel.

Gazing at the primate, John Waleis caught himself thinking of the story about the archbishop and the young king disguising themselves as merchants in order to travel abroad unnoticed. A man to be reckoned with, without doubt. John watched as Wevere the steward entered from behind the dais and whispered something in Stratford's ear. He saw him nod, ask a question and appear satisfied with the answer. But Waleis could hear nothing of the words spoken, for, without warning, the band of drum, flute, shawm, fiddle, psaltery and bagpipe took to playing with enormous enthusiasm. The banquet proper had begun.

Outside, the darkness of late afternoon crept round the palace but within there was warmth and light and laughter. The wine flowed freely and a succession of dishes were brought in for the guests, haunches of venison glazed with frumenty, roast swans done up in their feathers, peacocks and pheasants and a great, grinning boar's head.

But amongst all that noisy company, chattering like a flock of startled birds, one person was silent. The archbishop, drinking little and eating frugally, sat observing all. He saw John Waleis's eyes grow dark with wine and his wife's smile deepen; saw Robert Sharndene's glance run swiftly over the younger, prettier women; saw Piers work his fingers slowly from James Mouleshale's knee to his thigh; saw Nicholas le Mist return from outside, a second after Agnes atte Watere, a happy smile on his face.

Wevere the steward came and bent over Stratford's ear, asking if another cask of wine might be opened. The archbishop smiled and nodded, listening to the sound of music and laughter and seeing the fine clothes and jewels, though paltry indeed by the standards of the Court, that the assembly had worn in his honour. Then suddenly he stood up.

'You may feast throughout the night, my ladies, sirs. I must to my prayers and rest. It was a hard ride from Canterbury today.' Then without another word Stratford swirled through the archway and out of their sight. A dramatic gesture that left his assembled visitors gasping.

'Well?' said Robert Sharndene slowly.

'You're right,' answered John. 'No lily in a pretty robe. Have you noticed how he freezes suddenly, as if he's left his husk?'

'Yes. I believe he does it when he thinks. Strange trick though.'

'I wonder what he thinks *about*?'

'Murdered kings and powerful queens perhaps.'

'Careful Robert. I am the one with the reputation for speaking out. I wouldn't like to see you play my tricks – and get into trouble for them.'

Robert would have replied with a laugh – he had drunk

21

enough not to care too much for appearances – but a tug on his sleeve made him turn his head. Juliana de Mouleshale stood beside him, her eyes screwed up to look at him.

'Robert,' she said abruptly, 'I want to see you.'

Sharndene nodded discourteously.

'You do see me. I am before you.'

She glared at him furiously. 'I meant that I wish to call upon you next week about a matter of business.'

'I see. Well, when do you wish to visit?'

'Next Monday. In the morning. Perhaps if Margaret could also be present?'

'Margaret?'

'Yes, Margaret. Now I must be on my way. Goodnight to you.'

'One day I will strangle that old hag,' said Robert loudly to her departing back.

'Not that old, in fact,' answered John. 'She gave birth to James when she was scarcely fourteen. She is little more than thirty-five.'

'She looks older.'

'Because she is hideous.'

Margaret coming up suddenly said, '*Who* is hideous?' She was always sensitive if the subject of ugliness came into the conversation.

'Juliana. She wants to call on us on Monday to discuss business. And she wants you to be present. What can it be about?'

'I've no idea,' answered Margaret, 'unless ...' But she stopped short, refusing to put her thoughts into words – and no amount of persuading would make her change her mind.

But Alice had guessed.

'Juliana wants to marry James to Oriel,' she said, as she and John climbed the hill to Bayndenn, the house which was his home whenever he visited Maghefeld.

He turned to look at her, his dark face serious.

'God forbid!' he said.

'I'm sure I am right.'

Their two horses, side by side in the blackness, picked their way through the snow with delicacy.

'But, if I remember rightly, was not Oriel contracted at birth to Gilbert Meryweder's son?'

22

'He has not returned from a Scottish raid. He has been missing for nine months.'

'Christ's holy blood, Robert would never agree to James. Would he?'

The edge of doubt had come into his voice as the massive oaken door, the lower entry to the manor, swung open in response to their manservant's shout. Through the doorway they could glimpse the hall, and the servants sleeping round the dying embers on the hearth.

'Robert is ambitious,' said Alice, her eyes slanting at her husband. 'He has come a long way already. If he wishes to proceed further it might be of great help to ally his daughter with Mouleshale money.'

Both John and Alice shivered as the door closed behind them and a sudden wind moaned round Bayndenn and blew from the unglazed but shuttered slits of the windows above them.

TWO

A morning mist lay heavily over the valley of Byvelham, a white vapour clinging to the gentle sweep of land and dark-treed forest; while from the surface of Tide Brook and the moat of Sharndene, the fog rose like steam. Yet on the high plateau beyond the wood the sun shone like a parable. And even stolid Juliana, as her horse climbed upward, was struck by the thought of emerging from the Devil's shadow into the bright beam of God's goodwill. So much so that she reined in for a moment or two on the summit, gazing with difficulty about her, her eyes narrowed to slits in her plain and uncompromising features.

All around the land was transformed into a white sea, with trees sticking up like the masts of ships and the tops of hills little islands. The view was beautiful in its silent unearthliness, and so convinced was Juliana that she was alone that she thought, at first, that the great cross rearing up out of the clouds was an illusion of her inadequate eyes.

But then her ears, all the sharper for her dimness of sight, caught the distant jingle of caparison and she realised that a cavalcade was coming from the direction of Maghefeld and guessed at once that the archbishop was riding out. For no reason – for she had not seen the primate since the night of his arrival and had no real need to avoid confrontation – Juliana drew back into the fog.

The procession passed within a few feet of her – the men-at-arms, the monks, the man of God himself. Swathed in thick, warm fur, looking neither to right nor left, the archbishop's face had a curiously impassive quality, as if he contemplated something so mighty that he must give his whole mind to it. And yet, as he drew level with her, his light eyes flickered in her direction. For a moment she thought he must have seen her – but there was nothing. No sign that he had done anything but slightly alter his gaze. Unnerved, Juliana watched as the entire complement headed east, realising why it was she had not wanted to speak.

There was something about Archbishop Stratford that frightened her. She felt that neither her wealth nor her jewels would impress him; that all her postures and poses would be completely wasted on such an elusive and withdrawn personality as his.

Somewhat subdued by these thoughts Juliana descended from her vantage point to the edge of Combe Wood. Here the visibility was poor and she was glad to leave the trees again for the open country round Sharndene. She, who feared nothing - or so she said - had thought a voice had called her name as she first entered the forest's shadow.

So it was with a nervous glance over her shoulder that she finally went down into the basin of fog in the centre of which lay her destination. And a few moments later, as she entered Sharndene, she hugged herself with a little shiver of relief.

'Are you cold?'

It was the handsome Piers, whom James admired so much, bowing before her till his sleeves, tight to the elbow but then vastly flared, swept the floor. For all he was a country creature, the young man was well dressed to the point of caricature, sporting fine materials and fashions far too grand for his rural surroundings.

Juliana sparkled her tooth and dropped a curtsey. 'No thank you, God 'a mercy.'

Piers smiled a shade too broadly and said, 'Then God be thanked. And thanked too, dear lady, for the colour of your kirtle.'

Juliana looked at him suspiciously but decided at length that he was paying her a compliment. She fluttered a laugh and was fractionally annoyed to hear Robert Sharndene say, 'Good day to you. My wife awaits you in her chamber.'

Piers bowed his way out without another word and there was nothing for Juliana to do but follow her host.

Sharndene had been built by Robert's grandfather, John, in 1260 and was, to Juliana's darting eyes, grandiose indeed; even rivalling Mouleshale, which was but twenty years old and decorated with every kind of ornate embellishment.

From a passage behind the hall a wooden staircase led up to the family quarters above the kitchens. And there, dressed in her finest kirtle and cotehardie sat Margaret de Sharndene, playing at needle work, her small eyes anxious above her broad nose. She stood up as Juliana came into the room and said 'Welcome to Sharndene, Madam. Please sit down and tell us why you have honoured us with a visit at last.'

'Very well,' Juliana answered, folding her hands in her lap. 'I have come to see you about Oriel.'

'Oriel?'

Robert looked startled and Margaret doom-laden.

'Yes. It is now almost a year since Gilbert Meryweder's son vanished in Scotland and he has been mourned by his family as dead. I take it, therefore, that Oriel is without a contracted husband at this time?'

'Y-e-s.'

'I'll not mince words with you, Master Robert. I want her as a bride for *my* son James. And I am prepared to accept her without dowry in order to achieve that.'

There was a stunned silence broken by her host finally saying, 'Why?'

A curious expression crossed Juliana's face. 'For some foolish reason, my son has set his heart on Oriel. He says he is in love with her.'

'In love?' Margaret spoke for the first time, her voice rising with amazement. 'Why, I have never seen him so much as look at her. Are you sure?'

'That is what he said. To be frank, I am as surprised as you are.'

Robert shook his head. 'I don't know what to say, Madam. I cannot help but feel there is something odd about his declaration.'

'What do you mean, Sir?'

'If he had ever paid her any attention it would not be quite so startling.'

Juliana's features became slightly menacing. 'I have never contracted a bride for James, Sir, because it has always been my wish that he should have a free choice. When I was married to Martin de Mouleshale I cried for three whole months. He was already sixty and I just thirteen.'

'So?' Robert made an irritable movement, shifting his weight from one foot to the other. Juliana ignored him.

'James came to me as my salvation. He was my baby, my pet, my darling.' Her usual manner returned. 'And that is

26

why, unconventional though it might be, I want him to have the bride of his choice. I am making an exceptional offer. I will accept your daughter with no dowry at all. What say you?'

The sun pierced the grey world outside sending a shaft of light through the window, straight to Margaret's feet. She spoke without even looking towards her husband.

'We will consider it,' she said. 'We must talk privately. You have taken us by surprise.'

'Yes,' added Robert slowly. 'I had not thought of anything like this. I had wondered perhaps if a younger son somewhere ...'

Juliana gave a contemptuous snort. 'Younger son! I thought you to be an ambitious man, Sir. I thought you to aim high. Christ's Holy Body, you mention younger sons in the same breath as James de Mouleshale!' She rose to her feet. 'If it were not for his wishes I would tell you to forget what I have just said to you.'

She was seething with fury, her eyes angry knots and her brows drawn.

Robert calmed his urge to shout back at her and said smoothly, 'Please, Madam! Obviously we are very surprised. But it is indeed an offer to which we will give every consideration. We do realise the honour you have done us.'

He loathed himself, almost hearing Margaret say 'hypocrite'. Juliana, however, appeared slightly mollified and sat down again, taking a good draught of ale from the cup set before her.

'So when will you let me have your reply?'

Margaret spoke again, still not looking at Robert.

'In two days, Madam. You see, I should like in that time to ask Oriel what she thinks.'

'Oriel?'

It was Juliana's turn to look amazed.

'Yes, Madam. As you have given freedom of choice to James perhaps we, unusual though it might be, should give our daughter the same opportunity. Husband?'

Robert stared askance but Margaret's face had the heavy, determined look which he knew from long experience meant that she would not be shifted.

'Very well,' he said reluctantly.

Juliana rose once more. 'Then I look forward to a successful outcome and an early wedding.'

As the three of them left the chamber it suddenly filled with light, the sun emerging from the mist and painting the day golden. Juliana, the last to descend the stairs, gave a little cry of pleasure, made all the more heartfelt by a glimpse below of the handsome Piers, now dressed in fur and obviously preparing to ride out. Her heart beat slightly faster as he raised his eyes to hers and gave a flourishing bow.

And as she stepped from the house and her horse crossed the drawbridge, the widow heard Piers's voice behind her raised in song. She turned to look over her shoulder but the young man was climbing out of the hollow in the opposite direction to the one which she was taking. Juliana's pale eyes grew great with a sudden rush of tears before she turned slowly back again and headed purposefully home.

Far out in the fields beyond Bayndenn the hawk hovered above a mouse, its wings etched against the sun like gauntlets. Looking up at it Piers de Sharndene shielded his eyes with his hand, craning his neck back to watch its savage power. As it swooped he let out a laugh of joy.

It was a glorious late winter's day, the sweeping landscape bathed in pale afternoon sunshine. Everywhere the trees were in full ripening bud while the fields, the dark green of monastery herbs, made the hills, old and majestic as time, seem to rise above them like clumps of mint.

Piers laughed again and undid the top buttons of his cote-hardie, his dark curling hair bright beneath his wide-brimmed, feathered hat.

'I love you,' said James de Mouleshale.

'I know,' answered Piers, hardly bothering to look down to where his companion lay sprawled upon the ground, his hood rolled up into a cushion for his head.

'Do you like the hawk?'

'Of course I do. Why do you ask?'

'Because I want to hear you say so. It is important to me that you are pleased with the things I give you.'

James sat up as he spoke, his short-sighted eyes – almost identical to his mother's – blurring with anxiety. Piers gave him a narrow look and then squatted on his haunches, his face close to that of his friend. He adopted a sincere and earnest expression.

'You know how much I love your gifts, James. They are the most precious thing in my mundane life.'

James gave a grateful smile but said bitterly, 'Not as mundane as mine. Think of being cooped up in Mouleshale with my mother – and all the time just wanting to be with you.'

Piers looked sympathetic.

'Not a pleasant state I agree. But not for much longer. As a married man you can be out and about and Oriel must stay at Mouleshale doing women's tasks for the lady of the house. And serve her right.'

'Why do you say that?'

'Because she is so despicably weak.'

James stared at Piers curiously, his fierce battalion of spots red and sore-looking in the bright light.

'You won't ever grow to hate me, will you?' he asked.

Piers's face softened and he leaned forward and put one hand on the ugly youth's shoulder.

'No, James,' he said. 'For you are so harmless. Why, I believe you would sooner be dead than do me an injury.'

James put his bony hand over Piers's fingers.

'You know I would,' he said. 'I would gladly lay down my life at your feet.'

Piers turned away, the hawk swooping towards his wrist, its prey in its talons.

'I think I will go away,' he said casually.

'Next year, when you are eighteen?'

'No, I cannot wait that long. I am bored with relying on my father's money – I want my own. Will you come with me, James? You and I will be brothers-in-law soon.'

His friend looked ecstatic.

'How well that sounds,' he said. 'To be kin folk with you. Yes, of course I will come. It will be Oriel's duty to stay with my mother, not mine. But she has not agreed to marry me yet.'

Piers turned sharply.

'What do you mean, yet? She has no say in the matter. My father is too grasping to turn down your mother's offer. You are incredibly foolish sometimes, James.'

For a moment his friend looked mutinous. 'Not all the time,' he mumbled.

The hawk lurched off again towards the sun.

'Do not speak of it further,' answered Piers grandly. 'Let us go hunting like that creature. Who knows what we might find?'

THREE

In the dark hour just after midnight John de Stratford galloped his horse through the sleeping valley of Byvelham on his way to the palace. All about him night creatures stirred at the intrusion of thrusting hooves, but he ignored the slither of snake and scuttle of shrew, his expressionless face set firmly towards Maghefeld, his flowing mantle the only thing that pointed back in the wind towards Canterbury.

He was a complicated man, with as many layers to his extraordinary personality as there were in a flower bulb, lying beneath the dark soil and waiting to shoot forth colour. And though many people thought they knew the archbishop, believed they were able to judge his mood and varying thought processes, they were wrong. No one understood John de Stratford. He was an enigma. He had depths to him which he had not fully explored himself.

Above everything, of course, there was his very personal relationship with God. Unlike other men of his time Stratford was not riddled with superstition and fear; rather he stared God in the eye, not as an equal, but most certainly not as a shivering supplicant. For the primate thought of himself as one of the chosen. He believed – and had done from his youth – that he was destined for eminence. That he had been singled out to be raised above the heads of his fellows and that, provided he kept his bond with the mighty force that controlled destiny, nothing and no one could stop his inevitable sweep to greatness.

Yet, strangely, this concept had given him no complex of superiority. He merely expected, as his right, every door to open for him. In this way he was almost like a war horse, charging on to his fate unassailed.

But beneath this invulnerability there lay a darker side. For he was capable not only of thinking black thoughts but of putting them into deeds. John de Stratford was a plotter, a natural assassin. A man who would wait endlessly for revenge and, even after years, feel the thrill of its execution.

Yet alongside this facet lay compassion, a love of beauty and kindness. It was a strange, disturbing nature, hidden beneath the portrait that its owner wished the world to see. Stratford sometimes had the mystic idea that he was Thomas à Becket born again. That every emotion he felt had been experienced at some time by the martyred archbishop.

Now, as he headed for his palace, his heart began to race. Tonight he would kneel and pray in the small, private chapel where the saint had knelt before him. For though Stratford could walk in the very steps of Thomas at Canterbury, there was an intimacy at Maghefeld that somehow made him feel closer, more at one with the spirit of the murdered man.

Excitedly, Stratford left the woods and the territory of his neighbour John Waleis and took the first steps to his own domain. He was now little more than three miles from his destination, and a suggestion of a smile softened his otherwise impassive face. He rode alone tonight: no escort, no cross before him, except the one on his breast. In fact he had slipped quietly away from the cathedral's protection and taken the pilgrim's way, crossing the border from Kent to Sussex in the darkness. Not a star had glimmered, the night being full of rushings and stirrings and clouds racing overhead. But now, as the dark shape of Maghefeld Palace rose before him, brilliant points of silver threw an answering gleam from the canopy of pitch above.

The porter who took his horse looked startled.

'My Lord! You were not expected. All are sleeping. I must wake the scullions to prepare food.'

'No, no. Some fruit and wine in my chamber is all I require. Has Wevere gone to bed?'

'Long since, my Lord. Shall I wake him for you?'

As Stratford strode up the great staircase he shook his head again.

'Let no one be disturbed on my account. I shall retire immediately. If you will bring the food at once.'

The man bowed, withdrawing towards the buttery. But, having watched him go, the archbishop, instead of turning off to his own apartments climbed a stone spiral staircase to the floor above. Here he turned right and, walking through the huge and beautiful solar - situated directly above his bedchamber and occupying the whole of the palace's upper and southern storey - came to a series of smaller rooms. At the second of these he stopped, put his ear to the door and, after a moment or two, gently pushed it open.

The fitful moonlight, blotted out every few seconds by the bustling clouds, fell through the long window on to a small bed that stood inside and on to the face of the occupant. Stratford stood there silently, staring at the dark thatch of hair and pale features, and then he took a step forward. Impassively, he regarded the man who lay in an untroubled sleep.

The face at which Stratford looked could have been put together by a humorous god, for it had a snub nose, lips that – even at rest – seemed to be smiling, a sweep of thick black lashes curving down to the white cheek below. And the hands, one of which lay curled upon the pillow, were also comic. Small and broad, with short blunt fingers, they looked fit only to labour at the soil. But, nonetheless, despite his shortcomings, there was an air of fineness about the sleeper, showing that no ordinary villein slept here so peacefully in the presence of the primate of all England.

The moon disappeared totally and in the darkness the man, at last sensing a presence, began to whimper.

'Colin, don't be afraid,' said Stratford quietly. 'You are not being attacked, it is only John.'

'John? Why are you here? Wevere said you were in Canterbury and I was to be quiet.'

'Did he now? Is he unkind to you?'

'No, he likes me. And plays with me often. And he dances when I play the gittern.'

The moon flirted for a second and then came out in full. And in the rush of silver Colin sat up in bed. The archbishop looked at the tragicomic face and smiled. He had never made up his mind from the day of Colin's birth to this moment whether he loved or hated his simpleton brother. But now he only answered softly, 'I have brought you some pastries. No, don't get out of bed. You can have them in the morning.'

Colin hugged his knees with joy and then, spontaneously, kissed his brother's hand.

'You are so kind to me,' he said.

Stratford turned towards the window, his blank face for once twitching with emotion. Almost every day he wished Colin would contract some fatal illness and end the charade of his life. And, equally, almost every day the younger man would do something so sweet and innocent that the very thought of his death made the primate reel with guilt.

For here was a situation that the great and powerful archbishop could not control. For some reason that nobody understood – unless it was that their mother had been too old to give birth at forty years of age – Colin's mental age had remained that of a boy of eight, while his body developed into that of a man. Yet there was nothing in that childish nature of harm or spite. The truth was he was not quite mad yet neither was he sane. He was merely simple. A little boy encased in the shell of a man of thirty.

The archbishop turned back into the room.

'Go to sleep, Colin. I shall see you tomorrow after my morning prayers.'

'Can I pray with you?'

'No. You must remain secret as you always do. Just because we are away from London and Canterbury does not mean that you may show yourself.'

Colin's smiling mouth trembled slightly.

'Have I been naughty, John. Are you angry?'

Stratford, swinging wildly between revulsion and remorse, put his hand on his brother's shoulder.

'I will become so if you do not go back to sleep. Wevere will bring you to me when I am not busy.' He turned in the doorway. 'You are sure he is kind to you?'

Colin, snuggling into his pillow, said, 'Yes, quite sure. In fact I like it in the stone palace. I do hope we remain a long time.'

The archbishop did not answer but closed the door behind him as the moonlight faded into darkness.

That same night, less than three miles away at Sharndene, nobody except Piers – who had announced himself thoroughly bored with the entire situation – was yet abed. For upstairs Oriel was crying. And not crying quietly or circumspectly but, for one who was normally so gentle, sobbing with such a high desperate note that it could be heard even in the hall. So great was the sound that the servants had not taken their customary sleeping places around the hearth but huddled in groups behind the screens of the serving area.

In their place, Margaret, a mutinous look upon her ugly face, sat before the fire, holding her hands out to the flames and glaring at Robert, who was studiously whittling a piece of wood and trying to ignore her.

After what seemed an eternity she said, 'Well?'

'Well what?' Robert did not look up.

'You know exactly what I mean. What have you decided?'

Her husband continued to carve the wood as if there was nothing else of importance in the world. Margaret glared all the more, her heart thumping with emotion. In the few hours since Oriel had been informed of Juliana's offer, there had been a tremendous change in Margaret's attitude. The daughter of whom she had always been jealous had, for the first time in her life, become a figure of pathos. Beautiful, vivid Oriel had crumpled like a rag doll.

'Oh don't make me,' she had cried, dropping to her knees and clutching her mother's skirts like an infant. 'He is so horrible, so covered with blemishes. I would rather be in my grave than married to him. Oh help me Mother, please.'

'But he has offered for you,' Robert had put in sharply.

'No!' Oriel's voice had held a note of hysteria. 'He has never even looked at me. Why, he loves Piers more than he does me.'

Something in this remark had started thoughts going through Margaret's mind and then, looking at Oriel's face, all red and swollen and blotchy with weeping, she had felt the first stirrings of compassion. This had been followed, when she had put her arms round her daughter, with a great surge of love, almost as much as she felt for Hamon, in fact. It would seem that Oriel must be ugly in order to arouse her mother's affection.

But Margaret had not pursued this twisted path, merely glad for once that envy was not eating up her heart and resolving on the spot that Oriel should not be forced into marriage against her wishes. Margaret had then stuck out her bottom lip, put on her most intractable expression, and treated Robert to an icy stare.

Now she said, 'Are you going to answer me?'

Her husband looked up at last, though his fingers still went on working the knife over the wood.

'It is a very good offer,' he said.

'Is that all you can think about?'

She was blazing with fury.

'Margaret ...'

Robert's voice held a warning note but his wife went on undeterred. 'You know as well as I do that you despise Juliana. Yet you would consider selling your only daughter to her. Yes, I said *selling*. Nothing else but money would make you even consider allying the houses of Sharndene and Mouleshale.'

Robert looked as furious as she did, his wiry frame beginning to tremble slightly.

'Margaret, you go too far!'

'I do not go far enough! Robert, you have seen the girl. She is distraught. It would be monstrous to force her into this alliance.' Her tone became a little more placatory and she went on, 'Your father allowed you to choose. Surely that must soften your heart.'

'My father gave me the choice of two women: you or Anne de Winter. Your dowries were equal therefore it did not matter to him. That was the only freedom I had.'

Quite without bidding, tears sprang into Margaret's eyes.

'What a terrible thing to say. I had always believed you picked me because you had feelings for me.'

Robert looked contrite. 'I did, I did. All I am saying is that I was not allowed to act precisely as I wanted.'

He was making things much worse and was aware of it. He changed his tone. 'Margaret, do not look at me like that. You know I picked you because of your elegance. Why, Anne de Winter was a hay truss beside you.' Dropping on one knee before his wife, he planted a kiss on the end of her nose.

Mollified, Margaret said, 'But Robert, what of Oriel? Please consider carefully.'

'I shall, sweetheart, I shall. But look at it from my point of view – this is the best offer we shall ever have for her.'

'Perhaps, but I believe there is something strange about it. Our daughter says that James is a better friend to Piers than he is to her.'

Robert's head came up sharply and he gave Margaret a penetrating look. 'What are you suggesting?'

'Nothing. I am merely repeating what she said.'

Robert made no reply, sinking his chin into his hand and staring into the fire, only the distant murmur of the servants' voices and Oriel's muffled sobs breaking the silence. In the corners of the huge room the shadows seemed to deepen as the flames leapt in response to a falling log, and somewhere in that dusk one of Robert's hounds scratched and sighed. From the floor the smell of new sweet rushes wafted up to combine with wood smoke. If it had not been for the subject under discussion the room would have held a warm and glowing harmony.

Sensing the atmosphere was calming, Margaret spoke no more and it was some while before Robert said, 'You are right, of course. James has no thought of Oriel at all. This is either some political move of Juliana's or ...'

'Or?'

'Or there is something here we do not, as yet, understand.'

Margaret stood up. 'Then you have decided against it?'

Robert nodded his head slowly.

'Will you tell Oriel or shall I?' Her voice was matter-of-fact, hiding her feelings.

'We must both do it. Joan,' he called, 'go and bring Mistress Oriel to me.'

A little spiderlike servant scuttled from behind the screens and through the hall's dark shadows to the stairs beyond. As she disappeared from sight, Robert said quietly, 'You shall not be too soft with Oriel, wife. It is not right she should feel she has defied her parents. I shall make it clear that this is the last time she plays such a trick.'

Margaret said, 'Yes, Robert,' but inside her heart thudded; she had got her way, Oriel was to be saved from James.

And the smile on her mother's face must have told the girl everything for she rushed across the hall and flung herself into Margaret's arms, sobbing all the harder with relief.

Robert said sternly, 'Oriel, I have decided not to accept James's offer. It has been made clear to me by your behaviour and that of your mother that this match is quite unacceptable to you both. As you well know many fathers would have ignored this, but I believe in Christian mercy.' He paused importantly, then went on, 'In deference to your mother, therefore, the matter will be pursued no further.'

He was nearly sent flying as Oriel hurled herself at him, rubbing her wet eyes against his hard, cold cheek.

'Listen, my girl,' he went on. 'I warn you that I will not stand for this again. Next time a match is offered it will be your duty to accept. Is that completely clear?'

'Yes, Father. I will take anyone gladly. Nobody else in the

whole world can be as horrible as James. I promise this will never happen again.'

'No,' said Robert. 'It won't. You can be sure of that.'

As the household of Sharndene finally settled down to sleep, Isabel de Bayndenn – tenant of Sir Godfrey Waleis and keeper of the house of Bayndenn in the absence of Sir Godfrey and his son John, at their other estates – woke in the darkness. She had dreamed that her first husband, years older than she and long since dead, had stood at the end of her bed and wagged a reproving and skeletal finger. Then he had shaken his head and vanished.

Terrified, Isabel had struggled to consciousness to escape him and peered fearfully into the ink-black corners of her chamber, wondering if he had come back from the dead to stare, mean-mouthed, at Adam, her second husband, and to mock Isabel for her foolishness in marrying him. For foolish had been the word whispered when Isabel had bought Adam Guilot, a twenty-four-year-old villein belonging to Godfrey Waleis, and taken him for her husband six months later.

Looking down at him now, in the first faint light of dawn, Isabel smiled. He was utterly beautiful, golden looking, with not an ounce of fat on his handsome frame. He was also nearly thirty years younger than she and Isabel had done the most challenging thing of her life in marrying him. Still, time had not used her unkindly. Her body, which had never borne a child, was as perfect as it had been forty years ago. High in the breast, slim of the waist, lean at the hip, she could still turn the head of any man she rode past.

But her beautiful black locks were a different matter. Here she helped nature – or so she thought. Every morning, without fail, and before the servants were about, she would rise before daybreak and jump naked into the River Rother. Once in, she would draw breath and submerge her head for as long as she could. Repeating this ritual a dozen times, she would emerge and wash her face in the morning dew. She was convinced that this performance was the secret of her eternally youthful hair and skin. But of these things she never spoke to anyone.

Now Isabel, feeling the fresh winds of March whistling through the crucks – the curved wooden beams round which the timber house was constructed – thought that today might be too chilly for her ablutions, though in midwinter she had been known to break the ice rather than go without her youth-giving bathe. Nonetheless, she swung her bare feet out on to the stone floor. Instant cold sent her scurrying for her clothes and then, only stopping to pull a wimple and soft hat round her head, she proceeded, with a loving backward look towards Adam, out into the early dawn.

From where she stood she could see for miles along the valley. Eastwards and to her left, the first wild threads of pink suffused the mint-hued woodland, while before her rich green pasture sloped downward towards the gurgling river and onto the south, where the far side of the vale rose majestically in a great wood-covered slope. As always, Isabel caught her breath. She had been born and raised in the weathered house behind her but she would never, could never, quite get used to that irresistible view.

Her horse, through force of habit, started to wend its way towards the river and Isabel sat aloft, her face turned to the sunrise, her breath taking in the ice-crisp sharpness of the air. The morning was very cold indeed and her nostrils smarted with the sheer exhilaration of it all: the sun, the freshness, the incomparable vista.

But once at the riverside she lost some of her enthusiasm. The water was glacial; clear and icy and rushing along as if it were late. Very bravely, Isabel threw her garments onto a hawthorn but donned rapidly in their place a spare gardecorps. Then she jumped in and began her head dipping only to find, much to her chagrin, that she was not alone. In the far distance, and coming from the direction of Sharndene, she could see two figures on horseback.

Before they were able to realise her presence, Isabel had clambered out and clothed herself. But then instead of hailing them, for she could see by now that it was Robert and Piers de Sharndene, she stepped behind a great oak tree and watched, unobserved.

There was something menacing in the approaching couple's manner and Isabel wanted to escape but was forced to remain behind the oaktree, knowing that if she moved she would be noticed immediately.

'... suspected all along ...'

Robert's voice drifted towards her on the still air, only part of his sentences being audible.

'... fathered an apple of Sodom. Get off, you ...'

Horrified she saw that Master Sharndene had thumped his fist into Piers's stomach, knocking the young man from his horse.

'Get up ... knock you down again.'

Robert Sharndene had obviously brought his son out of general earshot to give him a sound thrashing. And this he proceeded to do, for Isabel could hear a great leather strap biting into the hapless Piers again and again.

'No ... no ... Father, please.'

'You can get out ... London ... give you horses ... make a man ...'

'Yes ... yes ... please stop!'

Grunting, Robert finally lowered his arm and stood looking at the weeping figure on the ground. Then with a curse he swung round, mounted his horse and headed off towards Maghefeld, leaving Piers gasping and bleeding.

Isabel stood stock still, wondering what she ought to do. To tend the wretch was the Christian answer but, on the other hand, to intervene in a family quarrel – and one of such vast proportions – was venturing into dangerous territory indeed.

After a few fraught moments, Isabel decided on the path of discretion. Quietly mounting her horse she walked it silently back up the wooded slope towards Bayndenn.

All the world was up early that morning, or so she thought, for a cheerful whistle drew her attention to Nicholas le Mist relieving himself behind a tree. Isabel lowered her gaze modestly but the little man, quite unabashed, called her name and waved to her with his free hand. Isabel gave him a reproving stare which only made him grin the more, his small gappy teeth resembling the crags of a rock-strewn ravine.

She had not gone another fifty yards before she heard evidence of someone else abroad, for, on the cold morning air, came the sound of a gittern most exquisitely played. Curious, Isabel followed the tune and, to her amazement, came across Wevere and a small dark man who sat cross-legged upon the ground, plucking the strings with short stubby fingers.

'Good-morrow,' she said, and both men looked up, thoroughly startled.

40

Wevere scrambled to his feet to acknowledge the greeting, but the other man merely gazed at her and continued to play. There could be no doubt that he was a genius, inspired. Isabel had never heard anything like the wealth of sound that poured from those blunt hands. It was as if the man had touched the gate of heaven and then communicated the anthem back to earth.

She could not help herself. Isabel dismounted and went to stand beside the stranger, staring at him enraptured. He did not acknowledge her presence but went on as if neither she nor Wevere were there. The steward caught her eye and saw by the slant of her fine dark brows that she was puzzled, but he said nothing. And so the three remained without speaking as the great wealth of sound filled the dawn.

Nicholas le Mist hurried up, his feet beginning to stamp and his knees bending into a jig.

'Come on, young man,' he shouted. 'Give us a tune for dancing.'

The player changed at once to the liveliest melody Isabel had ever heard. To stand still was an impossibility, so there – in the pinkness of the new day – she whirled about with Nicholas, laughing and breathless and acting half her age.

'Who is that man?' she gasped, as the music stopped.

'Why, that's mad Colin.'

'Who?'

'The archbishop's younger brother. He's kept well hidden, of course, but that's who he is.'

'How can he be mad when he can play like that?'

'Ah, there is the mystery of it all. Who could answer you that but God?'

Isabel had never heard Master le Mist quite so profound and she shot him a curious glance.

'*How* is he mad?'

'Not cruelly. He is just a simpleton. A boy trapped in a man's body. He would not hurt a living thing.'

Isabel stared at the player and was treated to one of the most beautiful smiles she had ever seen. For all innocence radiated from it, all purity, all joy. She knew that she was in the presence of something remarkable but found herself quite unable to say a word.

So merely giving a grateful smile in return, Isabel dropped a

41

respectful curtsey and allowed Nicholas to hold her shoe as she remounted. Then she set off towards Bayndenn and listened all the way back to a lark joining his voice with the wild soaring notes of Colin's music.

FOUR

The long unyielding winter of 1333 vanished overnight. There
had been no true spring, just bitter winds and frosts one day and
sweet breezes and flowers the next. The beautiful valley of
Byvelham burst forth like a jewel lifted to the sun. Bluebells
stood in regiments, armies even; buds – sticky, pushing, bursting with blossom beneath – clustered on high; the slopes of the
dales lost their wildness and glowed amethyst, sage and
brimstone.

And the gentle weather brought forth all those who had
huddled round their fires, avoiding the draughts and gusts of
their cold houses. Robert de Sharndene, nimble as a squirrel,
swung into his saddle and headed off in the direction of Battle
Abbey, where he would conduct the business of the archbishop.
For he held important posts, being not only Steward of the
Abbey, presiding at the manorial courts and supervising the
Abbey's vast estates, but also Bailiff of the Liberty of the
Archbishop, which necessitated much travelling and attention
to legal affairs.

But today Robert was not thinking simply of his many duties
as his horse climbed the hill above Sharndene. Instead his mind
was running over the fact that Margaret's lips had trembled
when he had announced his intention of being away a full week.
Had she guessed that he kept a mistress in Battle: that his love
was nineteen years old and widowed already, her soldier husband killed in Scotland? If so, his wife must be sick with anguish.
But yet he had been so careful, so discreet. Nothing would
induce him to hurt the mother of his children. It was simply that
he could not resist his sweetheart's laugh or eyes or eager-
mouthed embrace. With Nichola de Rougemont – so young and
free with her passion – he felt twenty again, strong and potent
and ready for challenge.

And this train of thought set Robert thinking about Piers,
and the depressing realisation that his second son was un-
natural. That the youth's wretched partner had been James

de Mouleshale had made the situation seem even worse. In fact Robert had been delighted to see Piers depart for London, nursing his wounds and muttering darkly of making his way in the world.

Yet the satisfaction at the removal of his second son had been short-lived. Within a week came the gossip – Juliana no longer deigned to speak to anyone connected with Sharndene – that James had left for London as well. The two young men had obviously planned to be reunited behind the backs of their families. Robert found himself wishing that he had broken Piers's neck on that morning when he had had the opportunity to do so.

As Robert of Sharndene headed for Battle thinking such murderous thoughts, his wife, pleading an aching head, plodded to her chamber and lay down upon her great bed. She had never felt more wretched having discovered, within the last week, a sarcanet glove of small and delicate design thrust into a secret pocket in her husband's gipon; a pocket that lay above his heart.

She had realised immediately that it belonged to a woman, for the perfume of expensive eastern spice arising from it was both overpowering and heady. After contemplating it with disgust, Margaret had thrown it onto the fire and said nothing to anyone.

But now, lying alone in her room, she faced facts. She was forty-seven and had not had a flux from her body for nearly a year, though the rapid and horrible heats associated with that great change were still an everyday occurrence. And she, who had never possessed a jot of beauty to start with, now felt herself to be growing puffy, seeing only too clearly the sagging lines of her eyes and chin. At that moment, ugly Margaret felt that she wished to die before her looks grew even worse. But before she did so she wanted more than anything to choke the life out of the owner of that small and scented glove, then dance a jig upon her grave.

Another tear ran from the far corner of Margaret's eye and trickled down her cheek towards the pillow. She could have wept all day then, stopped only by the thought that this would make her face swell till it resembled that of an adder. So instead she rose resolutely to her feet and thrust her burning cheeks into a little bowl of cold water that stood, with a jug, beside the bed.

Then she changed her kirtle for one of a brilliant and dashing blue, put on red wool stockings, and headed down to the stable. She would ride to Bayndenn and enquire as to whether Alice Waleis was in residence and would receive her.

As she mounted her horse Margaret saw, in the distance, Oriel and her serving woman heading off towards the woods, and frowned disapprovingly. She considered her daughter to be out and about too much for her own good and hoped that Oriel would never come across Nicholas le Mist energetically pursuing a maiden or – oh terrible prospect! – actually catching up with one! Such sights were not for the eyes of young and innocent girls.

But Oriel's thoughts were far from Master Mist. Instead she was wondering whether her father would be keeping a wary eye out for younger sons – those less likely to be pre-contracted from birth but nevertheless with prospects – on this visit to Battle. But such ideas were driven straight from her head as from deep in the wood came the sound of a gittern, brilliantly played. So brilliantly, in fact, that Oriel could truly say she had never heard anything quite like it.

For it was not really music – it was more a conversation between the player and God. Every note, every tone, every pluck of the wild wonderful strings, came from the depth of a spirit soaring up to touch the fingertips of the Almighty. Nobody who was not worshipping by the very act of his art could ever have poured out such glory.

As she drew nearer she dismounted and, leaving Emma to hold the horses, went through the bluebells alone and on foot, her shoes making no sound as she approached. In the near distance she could glimpse the musician, a dark young man sitting on a fallen tree trunk – his face rather comic and yet somehow sad – quite unaware of her presence and utterly absorbed in what he was doing.

Oriel suddenly felt an intruder and hid herself behind a tree, too polite to venture further but too taken up with the sound to turn away. She stood like that, quite still, for an age, hardly breathing, or so it seemed until, at length, the young man looked up and straight at her.

It was an odd first glance that they gave each other, for Oriel immediately had an overpowering sense of recognition, as if she had known the stranger all her life. So strong was this feeling in fact that, without being able to help herself, she gave a half-smile and held out her hand. Just for a fleeting second, just for a curious moment, she felt that he had recognised her too, and then his expression changed to one of blind and quite unreasonable fear. He scrambled to his feet shouting, 'Wevere! Wevere!' and with one more terrified glance at her, bolted into the protection of the trees.

Oriel stood transfixed, quite amazed by what she had seen. She could have been an ogre, a monster, a dragon – or even the ominous vision of St Dunstan working at his forge, the vision that supposedly killed anyone unfortunate enough to look upon the saint's holy features. All she could reasonably assume was that the musician had mistaken her for somebody else, somebody foreign and frightening to him. Rather sadly she turned away, walking slowly back to where Emma stood with the horses.

'Who was that playing, my Lady?'

'I don't know. A man I have never seen before. And yet it was odd, I felt as if I have always known him,' answered Oriel in bewilderment.

The riders from Gascony, leading their horses down the wooden plank of a ship – riding so hard at its moorings that it seemed likely at any moment to capsize – were nearly blown into the foaming race beneath. Everywhere they looked the sea was in strips of colour, jade plunging beneath iron, and cream leaping over turquoise, the noise of a million merpeople shouting in their ears. But dominating every other sound was the beating of the cruel and desolate rain, and the elder man pulled his black beaver well down upon him while the other raised his hood as they mounted their horses and turned their faces towards Canterbury.

The pair were an interesting study in contrasts as they rode silently, side by side: the elder rather fat, with short stout legs bulging against the flanks of his mount, his plump knees high and bent by the angle of his stirrups. Yet though heavily built it was obvious that he was still quite nimble, and the jowled face with its large nose and curving lips had once been handsome. His light brown eyes, as merry and sparkling as those of a harvest mouse, even now had great charm, set roundly and boldly in his moonlike visage. And his general demeanour was one of a sociable man, a *bon viveur*, yet a man who was nobody's fool and understood only too well the ways of a wicked and weak-willed world.

As the older man was bulky, so the younger one was spare. Tall, thin, he sat his horse as if he were a bird of prey, his shoulders hunched and his brilliant eyes turning, hawklike, from side to side. From his head a shock of full hair, the colour of cob nuts, hung to his shoulders, and a great strand of it, which he tossed back with an impatient hand, had worked its way loose from his hood. His fingers were long, bony, rather cruel-looking; his mouth hard as a rock. It was obvious that here was a man who was not to be crossed.

The two men went fast, covering the miles that lay between Dover and Canterbury as if they feared darkness might fall at any moment; for the storm had made evening out of afternoon and the crashing trees of the great woods forced the riders to lie low beneath the dripping branches, thus shielding them from what little light was left. It was with a sense of relief that they finally picked their way through the last of the springs and ponds, swollen to bursting point by the overwhelming down-pour, and saw the walls of the cathedral rising in the distance before them.

'We shall stay here,' said the elder. 'We can leave for London at first light.'

'I have heard that travellers may rest at the Abbey of St Augustine. Shall I enquire the way?'

As they reached the gates a bolt of lightning tore the clouds and the rain intensified, falling from the purplish sky in a solid sheet. Both men, strong though they were, shivered involuntarily and were glad to go in to the shelter of the abbey's stout and uncompromising building.

All about them, as they entered, they saw the dimness of old stone walls and flagstone floors, with light entering in shafts from high windows above; in their nostrils, meanwhile, came the smell of incense and fresh rushes, mixed with the pungent spiciness of garden herbs. The older man sniffed and the young monk who had acted as porter smiled.

'We grow many herbs here. The abbot believes that they are of medicinal as well as culinary value. He has a book of remedies said to be very old.'

'I should be interested to see it. I, too, believe in the power of plants' healing properties. But let me introduce myself – Paul

47

d'Estrange, knight of Gascony. And this is my squire, Marcus de Flaviel.'

The monk inclined his head slightly. 'You have travelled far. Come, let me show you to your quarters. Our repast is not for another hour and you will have time to rest.'

The younger man said abruptly, 'I'll see to the horses first. They have served us well, and must do so again if we are to reach London tomorrow.'

The monk nodded and asked, 'You have business there?'

'Great business,' answered Paul. 'Business that we must lay at the feet of the king himself if we are to get satisfaction.'

In the flickering rush light the private chamber at Bayndenn took on a new dimension, the walls spreading outward to a blur of blackness, so that the far corners appeared huge and cavelike. And in those places where the torchlight did not reach, the sound of the wind echoed, while the house creaked eerily like a cog in a tempest.

'I should not have come,' said Margaret Sharndene, shivering. 'I know I will have great difficulty in journeying back.'

'Then you can stay here,' answered Alice soothingly. 'With Robert in Battle there is no need for you to hurry.'

Margaret continued to frown. 'I should have been sensible and remained at Sharndene. I called on you yesterday, when the weather was fine, and was told by Isabel that you would not be here until today. But I wanted to see you so much. Alice, I need help.'

The younger woman looked at her sharply. 'What sort of help? What is wrong?'

'Nothing serious. That is, nothing serious to anyone except me. It is simply that Robert loves another, and the very idea is eating at me like a canker. I think of nothing else, day or night.'

There was a moment's silence during which the rain tapped on the window like a knocking finger and the wind blew a great gust of smoke throughout the house. Alice drew back into the shadows thinking how strange people were. If she had been asked to name the last person on earth to suffer jealousy, she would have said Margaret. In fact Alice would have wagered that her friend almost expected her husband to take a mistress in view of their life together.

'Why does it upset you so much?' she asked, hiding her

surprise. 'Most men have a lover – and many women too.'

'I cannot help convention. I am stricken to the heart.'

'Do you fear that he will leave you for her?'

Margaret considered for a second then said, 'No, I don't think that.'

'Then why do you feel so badly? If he has a little whore, so be it. Robert would never sacrifice his family – or his future – for lust.'

Margaret blew her nose overloudly, looking at Alice from watery eyes.

'It is all very well for you, Alice. Sir John loves you. Everybody knows it.'

'Perhaps because he looks on me as *his* mistress. After all, I am so much younger than he is and he chose me freely after his first wife died.'

Very softly, Margaret began to cry again, her broad nose swelling and reddening, her lips trembling slightly.

'But I love him, Alice. Robert may not love me but I love *him*. What am I to do? Which way shall I turn?'

Alice stood up, the hem of her kirtle falling heavily to the ground and swishing as she walked.

'For shame on you. I would never have thought to hear you say those words. Fight the girl with all the weapons in your armoury. You have Robert for husband, so hold on to him.'

Her friend, quite hideous with tearstains, raised her head. 'How?'

'Dress brightly, paint your face and charm his friends. He will soon wonder what has transformed you. You cannot slip into misery and middle life without a fight. Come Margaret, where is your courage?'

There was another pause during which her friend blew her nose once more, though this time with a certain amount of conviction. Then Margaret took from her pocket a cooling bag of mint with which she dabbed her cheeks.

'I will do as you suggest,' she said finally. 'But first I would like to know that my efforts will not be wasted.'

'Know? How can you know?'

'Alice, I want you to divine your magic stones for me. Read their message and tell me the truth.'

Lady Waleis went very still. 'You know how dangerous it is. Things like that are forbidden. Not only by the teachings of the

Church but also by my husband. His anger would be enormous if he knew what you had asked.'

'But he will never know. Please, Alice. I feel in need of guidance. Help me on this occasion. And then I promise I will do everything you have advised.'

'Very well,' answered the younger woman slowly. 'But know that it is against my better judgement.'

Taking a key from around her neck Alice Waleis opened a small wooden chest which she dragged from its hiding place beneath her bed. Margaret caught herself peering inside as the hinges creaked back, only to be disappointed. What lay within were no more than small stone tablets with strange carvings upon them. Nonetheless as she put her hand upon them they seemed to vibrate beneath her touch, and it was with a certain awe that she saw Alice throw them down at random upon the stone floor.

'Why are you doing that?'

'I am casting them.'

'How did you learn?'

'From my mother. They have been in her family for generations. I think they came from the old Norse land originally.'

The stones rolled and clattered and finally came to rest. There was a pause as Alice sank to her knees, the better to see them closely, her pointed face taking on a distant faraway expression. Then Lady Waleis swayed from side to side, a lock of dark hair escaping her wimple and falling down over her cheek. It cast a strange shadow, sculpting the face beneath to something not quite human. Quite inadvertently, Margaret made the sign of the cross.

'You will never be rid of your rival and yet you will be rid of her for ever.'

Margaret stared blankly. 'What does that mean?'

'I don't know. Sometimes the stones speak in riddles. But she will not bother you long, Margaret. Robert will return to your side and willingly.'

'God be thanked.'

'And there is something else.'

'What?'

'Changes are coming. Great changes that will affect not only you but all your family.' Alice looked up, her slanting eyes green as a cat's in the dim light. 'You must be careful, Margaret.

When the strangers come nothing will ever be the same again.'

A thrill of fear shot the length of Margaret's spine. 'What strangers are these?'

'Two men, both of whom you will love in vastly different ways.'

'Love? I? Alice, what nonsense is this?'

'No nonsense. Mark my words this night. They have crossed water to get here and they will never go away once they have found this place. Everything will be different when they arrive.'

'Will it be better or worse?'

'The stones say these men have power to change things. But they do not say more than that. We shall have to wait and observe in order to know.'

In the tense silence that followed there came a roar of laughter from the distant hall where the servants were gathered.

'I pray God the strangers are not evil,' said Margaret.

'Amen,' answered Alice – and then drew a frightened breath as the moon fought its way from behind the fierceness of the cloud mass and threw a sudden beam through the small, high window, lighting both the stones and the faces of the two women who crouched over them so intently.

That same faint moon could not penetrate the sky which loomed, thick as a hood, over Canterbury; and the evening meal of the monks of the Abbey of St Augustine – served in the later part of the afternoon – was eaten in a refectory lit by rushlight alone. As the abbot led the benediction shadows fell over the monks and the travellers who rested at the abbey that day, softening their faces and easing out the lines of weariness and care borne by so many of them, the men of God and journeyers alike. Even the youngest present, the lean and hawklike Marcus, was improved by the kindness of the light and, as he hungrily broke bread and wolfed it down, he looked boyish and gentle for a moment.

To the right of the abbot sat Paul d'Estrange, honoured thus as a knight of Gascony, and as the wine was poured and the food served, the two men were drawn into conversation. They were very different, the abbot being thin to the point of emaciation and eating sparsely, little more than the wing of a fowl and some watered wine passing his thin and somewhat mauvish lips, whereas Paul fell on his vittals like a trencherman.

51

He consumed a whole jugged hare, a duck, several spiced rissoles and half a pike before he finally sat back replete, patting his stomach and puffing out his cheeks in appreciation.

'A wonderful repast, my Lord,' he said. 'And rendered all the better by your cooks' use of spices and herbs.'

'The abbey prides itself on its board, Sir. Not that I care for a great deal of food. I have been plagued for years with an evil pain that strikes me if I have more than a few mouthfuls. I have tried many cures but none to any avail.'

A look of interest, quite at odds with his generally bland air, crossed Paul's face.

'You have taken herbal remedies, of course?'

'Many differing ones. Why do you ask? Do you have knowledge of the subject?'

'I was taught Arab medicine by a priest who had studied for many years. I venture to say that if I can find the right substances in your garden, or perhaps the meadows, I could mix you a compound that would cure your complaint.'

The abbot leant back in his chair, his thin face lit by a disbelieving smile. 'Then I enjoin you to try, Sir Paul. It would be a great relief to me and also to the brothers, who dare not eat their fill whilst their abbot is so abstemious.'

His voice, quiet though it might be, had carried down the long refectory table, and Paul found himself regarded with a certain amount of interest.

'Those are brave words, Sir,' said a sharp-faced monk, his brown eyes crisp as two withered leaves. 'I have tried for many years to cure our Lord Abbot but with no avail.'

Paul was instantly urbane, determined to make no enemies. 'It is but a thought, Brother. To cure your lord would be the least I could do to repay his hospitality. Certain roots, certain plants and herbs compounded together, can sometimes have the right effect.'

The doubting monk snorted and it was the abbot himself who put an end to the budding disagreement.

'I am willing to try anything. Sir Paul's knowledge of Arab medicine interests me.'

He stood up to signify that the meal was at an end and the monks obediently crouched in prayer, reminding Marcus of a row of mushrooms with their tonsured heads and habits like stalks. The abbot's voice, as thin and dry as himself, thanked the Lord for sustenance and for life, and then he walked out quietly followed by a smiling Paul. Marcus grinned to himself. His patron, the knight he had served as squire since he – Marcus – had been a boy, had won himself an important ally. The abbot of St Augustine's had invited the Gascon to converse with him further in his chamber.

The monks began to file out and Marcus, suddenly tired, made his way to the small cell which was to be his room for the night. There he removed his jerkin and his shoes and lay down upon the hard truckle bed, his hands folded beneath his head and his eyes open, gazing at the dimly-lit ceiling. He felt in a strange mood, neither elated nor sad but somehow suspended, waiting ...

He thought of the circumstances which had brought him to this sparse chamber on this miserably wet spring night; thought of how, like a parcel, he had been abandoned as a child in a strange village, on a hill above which stood a small castle. Remembered how he had been taken to Sir Paul, the owner, and how the knight had, without hesitation, agreed to let the boy stay in his household.

Marcus had puzzled about that for years: why a knight of Gascony should allow a homeless two-year-old to be brought up in his entourage, and why he should later single out the boy to become his squire. A boy who could remember nothing of his mother at all, only having an impression of a pair of long green-gold eyes and a perfume heavy as musk. She had pinned a ring to his hat: a man's ring which Sir Paul had removed and then returned to Marcus when he was fourteen. That had been the only clue to her identity.

He had hated his bastard state then – and still did to a certain extent – not even Paul's patronage and affection compensating for his lack of known parents. How many nights, Marcus wondered, had he spent staring at the ring on his finger, wishing that it would reveal its secret to him. But it never had and he was no nearer knowing his true identity now, at twenty-one, than he had been when he had first gone to Paul's home.

Marcus sighed and turned on his side. A long day lay before him and probably long weeks as well if he and his patron were to plead their cause with the English king. But plead they must, for Paul's lands in Gascony, an area which had belonged to the English crown since the marriage of Eleanor of Aquitaine to

Henry II had, only last winter, been invaded and seized by Philip de Valois. The French king's raids and incursions on this English possession had started three years earlier – yet another sign of the growing ambitions of an insolent France.

'I am not only a bastard but homeless too!' thought Marcus wryly. 'I wonder how it will end.'

FIVE

It was dusk, and John de Stratford sat on a stone seat in the palace herb garden, staring at the play of light on the ancient walls as the sky changed colour and listening to the sounds that helped to form the essence of this warm Sussex night.

To the east the evening had grown violet, but westward, behind the servants' tower, streaks of lilac blended with the jade of an early summer sunset. Beneath the tower, lights from the hall window glowed as *flambeaux* were lit, and the archbishop saw a sudden burst of scarlet which meant the central brazier had just taken flame. The sound of feet and clatter of platters told him that the table on the dais was being set, for the Sharndenes were to dine privately with him this night.

Beyond the hall lay the main buildings; the kitchens in the north wing – for the whole building was square, built round an open to the skies courtyard – sending forth a tremendous smell of roasting meat which mixed, not unpleasantly, with the heady perfume of wild flowers from the fields beyond.

Above these ground floor offices he could see the windows of his great chamber and above that those of the solar which, just now, caught the last rays of the sun, reflecting the gleam so that the archbishop could not see in. But he knew that Colin was sitting there, alone in the soft shadows, for, as if in incantation to the moon's rebirth, the voice of the gittern suddenly rose clearly above the household's cheerful domestic sounds.

Instantly everything seemed to still itself to listen, even the birds' evensong hushing beneath the rapturous sound. The archbishop found that he had, quite unconsciously, gripped the edge of the stone seat on which he sat, the problem of Colin coming to him even more poignantly in the uncertain half light.

And then Stratford's thoughts left his brother and began to race as the darker side of his nature rose in full strength to torment him. As always when this mood descended he saw a scene as clearly as if it were taking place now. And yet it had been ... how many years ago? Two? Three?

'No,' he thought in amazement, 'it was seven!'

He could remember the date now that he concentrated – 16 January 1327 – but he would never forget the grim events. No passage of time could dim the memory of the vaulted hall of Kenilworth Castle; the pitiful figure of King Edward clad from head to foot in a gown of jet, and the hard, set faces of the men looking on.

The deputation had been led by Sir William Trussel, he of the great big voice and little tiny eye, who had fought for Thomas of Lancaster and had pronounced sentence of death on the king's lover, Hugh Despenser. Then, those seven years ago, Trussel had opened his mouth to boom but before he could utter so much as a sound the king had fallen down in a dead faint, crumbling like the pathetic soft creature he was on to the stone floor without so much as a sigh.

It had been Bishop Orleton who had raised him to his feet: Orleton, who by his very brutality in private audience just beforehand, an audience at which the only other person present had been Bishop Stratford of Winchester, had reduced the king to such a pitiable state.

Here, here in the warm palace gardens of Maghefeld, the archbishop began to shake. He would never forget the moment when Orleton had thrust his fist into Edward II's face and said, 'You are finished, Sire. The whole country calls for your abdication. It comes of having too many sweet boys in your bed.'

Wretched bawd that the king had been, Stratford had never thought to hear God's anointed addressed so. But though he had not spoken insults himself, he, in the past, had been just as cruel to Edward. He had sided with Isabella the queen when the power struggle began: when she had had enough of her husband's humiliation. A humiliation that had begun when the king had given his lover, Piers de Gaveston, the best of her jewels and wedding presents, and which had culminated with her being abandoned, three months pregnant, as the lovers fled to Scarborough Castle to evade the wrath of the nobility.

That mighty insult had never been forgiven: from that moment the seed of revenge had been planted in sixteen-year-old Isabella's mind. The fact that Gaveston had been seized and executed without trial had not been enough; the king of France's daughter would not be content until she had, one day, brought her husband down. Not without reason would she earn the sobriquet 'the she-wolf of France'.

Sitting in the herb garden, the archbishop felt sweat pour from him, not just from the power of his wild thoughts but from the memory of the evil that had held England in its thrall. He recalled the sickness of the realm when the young Despenser had replaced the long-mourned Gaveston in the king's affection; how Isabella, who had until then managed to live in a state of marital truce, turned cruel with fury. It had not taken her long to welcome Roger Mortimer, Earl of March, into her bed and into dark corners where they might plot the king's downfall. They had gathered round them some of the mightiest people in the land, including John de Stratford, then Bishop of Winchester. The culmination had been at Kenilworth – the king a prisoner, Hugh Despenser hanged, drawn and quartered. Isabella and the Earl had won their bitter victory; her son, a boy of fourteen, waiting to seize the English crown.

Stratford saw again the crumpled heap that had once been his sovereign, lord of all England; remembered the bearded face, the colour of rennet, as Orleton manhandled the king back on to his feet, shouting, 'You must abdicate, Sire. You are finished and done. Only by your going voluntarily can you ensure the succession of your son.'

It had been pitiable to see a man weep, childlike, but this was what happened. With a great sob Edward had flooded at both eyes and mouth.

'Well?' Bishop Orleton had taken an angry step forward.

'Though I may be repudiated by my people,' came the choking reply, 'at least I rejoice that they see fit to crown my son.'

An indescribable roar had broken from Sir William Trussel. He had bellowed, with his mean and minute eye aglint, 'On behalf of the whole kingdom, I renounce all homage and allegiance to you. The reign of Edward – the second to bear that name – is over.'

As soon as he had finished speaking, Sir Thomas Blount, the King's Steward, had snapped his staff of office over his knee to show that the Royal Household was disbanded. And, without another word, the whole deputation had turned on their heels and gone, leaving the solitary figure staring hollow-eyed after them.

57

'If only it had ended there,' thought Stratford. 'If only that could have been the finish of the affair.'

He thanked God now that he had not been party to the last and most terrible plot of all; the plot in which the deposed monarch had been removed by order of the Earl of March to Berkeley Castle and where, after an almost successful rescue attempt, he had been thrown into the castle pit, along with the carcasses of diseased cattle, in the hope that the stench would kill him. But it had not: the king had survived, filthy and gibbering, covered in unspeakable things, his hair matted and disgusting.

Then came the announcement that Edward had died of natural causes. And, in truth, when dignitaries were called to examine the body there was not a mark on it. Yet there was a horrid and persistent rumour that the king had been murdered within the confines of the castle walls; and that the manner of his death had been of unbelievable savagery, an exquisite and cruel parody of the form of pleasure which he had once so much enjoyed. It was said that Edward died when a red hot poker had been inserted into his 'secret place posterialle'.

Stratford's face took on its customary frozen look, the ascetic side of his nature shuddering away from the contemplation of such a nightmare. Nor could he bear to think that he had, in any way, been an accessory to the deed, albeit before the execution. But the truth was that his hatred, first for Gaveston and then for Despenser, had led him into Isabella's faction and it had been he who had written the Articles of Deposition which accused Edward II of all manner of ills, culminating in the violation of the sovereign's coronation oath. As surely as if he had been present, John de Stratford had been partly responsible for the death of a king of England.

The sound of the gittern ceased abruptly and the archbishop glanced upwards. High above him his brother waved his arm, then turned away, his shoulders slumping a little. Stratford knew at once that Colin longed to join him, longed not to be kept so rigidly from palace life.

'And why not?' thought John, in a flash of clarity. 'What is the point of hiding him? Everyone knows of his existence. If they cannot see him they hear him play. Why do I try to deceive?'

Stratford had a moment of genuine sorrow that he should be

so ashamed of Colin's madness, for, after all, was not his brother just as much one of God's creations as he? But the feeling lasted only a minute, the survivor pushing the sentimentalist firmly down. Colin was assuredly an embarrassment to others and was, himself, happier kept quietly from the world's thrust. Nevertheless, it was a problem to know what should eventually be done with him. There would come a time when neither the archbishop nor his brother, Robert, would be able to cope with Colin's welfare. And when they died before him – as presumably they must – what then? What future for a child dwelling within a man's body?

The archbishop gave a deep sigh and rose from his seat. He could see by the sun's angle that it would be half an hour before he must attend the Sharndenes in the hall and his footsteps turned automatically towards the great chamber, and to the little chapel where Thomas à Becket had once bowed himself in prayer. This night, with thoughts of Colin weighing so heavily on his mind, Stratford felt that he must forget about the past and pray instead for guidance for the future. And what greater inspiration could he have than to touch the stones where once a saint had mastered his spiritual struggle and put his private devils behind him?

As the archbishop began his conversation with God, the Gascon knight and his squire walked into an alehouse in Bread Street and sat down at one of the crude trestles that were its only form of furniture. The squire, so tall that he had to bend almost in two to negotiate the entrance, called for ale and one of the daughters of the house – a pretty slattern with a curving red mouth – hurried forward to serve him. She was thirteen and not yet wed, and gazed at Marcus admiringly, thinking him arresting, with his exceptional height and hard hawkish features.

As she fluttered a smile, Paul whispered, 'I believe you have made a conquest,' but Marcus did not respond, merely raising one thin shoulder in dismissal.

'How much longer will this go on?' he asked. 'We have been in London a month now and barely glimpsed the king. I do not believe he is interested in our suit.'

Paul sighed. 'He is involved in his own affairs. His hands are full.'

'You mean Scotland?'

'Scotland, France, everything. The plight of a middle-rank Gascon knight must be very low on Edward's list of priorities.'

'Then what are we to do?'

Paul did not answer but finished his ale, banging the flagon on the table for attention when he had done so. Instantly the girl was at his side, leaning forward as she poured from the jug to touch the knight's arm. Now it was Marcus's turn to smile and his set features transformed spectacularly. But a commotion in the doorway of the alehouse brought both men's attention back to their surroundings as two elegants made an unlikely entrance into the squalid tavern.

'Or rather,' Paul thought, 'one elegant and one would-be.'

For though one of the newcomers was handsome, with crisply curling hair and eyes lustrous as darkened pearls, the other was ugly, his face a seething quagmire of yellowed pustules and angry blemishes. Yet even he, like the other, was dressed in the height of fashion with long pendant sleeves and pointed shoes – utterly out of place in such surroundings.

'Ale,' called one shrilly. 'Your best.'

Every head turned and there was a rumble of spiteful laughter. 'Your best!' mimicked a voice from a dark corner.

Ignoring the hostility the two sat down at the far end of the trestle which d'Estrange and Flaviel already shared with several others.

'Odious!' said the handsome man. 'Odious! If it were not that I die of thirst nothing would induce me to remain.'

He had an affected manner of speech which Paul found faintly comic but which obviously impressed the alekeeper's daughter, who now approached with a sinuous movement of her hips. As she leant forward, all eagerness, Paul noticed a flicker of interest in the stranger's black pearl eyes. So he did not mind which side of the bed he lay in!

So quickly that the movement was over before it had even begun, the man put up his hand and pinched the girl's rounded buttocks. She blushed and moved away but not before she had shot him a brilliant glance. He gave her a slow sweet smile in return, while his companion gulped miserably, riddled with jealousy. As if he delighted in his friend's misery, the stranger proceeded to give the girl a wink and beckoned her back to his side.

60

'How rare to find a rose blooming in such wasteland,' he said huskily. 'Allow us to introduce ourselves. I am Piers Sharndene and this is James Mouleshale.'

The girl made no answer, only turning a darker shade of pink. As her colour deepened, that of James drained away. He looked utterly bereft. Paul could almost see the working of James's mind as the young man turned to Marcus and said, 'You are a stranger in London, Sir?'

'Yes, I am a Gascon,' came the brief reply.

'You are here for a while?'

'At the moment it would seem indefinitely.'

James rose and made a florid bow, his sleeves dragging in the dirt of the flagstone floor. 'Then perhaps you would permit me to show you the City. I have only been here a month but already I feel I know my way.'

Piers gave a cluck of irritation, half his attention on the simpering girl, the other on James's pathetic attempt at nonchalance.

'No, I'm afraid not,' answered Marcus. 'I am squire to Sir Paul d'Estrange and am here simply to serve him.' Paul could not remember Marcus more frosty.

'James,' said Piers, 'be quiet.'

The miserable youth rubbed his hand over his spots. 'No, I won't,' he answered. 'I may speak to whom I please.'

Sensing that an argument was ripening, the alekeeper's daughter moved away to the protection of her father, who stood watching silently, his arms folded upon his chest.

'When you are in my company you will behave yourself.'

James's pale face flushed with passion. 'Do not speak to me so. Remember it is my money that keeps you.'

His voice had risen shrilly and other conversations in the ale-house ceased abruptly. Somewhere a chair was pushed back and those sitting in the dark corner came forward for a better view.

'I shall ignore that,' answered Piers, with an attempt at remaining calm.

Before James could reply Marcus stood up, his lean frame towering over the seated couple. 'It would be better if you continued this outside,' he said. 'You are disturbing Sir Paul.'

'Piss Sir Paul,' said Piers.

He did not see the fist come flying towards him until he was flat on his back on the stinking floor, something disgusting soiling the fine stuff of his cotehardie. There was a commotion as every man present rose to his feet and the alekeeper's wife hurried out her daughters.

Paul had a moment of terrible premonition and jumped up. 'Leave it, Marcus,' he said. But he was too late. Piers had scrambled upright and was hurling himself at the squire, a sharp bladed knife gleaming in his hand. At that James, who had scrambled on to the table, launched himself onto Marcus's back and there was a thud of bodies hitting stone as all three toppled over, then sprang up again.

Paul d'Estrange thrust in to protect his squire, pulling at the hapless James who still clung on to Marcus, but Piers, who had somehow managed to extricate himself, ignored the knight, wildly plunging his knife towards the Gascon's chest. There was the sickening sound of a blade entering flesh, then a moment of absolute quiet as James looked in surprise at the blood spurting from his heart, before he dropped to his knees and then fell sideways, broken and spent amongst the dirt.

'You've killed him,' screamed Piers. 'You've killed him as surely as if you held the knife.'

'No,' Marcus shouted furiously, '*you* are responsible. It is your hand that misjudged, not mine.'

'Get them out,' ordered the alekeeper. 'Get them all out before there is more trouble.'

The dripping corpse went first, hurled through the door as if it had been a toy, followed by the two Gascons and Piers Sharndene. Behind them they saw the throng pick up jugs, pans, chairs – any kind of weapon to see the strangers off. It was not dignified for a knight of Gascony to break into a run, nor for his squire to drag him along by the arm. Neither was it seemly for an elegant to kick off his pointed shoes and hurtle into the maze of alleyways in which the alehouse stood. But there was little choice and the three of them fled off in different directions without daring to look behind.

A voice echoed out of the alley into which Piers had vanished.

'I'll be revenged on you, Gascon. Even if it takes me years, James Mouleshale shall not go unavenged.'

But though Marcus turned to shout back there was no sign of the young man who had only a moment ago become his sworn and bitter enemy.

*　　　*　　　*

'. . . what do you say to that, Mistress Oriel?'

Leaning back in his chair the crimson-clad figure of John de Stratford – a gold and jewelled winecup twirling in his fingers, a smile, for once, lighting his wintery features – seemed to feast his eyes on Robert de Sharndene's fifteen-year-old daughter. In fact if the man had not been a celibate it might well have been thought that the archbishop was paying court to her. But she sat still, her hands folded mildly in her lap, her eyes averted shyly from his face.

'Well . . .?'

Oriel knew she must appear attentive but all she really wanted to do was stare at the dancing flames of the brazier and listen to the music. For a dreamy mood was upon her; a dreamy mood that had begun some weeks earlier when she had come across the strange young man who had sat alone and played the gittern.

But the archbishop's voice went droning on. '. . . you are fond of music? The Court has many minstrels.'

'Really?' Oriel smiled, trying hard to look alert.

The archbishop smiled back, his mouth twitching up at the corner as if he guessed she was day-dreaming.

'Yes. The king has five trumpeters, five pipers, two clarion players – to say nothing of a citoler, a tabouretter, a fiddler and a drum. In wartime, of course, they become a military band.'

'Does he have a gittern?' The question seemed to slip out almost without her thinking.

The archbishop frowned, his eyes suddenly dark.

'No, no he does not. Why do you ask?'

'I heard one the other day,' Oriel answered slowly. 'It belonged to a stranger, a young man. It was played more beautifully than I ever thought possible.'

She might not have spoken, so little response did Stratford make. Eventually, after draining his winecup to the full he said quietly, 'Yes, yes. I know what you mean.'

Oriel woke up at last. 'You know?'

There was another silence during which the girl found herself subjected to a strange scrutiny. The crystal eyes gazed at her as if they were seeing beyond her mortal flesh and into the depths of her soul. The man of God was frightening like that; a fierce and questioning archangel.

Eventually he spoke. 'Yes, I know the man.'

Robert, rather bored at being left out, entered the conversation.

'Is she being a nuisance, my Lord? She has not yet learned to hold her tongue in great company. Oriel, be quiet.'

Once again the archbishop's face changed. Before her gaze Oriel saw him grow sleek as the slinking black cat that stalked birds in the bluebell woods.

'Not at all, not at all,' he said urbanely. 'Your daughter was merely remarking on someone she heard playing the gittern the other day and asking if I knew who it was.'

'The gittern?' Margaret's thin eyebrows rose slightly.

'Yes, Madam. And it was my brother in fact. Though cursed with a terrible shyness he is a brilliant musician. Quite untutored, I might add. It is a gift from God.'

The master and mistress of Sharndene exchanged incredulous glances.

'Your brother?' said Robert eventually. 'I did not know that you had a brother, my Lord.'

'I have two. Robert, who resides in London, and Colin, who is here in Maghefeld.'

As Oriel's parents exchanged a series of startled glances, their daughter clasped her hands together with pleasure.

'Then it is possible I will hear him play again?'

The archbishop laughed, a rare sound. 'Anything is possible, my child. But Colin does not care for company. He has always been shy of other people.'

Stratford looked at his guests with an unaltered expression, but inside, his heart began to beat fractionally faster. 'But of course I shall ask him to play for you again, my dear. He would enjoy that.'

His guest went the colour of a hedgerose, the pale gold hair falling forward as she bent her head again.

'Thank you, my Lord,' she murmured, then turned her attention to the contemplation of her food.

The archbishop now gave his full charm to his Bailiff of the Liberty.

'How did you fare in Battle, Master Sharndene?'

Robert shifted uncomfortably beneath the glittering gaze. Did the man of God know something? Had some agency – human or otherwise – murmured into the archbishop's ear that Sharndene had visited the house of a certain young widow?

'I presided at the indictments and attended the gaol delivery, my Lord.'

'Yes, yes. And ...?'

Robert shrank within. If it had not been for Stratford's unusually urbane mood he would have thought some kind of trap was being set. And then he wondered if all the good humour *was* a prelude to disaster, whether the primate always smiled before he struck.

'And ... my Lord?'

'And what of William of Northrop? Was he also in attendance?'

Visibly relieved, Robert answered quickly, 'Aye, my Lord. And also John of Ifield and Thomas of Faversham.'

'Good, good.'

The archbishop was smiling again and Robert was once more unnerved.

'Now, Master Sharndene ...'

How unlike Stratford to use this formal mode of address; something was quite definitely in the wind. Finding himself unable to speak Robert merely inclined his head. He was horrified to realise that the archbishop had lowered his tone to one of confidentiality.

'I want you to come and see me, Sharndene. On a personal matter.'

Robert could not meet the primate's eye as he murmured, 'Very good, my Lord. When shall I attend you?'

Stratford purred out his answer. 'No hurry. It is nothing of urgency. Shall we say when you next return from Battle?'

'Certainly, my Lord.'

Robert wished himself a thousand miles distant as, with a secretive twitch of his lips, John of Stratford toasted the Master of Sharndene by raising his jewelled winecup.

On the morning after the death of James de Mouleshale, three riders left London shortly after daybreak. They rode swiftly, fearing repercussions from the accidental killing in which they had all been involved, and anxious to put as many miles as possible between them and the scene of the death.

The first to leave was Piers, his dark pearl eyes ringed through lack of sleep, his heart icy in his breast. To have to go back to Sharndene; to Robert and his narrow mind; to his flushed cross mother; to his fine-boned sister with her winsome ways, was a nauseous prospect to which he must find a permanent solution – a means of escape which would last forever.

London and, unbeknownst to James, the silken bed of a wealthy merchant had given him a full purse, but Piers knew his own extravagance; was aware that his craving for fine things ruled his entire life. He thought of bales of rich materials; tender meats and sweet red wines; soothing music played by handsome young minstrels, and felt desperation rise in his throat.

His mind moved on to the depressing prospect of telling Juliana Mouleshale that her only child was dead and, even as he thought of her, Piers shuddered. Those dim and peering eyes; the gawky shapeless body. Why, she could not have had a man in her bed in years.

The inspiration that came to him then was like a flash of lightning. At one moment he had been mulling over his lack of prospects, at the next he had seen the solution! Letting out a loud cry, Piers crossed himself in gratitude and spurred his horse on to Maghefeld.

Not far behind him on the same road galloped Paul d'Estrange and Marcus Flaviel, heading for Canterbury and the patronage of the Abbot of St Augustine's. The knight had left the abbot with a great jar of compound, the herbs picked and prepared by himself, and to enquire whether it had proved effective was as good an excuse as any to spend a few days away from prying eyes.

'Do you think there will be trouble?' asked Marcus, as they rode.

'No. It was an accident. You cannot be brought to account for brawling. Still I think it will be as well to vanish for a while.'

'But what of your suit to the king?'

'That will have to wait.' Paul looked at his companion, saw his pallor and the great purple bruise on his cheek where a flying fist had caught him. 'You look tired. A good sleep will do you no harm, Marcus. I shall give you a draught tonight.'

Marcus looked impatient. 'I am not concerned about tonight. It is the future that worries me.'

The fat knight smiled imperturbably. 'The future will take care of itself. I have a plan.'

'Will you tell me of it?'

The Gascon shook his head. 'No. Let us make haste to Canterbury. I feel the key to everything lies there.'

And with those puzzling words Marcus had to be content as they galloped through the dust along the pilgrims' way.

SIX

On the afternoon after his return to his father's house, Piers de Sharndene rose from the bed in which he had been lying throughout the day, and called for his men to bring the great wooden bathtub up the stairs and in to his private chamber. Then, whilst the servants laboured up and down with steaming pails of hot water, he idly strummed a citoler, looked at his clothes critically, and finally visited the garderobe, set in the ample thickness of the wall and boasting a vertical shaft which dropped straight to the moat below. Thus relieved he came back to his room, stripped himself naked before all and lowered himself into the tolerably warm water beneath a shower of rose petals thrown by a handsome young boy.

Piers closed his eyes and let the comfort sink into his bones, while his mind ran rapidly over the plan that was growing more and more acceptable to him. When Piers had heard it spoken that his namesake – young Piers Gaveston, the late king's lover – had walked at Edward II's coronation dressed in royal purple sewn with pearls and so decked out that he more resembled the god Mars than an ordinary mortal, Piers had known the direction in which his life must go. He too wanted to clothe himself sumptuously; to have glorious jewels and plate; to own a bathtub like that of the king, with four gilt bronze taps and four leopards' heads, screened off from the cold by partitions and paving tiles and thick, rich mats. Piers wanted music and laughter, poetry and song, and if ugly things must be done in order to achieve beauty and perfection, then so be it.

He looked down at his body with some satisfaction. As the dirt of London rolled away he saw firm skin and hard muscle. He was in excellent condition to put his plan into motion; to woo and win Juliana and thus get his hands on the Mouleshale fortune.

For his visit to the widow's home, having been dried carefully and rubbed with oils by the same young servant, he chose a rich black gipon with buttoned sleeves and a silver cotehardie with very long flaps, which he had purchased in London. On his legs he had black hose and shoes with pointed toes. And over all this he sported a crimson mantle and cap, rather like that worn by the archbishop.

With one last look at the splendid effect this created, Piers took his father's black stallion from the stable and, with no word to anyone, swung into the saddle. Then both horse and rider climbed the heights above the manor house, following a thin track skirting Tide Brook, until they reached the point where Mouleshale land became visible. Here Piers reined in. Twenty years before, Juliana's husband, a merchant, had built himself a grand house on the site. Narrowing his eyes Piers looked at it critically now for any signs of bad taste. Of these, alas, there were many and he fell to thinking how they could be replaced with finer things when he eventually became master.

But he had little time for more detailed contemplation, for no sooner had he entered the hall than the Mistress of Mouleshale was upon him. With a graceful move, Piers dropped to one knee before her, raising her fingers to his lips.

'Madam,' he said in a voice that, rich and sonorous though it was, contrived to tremble very slightly.

'I am told you returned to Sharndene alone last night,' she answered in a frantic tone. 'Where is James?'

Piers gave her a hollow-eyed stare, then let his eyes fall to the floor miserably. Without saying a word he conveyed all the anguish of a principal mourner.

'God's blood,' shrieked Juliana, clawing the air frantically. 'What has happened? Where is my son? Is he ill?'

Piers rose to his feet and made a motion to suggest that he would have laid a comforting hand upon her had not convention decreed otherwise.

'Alas . . .'

'He's dead, isn't he? Speak to me, Master Piers. Tell me the truth.'

He looked beyond her bleakly, his dark eyes misting over. 'Yes, Madam, I fear so. He lost his life in London.'

He paused while he weighed his next few words. To lay the blame squarely upon the Gascon squire was the obvious course. Yet Piers knew well that the truth had a cruel way of often coming to light. Better to be vague as to the manner of James's passing. But he was not able to utter a word as one look at Juliana's face frightened him to silence.

For a second or two she appeared demented, her jaw and lips working feverishly, a great torrent of tears flowing down her cheeks. Then she began to howl fiercely, at the same time gripping Piers's cotehardie and pulling at the material in a frenzy of anguish. Terrified lest the expensive stuff should rend beneath her grasp, Piers had to physically check himself from throwing her off, and only with a masterful show of self-control could he compose his features into a look of sympathy.

'Madam,' he said brokenly. 'Dearest Madam.'

But she was not listening to him. Releasing her grip she was threshing about the hall in despair.

'Juliana,' he tried tentatively, but was interrupted by a haglike old servant who flew to her mistress's side from nowhere and clutched her to a greasy bosom.

'There, there,' the beldam shouted. 'There, there, little sweet. Joan is here, old Joan is here.'

The sweat broke out on Piers's brow – he had never seen a more repellent couple. Just for a moment blind panic seized him and he thought that he could never bring himself to woo the Mistress of Mouleshale even were she ten times as rich. He turned to go but a fluttering motion attracted his attention. Juliana was flapping a pale hand at him.

'Stay,' she said, her voice muffled by the hag's embrace. 'Stay, dear Piers. Tell me how my boy met his end.'

He hesitated one second longer – this was the moment when he could have resisted the chance to change his fortune and gone from Mouleshale forever. But the thought of all that vast and glorious wealth was too much. He turned back towards her, his eyes sweetly sad.

'Madam ... Juliana ...' he answered. 'I shall wait here until your need for me is done.'

He said this without inference but hoping, nonetheless, that the words might quicken her attention. And, sure enough, that terrible grieving eye did glance at him briefly – and then away again.

'Yes stay, Piers, stay. I will be recovered enough to speak soon. Joan, see to Master Sharndene's wishes.'

She wandered from the room like a sleepwalker, the servant turning to Piers for instructions.

'Wine,' he said tersely. 'Your best. And food within the hour.' And then muttered to himself. 'I believe there is a long night's work ahead of me.'

As Piers began his repast so, too, did Paul and Marcus, dining late with the Abbot of St Augustine in the abbot's private chamber. They sat at a wooden table, the abbot at the head, the two men on either side of him, and while the knight and the cleric discussed cures, salves and potions, the squire looked about with interest at the personal possessions of their friend and benefactor.

The abbot's room in the abbey's west wing, though small and fairly spartan – there being no rug on the stone floor nor hangings on the wall – nonetheless held a carved desk of intricate design and a wooden chest of sturdy antiquity, a panel of which depicted a swineherd knocking acorns from a tree for his pigs, and another a sun risen in splendour. Marcus caught himself wondering if it held a secret compartment in which the abbot kept documents and valuables.

As with all the other parts of the abbey the smell of incense and herbs permeated the air, together with the soft green aroma which rose from the rushes spread beneath their feet. There was also a faint odour of musk, presumably coming from the abbot's garments and, as always, the scent conjured into Marcus's mind one of his few early memories. He saw again a slant-eyed woman pin a ring to a little boy's hat and then slowly walk away from him without looking back. He could remember, even now, the sway of her hips and the way she had moved, putting her feet down silently, as if she were stalking. He could remember, too, the anguish of standing still in the middle of the narrow, thronged street, waiting for her to return. And he could remember how he had cried, helpless and afraid, when she had not appeared.

Marcus looked across the table at his patron. Tonight the fat knight was at his most affable, basking in the abbot's praise. For the herbal compound Paul had prepared had cured the acidity that burned in the abbot's chest and restored him to full appetite, as he had claimed it would. In fact the hollow cheeks were already filling out and the emaciated body had a covering of flesh.

The conversation of the two older men had by now turned

71

away from medicine and Paul was smiling a little anxiously as the abbot said, 'But what of the future, Sir Paul? If the king is too busy to hear your suit, what is your plan?'

The knight spread his hands. 'I have no idea, my Lord. There seems little point in returning to Gascony. I thought perhaps of offering myself as physician to some great English household.'

'You are not married then?'

'I am a widower.'

'So there is no reason why you should not settle here?'

'None at all, my Lord. As long as my squire is welcome too.'

The abbot looked thoughtful, cupping his chin in a thin-fingered hand.

'My sphere of influence is limited, as you can imagine, but I will gladly write you a letter of commendation to the arch-bishop. He succeeded only last year and may still need men in his household. He is in Maghefeld at the moment ...'

'Maghefeld?'

'In Sussex. He has a palace there, rather a beautiful one in fact, and takes great pleasure in visiting it. It will be a pleasant ride for you in the morning.'

Paul nodded his head. 'It is God's will, my Lord, that you have spoken. I thank you for your suggestion and tomorrow will go to pay him homage.'

The abbot poured some white wine, the colour of sunshine, into two cups. 'I drink to your good fortune, Sir Paul,' he said.

The Gascon took the offered cup, obviously on the point of launching into a fulsome speech of thanks.

Marcus rose to his feet, 'My Lord, Sir Paul, if I might be excused. I would like to take the air before I retire.'

He bowed his way out, glad to be alone. Before him, beyond the abbey gardens, stretched the fields and, beyond these, a river flowed into the distance. In its cool, silver depths both the setting June sun and its sister moon – strangely at odds against the mazarine sky – were reflected. Marcus stared at them thinking that the same sun and moon shone over Gascony and over the lands that had once belonged to Paul d'Estrange. He supposed it probable that he would never see them again, never look on the places that were his only known background. He wondered what lay ahead of him and if he might, perhaps, join the household of the archbishop when he arrived in Maghefeld.

Rather alarmingly at that moment the abbey bells began to

toll the knell, calling the monks to evening prayer. With a slight shiver Marcus turned back to the abbey, glad to find the sleeping draught Paul had compounded waiting in his cell. He swallowed it in a mouthful, feeling its warmth fire his stomach. And after it came oblivion and no dreams and not even the thought of the youth who had died in London to trouble his sleeping mind.

SEVEN

The waking was harsh, swift and rather frightening. At one moment Oriel had been wandering in a dream-world: a world in which the noise of a gittern turned into the cry of a great white swan, and, at every step, a young man with long brown hair stood in her path; at the next she was wide awake, staring at the ceiling, her heart thumping crazily and her hands grasping the material of the bedcover in panic.

Yet there was nothing to be afraid of, for lying there in the chill of early morning she could see by the light thrown from the windows that all was perfectly peaceful and could hear the sounds of the awakening household. Chains crunched, bolts creaked and somewhere a servant's voice raised itself in song.

Oriel quickly got out of bed, her feet shuddering against the harsh wood of the floor, and crossed to where she could see over the moat to the land beyond. A silver sun, early and not yet full-blooded, was struggling up through the dawning mist, and the swans still slept on a moat bright as emerald. Smoke from the re-kindled fire in the hall hung thin and straight as a lance, and an answering thread from the bakehouse told her that fresh crisp bread would soon be pulled from the cavernous ovens.

Beyond Sharndene and its encompassing circle of water, the slopes of the basin in which it lay peeped through the mist like strips of ribbon, while on the heights above the full-leafed trees thrust eager fingers into the vapour. Within two hours it would be fine and hot; a day for riding forth. Eagerly, Oriel walked through to the chamber beyond to see if her mother stirred or slumbered.

Margaret looked younger in her sleep, her hair fluffed out on the pillow and the severe lines of her face softened. She slept alone – Robert being once again in Battle – and the empty bed diminished her, making her seem somehow more vulnerable. Oriel felt a rush of guilt; guilt for resenting her mother and her angry snappish ways. Without really knowing why, she put her arms round the slumbering form and dropped a kiss on its peaceful cheek.

'Robert?' said Margaret, not awake.

'No Mother, it is Oriel. Go back to sleep.'

But her mother was struggling to consciousness, her eyes opening slowly and taking in the fact that she was in her bedchamber and that it was her daughter who leaned over her and looked so kindly into her face.

'It is early,' she said at last. 'Why are you up?'

'I could not sleep. I was dreaming and it woke me. Mother, it is going to be fine. May we go out?'

Margaret sat up, yawning. 'I intend to go to the palace with Cogger. I have some fowl for the archbishop. You may perhaps accompany me.'

Yet though she knew she ought to take her daughter, there was once again the old sense of reluctance. If Margaret could have had her way she would never again be seen with Oriel at her side. She could imagine only too clearly the comparisons that even her friends must make. How they must think that it was the Devil's parody – a plain woman giving birth to such a rare and delicate beauty.

Through dropped lids she looked at her daughter in the white light of the misty dawn, saw the elegant sweep of cheek bones, the fall of pale gold hair, the eyes bright as harebells.

'You are beautiful,' she said.

Oriel turned pink. 'No, Mother. I am ordinary. It is *you* who are beautiful.'

Margaret stared at her. In all the times they had spent together their conversation had never gone down such a path.

'How can you say that, Oriel? Look for yourself. I am hog-featured: thick of nose and small of eye.'

'But Mother, you are vivid where I am pale. I am but a simpering shadow measured to your colour.'

Margaret savoured the words slowly. Was it possible that some knowledge of paints and a certain style in dress could pass for beauty? Or was it, perhaps, that when she wanted to converse her amusing turn of chatter could blind her listeners?

'Oriel,' she said suddenly, 'do you care for me?'

'You know I do,' answered her daughter without hesitation.

They regarded each other silently. Words of devotion between parents and children were not spoken lightly for, after all, times were not easy. A son was procreated to inherit, to fight, to emulate his father; a girl was useful for one thing only, to attract the best marriage possible in order to further the position of her family. Domestic life was entirely centred around these reasonings. There was very little room for anything approaching affection.

'We shall certainly go out today,' said Margaret, moved to generosity by a sudden upsurge of emotion. 'You may indeed ride with me to Maghefeld.'

Oriel shivered slightly, her cheeks pale where they had been dark a moment ago.

'I dreamt that there was a stranger in the woods, but still I would like to come. Nothing exciting happens to those who stay at home.'

Margaret gave her a reproving look. 'There will be plenty of time for excitement when your father finds you a husband, my girl.'

Oriel did not answer.

An hour before the ladies of Sharndene rose from their beds Marcus Flaviel was already fully awake and dressing himself for the day, his long fingers dealing swiftly with fastenings and buckles, his face set as he shaved away the night's growth of beard. Everything about him suggested a certain mistrust, his shoulders taut and tense, his whole body alert as if he would spring on an enemy at any moment. For to him victory had been too quick. The archbishop had accepted both himself and Paul into the palace entourage with so little questioning, so little fuss, that it was almost as if he had been expecting them before their arrival.

As he slipped on his jerkin, Marcus thought back to yesterday. He and his patron had been shown into the presence just as the afternoon sun had started to lower in the sky, only to find John Stratford already seated, reading the letter which had been sent up ahead of them. Finally he had looked up. 'The abbot tells me that you have cured his lack of appetite by use of Arab remedies, Sir. He also says that you and your squire seek some post in England while the king looks into your suit for redress.'

'Indeed, my Lord, that is so. I wondered if perhaps you might know of a household where we could be of use.'

Marcus thought of the archbishop's cool crystal eyes and frozen look as he had answered, 'A knight versed in the art of herbalism must be welcome wherever he goes. And as to your squire ...'

He had stopped, staring Marcus up and down thoughtfully. 'You look as if you fear nothing,' he had said. 'Do you?'

It had been a disconcerting question and Marcus had remained silent. The archbishop's expression had not wavered as he continued, 'Well, answer me!'

'My Lord, I fear what most men fear: dying in pain, being friendless, losing a limb.'

'But not the unusual; things that others might shrink from as strange?'

'It depends, my Lord.'

Stratford had then slipped into such a long silence that Paul had eventually ended it with a polite cough.

'You know of someone who might welcome us, my Lord?'

The archbishop had smiled, though the look in the wintery eyes had not altered at all.

'I think you might both stay here for a while,' he had said. 'I am sure that you could be of service as members of my personal staff.'

It had been too easy, Marcus thought now, as he walked beyond the confines of the palace. Something else lay behind the archbishop's decision. If it had been the household of any man other than that of the primate, the squire would have thought that they had been lured into a trap. And now, as he made his way into the quadrangle, the feeling recurred. What secret was it that these walls held? What was it that the archbishop really wanted them to do?

His hand flew automatically to his sword as a softly whispering voice startled him unreasonably. But as he could see no one he was about to make his way out of the courtyard to the palace gardens, when a rose fell from the skies above and landed at his feet. Marcus looked up, cursing the morning mist that shrouded everything and hid the higher branches of the trees from sight.

There was a mischievous laugh and a voice said, 'Up here, look!'

And there above him sat an impish man with a mass of curling dark hair, perched on a branch of a tree and holding a struggling cat in his arms. He gave a sweet smile, but it was immediately obvious to Marcus from the slightly vacant look in the stranger's eyes that there was something unusual about him.

'I'm coming down,' he called. 'Will you catch me?'

And without waiting for a reply he released the animal and shot from the branch straight into Marcus's arms. The feel of him was quite extraordinary: to the squire, so young himself that he could not have experienced such a thing, it was like holding a dearly loved and familiar child.

'Are you a new servant?' The simpleton was gazing up at him with uncannily light blue eyes.

'Yes, in a manner of speaking. I joined the household of the archbishop last night.'

'You belong to John?'

Marcus could not believe his ears. Who *was* the fellow that he spoke of the archbishop in such familiar terms?

'I belong to Sir Paul d'Estrange, a Gascon knight. I am his squire and we are in England seeking an audience with the king. We have become attached to the archbishop's retinue for the time being.'

'Oh good,' said the little man, clapping his hands together. 'Then I can play with you often. I am his brother, you see.'

'The archbishop's?' Marcus could not believe what he was hearing.

'Yes. It is very sad that he is so brilliant and I am so slow, but I do try to be good. If I *am* good will you be my friend? You always were my friend you know.'

Not understanding what he meant, Marcus said, 'Yes, I will be your friend. What is your name?'

'Colin,' answered the other. 'Or is it something else I can't remember? No, it is Colin.' He started to skip, leaping from one cobble to another. 'I knew you would come one day,' he said over his shoulder. Then he bounced off towards the kitchens and the smell of freshly-baked bread. As he reached the door, he waved. 'I shall ask John if you may look after me instead of Wevere,' he called, then vanished inside.

Marcus stared after him amazed, so lost in thought that, a few moments later, he did not hear the running feet of a servant until the boy was practically on top of him.

'Master Marcus,' said a panting voice, 'the archbishop

wishes to see you immediately in his chamber. Please come at once. And hurry!'

But on entering Stratford's private apartments the squire saw that he need not have made such haste, for the archbishop stood with his back to him, gazing out over the grounds as if he had all the time in the world.

'You wanted to see me, my Lord?' asked Marcus, bowing in the doorway and feeling fractionally annoyed with the imperturbable figure who had now turned and was appraising him with a glittering eye.

'Yes. I have been wondering since you entered my service yesterday what your duties should be, Flaviel. Now it is all quite clear to me and the hand of God is plainly visible.'

'My Lord?'

'You have met my brother and understand that he is ... different. He has been afflicted since birth, of course. But there is nothing cruel or unpleasant in his nature.'

'I realise that, my Lord.'

'He has been to see me already. He has asked that you may be his guardian rather than my steward, Wevere. Strangely, I was looking for someone. Now do you see the workings of God's plan?'

In a flash of clarity, Marcus did. He had been brought to the palace by a series of mighty chances which did, indeed, seem to have some overriding pattern. It was meant that he and the simpleton should meet. The words 'I knew you would come one day,' repeated themselves in his mind.

But the archbishop was speaking. 'Do you accept the task?'

'If Sir Paul agrees,' answered Marcus, 'it would give me great pleasure to be your brother's guardian.'

Stratford did not answer, merely nodding his head and raising his hand to bless the Gascon who, for no reason, had suddenly dropped on one knee before him.

As the moated manor house of Sharndene and the Palace of Maghefeld came to full and bustling life, so Robert Sharndene awoke in his mistress's bed in Battle and gave a sigh of pure contentment. To see that pretty face next to his on the pillow and touch the great cloud of spreading red hair, so long that it hung to her buttocks, was a joy of which he would never tire.

He did not know, of course, that she was little better than a whore, being utterly deceived by her tilting eyes and sweet rosy lips. He believed her to be nothing more than a tragic widow who had become his own dear love, little realising that from the age of seventeen – when her husband had fallen at the battle of Halidon Hill – she had sold her body for money and favours to middle-aged men.

But the sleeping girl, in her wakeful moments, did not regard herself in that light. Nichola de Rougemont saw herself simply as a mistress – young and sensual, uninhibited and pleasing, a skilled exponent of the art of love.

Now she woke, opening her eyes slowly, and saw Robert watching her. She read so much in his look – desire, love, his youth recaptured – that she smiled lazily. Then she sensuously slithered on to him, prolonging his delicious agony until he was a boy again, wet with dreams and wild with delicate sensation. It was a performance of consummate power and artistry.

Robert knew then, just before he fell back to sleep, that he could never give Nichola up. In the aftermath of lovemaking he made drowsy plans; plans that included Sharndene but somehow glossed over the futures of Margaret and Oriel, and most certainly did not encompass Piers. Yet plans that stopped short at the thought of Hamon – Robert's eldest son who had fought in the Scottish wars and had risen to serve in the king's personal retinue – and his monumental disapproval if anything should upset his mother.

No, he would not think of Hamon, only of Nichola, decided Robert, as he fell asleep beside her.

EIGHT

The unexpected laughter in the valley of Byvelham seemed to catch between the hills and echo round the moat and the manor house and through the thick wild flowers that grew profusely where the trees were thin. And to the horseman, riding fast from the direction of Maghefeld, the sound came as a shock which made him slow his mount and gaze about him to learn who was so carefree on that bright and gentle June morning. Much to his amazement the rider saw Margaret de Sharndene and a stranger over on the far ridge, their heads thrown back and every sign about them, even at this distance, of harmony and enjoyment.

John Waleis's big handsome face grew dark, for he was the archetypal man of substance, liking everything in its place, his houses, his steward, his villeins, and, most particularly, his wife. And, by the same token, the wives of his friends and contemporaries. It did not do for consorts to be out and about without proper escort. Nor for them to be laughing and enjoying themselves without the stabilising influence of their husbands.

Curiously, and as rather a jest of fate, John himself had the most deliciously individual wife alive. Alice Waleis had long since perfected the art of appearing to comply whilst actually doing precisely what she wanted.

But John realised nothing of this and now spurred his horse on to where Margaret and her companion went at walking pace down towards the woods.

'Good-day,' he shouted, bristling with importance at the possible discovery of an illicit meeting.

'Sir John,' Margaret was obviously pleased. 'Are you in good health? How is Alice?'

'Well enough. Well enough.' He stared at the stranger pointedly, obviously demanding an explanation.

Paul spoke. 'Paul d'Estrange, Sir John, a poor knight of Gascony, in England to seek redress for loss of his lands, having

81

joined the household of my Lord Archbishop the meanwhile – and there having met Madam Margaret. And, at this moment, taking some well-needed exercise in her company and delighting in the scenery. Alas, what it is to grow stout!'

He patted his stomach, which was as high and as round as an autumn pumpkin, with a pretended look of despair which slowly turned into a sheepish grin. It was obvious that he was a trencherman and would stint himself nothing in the way of rich foods and fine wines. John could almost hear the man smacking his lips as he talked. But there was something terribly likeable about him and the Englishman, who was also beginning to gain a little weight, found himself nodding sympathetically.

'What a joy it is indeed,' Paul went on, 'to see such glorious countryside.'

'You have not visited England before?' asked John.

'Oh yes,' Paul looked a little mysterious. 'Many, many times. But never to Sussex, never here. Never to this valley full of magic and merriment.'

Margaret and John stared at one another. 'How delightfully put!' they said, almost together.

Paul looked suitably gratified and made a bow from the saddle. As he did so his stomach vanished for a moment and Margaret thought, 'He was handsome when he was young. How wonderful to have known him then.'

She considered him quite the most fascinating and colourful character ever to have entered her life, and blessed the chance visit to the palace which had brought about their meeting. Robert, attractive though he had been when she had married him, had never had the charm that positively glowed from this Gascon.

She felt that John Waleis was eyeing her with some suspicion and forced her face into a serious expression. 'Perhaps we should go back, Sir Paul. Do you feel you that you have seen enough?'

The fieldmouse eyes twinkled. 'No, my Lady. If we might ride to the high point above us? I imagine from there the view would stretch for miles.'

He pointed to the plateau from whence John de Stratford had seen his stone palace for the very first time.

'I'll come with you,' said John abruptly. Then added, 'If you have no objection, Margaret?'

'Of course not.' Was her voice a little hesitant? 'Please do.'

The three riders climbed into the sunshine beneath a sky blue as a babe's sweet eye. Under the horses' feet the ground became coarse and scrubbish and then they reached the summit and looked down upon the sight before them. Field after field, wrested from the Wealden forest, stretched away in the colours of a herb garden. While beyond the cultivated land they saw fallow pasture, roamed all about by full-coated sheep and lambs and handsome brown cattle. But even then there were other splashes of colour; bluebells blazed splendour in the depths of a golden wood and out, on a distant hill, the rose-red coats of running wild deer were plainly to be seen.

'Paradise,' breathed Paul.

'But surely,' put in Margaret, 'your own estates in Gascony must have been equally lovely?'

'They were glorious, of course,' answered Paul. 'Gardens rolling down to the river beneath the ramparts of the castle. But here you have something unique: a rural magnificence echoed in the characters of those fortunate enough to live here.'

John's heart began to swell. 'What exactly do you mean?'

'A hardness of aspect, a fierceness of blood, combined with a mellowness of spirit, a gentleness of soul.'

The Englishman beamed at the man whom he had considered an intruder and seducer but barely fifteen minutes earlier.

'I would deem it an honour, Sir Paul, if you were to visit my father's house at Glynde. I know that he and my wife would be more than interested to meet you.'

John's recent thoughts of women in their place and men as master of the domain were now completely gone from his amazingly uncomplex mind as the party turned away towards the thick woods.

As they went down through the fields, Oriel saw them from her perch on the sloping hill above Tide Brook, where she had ridden with her serving woman. She raised an arm and gave a shout but, of course, the distant riders did not hear her, and went plunging on to where bluebells seemed to swallow them up and they vanished into a wave of flowers. She and Emma had ridden hard that morning, far harder than was Oriel's usual custom, for today there had been even greater enjoyment in the sound of pounding hooves and feeling herself, almost like a boy, leaning low over the horse's neck and shooting, arrowlike, towards the sun. But now Emma was showing signs of weariness and Oriel began the descent downhill that would lead them home to Sharndene.

As she came through the trees, she saw a stranger standing on the high ground and looking down to where the house lay surrounded by a moat full of sunshine. Though he had his back turned it was obvious that he was staring at the manor house, lost in admiration, and Oriel was at once reminded of her dream of a strange young man in the woods.

'Who is it?' she whispered to the servant.

'I think it must be the Gascon squire, Mistress. I've heard it said he's unusually tall.'

Oriel regarded him closely. Ever since her meeting with Sir Paul at the palace when the squire had been mentioned but not seen, she had wondered what he was like.

'Will you speak to him, Mistress?'

'Yes, of course. It would be rude to do otherwise.'

The horses crossed the ridge and at the sound of their approach, Oriel saw the Gascon's hand fly instinctively to his sword, before he realised that it was only two women who were coming towards him. He jumped from the saddle and bowed, and Oriel saw a bony face, a long lean body and bright eyes, gold as autumn apples.

'Mistress Oriel?' he said politely.

'Yes. Master Marcus?'

'At your command.'

They were both speaking formally as convention decreed and Oriel was wondering what to say next when a spectacular smile transformed the Gascon's features. Suddenly he looked young and amusing and interesting to be with. Oriel was perturbed to feel her heart quicken its beat. She willed herself not to blush but could feel the colour creeping into her cheeks.

The Gascon did not appear to notice and much to Oriel's relief started to look back towards Sharndene.

'What a beautiful situation,' he said. 'The house nestles so contentedly.'

She smiled. 'That is very poetic, Master Marcus. I have never thought of it like that.'

'That is because you are used to it. Rare beauty is treated as something quite ordinary by those who see it every day.'

Once again he gave his extraordinary smile and Oriel would

have looked away had not his eye caught hers so that she felt obliged to stare bravely at him. After a moment they stopped seeing each other as they really were and received impressions of eyes and features and hair. The air became alive with unexpressed emotions, with longed-for sensations, and both Marcus and Oriel believed at that moment that they had looked at each other like this before though neither could remember where or when.

How long they stayed like that nobody could tell for Emma, whose duty it was to protect her young mistress, found that she had to turn her head away, moved to tears by what she was witnessing. A hardened country-woman, brought up on rolls in the haystack and uncouth wooing, she believed that she was seeing that phenomenon she had only heard spoken about, falling in love at first meeting.

It was Marcus who finally broke the spell by saying, 'I will always serve you, you know that.'

To Oriel's shame she became an ordinary, prim girl again and said, 'We do not know each other, Master Marcus. You cannot serve a stranger.'

His features became hard and set and the smile vanished. 'We will never be strangers, Mistress. At least that is what I believe.'

Oriel would have answered something unworthy of her but was saved by a sight that attracted the attention of all three. A distant brown dot was coming from the direction of Maghefeld and heading for Sharndene at a great rate. They stared at it silently and as it reached the edge of the moat saw that it was the small and wizened monk who acted as secretary to the archbishop, riding a horse that seemed far too big for him.

'I wonder what he wants,' said Oriel, turning to Emma.

The monk clattered over the drawbridge, his funny round shoulders slumped within his habit like a pudding in a cloth.

Turning to look at Marcus again, she said, 'My mother is out riding with Sir Paul d'Estrange. I must go and receive him.'

'Then I will take my leave of you.'

He raised her hand to his lips and the touch sealed everything between them. They were on fire for each other, longing to be together embracing and loving, never wanting to be separated again.

All the way home, Oriel turned to stare over her shoulder at the departing horseman and as he disappeared into the trees on the track to Maghefeld, he waved. Oriel waved back till he was lost from her sight and Emma said, 'You shouldn't let him know you like him so much.'

A pair of blue eyes that held a sparkle the servant had never seen before, turned to regard her seriously.

'I could never hide my feelings from him, Emma. I feel that he is already part of me.'

'Be careful, Mistress, I beg you. Your father would be furious to think you had a light-of-love.'

'He's not that – yet,' answered Oriel, smiling. And Emma was left to keep her worries to herself as they crossed the drawbridge and went into Sharndene.

That night, soon after midnight, Alice Waleis, asleep in Bayndenn, had a strangely vivid dream. She dreamt that she stood on high ground above the moated manor and looked about her. Everywhere were colours that she had never observed in real life: stars of crystal were ice-white in ebony skies; purple hills rose up from lakes of deepest indigo; and streams flowed silver amongst jade-green pastures.

As Alice looked at these awesome shades she wondered whether she was, in fact, dead. Whether she had breathed her last in her sleep and it was her wandering soul which now stood alone and looked down upon the beauty of the magic valley at night.

In her dream Alice wore dark blue and held in her hand the mystic stones, wondering, as she looked at them, whether their secret was the eternal search for God, or whether they were the playthings of a darker power. And as she puzzled there came into view, almost as if it symbolised something, a strange procession. Seated on a white horse was Oriel de Sharndene, behind her two men, neither of whom Alice recognised. One was tall, thin, hawklike; the other short, dark, tragic-faced. There was also a man holding Oriel's bridle and as he stepped out of the shadow Alice saw to her amazement that it was Adam de Bayndenn, the man whom Isabel had bought out of serfdom and married.

Without seeing her they passed quite close to where Alice stood and it was then that she witnessed the events which filled her with a sense of danger. She saw Oriel's horse miss its footing

86

and the girl be thrown forward, only to be seized instantly by Adam and lifted to the ground below. Then, without warning, the man suddenly crushed her to his great frame and poured kiss after kiss upon her trembling and frightened mouth. In a flash the younger man was upon him, knocking Adam to the ground and smashing his fist repeatedly into the other's face.

Alice began to cry out but realised after a second that she was making no sound, that nobody was turning to look at her. Then she saw Adam's massive strength prevail. He rolled above the younger man and began to batter him like a puppet. At this the small man joined in, punching ineffectively at Adam's back like a child caught between two fighting adults.

Even from where she watched, Alice heard the terrible gasping sound of strangulation – and then the moon went behind a cloud. She was in total darkness, her eyes searching wildly for what she dreaded most to see. Somebody had been killed in that deserted place, but as to who it was she had no idea. She took a step forward, tripped over a hummock and began to fall down and down into the valley's secret heart.

'Oh help me,' she cried. 'Evil is at work this night.'

'Shush,' said John's voice beside her. 'It is a nightmare. You have been calling out these past few moments.'

Alice opened her eyes and saw daylight streaming into her bedchamber from the windows above.

'Oh,' she said, 'oh thank God! It seemed so real. I thought my soul had taken flight, for there were colours in the earth I had never seen before.'

'The fault lies in those sinister stones,' said her husband abruptly. 'You will see strange colours and hear dreadful things as long as they are in the place. I believe them to be Devil's work.'

'Or God's,' answered Alice slowly. 'Maybe we receive divine help and guidance through their auspices.'

'Never. They should be crushed to nothing and buried deep.'

She ignored him, climbing onto a stool to look out of the high window. In a different voice she remarked, 'It is a rose-bowl morning.'

'What do you mean?' he asked.

'There has been rain in the night and the flowers are newly-washed. And there is a smell in the air as sweet and sharp as any fine perfume. I must go out at once.'

She jumped down and began to splash her face with water, pulling on her stockings and kirtle – a long-trained dress which fitted tightly to her body – at the same time. Over this she drew her cotehardie – a tunic with elbow sleeves, fancifully trimmed – while on her head she thrust a linen wimple, swathing it round the front of her neck and chin and pinning the ends to the hair above her ears.

John, watching her rapid attempt at dressing, said, 'Where are you walking?'

'I thought I might go to Sharndene and talk to Margaret.'

'In that case I will come with you.'

He swung himself out of bed and put on his clothes. Like Alice he wore a long-sleeved cotehardie but beneath this was a gipon, a close fitting garment with kneelength skirt, which displayed his leg hose, cut on the bias and parti-coloured. On his head, instead of a hood, he drew a soft fur-trimmed and beret-shaped hat. Both he and his wife dressed fashionably for country folk and this morning was no exception.

'I really *do* want to walk,' said Alice as her husband turned automatically towards the stable.

His fondly-imagined look of mastery played about his big dark features momentarily, then he answered, 'Oh very well. It is a fine day, after all.'

They stepped out into a world washed clean by the rainfall of the previous night. All about them, upon every branch and leaf, raindrops trembled as clear and fine as jewels, reflecting in their lucence a host of little rainbows, while in the heart of a wild rose a spider's web was transformed to a silken net aglimmer with silver. Above their heads a dim, green arch had been formed by the trees so that, as Margaret and John walked through the Rother valley, they felt themselves to be in a holy place.

But it was the smell that made the morning bright as trumpets and fine as gold. From all around came the aroma of every kind of flower: apple blossom mingled with honeysuckle and rose, while the smaller plants sent up a strange keen perfume of their own. The combined scent of rain-washed petals and earth was almost overwhelming.

And as the Waleises approached Sharndene they saw that the moat, too, gurgled fresh and swollen with rain, the cob and pen riding high and on a level with the house.

'That should clean it,' said John hopefully.

The drop shafts from the Shardene garderobes fell directly into the moat below and a good rainstorm could always be relied upon to shift the sewage – in one direction or another. But further speculation was not possible. From one of the small upstairs windows a banging could be heard and, on looking up, they saw Margaret knocking frantically and sneezing like a pepper cook. As the banging grew Alice hurried into the house, through the hall and up the stairs to where Margaret waited at the top.

'My dear, are you ill?' she asked.

'No,' replied her friend, blowing her nose violently. 'It is this wretched complaint I get in summer, and it has come at quite the most inconvenient time. The archbishop has invited both Oriel and myself to the palace to dine with his brother today.'

Alice's mouth fell open. 'His brother? You mean Robert de Stratford?'

'No, no! The youngest of the three, Colin. He is very shy and rarely seen in public, but apparently he has lived at the palace since the archbishop's arrival.'

Alice shook her head as if she could scarcely believe it and Margaret went on, 'But I cannot go. I would sneeze all the way through the meal. Alice, would you be able to accompany Oriel?'

Margaret's face fell as her friend shook her head. 'John and I are to ride to Glynde this day. We will stay some time.'

'Then what's to be done?'

'Might you not send her with a servant?'

'No, Robert would not approve of that. Alice, do you think I could ask Isabel de Bayndenn?'

The dream came back to Alice with horrid clarity. She saw Adam's great body crushing that of Oriel as a bear might smash a flower. 'Oh no!' she said. But it was too late. Margaret had already rushed to the top of the stairs and was calling, 'Cogger! Cogger! Find me a rider immediately.'

Very slowly Alice Waleis made her way into Margaret's chamber and there took the unusual step of pouring herself a goodly cup of wine. It seemed that day there was a canker in the rose-bowl morning of Byvelham.

The town of Battle, which sprawled out from the gatehouse of the abbey, was wet that morning. The rain ran all over the rooftops of the great abbey built at the command of Duke William to commemorate his glorious victory, victory at which Christian blood had been spilled, including that of the English king. The abbey's high altar had been raised – over the very spot where Harold, son of Earl Godwin and last of the English rulers, had been cut down – as William's act of atonement.

Yet Robert de Sharndene, leaving his mistress's little house, which stood with a handful of others some quarter of a mile from the abbey itself, thought nothing of the place's violent history but only of his own misery, as he passed the mighty building which had been the Norman's visual penance for the terrible slaughter.

He was infinitely depressed. He would, at that moment, gladly have changed places with the poorest villein in the town. And ahead of him, too, lay a grim prospect, deepening his gloom. First must come his interview with the archbishop at which, he felt sure, accusations would be made about his guilty secret. And then – and far, far worse – he must face Margaret and tell her that he wanted to be rid of her. Even now, as he mounted his horse and rode away, he could imagine her ugly face – flushed and trembling, the eyes beginning to spout – as he told her that their marriage was over and done.

If only she did not love him so much, he thought with a sigh. If only she had not devoted her life to him and to the raising of their surviving children. If only, like that elf of a woman Alice Waleis, Margaret had some interests outside the home. And it was then that Robert adopted the comforting attitude of every faithless husband: he justified his actions with the conviction that it was his wife's own fault. For, after all, if she had remained young and slim, lively and on fire with passion, he could not possibly have strayed. It really was Margaret's responsibility to stay desirable in every way. Slightly happier, he spurred his horse on.

Approaching him from another track that led from Battle to London he saw, as he rode, a distant group of horsemen, their banners denoting them as being on the king's business. Robert narrowed his eyes. Was it possible that his eldest son was in their midst? But they were too far and too fast, their horses swirling up a cloud of dust even from the newly dampened highway, for him to identify anyone. He toyed with the idea of pursuing them but the possibility of Hamon being amongst them was remote and he turned his head away and continued his progress to Byvelham.

But he was wrong, for Hamon de Sharndene, tall and broad and handsome – a larger, tougher version of Piers in many ways – *was* in the entourage heading for Battle, and he and his father passed one another unknowingly. So it was the younger Sharndene who now rode through the gate at the western end of the abbey's precinct wall and, dismounting, went into the stone-built guest range that stood next to the great barn in the abbey's west courtyard.

Hamon was an interesting man, his dull exterior masking complex emotions and beliefs. For he, to whom killing was second nature, believed in pure love with a fervour that was fanatical. Yet hand in hand with his romanticism walked lechery, though this extraordinary dichotomy in his character was hidden by his generally tough appearance. Hamon was one of a group of men who were the hardest fighters in the world, with their Welsh long bows and heavy cavalry of armoured knights, to say nothing of their machine-like infantry. No one suspected the ale-swilling, laughing soldier's longing to die, metaphorically, for love.

But now this day, here in Battle, lust was upon him and calling to the villein who was humping in the accoutrements, Hamon said, 'Where can I find a woman?'

The servant, who was immensely gnarled and smelt quite rank, answered slowly, 'You are young Sharndene, aren't you?'

Somewhat startled, the knight replied, 'How did you know that?'

'I saw you once with your father, the bailiff.'

'I see.' Hamon had ceased to be interested. 'Well, are there women in this place?'

A strange glint formed beind the villein's bleary eye. 'Indeed, yes. There are plenty of women in Battle.'

Hamon frowned impatiently. 'You know perfectly well what I mean. A woman whose body I can hire.'

The villein clutched his sides in a sudden soundless cackle, his rotten gums fuming decay as he opened his mouth. Hamon waved his hand in front of his face.

'Speak up you old wretch or I'll give you a beating.'

The villein straightened, his face a wrinkled walnut, each crease etched in dirt. 'I can think of one to suit you fine, Sir,' he said. 'She lives a little distance away, which the gentlemen find convenient.'

'Then she's available?'

'Oh yes, Sir, very available. She has a little house of her own. I'll point you out the way.'

'Good. I'll go as soon as I have eaten.'

'Very well, Sir.' The villein was bowing in a cringing manner. 'But if you'll listen to an old man, I would not tell her your name.'

'Why not?'

'She might be afraid of the bailiff's son.'

'Oh, I see. Very well.'

Hamon turned away and did not see the villein once again bent double in mirth behind his back.

The rider from Sharndene, in a hurry to deliver his lady's message, followed the Rother valley as far as he could and then turned towards Maghefeld and the soft green lands tenanted by Isabel de Bayndenn. Climbing up the slope he picked his way through the bluebell wood, then up again to the field and out to where Bayndenn stood overlooking one of the finest views in Sussex.

There the rider halted, tied his horse to a post and entered the hall in which Isabel and her servants lived. This afternoon there was no one about except Adam, who lay asleep on a bench before the central fire, one foot crossed over the other and his head back and snoring. He woke as Ralph entered noisily.

As always when he saw Adam, Robert's servant felt a wave of acute embarrassment. To him Isabel's husband was still a villein – as was Ralph himself. But there was one insurmountable difference between them: the younger man had been bought and then married by a freewoman; Ralph had remained the servant he had been born.

Now, feeling this difference strongly as he stood in Adam's hall, Ralph gave a slight nod of his head – nothing on God's earth would have induced him to bow – and said, 'I have a message for your wife from the Mistress of Sharndene. Can I possibly see the lady?'

Adam went slightly pink. 'My wife,' his tongue fumbled and tripped round the words, 'is busy outside. You'll find her there.'

Ralph's look said, 'So what are you doing sitting by the fire?' and as if he had read his thoughts Adam added, 'I have been ill with the ague and she wished me to stay indoors.'

Suddenly and quite inexplicably, the messenger felt sorry for him. Adam was no more his own man now than he had been when he was the property of Godfrey Waleis. He had simply gone from one kind of serfdom to another.

'I'll wait with you if I may,' Ralph said, guilty because he had just had uncharitable thoughts, but had done no more than take his place by the fire before the archway darkened and, smiling at them both, Isabel stood in the entrance.

With the afternoon light falling full on her face, Ralph studied her carefully. He knew, could calculate, that she must be approaching sixty and yet she could have been mistaken, by a stranger, for twenty years less. Her clear, fine skin bore only the slightest suggestion of wrinkles and the thick dark hair, visible in strands peeping from her wimple, carried no sign of grey. Her blue-stockinged legs – clearly to be seen as she had tucked her kirtle into her belt in order to walk faster – seemed also those of a far younger woman. And as she released the skirt to fall once more to the floor, a firm and marbled thigh could be glimpsed.

Ralph rose. 'Madam, I come from Sharndene to ask a favour. Mistress Oriel is to dine with the archbishop today and her mother is sick with the great summer fever. She asks if you and your husband would accompany her.'

Isabel wiped her fingers across her cheek and a tiny smudge appeared; she worked the land she tenanted with her own two hands and cared not a whit who knew it. But the gap between Adam and herself gaped vastly as she answered, 'Yes, of course we will.'

In any other marriage the wife would have turned to her partner and asked him if it was convenient.

In fact, Ralph thought, in any other marriage it would have been the master of the house who would have made the decision.

His anguish for her husband grew as Adam, to cover up his position, mumbled like an echo, 'Of course we will.'

Isabel gave him a beaming smile as though he had just made a clever and original remark. 'Good,' she said.

Ralph nodded again. 'In that case, Madam, I shall return

at once for I know my mistress is anxious for your reply.'

Isabel smiled once more, looking beautiful. 'Then I must get the great tub filled if I am to dine with the archbishop.'

Without thinking, without even being consciously aware of what he was doing, Adam, bowing, said, 'I will see to it,' and left the room.

Nichola's little house was quite easy to find, even to a stranger on foot. Hamon went through the abbey's western end, passed the pilgrims' house, known locally as The Hospital, and proceeded down the broad track that ran through the midst of the village dwellings. Then he turned right, as instructed by the villein and found, standing on another track with rolling fields behind them, a few more buildings. The first he came to was the house described to him as that of the woman, and there he stopped and gave a most peremptory knock on the door.

At first there was no response, but after he had banged his fist upon the wood again, someone called 'What is it?' and standing back a few paces and tilting his head, Hamon saw that through the unglazed slit a girl was looking out.

'I was recommended to come here,' he answered fairly softly, aware of the presence of a damp-nostrilled child who stood outside the nearest dwelling to the little house.

'What?' The girl bent her head forward.

'I'm staying at the abbey.' Hamon spoke rather more loudly, sure that the child was now regarding him beadily.

'What? I can't hear you.'

The glimpse of head withdrew and after a moment or two the door opened to reveal a young and fetching female, her red hair loose and streaming to her buttocks. She wore nothing but a cloak thrown around her, having obviously just woken from sleep.

'I'm sorry to disturb you. I was recommended to come here,' said Hamon, rather abashed.

She stared at him and he went on, 'I was told you were available.'

An extraordinary look crossed her face and then she said, 'Oh, were you!'

'Yes.'

Under her silent scrutiny young Sharndene felt himself grow hot. She really was very desirable. Yet he could not understand why a harlot should be subjecting him to such a cool and appraising stare.

'Have I made a mistake?' he said at length. And then he smiled, rather sheepishly.

Despite her anger at his impertinence, Nichola smiled back. There was something she liked about this man, with his rough cropped hair and scar slanting upward from one eyebrow, and the bony wrists showing beneath the sleeves of his jerkin.

'Come in,' she said.

He dominated her doorway being too tall and too broad to pass through easily.

'Now . . .' she said, but never managed to speak another word. As if her invitation to enter had been the sign he was looking for, the soldier gathered her into his arms with a kiss so ardent that Nichola felt swamped – not one of her lovers, nor even her young husband, had ever aroused such an instant response in her.

She knew that she should push him away, tell him that he was making a terrible mistake, pretend that she was a woman of virtue, but her body was growing limp and she wanted nothing more than to let this strange young man share her bed.

Eventually he loosened his grip and said, 'You are so beautiful that I feel you must be expensive. I am not sure that I will be able to afford you.'

This was the moment when she should have turned him out of doors but instead Nichola said, 'Most of my clients are soldiers. I charge only what they can pay.'

'Then may I stay?'

She could not bring herself to answer no but instead let him kiss her again and go with her to her bedchamber, where she threw off her concealing cloak and teased him with her pretty figure until he could bear it no longer and entered her. Neither of them had ever experienced such passion or such fulfilment, they were at one from his first touch to the climax of love. And afterwards, before he returned to the abbey, Hamon kissed her tenderly and wondered why she smiled so secretively when he pressed his entire purse into her strong little hand.

As her brother Hamon fell contentedly into his bed in the abbey guest house, Oriel Sharndene was making her way through the palace doors and up the stairs to the great antechamber, where, in all his glory and power and arrayed with a ruby ring that flashed at his slightest move, the Primate of all England, the Archbishop of Canterbury himself, stood awaiting her arrival.

Both she and Isabel de Bayndenn, who followed one step behind her, paid their respects and with his own hands Stratford raised them up after they had saluted the archiepiscopal ring.

'My Lord,' said Isabel, giving a grave and beautiful smile. 'My husband and myself accompany Oriel as Master Sharndene is not yet returned from Battle and madam is ill with the great summer fever.'

Behind the archbishop's frozen face an expression – surely not of relief? – gleamed for a second before he said, 'You are most welcome, my Lady, and you also, Adam. And Oriel, of course my dear, you are my honoured guest.'

'My brother Colin will be joining us shortly,' de Stratford went on. 'I must warn you all that he is extremely shy and unused to company. His great love is playing the gittern at which, I must say, he surpasses all but the very finest.'

In her mind Isabel was back in the woods beneath Bayndenn, listening to a stranger with little stubby hands pluck glorious sounds from the instrument's rosewood heart. She remembered Colin's innocent smile, all purity and joy, and started as she saw it again from the doorway, where the archbishop's brother had obviously been waiting some while in silence.

He advanced into the room, his eyes to the floor and his dark hair brushed neatly into curls.

'Ah, Colin!' said Stratford. 'Here are our guests.'

Slowly, and with the utmost care, the archbishop's brother bowed and Isabel was reminded of a child aping its elders. She gave him a kindly smile but saw that the man's light blue gaze had fastened on Oriel in fascination. And then Isabel witnessed the most touching thing. Oriel stretched out her hand and Colin took it and pressed it to his cheek. Isabel was seized with the ridiculous notion that the couple had known one another a long time.

'Will you accompany me to dinner, Madam?' said Stratford loudly, not leaving a second for her to form a more lasting impression.

'Of course, my Lord.'

Isabel went to walk beside him, shooting an affectionate glance at her husband as she did so. Much to her consternation Adam appeared to be in a daze, gazing at his feet, then shuffling miserably. And as the feast progressed he grew worse, staring first at Oriel, then Colin, and finally just at his platter. Isabel could not help but notice he ate barely nothing at all.

It was a great relief to her, therefore, when the archbishop finally waved to the minstrels to be silent and said, 'Colin, will you play for us? It is at the express wish of Mistress Oriel. She heard you once before and would like to do so again.'

Into the sudden silence Colin said, 'Was that the day I ran away from you?' and Oriel answered, 'Yes.'

The words in themselves were not particularly unusual but yet everyone present knew, by the very tone used, that Colin was simple, retarded – a man for whom there was no possibility of manhood.

All the guests remained frozen, waiting for somebody to show them what to do. Finally it was the archbishop who spoke.

'Colin's shyness is profound,' he said, adding slowly, 'So much so that sometimes he is inclined to withdraw from strangers.'

It was Stratford's obvious wish, then, that his brother's idiocy be regarded as modesty. The two women smiled and the moment passed. Without moving a muscle Stratford said, 'But Colin will make recompense now. Come along, brother.'

Was that flat, unemphatic voice hiding deeper emotion or was God's representative on earth incapable of human feeling? The question remained unanswered as Colin moved a little way away from the great table and picked up his gittern.

As soon as he touched the instrument a change came over him. It was as if he listened to a signal, a voice, that nobody else could hear. His eyes looked up and then closed; his fingers swept the strings with a tenderness bordering on love, as though he touched a human child. And then great volumes of sound poured out as Colin played a melody fierce and sweet, full of the passion he could never hope to know.

Nobody moved; nobody could have moved. And it was only Adam who felt something stir in his heart which he was later to identify as hatred.

'He should have been strangled at birth,' he thought. 'Put out of his misery, and not be seated here playing to Oriel de Sharndene as if he were a suitor.'

Without knowing at all why he did so, Adam began to shake as violently as if he still had the ague.

97

And this is what he said to his wife when he felt her enquiring gaze turn upon him. 'The fever,' he muttered. 'It has returned. I shall sit in the kitchens until you have done.'

Standing up he made a bow to the archbishop – who nodded his head imperceptibly by way of acknowledgment – then Adam left the hall, only too painfully aware that neither Oriel nor Colin had even so much as noticed his going.

NINE

On his way back from Battle, Robert de Sharndene stopped at Lewes, spending the night there alone, imagining Nichola also alone and thinking of him. And though he had set off early for Byvelham the next day, his mare had cast a shoe on the journey and he had walked her the few remaining miles home. As he had entered Byvelham Woods he had thought – most cynically, for he did not believe in the legend at all – that the dreadful vision of St Dunstan working in his forge would come in very useful at that moment. But he had seen nothing and had made his slow progress to Sharndene pondering how gullible, superstitious and ignorant were the native people of Sussex.

And now, as his villeins bowed before him, he caught himself despising them for being so dull and cloddish, and thanking God that he was of superior intellect.

As if the very same God promptly punished him for the sin of pride, Alice said, 'You are to go to Maghefeld at once, Robert. The archbishop's secretary has been here and demanded that as soon as you return you must attend his audience.' So there he was, just as menial as anybody else, and jumping to attention at the thought of the primate sending for him.

'What is it about? Why is it so urgent?'

'I don't know. He gave no indication. All I can tell you is that it *is*.'

'Well I must change – and have a drink! I've walked the last four miles. God help us, I wonder what the man wants.'

Margaret shrugged her shoulders and turned away. 'The sooner you go, the sooner you will find out.'

It was a cool reply and Robert was startled. 'I am aware of that,' he said icily. 'I shall go as soon as I am ready.'

'Good,' came the answer. 'Promptness is of the essence, as you are constantly reminding us.'

What was the matter with her? She had not been so crisp in the last ten years! Robert narrowed his eye and studied his wife carefully. Was it his imagination or had her appearance altered slightly? She certainly looked well; quite rosy of cheek and lip, with sparkling eyes that were very well painted. She had changed their shape somehow by the use of a darker tint.

'How have you fared in my absence?' he said, with the faintest hint of an undertone.

'The time has gone in a flash. I scarce noticed you were not here.'

For no reason that he could understand, Robert was furious. 'I see I need hardly have bothered to return,' he snapped, and stamped off towards their private chamber, his face flushed.

Normally Margaret would have gone chasing after him, cajoling and pleading with him not to be angry. But now she ignored him and went on her way, hurrying outside as if she had an appointment to keep.

'You wait!' said Robert under his breath, and then thought, 'I must be charitable at all costs. After all she has no youth and no looks to help her.'

Yet today she had seemed vivid; not pretty – she could never be that – but arresting and colourful; the sort of woman it would be interesting to know. Robert turned to see if he could catch another glimpse of her but Margaret had disappeared from view, only the scent of an unfamiliar musky perfume hanging in the air to remind him where she had recently been.

And on the journey to the palace Robert found himself still pondering the change in Margaret until he was ushered into the archbishop's chamber, full of sunshine and shadows and the smell of the herb garden beneath.

From one of these shadows a white hand motioned Robert to sit down and, looking closely, he saw that Stratford was already there, barely visible in the brightness. The bailiff bowed, suddenly terrified of the still and menacing figure regarding him with a strangely impassive face and so sharp and unblinking an eye. It was not difficult in that moment to imagine Isabella the queen and my Lord Bishop of Winchester huddled together like two black rooks as they plotted the downfall of Edward II with wicked words and hard dark faces.

But when the primate spoke it was in gentle enough tones. 'My dear Sharndene, how are you? How is everything at Battle?'

Was he playing with words? Did he really speak of Nichola de Rougemont?

'Very well, my Lord. And in Canterbury?'

'I have not been there for several days. Matters of import have kept me here in Maghefeld.'

There was a silence broken only by the sound of Robert shifting uncomfortably in his seat. Finally Sharndene said, 'You sent for me, my Lord. I was told the matter was urgent.'

Stratford tensed slightly.

'Really? I apologise. My secretary tends to exaggerate and sometimes grow confused. But he is a loyal servant of long standing – he was with me in Winchester you know – and I am loath to dispense with his services.'

This remark was unanswerable and Robert said nothing, hoping that he would be able to counter Stratford's next ploy.

'You know, of course, Sharndene, that you are the man most likely to be chosen as the next Sheriff of Sussex?'

'Really, my Lord?' The right ring of enthusiasm was not in his voice. He knew perfectly well that the archbishop was merely dancing on the edge of what he actually wanted to say.

'Yes.' Still that same flat voice. 'Obviously there are others who will be considered but naturally in the end the king's choice will fall on whoever has the highest connections and most proven loyalty. In short someone who can be relied on absolutely. A man such as you, Robert.'

'My Lord, so great an honour for me?' Robert bowed his head, thus hiding his puzzled expression. Could the archbishop possibly be sincere?

'Why not? You are no fool. You have served me well and, of course, with the right family connections ...'

Robert looked up again. 'What connections would those be, my Lord?'

Stratford sat immobile, only his black gown moving over the floor like droplets of ink.

'Those of marriage, Robert. I am saying that you could strengthen your house in one stroke. My brother Colin is offering for the hand of your daughter, Oriel.'

Robert stared aghast, his jaw dropping almost to his chest.

'Why so astonished? He is but thirty years. He is not pre-contracted and he says he has fallen in love. Where's the strangeness in that?'

'But my Lord ...'

How to say aloud that gossip spoke of Colin as an idiot, that stories of his lunacy circulated even in the valley of Byvelham?

'Yes?'

Robert shook his head. 'I do not know what to answer.'

Suddenly and visibly the archbishop lost patience. 'I must comment, Sharndene, that I am not flattered by your reaction. I would have thought that an alliance with the brother of Canterbury would have pleased the hearts of most men in the Kingdom.'

The ruthless opportunist in Robert rose rapidly to the surface.

'My Lord, I meant no offence. It is the very honour you have paid me that has rendered me speechless. Naturally, for me to have met Master Colin would have been an advantage ...'

'Yes.' The archbishop rose up like a wraith, reaching for the wine flagon with a pale hand and poured out two golden measures. 'You will no doubt have heard, Robert, of my brother's excessive shyness. Much of what is said is exaggerated of course! But the truth is that he does not care for people as a whole.'

'But what about Oriel?'

'Your daughter seems very fond of him, and he devoted to her. In fact they are well suited. Or so I thought when Oriel dined here yesterday.' The archbishop paused and sipped his wine, the thin lips savouring the drops with ascetic enjoyment. 'Naturally, as my brother has this social disadvantage, the question of Oriel's dowry would be totally waived. Now what say you?'

Robert reeled with shock: first Juliana de Mouleshale and now the Archbishop of Canterbury himself! 'I shall have to consider, my Lord,' he answered cautiously.

Without moving a muscle Stratford hardened his eyes. 'I would have expected a more positive reaction from you, Sharndene.'

Robert hung his head. 'My Lord, I can go no further. My conscience tells me that I must ask Oriel if Master Colin's timidity ...' He cleared his throat. 'Gives her any ...'

He never completed the sentence for from the courtyard below, the sound of a gittern, strange and joyful, rose on the quiet air.

'There,' said Stratford abruptly. 'That is him. See for yourself.'

Crossing to the window Robert looked down. A harmless creature sat below, his head bent to the instrument as if it were his life's heartbeat.

'Colin!' Stratford called. 'Come up here at once. Master Sharndene wants to see you.'

Startled, the young man stopped playing and Robert saw a pair of light blue eyes give him a frightened glance. And they were no less afraid when, a minute or two later, Colin stood before him, bowing awkwardly.

The archbishop suddenly appeared savage, bellowing at the poor wretch, 'Go on! Tell Master Sharndene of your love for his daughter. Speak up. I have made the formal offer on your behalf, now it is up to you.'

His brother went crimson and shuffled his feet while the archbishop looked as if he would like to strike him. Hard man that he was, Robert Sharndene could not help but pity the creature.

'So you wish to marry Oriel?' he asked in gentle tones.

'Yes,' said Colin, dropping on one knee and embarrassingly kissing Robert's hand. 'Please permit this, Sir. I would be very kind to her all the time, I promise you.'

Sharndene's heart sank, that the young man was backward was glaringly obvious.

'I will speak to her,' he said. 'That is all I can do.'

'If I can have her,' answered Colin, 'I will serve her with my life – as I always have.'

As Robert de Sharndene left the palace by the main door he saw Colin come round from the kitchens in the company of a tall young man whom Robert had never noticed before. And as he mounted his horse, so, too, did the stranger help Colin into the saddle and then mount himself.

Seeing the direction of Robert's eyes Cogger, who had accompanied his master to the palace said, 'That is a new member of my lord's household; a Gascon squire here with his patron, the knight.'

'For what reason?'

'To seek redress for the loss of their lands. But as the king is too busy to hear their suit they have sought help at the hands of the archbishop. It is said that the squire has been appointed Master Colin's new keeper.'

'Then he *is* mad?'

'Oh totally, Sir,' answered Cogger cheerfully.

Robert shook his head, keeping his thoughts to himself, but as he and his steward headed in the direction of Sharndene he saw the Gascon turn with the archbishop's brother towards Bayndenn.

'I wonder where they are off to?'

'I think they go to the river, Sir. I think Master Marcus is teaching the half-wit to hawk and to fish.'

'And the knight? What does he do?'

Cogger looked at him straight-faced. 'Become a firm favourite with everyone he meets. He has already been invited to Glynde and I know that Madam Margaret is only awaiting your return to ask him to dine at Sharndene.'

Robert gaped. 'Margaret knows him?'

'Oh yes indeed, Sir. They have been out riding several times and she is showing him various local landmarks.'

Robert's eyebrows rose. So here lay the explanation of his wife's rediscovered vivacity and careful use of cosmetics. The poor thing was flattered by the attentions, probably all imaginary, of a landless Gascon. Nonetheless a slight pang of annoyance swept him and his bright eyes grew calculating.

'I hope he is duly appreciative.'

'I think he is most grateful to Madam Margaret, Sir. He has already mixed her several compounds which, so her woman says, are Arab potions for health and beauty.'

Robert would have loved to ask more but a certain dignity forbade him from gossiping with his steward. Instead he said, 'I shall be most interested to hear about it from madam herself. Thank you, Cogger.'

Duly chastened the steward relapsed into silence as he and his master cantered towards home.

'Who is that?' asked Marcus, watching the horsemen disappear.

'Master Sharndene.'

'Oriel's father?' The squire looked at the distant figures with newly awakened interest.

'Yes. Soon to be mine, I think.'

'Who? What do you mean?'

'John has offered for Oriel's hand on my behalf. He wants her to be my wife.'

Marcus's stomach turned so suddenly that for a moment he thought he would vomit, and he was forced to clap his hand over his mouth as he retched.

'What is it, Marcus? What is wrong? Are you ill?'

The earnest blue eyes stared at him anxiously and the little man began to mouth with distress.

'No, I'm all right. It will pass.'

Marcus stood still, reining his horse in and slipping from the saddle in order to lean against its comforting brown flank. The smell of its skin was the thing he would always associate afterwards with pain in his chest, a pain which was, he presumed, generally termed a breaking heart.

His eyes slid sideways and he regarded Colin with a hard, black stare. He had heard it said that madmen could be wild in their passion, as cruel and base as the beasts of the field.

'Why are you looking at me like that?' asked Colin. 'Have I been naughty?'

Instantly Marcus felt guilty. What right had he to react like this; he had done no more than talk to Oriel Sharndene. If her father wished to strengthen his position with the archbishop, what business was it of a humble Gascon squire whose master no longer even had estates?

'I'm sorry,' he said. 'I was thinking.'

Colin's smile was guileless. 'You are thoughtful, yes. Then too.'

'What do you mean? When?'

'Oh, just then,' answered Colin vaguely.

They had reached the lands tenanted by Isabel, and Marcus found that he had dismounted by a large pond, heavily grown with willows which bent their heads to its dark green waters. Though there was no sign of anyone about, someone had started to build a cottage on its secluded shores for he could see its mud walls already taking shape.

'Come on,' he said, resolved not to punish the little man further, 'I'll show you how to skim a stone across the water.'

He picked one up and watched it bounce across the tranquil surface, making little splashes as it went.

'Here, let me.' Colin was eager as a child; surely lust must be unknown to such an innocent?

The half-wit's stone sank but, grimly determined, he picked up another, his teeth biting his lower lip with the anxiety of perfecting this new game. Smiling, Marcus sat down, his back to one of the trees, removing his jerkin as he did so. He rolled it up and put it behind his head and, just momentarily in the heat of the day, closed his eyes.

He must have dropped straight off to sleep for he had a curious dream almost immediately. It was that he opened his eyes and saw the cottage built and standing outside it a girl; a tall, lean girl with black hair hanging loosely to her waist. She was humming a song to herself and picking some flowers that grew in the shallow water. From inside the cottage came the clack of a spindle and a white cat sat on its step, washing its face with a long thin paw.

In his dream Marcus stood up and the movement must have attracted the girl's attention, for she looked over to him. He saw her face then; saw the angular bones of it; how the hair grew from a point on her forehead; and how her eyes gleamed against her skin.

'You've come then,' she said.

He was so frightened that Marcus woke himself up, and sat panting and gasping beneath the tree. Colin looked at him curiously from where he stood skimming stones with ease.

'I've learned how to do it,' he said.

'You've mastered that quickly.' Marcus got to his feet, amazed at how stiff he felt.

Colin regarded him seriously. 'I thought it took me a long time. Look, the sun has started to dip.'

He was right. The waters of the pond were shimmering, reflecting the light of a sinking sun, their stillness broken only by two wild ducks which silently emerged from the tall reeds and made rhythmically for the opposite bank. Marcus's glance at the cottage confirmed that it was nothing but a shell, needing thatching and shaping and completion.

'I must have slept for some while,' he said.

'Yes, though your eyes were open. You were staring.'

Marcus felt a frissance of fear. 'At what?'

'At that little building.'

'Was anybody there?'

'No, nobody. We have been alone all the time.'

Marcus suddenly shivered. 'Come on, it's getting chilly. We must get you home.'

'Can we come here again tomorrow?'

'No, not here. We shall go to the river as we usually do.'

They mounted their horses in silence and turned back towards Maghefeld.

As they arrived at the top of the hill from where they could look down on the palace, a man and a woman, very brightly dressed, came out of its main door. Marcus felt a sense of unease, the figure of the man was unpleasantly familiar.

'Who's that?' he asked.

Colin squeezed up his light eyes. 'Piers Sharndene, Oriel's brother.'

Marcus's heart sank. The last time he had set eyes on Piers had been over the dripping corpse of James Mouleshale.

Without looking at Robert, Oriel swallowed and stared at the floor.

'Say something.' Sharndene could feel irritability rising in his throat. 'Go on girl! Don't stand there tongue-tied. Will you marry the archbishop's brother?'

Without waiting for her reply he went on, 'I am giving you the chance to say no, Oriel, not holding you to your promise never to disobey me again. And why am I doing this? Because I believe Colin de Stratford to be a raving lunatic, that is why.'

'That he is not.'

'What did you say?'

'He is not mad, only childlike.'

Oriel's vivid eyes – usually so unclouded – looked fierce for a moment before she dropped her gaze once more to the ground.

Robert lowered his tone and said soothingly, 'So you do not find him offensive?'

From somewhere behind him Sharndene was vaguely aware of the twitch of a blue-stockinged leg as Margaret signalled to Oriel with her foot. Ignoring the move he went on, 'In that case it would be a great honour for us all if this family were to be allied with that of the archbishop.'

He cleared his throat, 'You realise I am being considered as Sheriff of the county. Stratford can influence the king enormously when the day comes for a choice to be made.'

He paused and Oriel answered softly, 'Father, thank you for giving me the right of refusal. However, Colin is kind and I accept.'

Out of the shadows, Margaret spoke. 'Oriel, you are quite

certain about this? Your father's future prospects are of little consequence compared with a lifetime tied to a man who is, at his best, retarded.'

As Robert turned to glare at her, Margaret met his eyes with the boldest look he had seen in them for years, and he thought briefly that she was turning into a considerable woman.

In the silence that followed, Oriel spoke again. 'It is unnecessary to consider further. I shall have to marry someone soon and Colin will do as well as any.'

'Then I shall leave at once to tell them,' said Robert, turning to the window that Margaret might not see the conflicting emotions which swept his face.

But he had no time to think, for immediately his eye was caught by an extraordinary cavalcade wending its way down into the hollow in which Sharndene nestled. With their backs to the setting sun and riding in quite the most excellently caparisoned splendour came Piers and Juliana de Mouleshale, accompanied by a host of out-riders.

Even from this distance Robert could see that his son was dressed sumptuously in fine white clothes sewn with brilliants, a scarlet trimming around his hat and, on his feet, soft shoes with pointed toes. Juliana, too, was tricked up as finely as her escort, sporting a high pointed hennin from which floated a gold-threaded veil.

'God 'a mercy!' said Robert as Margaret and Oriel crowded beside him, the discussion of a moment ago completely forgotten in the excitement.

'So *that* is where he's been!' said Margaret grimly.

'Comforting the bereaved mother!' Robert did not need to put an edge in his voice.

The procession began to clatter over the drawbridge and from the hall below Piers's shrill and excited tones could be heard as he dismounted and made his entrance.

'Where is my father?'

'Here,' cried Robert, striding down the stairs and into the hall. 'Where the Devil have you been?' He ignored Juliana who was making her way a few paces behind.

'Sir.' Piers had decided to be effusive and had sunk on one knee as his father approached.

'Get up, get up,' said Robert irritably, and was horrified to see that Juliana, too, had dropped to her knees like a penitent.

'We crave your blessing, Father,' said Piers sweetly.

'God's Holy Blood,' cried Robert. 'What have you done now?'

'I have wived, Sir. Wived!'

'I don't believe this,' shouted Margaret from the stairs. 'Madam, what has been going on?'

For answer Juliana rose from her kneeling pose and hurled herself at Margaret crying, 'Mother! Mother!'

Robert sat down heavily on the dais. 'Cogger, bring me a flagon. I feel my only escape is to lose myself in drink.'

Oriel, wide-eyed, turned to her mother. 'Is Juliana really my sister-in-law?'

'Aye, aye.' Piers rose to his feet, patting his sister on the head a fraction too hard. 'We were visited yesternight by Sir Priest and are wedded and bedded and have told the archbishop. All we need is the blessing of you both to seal our joy.'

He shot Robert a look which said, 'I've done it! I've married the Mouleshale fortune and you can go to hell in a bucket if you don't approve!' But his lips continued to smile winningly as Juliana, gawky as a pole, curtsied to her new parents-in-law.

'Oh God, God, God,' said Robert, drinking deeply. 'Two of them in one day! It is too much for human flesh to endure.' And in reply to Piers's puzzled frown, he went on, 'Your sister has but an hour since consented to marry Colin de Stratford, the archbishop's younger brother.'

'The half-wit?' Piers's charming expression slipped noticeably.

'You must not speak of him like that,' shouted Oriel. 'He is kind, and clever at music, and I feel as if I have known him always. He is already a friend to me.'

And with that, Oriel turned and left the hall without a word of farewell.

TEN

The sun dipped beyond the wooded hollow in which Sharndene nestled so snugly, as a roll of thunder sounded from the hills and a dark race of clouds blew inland from the sea. Then came silence, broken only by the cry of a distant storm-bird. The beautiful June day of 1334 was ending ominously.

To the great relief of the household, Piers insisted on leaving at once for Mouleshale, making a vast amount of noise about the danger of his bride getting drenched. Bidding his family a rapid farewell, he bundled Juliana on to her horse and carefully took to the saddle himself, adjusting his sleeves so that they could in no manner brush against the flanks of his mount.

'I don't know what to say,' gasped Margaret, having seen him off.

'I do,' answered Robert tersely. 'Piers has achieved his ambition. He has acquired a fortune by marrying a wretch. I would like to disown him.'

'Then why didn't you? You had your chance when he asked for your blessing,' answered Margaret roundly.

Yet again Robert was struck by the change in his wife. 'I hear that the Gascon knight is mixing you potions for your beauty,' he said abruptly. 'And what, pray, brings him to have knowledge of such a subject?'

Margaret blushed but answered, 'I did not know that you had stooped to gossiping with servants, Robert. But yes, it is true; Sir Paul *is* making me compounds. He was educated by a priest who crossed the Pyrenees and studied Arab medicine.'

Robert felt that he disliked the man before he had even met him. 'I must look out for this paragon when I go to the palace tonight – this man of arms and medicine and charm and learning,' he said irritably.

Much to his annoyance, Margaret laughed. 'I can see that you have taken against him, which is a pity for you. You will miss the companionship of a witty man.' She changed the subject before her husband could argue. 'If you are leaving for the palace I think it would be best if you did so soon. I believe we are in for a bad storm.'

Oriel stood up from where she had been sitting.

'You are going to tell Colin of my decision?'

'Yes.'

She smiled a little wearily. 'I hope he receives the news well. Goodnight. I will go to bed before the tempest begins.'

She turned and left the hall quietly, suddenly as small and defenceless as a flower. Staring after her Margaret said, 'I do not like it. I do not like it at all.'

Robert got to his feet. 'You heard what she said for yourself. She told Piers to hold his tongue; she claimed that Colin was already her friend. You cannot argue with that, Margaret.'

But his blustering words hid what he was really thinking and as his horse crossed the drawbridge, he almost turned back to tell his wife that he had changed his mind.

A wind had come up and howled round Robert, plucking his mantle and snatching at his horse's mane. As he rode through the woods it cried amongst the trees, as sad and forlorn as a dejected child. Even bending low and urging his mount to hurry could not take the sound away.

'But she swore that he was a friend to her. I gave her the chance to refuse,' he called out loud. But the wind ignored him and Robert was relieved to leave the trees and head for the open countryside and towards the palace. As he went through the door the rain started again, pouring down in a solid sheet, and he hurried inside and peered out again, making remarks about 'Evil night,' and wondering if the great Sir Paul d'Estrange were on hand and ready to receive a withering glance from Robert Sharndene.

And, sure enough, as he climbed the stone staircase he heard the sound of voices and on being shown into the great chamber discovered that, seated beside the brazier, the chess-board and pieces set out before them, John de Stratford and a stranger sat discussing a move.

They looked up as he entered and Robert thought, 'That funny little fat man can't be him!' Yet as the stranger leapt to his feet and bowed, Robert reconsidered. The penetrating mouse-bright eyes suggested someone who could not be overlooked.

Robert returned the bow and said coolly, 'Robert Sharndene,

Sir Paul. You are already spoken of with awe and I am happy to meet you at last.'

The Gascon smiled. 'Master Sharndene, my lord has also told me of you. It is an enormous pleasure to actually see you.'

John de Stratford, still with a chess-piece in his hand, said, 'Take a seat, Robert, do. I expect you have come with news for me.'

'Yes,' said Sharndene sitting down heavily, his mind suddenly removed from trying to put Paul d'Estrange in his place. 'I have indeed.'

On the top floor of the palace the storm seemed to scream and rage all the louder, the wind tearing at the rattling panes like marauding fingers and the rain lashing dementedly against the shivering walls. The noise was such that Marcus imagined the heralding of the last trump as he peered out of the window, only to see a lightning-streaked sky deep as an ocean and full of racing black chariot clouds. Behind him Colin shivered as a clap of thunder burst overhead.

'Has Master Sharndene really come to see John in this weather?' he asked wonderingly.

'Yes. I think he has come to tell the archbishop his decision about your marriage,' Marcus answered, trying to appear uncaring.

With the uncanny perception of the mad Colin said, 'It doesn't please you that I am to marry Oriel, does it? But it will not mean that we can no longer be friends.'

He looked pathetic, his face wrinkled as a walnut in his anxiety and his steadfast eyes glassy with unshed tears. Impulsively, Marcus crossed to the bed and, sitting down upon it, took Colin in his arms.

'I want you to be happy, you know I do. It is just that ...'

'You are afraid I will prefer Oriel to you? I won't, I promise you. The three of us will always be together.'

He was growing tired and, after a moment or two, his eyes closed and he fell asleep, still with Marcus's arms around him. Gently the squire put Colin down on his pillow and then flung himself on the floor beside his bed, lying fully dressed and listening to the storm, before slowly beginning to drift towards sleep.

*   *   *

The wicked weather blew itself away in the night, and the next day found clouds running like hounds in the sky and the sun slashing fire onto the hills. In the darkness before first light, John de Stratford rose from his bed and avoiding the chapel situated between the hall and the tower directly above the porch, went to the tiny place in his great chamber where Thomas à Becket had once knelt to pray. Here he was solitary and in the dim candlelight could think in peace.

First he let his mind wander over the past: his part in the downfall of Edward II; his subsequent imprisonment at the hands of Roger Mortimer, the queen's lover; his emergence into favour again when the young monarch had personally arrested Mortimer, storming into the earl's bedroom and dragging him from the bed where he slept with the king's mother. Stratford had heard that she had begged her son not to execute her lover on the spot and Edward had reluctantly agreed. But the archbishop knew full well that his youthful king had never intended that; was far too clever to spill blood himself. Instead Edward had let Mortimer stand trial for his life and had appointed his trusted friend John de Stratford as his Chancellor and principal adviser.

In the darkness Stratford felt – just as the great Thomas before him – that though he loved his king yet he feared him. Like his ancestor Henry II, an enormous confidence, bordering on brashness, flowed in Edward's veins. One could never be quite sure what he was going to do next, or whether one might suddenly find oneself his enemy.

Preparing himself for prayer, Stratford guided his thoughts away from such matters and on to his own family life. And, as if God were already listening to him, a great pang of guilt swept him for his manipulation of Sharndene. Quite cruelly, quite coldly, quite without mercy, he had condemned a young and lively girl to a marriage that could bring her no joy. For kind and endearing though Colin might be, his brain was that of a child in every sense. Though his body might suspect the existence of a physical union between man and woman, unlike many madmen Colin would be incapable of the act. Oriel de Sharndene was destined for a life without love.

Or was she? In the dim light Stratford felt a shiver of disquiet. Forces were at work, things over which he had no control.

'Oh God help me,' he murmured. 'I am Your most powerful

113

servant, and yet the most humble of them all. Help me to know what is right.'

He shivered more violently than ever. He felt that a man knelt beside him, could almost feel the penitent's hair shirt beneath the finespun robe. It seemed that a voice breathed to him, 'Let events take their course.' In glorious terror Stratford crossed himself and closed his eyes fervently, lest he should actually see the great Becket and die of joy.

But an hour later as dawn came up he was himself once more. As he led the prayers in the larger chapel, his eyes were without expression in a face blank as a mask.

'I shall leave for Canterbury,' he told his wizened secretary afterwards. 'Be prepared to go within the hour. And see that Sir Paul d'Estrange is roused. I think on this occasion it might be as well if he accompanies me.'

The palace was in an uproar, servants hurrying about and a great many monks rushing to and fro with papers and books.

'What is happening?' Marcus asked Wevere.

'My lord is leaving for Canterbury with no prior warning. We must be ready within the hour.'

Knowing how dishevelled he must appear, Marcus nonetheless went at once to Paul's chamber, where he found the knight dressed for riding, pulling a pair of boots on to his plump legs.

'Marcus, where have you been? I needed help to dress but when I went to your chamber you were not there.'

Rather irritably, Marcus answered, 'Colin was afraid of the storm and I spent the night in his chamber.'

'Well, those kind of duties won't befall you much longer. He is soon to be a married man. Robert Sharndene came here last night to give his consent to the match with his daughter.'

Marcus did not answer, bending down to help pull on Paul's boots.

'An odd business,' went on Paul, unaware of his squire's frozen manner. 'There will be no joy for her in that relationship.'

Marcus's face appeared wearily. 'Do you mean that the marriage will go unconsummated?' he asked.

'Either that or Colin will not leave her alone. Whichever way it turns out it will not make for a happy situation.'

Something of the taut and narrowed lips, and the patches of white that appeared round Marcus's nostrils, made Paul pause.

114

Was it distaste that brought about such violent reaction? The Gascon's voice took on a soothing note, much as it had to a solemn-faced little boy with a ring pinned to his hat. 'What is the matter? Do you not approve of the match?'

The squire flung himself violently to his feet. 'The very idea revolts me. I do not like to think of a young girl being sacrificed.'

'Young girls are sacrificed every day and yet none of us are incensed. Why are you so concerned about this one in particular? I did not realise you had even met her.'

'Well I have, briefly.'

Paul looked thoughtful. 'I believe you have formed some sort of attachment already. Be careful, Marcus.'

'What do you mean?'

'What I say. Danger lies along that path. Robert Sharndene is a hard man.'

Almost savagely Marcus answered, 'I care nothing for him but I will not see his daughter suffer.'

'And how will you stop it?'

'I don't know yet. But I shall try.'

The knight's mouth was a mere line in the folds of his jolly face. 'You are not to lay a hand on the archbishop's brother. Stratford is our patron in this country and you will remember it.'

Marcus nodded. 'I *will* remember it.'

Paul stood up. 'Marcus, I know you too well. Give me your oath that you will behave while I am away.'

'I swear it.'

But there the unpredictable side of the squire's nature over-ruled his promise, for no sooner had Paul left the room than Marcus picked up a jar of ointment intended for Margaret and hid it within his jerkin. He fully intended to see Robert Sharndene's daughter again before the day was out.

Oriel sat before her mirror and thought, 'Is that solemn creature really me? Is that Oriel Sharndene who gazes out at me without a smile?'

She studied her reflection carefully, seeing the fall of gilt-coloured hair, the mazarine eyes, the red mouth with its curving lips. She thought, dispassionately, that today she looked well. She had drunk wine to cheer herself and her cheeks were pink

and glowing; her eyes sparkled like fine-cut gemstones. Yet still
she had a sad air, the air of one resigned to settle for whatever
fate was about to mete out.

Oriel sipped the wine again, relishing its fine heady taste, and
leant forward to trace the lines of her nose with her forefinger.
Yes, she had beauty; a healthy golden beauty that she had
hoped would bring her a man with whom she could taste all the
dangerous and delicious fruits of love. But that was not to be her
fate, she must settle instead for life with a good companion.

A noise in the hall below had her starting to her feet. Surely
that was the voice of the Gascon? Putting her head on one side
Oriel listened carefully. Yes, Marcus Flaviel had come to
Sharndene and was speaking to her mother. With a lift of her
heart Oriel whirled to the mirror again. She saw eyes more
brilliant than ever, and lips already beginning to smile. Satisfied, she hurried down the stairs.

Marcus caught sight of her and she stopped where she stood
in the hall entrance, faltering beneath his gaze. He was not able
to conceal his admiration, nor his desire for her. It was only the
second time they had met yet Oriel knew for sure that Marcus
Flaviel was already in love with her.

The hall crackled with feeling and there was silence as
Margaret's words died on her lips. She was aware, as was her
serving woman, that the young squire was staring at her
daughter as if, at any moment, he would snatch her in his arms.
Margaret cleared her throat remembering suddenly how
Robert had once looked at her, all those years ago when he had
chosen her rather than Anne de Winter.

'Master Marcus,' she said, 'I thank you for bringing this
ointment and would ask you to take refreshment with us if it
were not for the fact that we are going out.'

It was a lie and everyone knew it. With an effort Marcus
collected himself. 'I thank you, Madam, but I could not stay in
any case. Master Colin will soon be requiring my services.'

'Are you to remain his ... er ... companion after the wedding?' Margaret asked, her voice unusually loud.

'I do not know, Madam. The archbishop has given me no
instructions. But I do not suppose so.'

'But you will be staying on at the palace?' This from Oriel
whose voice, in turn, sounded unnaturally high-pitched.

Marcus bowed. 'Again, I do not know, Mistress Oriel. I

116

am in the hands of my patron, Sir Paul. I can only await developments.'

There was another breathless pause during which Margaret was horrified to see her daughter blush furiously and murmur, 'I hope you will remain.'

'In a minute,' thought Margaret, 'they will kiss one another. Oh Jesu, that this should happen just as she is to be married! I must speak to Robert. The Gascons must go from the palace.'

But even as she thought it, Margaret knew that she would do nothing of the kind; that she would rather see her daughter go into deep water than lose the companionship and advice of Paul d'Estrange at this stage of her life. Why, the mirror told her how her looks were improving and her heart said that she no longer cared if Robert had a hundred women with sarcanet gloves.

Almost against her will, Margaret found herself saying, 'Yes, I do hope that you will remain with us.'

He paid no attention to her, lost as he was, in the look that he and Oriel were exchanging.

ELEVEN

On the evening before her wedding Oriel Sharndene vanished for a while and nobody could find her within the vicinity of the house. It was Marcus who by chance saw her, sitting by the Rother at the point where the pastureland joined the water in a profusion of flowers. He saw green moss and silver willow and spun-gold hair, all reflected in the water's glassy surface and he knew that fate had sent him this way to come face to face with Oriel on the night before she married.

She sat with her back to him, her knees drawn up to her chin and her arms clasped around them, so that she did not hear his approach. It was only when his shadow fell over her, blotting out the August sunshine, that she turned and regarded him steadily, no smile playing round the curving mouth or lighting the bluebell eyes.

They stared at each other in silence, conscious of the sound of birds all about them and the distant call of cattle from the meadows. Eventually Oriel said, 'Why have you come? Did you know I was here?'

Marcus did not answer, but asked instead, 'What are you doing by yourself?'

She turned her head away from him. 'Thinking.'

'Oriel, do you love the archbishop's brother?' asked the squire abruptly.

'I don't know,' came the reply. 'I know nothing of love. How could I? All I know about is my duty – and that is clear. I have been promised to Colin by my father.'

'Then there is no tenderness in your heart for your betrothed?'

Oriel turned to look at Marcus once more. 'I have great affection for him. In fact I believe he will become my greatest friend. But I do not love him as a woman loves a man, if that answers your question.'

'Yes, it answers it,' answered Marcus, gently raising her to her feet. 'So now may I ask another?'

'What is that?'

'That day, four weeks ago, when I called on your mother at Sharndene ...'

'Yes?'

'Did you not feel then, as I did, that there was great affection between *us*? An affection that could easily turn to love?'

Oriel's colour heightened. 'I felt ... drawn to you, yes.'

Marcus took a step closer and placed his hands on her shoulders. He was so tall that Oriel had to bend her head backwards in order to see him.

'In my case it did change. The affection *has* become love.'

She looked at him very seriously, 'Are you teasing me?'

For answer his lips touched hers, so gently that it was like the brush of birds' wings, then slid down to embrace every curve and hollow of her neck until finally they returned to her mouth. Suddenly the manner of the kiss changed and her lips parted beneath his as Marcus swept Oriel into his arms, the hardness of his body pressing against the softness of hers.

Finally they drew apart and he said, 'By Christ's Holy Blood I am not teasing you. I love you and want you – and have from the first moment I saw you.'

Breathlessly Oriel drew back. 'But you cannot have me. You know that. Tomorrow is my wedding day.'

The strength of his feelings aroused Marcus's anger. 'Damn your wedding. Colin shall not be your husband. If he lays a finger on you he is a dead man.'

Oriel froze where she stood. 'You must not harm him, it would be base and wrong. Mentally he is still a child. I shall be his wife in name only.'

There was a silence while they looked at one another searchingly until finally Oriel added, 'It is not going to be easy for either of us. I think, perhaps, we have chosen the path to destruction.'

The hawk features were set in hard lines as he answered, 'I can bear destruction if your love is my reward. Will it be?'

'Yes,' she said quietly.

They drew close to kiss once more, this time quite gently, knowing that they must leave each other's company and that he would not see her again until she was a bride. Then he lifted her onto her horse and watched as Oriel began the journey home.

When she vanished from view, Marcus mounted and rode slowly through Isabel's lands until he was almost within sight of

John Waleis's manor house, then the sound of a horse thudding behind him made him turn swiftly, thinking that Oriel had come back. But he was disappointed, for there riding hard towards him, his handsome face drawn into a scowl, was her brother, Piers.

As if to underline the contrast between himself and his sister, the first thing young Sharndene did was to spit upon the ground with deliberation.

'When I was told two Gascons had joined the archbishop's retinue I had my suspicions. And when I heard you described, I knew. The fat man and the tall thin hawk – there could be no other! So it won't be as difficult for me to avenge James as I thought. You bloody murderer!'

Marcus was off his horse so fast that Piers had not time to draw breath before the squire had grabbed the collar of his beautiful mantle, newly purchased in London, and had half pulled him out of the saddle. If it were not for the fact that one of Piers's feet had caught in his stirrup, he would have been flat on his back on the ground.

'Listen you prick,' hissed the Gascon, pulling Sharndene's face to within an inch of his own, 'it was your hand that held the knife, and don't forget it. If you heard a rumour that my patron and I were here, then so did I hear a rumour. It was that you had married your lily boy's mother and in return for frequent servicing she had dressed you like a whore in spangles – and so she has.' The hard fingers deliberately tore the velvet collar and Piers let out a furious cry. 'One word of trouble from you, Sharndene, and I shall go straight to your keeper and tell her the truth. How, in a brawl, you were not even capable of killing the right man. How you missed me and struck her son instead.'

Piers struggled furiously in his grasp. 'By Christ, I'll kill you one day, Gascon. And when I have done so I'll bury you six feet deep and piss on your grave.'

'The more you threaten the greater fool you look. It is those who talk most who end up dead themselves.'

Marcus released Piers so violently that he fell the rest of the way, and lay on the ground staring angrily up at the squire. 'Sleep with your sword, Gascon. You'll not last six months.'

Marcus remounted, his horse wheeling round as he did so, pointing its head towards the palace. '*Au revoir*. Try to be civil at the wedding feast.'

Piers struggled to his feet. 'A wedding or a funeral, we shall have to wait and see.'

'Indeed we shall,' called Marcus over his departing shoulder.

The wedding morning dawned in a soft glow of lavender. Mist had rolled down the hills during the night and through its gentle veil the sun could be seen rising and burning, gilding the hours which should have been the brightest of a bride's life, and casting warmth on all those at Sharndene preparing for Oriel's marriage. When the vapour finally cleared, the land was subjected to the fierce heat of August, and the wedding guests grumbled aloud as sweat began to run against their skin and soak into their clothes.

Naturally the most finely garbed was Piers, clad in saffron and white, his hose so tight that his buttocks were stretched round and high as Lombard puddings in a buckram cloth. Juliana wore tawny and morello which only served to make her look gawdy, while Hamon, who had journeyed from London on the previous day, seemed, by contrast, sombre in dark grey, his short and jagged hair hidden beneath a hat of blue.

So it was, on that hot and merciless day, that they left the shade of Sharndene in a procession which wound its jingling way up the valley towards Maghefeld. First came the musicians: the pipers from Robert's household augmented by villagers banging neckeners and drums. Behind them rode the men of the main party, surrounded by servants, the litters which carried Margaret and Juliana swaying aloft on two stout horses. Last of all and accompanied on either side by the Gascons came the blue litter bearing Oriel, modestly curtained off from the world.

Yet she could see out to where Marcus rode but a foot or two away from her, his face set and determined, his hands gripping the reins too hard, his gaze directed straight ahead. Oriel would have given anything, then, to reach over and touch him.

The cavalcade swept down the hill and out of the valley of Byvelham, then climbed up on the other side to the village of Maghefeld. As with all communities built around a religious house, the scene was dominated by the main building. For the cluster of cottages, the church and the near distant mill were all strung out from the archbishop's residence down a long central street atop the ridge. From the doors of the thatched, mud-walled cottages, the curious inhabitants now stepped forth to see the daughter of Sharndene pass by to her wedding, and to listen to the music of her musicians, knowing that beer and food from the great banquet would be passed amongst them later in the day, and cheerful because of it.

They watched eagerly as the wedding party drew up before the church of St Dunstan.

The saint's original wooden building had long since vanished and now a stone church, built some hundred years earlier, stood on the same site. Waiting outside it, clad in vestments usually only seen in Canterbury so gorgeous were they, stood the archbishop himself, while Colin peered nervously from the porch.

With fingers that trembled as she moved, Oriel drew back the curtains and found, before she could say a word, that Marcus had his hands at her waist and was lifting her to the ground below. She slid down his body, so close to him that she could feel his thudding heart. But she could make no sign to him. Almost as if he feared she might run away the archbishop had thrust Colin's hand into hers and was beckoning them both forward.

Then she was in the cool of the porch, the smell of incense in her nostrils and the sound of music and voices suddenly hollow beneath the vaulted roof within. Beside her Colin began to tremble and she turned to look at him enquiringly. He was very pale. A fact accentuated by the silver tissue clothes he had been given to wear and the darkness of his hair, recently washed and rubbed with herbs.

Oriel smiled at him and he gave her a timorous glance. He suddenly seemed so vulnerable that the thought of Marcus's threat was dreadful. Standing behind her she could sense the presence of de Flaviel, his hands clasping and unclasping the hilt of his sword as if he would draw it at any moment.

A sudden hush told her that the wedding party was ready and that Archbishop Stratford – was it possible that in minutes he would be her brother-in-law? – was speaking to her, asking her to make her vows, looking 'at her penetratingly when for a moment she seemed nonplussed and did not reply. And then it was Colin's turn and as he mumbled and muttered incoherently, staring at the ground and going whiter and whiter with each passing second, Oriel's heart bled for him. Frantically he pushed the wedding band on her finger, wrenching it down over her knuckle like a child, and as it finally slipped into place she realised that it was done; that she was Colin's wife now and that truly only his death could ever set her free.

She was in a trance through the rest of the nuptial mass, the archbishop at his most astringent as the long ritual dragged on. It seemed to her that she took in nothing more until she found herself at the high table in the hall, staring out at a sea of faces turned towards her as winecups were raised in a toast.

'To the bride and groom,' came a chorused shout, and in response the archbishop rose to his feet and said smoothly that his brother would not be addressing the guests owing to hoarseness in his throat. Almost as soon as he had sat down again the palace musicians burst into abandoned noise and the first course of tasty cherries – to stimulate and awaken the appetite – was commenced.

As was customary on these occasions the most important people sat at the high table with the family and the low tables along the sides of the hall were occupied by the less influential. At the farthest board of all sat thirteen poor people of the manor feeding at the archbishop's expense; a practice he had started of late along with giving bread to the needy with his own hands.

The fruit done, the first serving of eleven different dishes was carried in on high platters. A boar's head with tusks was accompanied by cygnets, pheasants, herons, to say nothing of Crustarde Lumbarde – a pie made from cream, eggs, dates, prunes and sugar – together with sturgeon and great pike. The company fell on the feast like wolves, only the bride and groom sitting withdrawn, overwhelmed by their own feelings, scarcely touching a mouthful.

And, as the second course was brought on, Hamon de Sharndene, looking towards his father, mother and sister, wondered about them. He wondered if Robert had ever tasted passion as raw as that which he had experienced with Nichola de Rougemont and then pitied his father that he had grown old and past such things. He wondered if his mother – looking far more vital of late – knew what it was to feel flirtatious and wicked, as he and Nichola did when they were together. He wondered, most of all, seeing how pale she was, whether his sister could cope with a lifetime tied to an idiot, passion, flirting and wickedness all pushed away as if they did not exist.

As the second course of venison – presented with a gruel of cream, wheat and eggs – accompanied by sucking pig, peacocks in their plumage, cranes, bitterns, great pies and Leche Lumbarde – small spiced date cakes from Lombardy – were served, Hamon's eyes turned away from the banquet and towards Gilbert Meryweder's thirteen-year-old daughter. She was everything that he should, in truth, desire. Young, good-looking in a docile way, obviously virginal and pure of heart, he should have been, at the least, interested in her. But she bored him to the roots of his feet.

With a shock Hamon realised that 'the sweet slut of Battle' as he had secretly named Nichola was, yet again, in his thoughts and he forcibly dismissed her, concentrating instead upon the great portion of Pome Dorreng – the spit-roasted and herb-crusted rissole to which he had helped himself. As he bit into it, the archbishop's musicians struck up a trotto and the wedding guests, full of drink and forgetting or recalling their own wedding day, were upon their feet in a body and capering between the tables and around the brazier which still, even on this hot August night, threw its smoke and flames towards the blackened ceiling. To eat more was impossible. The music gained in momentum and everybody was dancing with the exception of the archbishop and the bride and groom who sat in silence at the top table.

If Hamon had been a man more concerned with people, if he had been able to think of anything other than his own affairs, he would have noticed his sister's frightened expression and her husband's pitifully white face. But as it was he observed nothing and went galloping on, pressing Matilda de Aylardenne close to him, and wishing that she were Nichola and that, when the festivities were done, he and the little slut could roll together in a delicious bed of sin.

Without warning, the archbishop suddenly stood up, signalling to the musicians as he did so. There was a sudden hush and Stratford announced, 'It is time for the bride and groom to leave the feast.'

There was a general snigger and Oriel felt sick with shame as Colin gazed at her in fright.

'It will be all right,' she murmured to him. 'It only means that we must go to sleep now.'

Reassured, he took her hand in his – at which there was delighted applause from some of the onlookers. Then suddenly the pair were surrounded by well-wishers; backs were patted, remarks passed with double meanings, somebody banged a neckener loudly, and a young girl fainted at the thought of it all.

Then they were marched up the stairs and Colin taken to one chamber, Oriel to another. Just for a moment she and Margaret were alone.

'My child,' murmured her mother, her face grim. 'I feel I must . . .'

'It will be all right,' answered Oriel in great distress for, as the door had opened to reveal Colin being pushed forward, his face a study of misery, she had caught a glimpse of Marcus hovering like an avenging angel in the corridor outside.

'Oriel,' Margaret tried again, her voice quite harsh with anxiety, 'you know what is likely to happen to you? You understand, don't you?'

Oriel nodded her head, too nervous even to speak as Stratford himself entered the room, and headed purposefully for the great bed by which she and Colin went to stand in silence.

His voice sibilant, the archbishop said, 'I bless this union and this marriage bed in the name of our Holy Mother and Her Blessed Son. May the fruits of Colin de Stratford and Oriel de Sharndene grow in Christian love and compassion in the years to come.'

Just for a second Oriel caught his eye and just for a second it was unshuttered, the thoughts behind it clear for her to read. She knew very well that he did not believe the words he said, that he knew the chances of consummation were virtually nonexistent. She wondered, in amazement, what scheme could be running through that devious mind.

But as she and Colin climbed into bed, Stratford was already making the sign of the cross over them, then leaving the room in a swirl of vestments, leading out the other guests, until at last everything was silent. Oriel realised in fright that she was completely alone with her simpleton husband in the darkness.

Very endearingly but rather shockingly in view of her racing thoughts, Colin said into the quietness, 'Need we go to sleep yet? Could we not play for a while?'

In the light of the flickering candle which she lit at once, she looked at him wide-eyed. 'What do you mean?'

'I could play the gittern if you like. Or we could have a battle with my little knights and horses.'

She did not know whether to laugh or cry. 'The gittern, Colin. That would be best.'

She leant over and kissed him on the cheek and he said with pleasure, 'Is this what having a wife means? That you will always be here to play with me and share my bed?'

She nodded.

'And there is nothing more?'

Once again she asked, 'What do you mean?'

'The kitchen scullions were teasing me. Speaking of my having to jig all night. And to see that you do also. Must we dance instead of sleep now that we are married?'

'I don't think so,' answered Oriel gravely.

Colin turned to where his gittern lay on a table beside the bed. No sooner was it in his hands than the usual transformation took place. He seemed to grow in stature, the composition of his features altering to those of a fine-boned adult. In a second the wealth of music began to pour out and it was then, with Colin totally immersed in playing and unaware of anything else, that Oriel saw the door open slightly and Marcus de Flaviel stand in the entrance.

'No, no, he has not touched me,' she whispered, but he ignored her. In what seemed like one stride he was across the room and, as one of his hands clapped over Colin's mouth, the other held a dagger, blade lengthways, to the simpleton's throat.

For some reason that Oriel could never afterwards understand, Colin went on playing. The welter of sound filled the room and Oriel saw Marcus hesitate. She seized her chance and flung herself headlong out of bed, throwing herself at the squire's feet and winding both arms around his knees.

'Don't kill him,' she sobbed. 'Listen to him. He is gifted, a creature of God. You must not harm him. It would be a crime I could never forgive.'

It was then that she saw something for which there was no explanation. Colin played a note and laid down the instrument. Then still with the wicked knife blade across his throat he rolled his gaze up to see who grasped him so menacingly. For a long moment he and Marcus stared into the depths of each other's eyes.

From behind Marcus's hand Colin tried to speak and as the Gascon loosened his grip the words became audible. 'Why are you so angry? I promise I have not been wicked.'

And with that he went into a dead faint, falling forward over the bed like a broken toy. In the silence that followed Marcus and Oriel stared at each other and then she saw what she would not have believed. Quite suddenly Marcus dropped the knife and buried his face in his hands, convulsed with sobs.

'God damn him!' he said loudly. 'God damn him! I cannot kill him any more than I could kill you. Oh Oriel, what are we going to do with him?'

She put her arms round Marcus gently, as if he were a little boy.

'We can only love and cherish him.'

'But what of us?'

'We must love and cherish each other too.'

'And what of the future?'

'The future will be that the three of us . . . remain together.'

Marcus nodded slowly as somewhere at the back of his mind three boys on horseback raced across a glowing strand.

TWELVE

The great solar of the archbishop's palace seemed a web of grey shadows, drawn together tightly by a central knot, in which sat a crimson spider. For in the gloom of a sunless afternoon Stratford waited alone, clad in his travelling mantle, his finger-tips together and his face so devoid of life that he appeared in a trance.

In response to a knock he called out 'Enter,' though altering his expression not at all. It was as if he acted automatically, his soul removed to another plane. Yet the eyes that ran glitteringly over Marcus de Flaviel, who stood bowing in the doorway, were appraising enough and the voice that said, 'Sit down, if you will,' was brisk and incisive.

'You sent for me, my Lord?'

'Yes, Flaviel. I want to talk to you, principally to ask you how you see your role here now that my brother has become a married man?'

Marcus hesitated. 'I am not certain, my Lord. You have given no instructions. I am not sure whether you wish me to continue as his guardian, or if you would now prefer that my duties were changed?'

There was a long silence, a silence during which the light eyes fixed on Marcus unblinkingly and it grew so quiet that every distant noise of the palace, from an argument between Wevere and the baker, to the cry of a young hound kennelled below, was magnified out of all proportion.

But Stratford sat immobile, looking at Marcus so directly that the squire had an uncomfortable feeling the primate could read thoughts.

'I wish you to continue to watch over him – and over madam as well,' Stratford said finally.

There was another pause during which Marcus asked stiffly, 'You wish me to be her bodyguard also, my Lord?'

Stratford nodded, a shutter opening behind his eye.

'Did you know that many madmen are like ravening beasts,

Marcus?' he said finally. 'Beasts who satisfy their appetites – *all* their appetites – as greedily and as often as they will?'

Marcus grew rigid beneath the terrifying gaze. 'My Lord?'

'My brother is not one of that number. In all things he is ascetic. You understand me?'

'Not completely, my Lord.'

'I want you to do what *must* be done, Flaviel. I want it to be your principal concern that my brother – and his wife – lead a fulfilled and contented life.'

There could be no doubt now as to the message that lay beneath the words, but still Marcus persisted, terrified that he might be making a mistake.

'You want me to ensure that their marriage is a happy one, my Lord?'

Without moving a muscle Stratford altered his expression and, as he did so, a white hand shot out from the depths of the red mantle and pushed Marcus on to his knees before the primate.

'Now, vow before Christ that you will remain forever silent on this matter, as must I.'

The whispered voice was fierce.

Marcus bent his head and put his lips to the extended hand before him, his mouth brushing the great ring of the archbishops as he did so.

'I swear it, my Lord.'

'Then may God protect you, my son.' Stratford stood up, his voice altering to its normal tone, and the customary blankness returned to mask his features. He said, without emotion, 'Affairs will keep me away from Maghefeld this autumn and I shall leave the management of the household in the hands of Wevere; its safety in those of you and Sir Paul.'

Marcus bowed, his shock of hair falling on either side of his cheek bones. 'I will try to guard everyone well, my Lord.'

'Do what you think to be right, Flaviel. As long as we are all true to God there can be nothing amiss in any of our actions.'

He was gone from the room leaving the squire to stare after him wonderingly. What man could order another to sin with so clear a conscience? What servant of God could possibly take such a stand? And then, in a flash, he realised that Stratford saw the greater evil as the greater sin. He had plotted against the late king in order that England might have a young and vigorous monarch. Now he had virtually ordered Marcus to take possession of Colin's wife.

Slowly Flaviel left the solar, and was in time to see the archbishop's retinue move over the cobbles as it headed towards London.

'God speed,' he called.

Stratford turned to give Marcus an unreadable look. Then the archbishop gave an abrupt nod before he turned his back on Maghefeld and all those left behind. Shaking his head Marcus went inside.

From a chamber above the sound of music and laughter rang out and, going up the great staircase, Marcus followed the noise to where, in a room that had been given to them for day time use, Colin and Oriel were dancing. As he came in their heads turned simultaneously.

'I am to be your special protector,' he said. 'My Lord of Canterbury has commanded that it be so.'

'*My* special protector?' asked Oriel.

'I am to look after you both.'

She became thoughtful, the colour in her cheeks heightening a little. 'What will it mean?'

'That I am to keep the pair of you safe and happy.'

'Why has he ordered that?'

'Because I love you both,' answered Marcus, pausing for a moment before he added, 'As I believe does my Lord of Canterbury in his own particular way.'

Adam de Bayndenn looked up as the archbishop's calvacade passed, shielding his eyes with an earth-stained hand and watching until it had vanished from sight. Then he sighed deeply, his handsome face set in hard grim lines.

He had never been unhappier in his life, imagining what all the world must be saying. That he was a stallion, bought to service a wealthy woman. And to add to his burden he had, of late, grown almost incapable of that, lying beside Isabel apologetically as his powerful body failed to show the least enthusiasm for her. How much he would have liked to confess to his wife – whom he loved in his own way – what lay at the heart of his difficulties; what it was that caused this cruel and mocking shortcoming in such a mighty man. Poor, poor Isabel! What a tragedy for them both that Adam had fallen in love with the unattainable Oriel and could speak of it to no living creature.

The realisation of the truth had come to Adam suddenly, on the night they had all dined with the archbishop. He had sunk his head into his hands then, overcome with emotion, and now he did so again. What hope was there? It seemed to Adam that he had no purpose left; that his life was meaningless. And now his dreams were further shattered by the fact that Oriel had yesterday become the madman's bride.

A deep sob shook him before he raised his head again and put his great hands once more to the plough, shouting at the oxen to get on. He was utterly without hope as he resolutely cut another furrow into the dark, rich soil of Sussex.

Just as Isabel's black mare picked her hooves through the fields there was a roll of distant thunder and a flash of lightning cracked through the sky like a spear. Madam Bayndenn pulled in her horse at the sound and looked about in awe, unaware of the first light raindrops that had begun to fall.

From the high field in which she stood, the valley stretched out into a bluish haze; on the ridge above, a line of deer hastily threading their way to the shelter of the trees, while the river weaving through the valley's foot like a gypsy ribbon, had turned periwinkle blue as it took on the reflection of the storm.

It was a sight to make mortals shiver, dangerously beautiful as the distant tempest took hold, and Isabel made her way cautiously through the wood and from there picked her way downwards to the fields beyond.

Even from the distance where she stood she could see that Adam had stopped ploughing and had buried his face in his hands. Instantly her heart sank, her mind running like a hare in a trap, over and over the same wretched course. What was it that ailed him? Why could he not be happy? She had freed him from serfdom; she had given him a home in Sir Godfrey's house; he had good food and good wine and warmth and clothes and comfort.

Isabel's thoughts shied away from the next possibility, her full, warm mouth drawing down at the corners at the very idea. Of course he could not consider her too old; by her rituals, by her suffering ice-cold water and dancing naked on the river bank – rituals that would have had her branded a witch had she been observed – she had kept the years at bay. She was as desirable now as when she had gone as a virgin bride to her first husband. Isabel straightened her shoulders, telling herself she had nothing to fear. But even as she did so she saw Adam savagely kick the side of the plough and wave a clenched fist at the sky. Without warning she lost patience. What had the great fool to complain of? As she stood watching him, Isabel felt the first drops of rain turn quickly into a heavy shower. She could see the cold rain soaking through Adam's shirt and Isabel wrestled with the temptation to let her husband be, to let him get drenched as befitted such an ungrateful clod. Then her maternal instincts came, most infuriatingly, to the surface. Angry with herself she nonetheless called out, 'Adam, come home! There is no point in staying out here.'

He spun round, unaware that he had been observed, and she saw the deep scowl that hung over his features.

'Oh, it's you,' he said abruptly.

Isabel lost the last vestige of patience. 'Yes,' she answered. 'Who else did you expect? If it was some secret love then you are bound for disappointment.'

Much to her amazement Adam turned the colour of the mistletoe that grew about the trunk of the ripening apple tree beneath her window and did not reply.

'You are welcome to her,' Isabel shouted furiously, heading her horse towards Bayndenn without a backward glance.

'What a summer of storms,' said Colin. 'It thundered the night your father came to the palace to say we were betrothed. Do you remember, Oriel?'

'No,' she answered, half smiling, 'I was asleep.'

'So was I. But I heard him arrive. You remember that night, don't you, Marcus? It was when you slept on my floor.'

The squire nodded his head. 'Yes, I remember,' he said.

The three of them had ridden out of Maghefeld, heading north-west, and were on a thickly wooded slope which climbed steeply up above a lush green valley. Far below them a herd of black and white cows grazed contentedly, oblivious to the driving rain.

'Quickly,' said Marcus, 'there's a hovel by that field. We'll take shelter.'

Most surprisingly Oriel answered, 'Take Colin there. I must speak with you alone.'

He turned to look at her but was unable to read her face, the brilliant eyes masked and inscrutable.

'But you'll get wet?' said Colin.

'It won't matter,' she replied quietly.

'I see.'

And just for a moment it seemed as if Colin was more aware than Marcus of what Oriel meant, for a glimmer of understanding appeared on his face.

'You never did mind getting wet,' he said.

Oriel imagined a boy splashing through the brilliant water of a foreign shore, his horse's feet kicking up the spume which shot into the air in a million droplets and showered his tunic through.

'. . . hurry then,' Marcus was saying. 'Oriel, wait for me under this tree.'

His eyes were full of questions as he rode off with his charge but Oriel would not meet his glance. For once she was in control of her destiny. It was her decision, and her decision alone, that here in this remote place, with the warm rain soaking through to her skin, she would leave her girlhood behind and step through the gateway from which there could be no return.

When Marcus returned he found her naked, looking up at him, the boldness in her eyes masking an inner fear.

'Let it be now,' she said.

'Here, in this storm? Are you not afraid?'

'I am afraid of everything – and nothing. Is Colin safe?'

'Safe and happy.'

The squire dismounted and stood before the girl, his eyes taking in her body from the sweep of neck to high, firm breast, the small waist and finely-shaped limbs. Without speaking further he led her by the hand into the heart of the glade and there laid her down on his cloak, seeing her watch him in wonderment as he slowly revealed his body.

The rain ran down his bare back as he dropped to his knees beside her and kissed each delicate undulation from neck to ankle, preparing to take his love through the threshold of pain to the bliss that could lie beyond. They fitted one another in every way, their rhythm quite perfect until at last it was over and they

133

climaxed together as though they were lovers of many years understanding.

There was no guilt as they lay entwined afterwards, drawing comfort from each other's rain-wet bodies. For mixed with the drops were not only the body's natural dews but also Oriel's tears and the precious blood which she had spilled so willingly for Marcus de Flaviel.

As they lay in silence, not needing to speak, over the voice of the storm rose another sound, so sad and sweet that they knew at once what it was.

'Colin is playing,' said Oriel. 'Playing for us.'

'Do you think he knows?' asked Marcus.

'He knows something,' came the reply, 'but he is not sure what it is.' She half sat up. 'You will never hurt him, will you?'

'No, I will never hurt him. I was jealous then; now I never can be so again for he has given me his greatest gift.'

'And what is that?'

'You, Oriel,' said Marcus. 'He has given you to me – once more.'

THIRTEEN

That summer, that strange and eventful summer of 1334, at first gave way so slowly to autumn that the signs were barely perceptible. The trees took on the merest tinge of ochre; the creepers that consumed the walls of the palace only hinted a glow of red; the change in the sky was hardly discernible as a deeper and more vivid blue; the afternoon shadows could scarcely be seen to grow purple as the great sun circled lower in the heavens.

And then suddenly, as nobody looked, the season was upon the inhabitants of the village and the valley: leaves crackled beneath feet in the palace's cobbled courtyard; chill winds blew through the houses; rain hissed on to the hearths; and there was a general gathering of garments to the neck as the landscape burst forth in all the magic colours of topaz and amber, crimson and flame. The year was dead. It was over. They must all look to new beginnings and new ideas, for soon the birth of a new year would be facing them all.

Challenge came then. Everyone thinking of the winter that lay ahead and of survival: survival from the cold, survival of the herds and crops, survival from illness, survival of life lived out on a land hard as iron. And with that prospect still to come, Stratford, raised up in pomp and glory before his king and fellow clergy, heard the choir of Canterbury call out that a new archbishop was being enthroned, and knelt down humbly to pray for guidance in the place where the great Thomas had bowed the knee so long ago. And while he did this his brother Colin, sitting amongst the assembled company and trying very hard to concentrate, thought of warm soup, and his gittern and, above all, his friends Oriel and Marcus who had transformed his humble life to one of infinite contentment, and for whom he would have laid down that same life on the instant, if one of them had so asked.

But thoughts far less tranquil were also abroad on the day of the archbishop's raising up. Robert de Sharndene, now a

135

candidate for the post of Sheriff, silently railed against the fact that he was getting older; that commitments had kept him away from his mistress; and that on the one occasion he had managed to have free time in Battle, Nichola had been mysteriously out. And Robert also grumbled to himself that, since Oriel's wedding, Margaret had spent little time at Sharndene and had become, instead, a constant visitor to the palace. The horrid suspicion that she might be meeting Paul d'Estrange continually crossed Robert's mind and this, together with her increased vivacity and attractiveness, gave him disquieting food for thought.

And it was true that Margaret had never been more at ease. Gone her old jealousy of Oriel, gone the fears of her ugliness, gone, too, the worry about losing her husband. And all because the Gascon knight, with his lotions and potions and obvious admiration, had at last given her confidence.

Also at Canterbury that day, Sir John Waleis, representing his ancient father Sir Godfrey, sat flanked by his wife, Alice, and all four of his children: the eldest two, stolid Andrew and William, the product of his first marriage; the younger, Hugh and Richard, Alice's sons, all long legs and bony wrists and fine coltish ways.

As the mitre of the archbishop was placed on Stratford's head, 'Gloria,' sang the cathedral choir. 'Gloria in excelsis Deo.'

It was done. England had a new archbishop – the second most powerful man in the realm was now John de Stratford.

The autumn passed and snow came early, silent and waxen, falling slowly at first. Then came chilling winds and mutinous skies which spoke of further heavy falls and, during the next few days, the landscape was blotted out by deceptively gentle gossamer flakes which left in their wake a grip of drifts and ice. People huddled in smoke-filled rooms, unable to venture forth and hardly knowing night from day, so dark and ominous was the brooding sky.

The snow fell for a week without stopping and finally fluttered to a halt during the darkest of nights. The next morning, winter lay on the land. Everywhere there was glittering frost and glinting ice, and the berries on the holly were as red as the sunset. At Sharndene the moat was frozen and the swans lay on the snow. White feathers on white flakes and a white world beyond; a world in which people could at last venture forth but in which a pair of forbidden lovers found it hard to discover a secret place where they might go unseen. For even Oriel's grey horse showed up in the bleak landscape and the naked trees gave no protection from curious eyes.

So for this reason, with Colin left safely at the palace by the brazier, the couple set out on foot, the squire leading his lady over the bleak terrain to a deserted woodcutter's home, where he spread his cloak for her on the floor and lit a fire in the small hearth within.

This day he played lovemaking to the full until he and Oriel moved, as one, beyond return. Together they called out joyfully and it was at this moment that Marcus thought he heard a noise in the doorway and, turning his head swiftly, caught a glimpse of something moving hastily out of sight.

Jumping to his feet, the squire straightened his clothes and rushed out. There was nothing to be seen, only a track of footprints leading off to the woods to tell him that the incident had not been a trick of his imagination.

'Is there anything wrong?' called Oriel from within the hut.

'I thought I heard something, that is all,' answered Marcus, as he went back inside.

'Was there anyone there?'

'No, no one.' He could not bring himself to sicken her with the thought of a peeping Tom. As he smiled Oriel stood up, then swayed a little.

'Are you ill?' he said anxiously.

'No, just cold. We must return home. Colin will be anxious.'

'Yes, he will. Come, walk close to me. Let us get you back to safety.'

Oriel did not think to question his words as they stepped together into a crystal world, already turning dark beneath a glowing winter sky.

So cold was that evening that Hamon de Sharndene, in residence at the King's castle at Windsor, sat crouched virtually on top of the brazier of logs, playing a game of chess with a fellow soldier.

But his mind was not on the board before him. Nor indeed on the bitter night beyond the castle's stout walls. Instead Hamon thought about himself and admitted, in a moment of blinding

137

truth, that he had fallen in love with a slut and was powerless to do anything about it.

With a sigh, Hamon moved a piece on the board and considered recent events. Ever since Oriel's wedding he had tried to put Nichola from his mind, even going so far as to call on Gilbert Meryweder unexpectedly, and running an appraising eye over his virgin daughter. But the girl's innocence had bored him and he had soon returned to Windsor and the arms of the most uninhibited creature in the brothel that nestled at the foot of the walls. But he had been bored even more.

It was then that the truth had finally dawned on him. He had arrived at a point in his life when only the little strumpet from Battle – with whom he had managed to spend one incredible week's leave during the summer – could satisfy him. Yet the thought of his parents' reaction to such a situation made him sigh aloud.

At the sound his companion asked, 'What's the matter? Are you ill? I've never known you to play worse.'

'My mind is not on the game,' answered Hamon shortly.

'On a new conquest I suppose?' Hamon's reputation was spoken of in awed tones even among the men.

'Tom, I believe I might have fallen in love at last,' came the unexpected reply.

Much to Hamon's annoyance his companion burst into uncontrollable laughter, slapping his thigh and wiping his eyes on his sleeve. 'I never thought I would see the day! Who is she?'

'A widow from Battle.'

For some reason this struck Tom as even funnier and he roared all the more. Hamon had a strong urge to punch him.

'There is something about this story I do not trust,' Tom gasped eventually. 'I believe you have fallen in love with a whore.'

'She is nothing of the kind.' Hamon stood up, snatching at his dignity like the threads of a well-worn robe. 'She is a respectable woman and I intend to marry her. In fact I shall ask for leave and, as soon as it is granted, I shall go to Battle and arrange for us to see a priest.'

Tom quietened, Hamon's serious expression at last penetrating his hilarity. 'I am sure your parents will be delighted after all these years,' he said contritely.

His friend, with absolutely no idea of the import of his words,

138

answered, 'My mother very probably; of my father's feelings, I am not so sure.'

'In the spring I am to bear a child,' gushed Juliana. 'Do you know you impregnated me the very first time we lay together? Oh my dear Piers, you are so virile.'

She smiled at him lovingly.

'That is because you are desirable, my sweet,' he answered automatically, his mind planning the early stages of an affair with a youth.

If he brought a young man into the household and an amorous adventure were to begin, would it mean – if he continued to sleep with Juliana – that he was utterly beyond hope? Would his life's ambition of total debauchery at last be realised?

The idea was so intriguing that Piers hardly heard the steward step into the hall and say to Juliana, 'There is a traveller at the door, Madam, desiring to know if Mistress Oriel is within.'

'Oriel?' Piers came back to full attention. 'Why should she be here?'

The steward coughed slightly. 'It is her husband who enquires. He seems to be somewhat bewildered.'

Piers groaned. 'Oh no, not the half-wit! What can he be doing out alone?'

'You had better show him in,' said Juliana, and as Piers frowned added, 'We can hardly leave the poor wretch standing in the cold.'

'No,' Piers answered reluctantly. 'Bring it in.'

A moment later, Colin entered the hall in total silence, his dark hair flattened, cowl-like, to his head and his clothing all but frozen to his body.

'Is Oriel here?' he asked abruptly, his teeth chattering as he made a clumsy bow.

Juliana stood up, startled yet again by his simplicity. Nobody but a dollard would have addressed her so peremptorily and stared about quite so wide-eyed.

'Master Colin,' she said, her voice plumlike. 'What brings you to Mouleshale out of the storm? Why should Oriel be with us?'

Colin shuffled even more, sensing her condescending manner.

'I am looking for my wife and Marcus, Madam. They went out some hours ago and still have not returned. Usually I do not worry but tonight the weather is so bitter I fear for their safety. Madam, I have come to you alone through the cold and the darkness.' His lips quivered. 'Please help me.'

Piers, who had been sprawling in his chair, a look of great distaste about his mouth, suddenly leapt to attention.

'What do you mean, Oriel and Marcus went out, Master Colin? Are they in the habit of doing so?'

'Oh yes,' said the wretched innocent. 'They frequently go off together but always come back quite safely, yet today the cold is so intense I am afraid for their lives. If anything should happen to them I ...' His voice trailed miserably into silence.

'Sit down,' purred Piers. 'Pray do not distress yourself. Some strong wine might help matters.'

He jerked his head at Juliana who rose to pour a goodly measure from a jug.

'Now Master Colin, let me hasten to assure you that all at Mouleshale will do their best to find the missing pair. Tell me when you last saw them.'

'At noon. They told me they were going for their usual walk – and I stayed at home to play with my little wooden knights.'

Piers and Juliana shot each other a meaningful look and he said, 'When they go out together do they often leave you behind?'

'Oh no,' said Colin. 'In the fine weather I go with them and then I go off to pick flowers while they talk.'

'Really?' Piers uncoiled like a snake. 'And have they been doing this for a long while?'

'Oh yes,' answered Colin happily, swigging his cup with relish. 'Since the day after the wedding.'

Piers rubbed his hands together. 'Then may I suggest,' he said, smooth as silk and smiling sweetly, 'that you stay here this night and tomorrow we go together to the palace to see if they have returned.'

'Oh no,' answered Colin, putting down the cup, 'I could not risk their being lost. I must find Oriel and Marcus tonight. You see, there is no life for me without them. And anyway none of us mind about getting cold or damp.'

Piers raised an eyebrow in the direction of Juliana and stood up, his robe falling back to reveal a bare chest and stomach that were beginning to gain weight with all the comforts of married life.

'Well, there's no help for it,' he said. 'I must ride out into the night. Juliana, you stay here. You must not risk the babe.'

His voice dramatically fell as she clasped her hands together in delight. 'Oh Piers, Piers, you are so good to me.'

'Who could be other to a wife like you?'

She smiled unattractively, baring her tooth, and even Colin looked startled.

'Come then, brother-in-law, let us make haste to find your wife – and her friend. And you can be assured that when I do so I shall have words to say.'

'What do you mean?'

'That I shall greet them as they deserve to be greeted.'

'Oh!' said Colin wonderingly, and trotted out behind Piers into the freezing night.

'Look Adam,' said Isabel, 'it's freezing hard. See the ice in the valley? In the morning it will be cut off.'

She stood beside her husband in the doorway of Bayndenn, gazing down on a vista transformed by the magic touch of winter's hand. Below and beyond her the slopes of the Rother fell away in an eternal sweep, broken here and there by the iced diamond branches of the distant trees. It was a view of complete purity, of gleaming frost-capped hills, of a silver river scurrying through a glint of deepening rime.

As they stood there in silence, looking out, the flame of torches appeared in the distance, wending their way up from Maghefeld and breaking the great stillness of that sparkling night. The lights lit the snow with circles of saffron, turning the darkness into a fantasy of fire and ice. In the distance could be heard the wild, high yelping of dogs.

'What is it?' asked Isabel.

'A search-party,' came the brief reply.

'Who is missing?'

'Oriel, I suppose. Oriel and her friend Flaviel.'

Curiously Isabel turned her attention to her husband. He stood with his face set grimly, gazing to where the lights lit the distant view.

'How do you know it is them?'

'I don't.' He turned to look at her and just for a second Isabel felt afraid of him, so stern were his features. 'I only think so because they are in the habit of wandering off together, regardless of the weather.'

'What for?'

Adam gave a bitter laugh. 'Who knows? Perhaps they enjoy such things.'

The way he said that told Isabel everything. She knew at once the two young people were lovers; that her husband was not only aware of it but seething with jealousy as a result. In one terrible and icy moment – as cold as the night into which Isabel gazed – everything fell into place: Adam's strange behaviour during Colin's pathetic courtship, his misery since Oriel had become a bride, and his recent and almost total inability in the bedchamber.

A great wave of tenderness swept her. She had bought the fellow so that she might have a young and vigorous husband and had given no thought to his feelings, to his capability for falling in love.

Very gently she put her hand on his arm and said, 'Whatever they do I think we should speak of it to no one.'

From his vast height Adam looked down at her, 'Oh, never worry about that. I will not mention it again. It was difficult to say even to you that Oriel is a slut.'

In a voice that was only barely beyond a whisper Isabel said, 'You must love her very much.'

Equally quietly he answered, 'If only you knew ...' And then he seemed to collect himself, shaking his head and staring about him as if he had just awoken. 'Isabel ...' he said wretchedly.

'Speak of it no more. Come inside by the fire.'

'I would rather go and search. Would you mind?'

A terrible feeling of unease, of things awry and getting worse, swept the tenant of Bayndenn. So much so that she said, 'I think it would be better if you did not, Adam. I think your feelings are too confused tonight. In the morning we will ride to the palace and see that all is well.'

He gave her a long, dark look. 'Things will never be well at the palace until those Gascons are gone.'

'Don't speak so. It is dangerous. They are here to stay and nothing can change that.'

Adam made no answer, striding ahead of his wife into the warmth of the hall, without a backward glance.

It was on the track above the heights of Sharndene that Marcus, who was leading the search party from the palace, finally found Colin, wandering on his own and looking near to death. As the squire approached, the simpleton came running forward, his feet shuffling through the snow, holding his arms out to Marcus and weeping silently.

The Gascon picked the pathetic creature off his feet. 'Where have you been, you naughty boy? We have looked everywhere for you.'

'But I have been looking for *you*. I thought you and Oriel were in danger so I stopped playing with my knights and went searching. I went to Piers and he came to help me but he said we must separate to widen the net.'

Marcus shook his head fondly. 'We were out a little longer on our walk than we intended, that is all. And when we got back you were gone.'

Out of the darkness a voice said, 'Of course it is wonderful weather for walking, is it not?' It was Piers, expensively dressed against the cold, and sitting astride a sturdy horse which had come upon them quietly.

He looked down at the pair and said, 'A word in private with you, Flaviel. Before the rest of the party catch up.'

'Then dismount and come over here. Colin, hold the horse's bridle and do not move from this spot.'

Through the ankle-deep snow the two men walked just out of earshot, their eyes still on the simpleton who stood transfixed, obviously terrified of being alone.

'You do not deceive me for a moment,' said Piers without preamble. 'You are leading my sister into wickedness and depravity – and by God's Holy Blood, I shall see that you pay for it.'

'What are you going to do?'

'Speak to the archbishop of course.'

The collar of Piers's mantle was suddenly pulled tight as Marcus seized it furiously.

'I'll kill you first, you son of Sodom. One move to tell de Stratford and I'll string you up by your privy parts. Do not think I would hesitate – nothing would give me greater pleasure.'

'You would not dare.'

'Oh no? I will spare you now for the sake of your sister and your mother. But one mistake and you can count your days, Sharndene. There is nothing more disgusting than a peeping Tom.'

Piers's eyes rolled wildly. 'What do you mean?'

'You know perfectly well.'

'I have never spied on you. I guessed all from Colin's chatter. Besides you foreigners are all the same. Your mind never gets any higher than the place between a woman's thighs . . .'

But he said no more as a mighty blow sent him reeling backwards into a drift.

'Damn you, Marcus de Flaviel,' he said from where he lay. 'I wish you in hell and I promise you that I shall bring that journey about ere long.'

For answer Marcus turned on his heel and strode to the place where Colin stood, lifting the little man onto Piers's horse and leading him away.

'Wait!' shouted Piers, struggling to his feet. 'How am I supposed to get back?'

'You can walk,' called Marcus's distant voice, 'or die in the darkness for all I care.'

'Flaviel!' screamed Piers, saliva flecking his mouth. 'Start to count your days.'

There was no reply as the distant baying of dogs told the limping Piers that the search-party was on its way back to the palace, and that he was alone in the treacherous night with only his hatred to spur his safe return.

FOURTEEN

There was much suffering during that terrible winter. Many died of hunger and many more of cold, lying stiff and silent in their dwellings while outside a shroud covered all the earth in a great pall of white. The bleakness took babies and old men alike; wasted young girls and brought hardened men to their knees with starvation. And then, gradually, the cold, clear air had a smell in it like sea-salt; buds thrust their way through the pearls of ice; the Rother roared at full spate, swift with its icy cargo. It was over: life had begun again; the cycle had swung into its rightful place; the winter was finished.

Everything returned to normal. Tenants hastened to their holdings; the sheep – penned for their own protection – were turned out to graze; freshly-killed meat was brought to the archbishop's palace; and Nicholas le Mist once again seduced a willing wench behind the barn. Spring had come to the village and valley.

And so it was that the first manorial court of the year was called at Sharndene and as the Lord of the Manor strode purposefully to the hall, Cogger called out, 'Let all be upstanding.'

Robert saw before him a sea of faces, some dark and lean, others pink and round, but all watchful and wary, wondering what mood he would be in and what ear he would give to their suits. The colour of their clothes, lit by the glow of the flames, seemed to him to blend with their skins. He saw shades of tan and brown; nature's hues echoed in the rough woollen clothes and weaves of his tenants. The hounds before the fire; the smoke wafting through the chamber; the mud-caked rushes where forty feet had recently trod – all this and the strangely comforting smell of sweat and dirt and candles conjured up for Robert de Sharndene the raw bones of his entire life. He felt a great lift of his heart. 'You may be seated,' he said.

'Oh yea, oh yea,' called Cogger, opening the formal

proceedings. 'Let all those with business at this court draw near and give your attention.'

The official procedures had begun and Robert sat back, his elbow resting on the table and his chin in his hand, as the defaulters were noted by the clerk and subsequently fined twopence by the jurors.

Sir John Waleis – not a usual visitor – rose to his feet. 'I propose to construct a certain park at Hawkesden and have come to this court today to seek the assent of the Lord and his tenants at the ford whose lands and enclosures adjoin the said enclosure.'

Robert nodded. He had already privately agreed to the park's creation, but formal application was essential if John's plans were to go through. His friend continued to plead his case and Robert switched his brain from the matter at issue.

Instantly he thought of Margaret. Where was she, he wondered? She had set off within an hour of daylight, saying that she must make some charitable visits, but her horse had turned in the direction of Maghefeld.

Robert moved his shoulders irritably. He positively detested Paul d'Estrange, who struck him at once as a posturing and opinionated windsack. For how could one overlook the fact that Margaret's constant visits to the palace, ostensibly to see her newly-married daughter, must also allow her to indulge in witty conversation with the Gascon. With a feeling of betrayal Robert caught himself thinking that Nichola was not witty. In fact, even worse, she was rather stupid.

'My Lord?' said John.

'Eh?' Robert returned to the present with a start.

'Is it your wish, my Lord, that I proceed to create such a park under the terms just stated?'

'Er ... yes.'

'And that such an agreement may be drawn that my heirs and assigns may proceed should my decease come about before the completion of such a park?'

'He's being terribly pompous,' thought Robert, but replied, 'Permission granted to draw the agreement.'

John sat down, smiling, and the business of the court moved on.

'Presentments for lerywite, my Lord,' said Cogger.

Robert always found the fines for immorality amongst the

villeins faintly amusing and his full attention was restored as he nodded consent.

'Simon Lukke, drunkenness.'

'Twopence,' answered the jurors without conferring.

'William Dosy, stealing Widow Button's hen.'

'Sixpence.'

'Peter de Chillhop, adultery with the wife of Walter Cokerel of Maghefeld.'

'Fourpence.'

'John Wynter, adultery with Margery Swetyng, Matilda le Coche, Christina Colyn, Alice de Eversfield and Matilda atte Red, and persistent fornication with the Relict of Steld, the Relict of Chomcels and the Relict of Button. Also the impregnation of Julia Serymond.'

'Good God!' exclaimed Robert. 'John Wynter, where are you?'

A little man with a leathery face and hangdog expression stepped forward and said plaintively, 'I only did it to please them, my Lord, because they did keep pestering so. Particularly the three widows.'

He wiped his hand across his brow and Robert said, 'You should know better. Can you not control yourself, man?'

Wynter gulped convulsively and said, 'Only with great difficulty, my Lord.'

'Who am I to judge him?' thought Robert guiltily as the jurors announced, 'A penny for each adultery and a further presentment when the child is born. The widows free of fine.'

There was a muffled laugh as Wynter vanished into the throng, his leathery face turning from crimson to white and his eyes firmly fixed on his feet.

The business of the court droned on as Robert found his mind once more on Nichola. Then from what seemed a great distance he heard the jurors pronounce sentence on the final case and Cogger accept the last fee from a tenant. The court's first session of 1335 was over.

The Lord of the Manor got to his feet, looking at his tenants narrowly before he swept away from them and out of the hall. They were going, that pack of people whose lives depended upon him. He paused for one final glance before they trudged off into the waning light of the chilly February afternoon.

*   *   *

As the winter finally died and spring leapt into life over the beautiful land of Sussex, Oriel, hugging her arms tightly around herself and circling silently in a private dance of joy, realised that the great rhythm of the seasons was being echoed within her own body. That the absence for two consecutive cycles of the flux controlled by the moon's mysterious path could mean only one thing. The wonder had taken place. The seed of Marcus de Flaviel had flowered within and had formed a new being; from the great love of two people an individual had been created. She felt as humble as the recipient of one of the miracles, and cried with the splendour of it all.

She knew exactly when it had been, that day last winter in the bitter cold. As she stood upright she had felt a moment's weakness and this – or so she believed – had been the moment of conception. Even as she had walked back through the ice to the palace, she had already been pregnant.

She felt alive with the news, longing to run from room to room and tell everyone – servants, guards, kitchen lads, anyone. But there was no one to be seen as she hurried down the great stone staircase; and when she ran outside only Paul d'Estrange was there, sitting on the seat in the herb garden and turning his face towards the feeble sun, his eyes closed.

'Oh dear me,' he said, jumping slightly as she came up to him. 'Oh, Oriel, it is you. I must have fallen asleep.'

She smiled at him and he patted the silver-gilt hair affectionately. 'My dear little girl. How happy you look.'

Oriel could not help it. She knew even as she spoke that it was not discreet to do so, but could conceal her joy no longer. Kissing him on the cheek, she said, 'Oh Sir Paul, I *am* happy – because I am with child.'

He stiffened and drew away from her. 'Oriel, what are you saying? Have you told anyone else of this? Does your mother know?'

Oriel felt sudden tears. 'No, not yet. Why are you not pleased?'

'Because the possibility of Colin having fathered this babe is too remote to be considered.'

She stared at him, aghast. 'But he is my husband. Surely no one will suspect . . .'

'The truth. That you and Marcus have been lovers for months. That it is his child you carry.'

The sun suddenly went in and Oriel realised it was cold.

'How did you know?' she asked sullenly.

'Because Colin is a child in every way. It stands to reason that your lover is Marcus.'

'Will other people guess?'

'Most probably. But you must not give them a scrap of evidence. They can whisper all they wish but there must be no grounds for them to point the finger. I beg you in your exalted position as kinswoman of the archbishop not to allow a breath of scandal to besmirch your name.'

'But how can I stop it?'

'By ending your affair with Marcus at once.'

Oriel did not answer, merely turning on her heel and walking back into the palace. Paul stared after her, shaking his head from side to side but after a few moments seemed to come to some sort of decision and followed her slowly into the palace.

Calling to a servant, he said, 'Saddle up your horse. I want you to take a letter to Sharndene. The matter is urgent.'

'Very good, Sir. Shall I await the reply?'

'Yes. It is imperative that we make haste.'

The man looked puzzled but was given no further information as Paul disappeared into his chamber and picked up a quill pen.

Market day in Battle, and the approach road taken by Hamon de Sharndene – whose visit to Nichola had been delayed by the impassable weather conditions – was crowded with people, some herding cattle, sheep and pigs; others struggling beneath baskets of eggs and produce; more yet clutching squawking hens and honking geese; but all watching the antics of a dark-skinned girl with a twirling skirt and long naked limbs, who danced to the music of a pipe played by a man with a wooden stump in place of his leg.

In normal circumstances, Hamon would have enjoyed being part of the excited throng heading for the Abbey Green. Would have loved the sights, smells and company of the heavily-painted women entertainers who had joined the ranks of the market-goers. But today he was anxious to see Nichola without delay and he cursed as a fluttering hen caused his horse to rear up, knocking over a woman with a great pannier of fresh loaves, tipping her flat on her face in dung, her baking ruined.

She shouted and waved her fist, and it was only by dismounting and pressing more money into her hand than she could possibly have earned, that Hamon managed to avoid the angry throng turning on him.

Meanwhile the dancing-girl had approached him, and smilingly offered her services. It was with a sigh that Hamon refused. Before the advent of Nichola he would have carried the girl off at once and delighted in her for the rest of the day.

She winked a vivid eye. 'Another time perhaps.'

'Perhaps.'

Much as he had guessed, Nichola's little house was empty, and Hamon, on foot and leading his horse, joined the vast crowd thronging towards the market. Tying his mount to a ring in the wall, Hamon walked amongst the stalls, seeing, with some amazement, everything on sale that anyone could possibly need. Mounds of herrings spilled over sweet confections, and apples rolled amongst great and glistening cheeses. There were trays of delights: hot cakes to be consumed with wine, pies oozing with meats, vast heaps of dumplings, sugared sweets and barrels of sweet-smelling ale. It was as good a market as he had ever seen, even in the City of London.

Happily, young Sharndene jostled his way through the crowd, swollen in number today by a horde of pilgrims – complete with their personal entertainers – who had come to kneel at the high altar erected on the very spot where Harold, last of the Saxon kings, had fallen. Of Nichola there was no sign in the throning multitude but Hamon, believing that at any moment he would catch a glimpse of her, contented himself with watching the antics of two little dwarves who were dancing before a wretched bear.

Suddenly he felt himself swept into the very essence of the place. He heard the abbey bells; he heard whistles, shouts and screams; the barking of dogs, the screaming of babies, the high silly laughs of the dwarves. He saw the brightness of spices on a plain wooden stall and the shabby dark brown of the old bear's coat. He smelled roasting meat and unclean bodies, manure and ale and musky scent. He saw and touched and felt joyfully at one with the whole glowing pageant of the heaving, shoving, roaring, jostling company that had come to Battle market on that crystal-bright spring day.

And then he glimpsed Nichola wearing green, cool as a wood-nymph.

'It's Hamon. I'm here,' he called out.

An eddy of people swept before him as the pilgrims' singer launched into a noisy song and the bear finally succeeded in swiping a dwarf – a fact which pleased Hamon enormously – and temporarily he lost sight of her.

'Nichola,' he called at full voice.

Once more she came into view and he saw that she had not heard him and was deeply in conversation with a man, a man whose back was turned and yet who had a vaguely familiar look.

A thrill of unease swept Hamon and he began to push towards her, cursing those who stood in his path. Once again he shouted and this time she did hear and turned to see who had called her name.

He saw a look of amazement, followed by one of horror, cross her features. Then her companion turned as well. Hamon froze where he stood, unable to move. He was staring into the face of the man he knew better than any other on earth. Robert de Sharndene was also in Battle that day.

That evening a great mist came up from Tide Brook, spreading shroudlike through the length and breadth of the valley of Byvelham, and then creeping on to Maghefeld, where it swirled round the palace like a ghost.

There was something about this particular fog that seemed to shut out sound. Everything became hushed in its wake and even the most adventurous creature stayed silently in its lair. Not a hare twitched; not an owl raised hollow voice; not a mouse scuttled amongst the dead leaves of a long-forgotten autumn.

Yet two people were out in it, choking and coughing in the moistened air and straining their eyes without the benefit of a lantern to see where, in the vast and rambling woods, they might possibly be. Marcus and Colin, returning from a hunting trip, had realised that not only were they thoroughly lost but that they had little hope of finding their way before daybreak.

'Must we sleep here?' asked the simpleton nervously.

'Not yet. We will go on a while longer. Come on, don't be afraid.'

At once Colin was happy, the lynchpin of his existence bringing him all the comfort he needed.

Colin could no longer remember what life had been like before he met Marcus and married Oriel. To him they had always been there. And he was not sure, in his blurred strange mind, whether this was because he recognised both of them as friends of old, or because they filled his little, undemanding life with so much joy. And yet, like driftwood in a great ocean of nothing, memories sometimes came to him. Memories that would slip away as he sought to focus them more clearly. It was then that he would turn to his gittern, plucking the strings and trying to concentrate on what it was he really knew.

Now he said, 'I am not afraid.' Then added, 'Did I shoot well with the bow?'

'Very well.' Marcus was not concentrating, straining his eyes through the solid wall of grey that hung about them. It was just growing dark, the most deceptive light of all in which to be fog-bound.

'I used to once,' said Colin.

'What?'

'When we ran in the hills.'

'Oh.' Marcus was not listening, thinking that he had noticed the glow of a light. 'I believe I can see something,' he said.

Colin smiled. Not long now till he sat before the fire and was given warm soup and hot bread and could relate to Oriel all the day's events: they had seen a heron flap his wings; he had shot three arrows into the bull's eye; Marcus's face had creased when they had come across Nicholas le Mist. And not long to wait to see her smile; see the toss of her lovely hair when she loosened it; feel the warmth of her sweet lips as she kissed him on the cheek. Not long now.

In the dimness he felt Marcus pull upon his sleeve. 'There *is* a light. Do you see it?'

Colin screwed up his eyes. 'No, I don't think so. Where, Marcus? Where?'

'Over there.' The squire pointed to a place, through the thick trees and confident young saplings, where it seemed to him a clearing was visible in the mist.

'I can't see anything.'

'Well, I can.'

Marcus went forward. Now there could be no doubt. Through the haze he could distinctly see a forge, the furnace glowing scarlet in the dullness, the anvil ringing with sound.

152

And then he saw the smith. Dressed as a monk, in roughspun habit, the man stood with his back to him, the great blacksmith's tongs clasped firmly in his hand.

'Hey there,' called Marcus, 'can you help us? We're lost in the fog. May we take shelter with you till daybreak?'

The man apparently did not hear, for he remained stock-still, standing in a strangely frozen manner, looking neither to the right or left.

'Hey,' Marcus called again, 'can you shelter us for the night?'

At last he seemed to understand, for the blacksmith slowly turned. A light so bright that Marcus thought he would be blinded appeared to shine from his face; his eyes were glowing orbs of starlight.

'Oh God,' cried Marcus.

They stared at one another and into the silence Colin spoke, 'What are you looking at, Marcus?'

'Can't you see him?'

'Who? Where?'

'The blacksmith. Over there.'

But the man had turned away again and the mist had come up so thickly that the smithy was lost to sight.

'I must have missed him,' said Colin apologetically.

But Marcus could not answer, too full of fear – and of something surpassing that. He felt that he had peeped, just for a moment, at immortality and wondered, in tremendous dread, if it would be possible for him to ever be quite the same again.

FIFTEEN

A wild and blustering March morning and a wind coming in from the ocean, full of crisping brine and the distant cry of sea birds, a wind that swept inland, puffing full-cheeked at fogs and vapours, bringing in its wake skies the colour of an angel's eye and clouds the shape of wings. There was a high bright sunshine everywhere and trees leapt to dance as the breeze hurried past and the world drew a sweet breath of springtime.

'It's daylight,' said Colin. 'Look Marcus. The mist has gone.'

There was no immediate answer and for several moments the simpleton sat in silence staring at his sleeping friend. He saw the bony cheeks, the hawk face, the heavy-lidded eyes, relaxed, at peace, almost as if the squire were dead. He saw the long brown hair lift of its own accord, ruffled by currents, and he saw the thin fingers of Marcus's hands, the smallest of which wore a ring, curling like the petals of a flower.

The hands lay innocently, in quietness, and, looking at them, Colin felt in a terrible and frightening way that he was seeing something that was yet to come; that one day Marcus would lie like that on the forest's ferny floor, with nothing to comfort and love him but the rustling grass snake and the short-sighted hedgehog.

'Oh God,' said Colin, hugging his knees to his chest, 'if that happens, make me die too. Don't let Marcus go away.'

The sweet, wild wind teased Margaret de Sharndene all of her journey home to the moated manor. And when she paused a moment on the hill above and looked down to the house she saw that the breeze had made playful little waves on the moat and that the swans bobbed joyfully, enjoying the excitement, and stretching their primeval necks up towards the gate of the sun.

Margaret felt such a love for life at that instant, such a stirring of warmth inside her. Paul d'Estrange, by his obvious fondness for her, had brought about the final metamorphosis:

she had at last become the mature and considerable woman she was always destined to be.

Much to her astonishment, as she sat enjoying the morning, she saw Robert approaching Sharndene from the opposite direction. She wondered instantly what was wrong, for he had stated clearly that his duties at the abbey would keep him away at least a week. She concluded at once that he had quarrelled with his mistress and could not resist a triumphant smile.

Her husband had still not noticed her presence and Margaret kept her horse motionless, observing him through the eyes of a woman cherished by another man.

'He's grown old,' she thought. 'He looks like a miserable squirrel. I wonder what I ever saw in him? Or what the owner of the sarcanet glove can possibly do? I vow he's a silly, hunched figure.'

And Robert certainly looked depressed, slumped in his saddle, his face like a gargoyle, plodding forward slowly towards his home.

'She has thrown him to one side,' Margaret decided certainly. 'He's too weary and boring for her despite his money and position. And serve him right!'

It was not in her nature to be vindictive but she had suffered too greatly when he had grown away from her not to feel a thrill of spiteful elation.

Quite unable to resist the urge to rub a little salt in a well-deserved wound, Margaret called out, 'Robert I am here. Opposite you. You are returned quickly.'

'Yes,' he shouted back, having at last seen her, 'I have some news to impart. Come to the house and I will tell you of it.'

They trotted down the opposite slopes and met at the drawbridge.

'Well, well,' said Margaret, grinning somewhat, 'you look a-brim with worry. What is wrong?'

'Nothing,' answered her husband, bearing a patently false smile. 'In fact quite the reverse. I met Hamon in Battle, absolutely by chance, and he has finally found himself a bride. A widow woman whom I vaguely know. I have come back to tell you to prepare; there is to be a wedding this week.'

Margaret stared at him in amazement. It was such an odd story that it seemed more than likely to be true. And yet...

'How old is she, this widow?' she asked. 'What is she like?'

'Er...: about nineteen or twenty, I believe, and reasonably pretty from what I can remember.'

'You do not know her well, then?'

'As I said, hardly at all. But you can shortly judge her for yourself. They are only a few hours behind me.'

He laughed hollowly and Margaret peered into his face narrow-eyed.

'Why do you stare at me like that?'

'It is only that you appear ill at ease.'

And with that she walked her horse across the drawbridge, Robert following behind wishing that the planking would open up and let him drop into the moat below. He supposed, at that moment, that the word misery must have been created especially for him. To be told on arriving at Battle that Nichola no longer wished to consort with him was bad enough, but to discover that the object of her changed affections was his own son was more than a human should have to tolerate.

He had felt instantly old, gazing into a bronzed mirror that very day and noticing the pouches beneath his eyes, lines around his lips, and the hangdog expression on his face; to say nothing of the profusion of grey suddenly and quite clearly visible throughout his hair.

'God 'a mercy,' he muttered now. 'I may as well give up and sit in the corner for the rest of my days.'

But small hope of that. Shortly he must fulfil the promise that Nichola, in the last few private moments they had had together, had begged him to make.

'He must never know,' she had said. 'Please Robert, if you have any thought for me left, do not tell him.'

He had looked pompous. 'Why should he not be told? Is he not man enough to know that his father is still vigorous?'

The expression on Nichola's face had been the final insult. In one quick glance she had managed to convey that, in comparison with his first born, Robert's idea of lovemaking was that of a schoolboy.

He had grown instantly furious. 'To hell with him – and with you too. You are a whore, Nichola Rougemont.'

She had looked at him coldly. 'Think what you will – it is of little consequence. However, as I am to be your daughter-in-law within the week you had better decide whether or not you will give us your blessing.'

'You are very confident, Madam. Suppose he throws you aside when he learns the truth?'

A sly and secret smile had spread over Nichola's face. 'I do not think that is likely to happen,' she had replied. And he had known then that she and Hamon had found the kind of bed magic together that meant they would never give one another up.

He had been about to give a cutting reply but at that very moment Hamon had walked in, looking so absurdly happy that his father had not had the heart to say a single word.

And now here Robert was at Sharndene, with Margaret peering suspiciously, and the bridal pair probably no more than three hours away.

He sighed deeply and Margaret, who had come up to him silently, said, 'I learned last night that we are to be grand-parents.'

He gaped at her. 'Not Juliana?'

'Not as far as I know, thought she *does* seem to be gaining weight. No, it is Oriel.'

'But surely the idiot is not capable!'

Remembering her secret conversation with Paul when he had called her to the palace on the previous evening, and their pact, to reveal the truth to no one, Margaret smiled and said, 'Apparently he can play the husband occasionally. Oriel tells me in the cold weather he stayed with her for warmth and the result of that will be born in the autumn.'

Robert shook his head. 'So it is all weddings and beddings?'

'Yes.'

'Well, well. A cycle has ended. Now I suppose we must learn to endure our advancing years.'

Margaret swished her gown. 'You may do as you wish. I personally have a great deal of living ahead.'

Robert sighed again. 'You have changed so much. Why, at one time you were so besotted with Hamon you would have gone into mourning if you had not picked his bride yourself.'

'I was foolish then. I realise now that one cannot live other people's lives for them.'

Robert sat down, suddenly very tired. 'I believe it is that wretched Gascon who has influenced you in all these things. You have not been the same woman since he arrived at the palace.'

Margaret nodded. 'It is true he has opened my eyes to much philosophy.'

'And has he also opened his arms to you in bed?'

Robert had never spoken to his wife in such terms and now she turned on him a disdainful glance, ready to trade insult for insult.

'We are not all of your stamp, Robert. I know full well that you have had a mistress in Battle for months and have almost exhausted yourself with her. Why, you have aged ten years in as many weeks.' A curious expression crossed Margaret's face. 'I suppose that by some curious mischance she and Hamon's bride are not one and the same person?'

Robert glared furiously at his wife and marched out of the hall without looking back, leaving Margaret to stare at his retreating form.

'Very convincing,' she said to herself. 'But I wonder. Anyway, I shall know as soon as I see her. I could never mistake the owner of that horrid little glove were I to live to a hundred years.'

And with this thought, Margaret went off to confer with Cogger about the wedding feast.

In the afternoon that Hamon brought Nichola to Sharndene, Oriel and Marcus walked in Byvelham woods for the last time. Hand in hand they went to the place where they could climb up and stand on a high ridge, looking out to the distant hills behind which lay the sea. They stood in silence, gazing at the view and thinking about their lives and the odd twist of fate that had brought about their meeting.

Eventually Oriel said, 'Another path, another destiny, and everything might have been different. The child that I am to bear might never have been created.'

'A child?' answered Marcus. 'You are carrying my child?'

'It will be born in October, or thereabouts. It was conceived last winter on that bitterly cold day. Do you remember?'

But Marcus did not answer, his spectacular smile lighting his eyes and softening his face. 'Something of my own at last,' he said. 'People who have no parents feel the need for that more than any other. I thank you, Oriel.'

He dropped to his knees before her and kissed the place where the baby grew. 'I greet it with love,' he added, looking up at her with an expression that she would remember for the rest of her life. 'And I greet its mother also.'

He took her in his arms and they kissed each other solemnly, then made love most beautifully, like a ritual for dancers, as if each had a premonition that time had turned against them. Afterwards, they lay quietly, until the angle of the sun told them that it was the hour to return to the palace. Then they dressed and walked through the woods hand in hand.

'You realise I was lost here only last night,' said Marcus. ' I wonder where the forge really is.'

'What forge?'

'In the fog I came across a smithy, the blacksmith standing by his furnace.'

Oriel gasped. 'But there is no smithy here – and never has been. Though there is a foolish legend that the lost forge of St Dunstan sometimes appears in the valley, and that to look on his face means death.'

Marcus shivered violently. 'But the smith *did* look at me, with eyes like suns.'

Oriel went pale. 'It could not have been. You were mistaken. You imagined it.'

'Yes,' said Marcus slowly, 'I probably did. For Colin saw nothing.'

But neither of them was convinced and there was a strange silence between them as they made their way to where Colin patiently sat, his tongue poking from his mouth in concentration, as from his blunt fingers a little wooden boat began to take shape.

No sooner had she clapped eyes on Nichola, no sooner had she sniffed the musky perfume so reminiscent of the sarcanet glove, than Margaret Sharndene knew at once that this was she. That Robert's mistress, by some twisting irony of fate, had succeeded where all others had failed and had persuaded Hamon to offer her his hand in marriage. And it was not difficult to imagine how, at that. For here was a strumpet if ever she had seen one – long of leg and red of lip, and very merry of eye indeed. Margaret disliked her thoroughly. But still, it was amusing to see the performance coming from Robert, who, by adopting a terribly bluff manner, clasping the hands of all the men present and being over-attentive to the women, truly imagined that he had disguised the whole situation.

In a way Margaret felt sorry for him. She gave him a distant smile as he conversed with Oriel, who had ridden over from the palace with Marcus, and then turned her full attention to Hamon's betrothed.

'You have lived in Battle long?' she asked.

'Several years, Madam.'

'So then you would know my husband?'

Nichola shot her a questioning look. 'Everyone knows the Lord Bailiff.'

'Quite. But some better than others, I dare say.'

The widow looked somewhat disconcerted. 'I expect so.'

There was a fraught silence into which Hamon burst with, 'My sister with child, I cannot get over it.'

Oriel went very pink and said, 'It is not so surprising. I have been married since last year.'

'Yes, but I had not thought...'

His voice trailed away as he felt everyone turn to look, and it was left to Piers to drawl, 'Fatherhood must be in the air. What do you say, Flaviel?'

'It is probably the time of the year,' answered Marcus calmly. 'I believe that many a baby is sired during the winter months.'

'I hope so,' said Hamon, looking at Nichola so lovingly that Margaret felt her heart wrench.

'I must try to be kind,' she thought.

But she could not resist one final dig, one final hint to Nichola that she might know more than she was prepared to reveal. Leaning across the table she whispered confidentially, 'My dear, Hamon has been a great womaniser in his day. That is why his father and I never forced him to marry. But, if I may advise you, should he start to wander when you are saddled with several babes and no longer able to give him all the attention he needs, try to ignore it. I am quite sure that he will come to heel again in time. It is a family characteristic.'

And with that, rewarded by Nichola's thoroughly startled face, the Mistress of Sharndene set about forgetting the past and thinking only of the fulfilling times to come.

The guests finally departed from Sharndene into the blackness calling out to one another as they went their various ways, lighting torches of flame which could be seen bobbing about the valley for a while and then were gone, leaving nothing but the sleeping house and the swans skimming silently on an indigo moat.

Only Marcus rode alone and that by mischance. For Oriel, whose safe passage to her parents' home and back had been the squire's responsibility, had lost consciousness as they had crossed the drawbridge. He had only just saved her from falling to the wooden planks below, catching her as she slumped forward out of her saddle.

'Don't...' she had whispered. 'Marcus... the blacksmith.'

Then she lapsed into silence and he had had no choice but to carry her back into Sharndene and make his solitary way home.

Now, as he rode, Marcus's thoughts turned, yet again, to the mystery of his parents and it occurred to him for the very first time that his mother could have pinned a ring to his hat in order that he might be recognised. This would mean one of two things: that the ring was so famous a child carrying it would be known at once, or that it held some particular significance for the boy's father.

With a thrill of elation, Marcus realised that it must be the latter. The ring was cheap, a trinket, a bauble from a pedlar's tray. Had it been a gift for his mother which she was returning with her son? But why there, in that small town in Gascony?

The answer came like the lifting of a veil. Of course! Why had he never thought of it before? Now that he realised, it was so obvious. He was Paul's son; he was the flesh and blood of the man he loved more than any other. His mother had taken him there in order that the knight would find him.

Marcus shook his head and realised he was weeping. How clean it felt for those tears to course down into the blackness. He was a bastard and yet he was not. He had been brought up in his father's house as respectably as any acknowledged son. And then Marcus thought of *her*, whoever she might have been, and what had prompted her to abandon her child in the middle of that narrow, crowded street, walking away from him and never daring to turn her head for a last look. He saw the place again: the jostling people, the high, gabled houses, the shopkeepers shouting their wares. And there, in the middle of it all, saw the son of Paul d'Estrange grubbing at his eyes and wondering

161

when he would next smell that musky perfume that meant his mother was somewhere near.

Marcus narrowed his gaze, realising that he was almost at Bayndenn and that in the high wood above him a strange light was weaving amongst the trees, and that someone was walking there in the blackness.

'Ho there!' he called out. 'Who is it? Is anything wrong?'

There was no reply and Marcus had no option but to climb the rise swiftly and enter the intense shadow. The light had vanished and so he was unprepared when his horse suddenly reared in terror as, in the darkness, something lacerated its front legs. As he fought to keep his seat a pair of arms, strong as bars, grabbed Marcus from behind, pulling him down to the earth below.

He never saw who attacked him, had no time to do more than reach for his sword, before a crushing blow smashed his skull and he sunk to the ground in silence. After that there was no noise at all except for feet running through the woods, a horse hurrying away into the darkness; and Marcus's mount steadily cropping the grasses, accompanied only by the cries of a distant barn owl.

SIXTEEN

The seasons changed; the earth and the sun continued their great conversation; high summer triumphed in the valleys and hills; and in Oriel's womb her baby danced in a dark, silent world.

It was only now, now that some months had passed since Marcus had vanished, that she had begun to accept the fact that he must be dead, that somewhere in the forest – still, as yet, undiscovered by the search-parties – he lay rotting. That all the sweet, strong youth of him had started to decompose and return to the earth on which he had once walked.

At the beginning she had thought him on a mission for the archbishop, a mission so secret that he had been able to tell no one. And then came the bleak idea that he had deserted her, that all his sweet words had been falsehoods and that because she was with child he had run away to escape the consequences. Then something Colin had said had made her change her mind. He had looked at her with eyes like sheet-ice and had announced, 'Piers killed Marcus. He told him to count his days.'

'My brother said that?' Oriel had exclaimed.

'Yes.' Colin had hesitated, then said, 'Please may I tell you about something else too?'

'What is it?'

'The kitchen lads keep teasing me. Patting my back and saying that I knew what it was for after all. That I understood how to keep myself warm on a winter's night. What does it mean?'

He had been so earnest and Oriel's heart had bled for him that he should be the butt of the cruel and the ignorant. For answer she had taken his hand and laid it on her stomach.

'There, do you feel that? Do you feel how round it is getting?'

'Yes. Why is it doing that?'

'A baby is growing in there. Just as the mares in the stables have foals growing within them.'

'How did it get there?'

Oriel hesitated and then said, 'Marcus put it there by loving me.'

Colin said nothing and she went on, 'But that is a secret we must tell no one. Not even John; particularly not John. Colin, we must pretend to all the world that you are the father of this child.'

He had suddenly looked wise. 'Perhaps I am because I love you just as much as Marcus did.'

She had smiled and answered, 'If you want to think so.'

They had been happy for a while after that but Oriel had been unable to forget Colin's words and now she rode in her litter, her pregnancy too far advanced to allow her to go on horseback, through the green and gold of the valley in late summer, on her way to see Piers. To her right she saw the colours of the fields – the amber of harvested corn, the emerald shoots of winter grain, the dark red soil of the fallow field.

There was an odd sensation in her head as, just for a moment, she raced across the sands beside an aquamarine sea, listening to the laughter of her two companions, and watching a brown hand reach out to seize her bridle. Then the laughter grew louder as the owner of the hand drew level with her.

'Marcus!' she shouted, only to see the curious expressions of those leading the litter horses. She had been day-dreaming again but this time she had actually called out.

'Are you not well, my lady?' asked her servant, drawing alongside and peering anxiously through the litter's opened curtains.

Pretending faintness to cover her embarrassment, Oriel put her hand to her brow murmuring, 'Just a little tired,' and remained quiet for the rest of the journey. But on going down the track to Mouleshale such a weird assortment of noises greeted her ears as the little cavalcade turned towards the house that Oriel found herself exclaiming out loud again, this time in surprise.

Above the din and overwhelming everything else by its sheer ferocity, came the yells of a baby. For Juliana had produced a bouncing daughter.

Beneath this raucous cry could be heard the sound of a gittern, not played very well, and the high-pitched shriek of laughter. Between these bursts of giggling were rendered occasional snatches of song, from the tone of which it could be deduced that Piers, slightly drunk, had found himself an extremely youthful companion. On a lower key altogether to this ill-matched clamour came an occasional moan from the mistress of the house, presumably driven crazy by the uproar around her.

In the hall Piers, growing fatter with good living, lay back upon a sheepskin rug, clad in extremely tight hose and a long velvet robe which gaped at the front; while fawning attendance upon him and gurgling with delight was the prettiest boy Oriel had ever seen.

'This is Crispin, my protégé,' announced Piers.

Ignoring the youth, Oriel said, 'I have come here to speak to you privately. May I do so?'

Piers nodded, saying, 'Crispin is privy to my secrets.'

Reluctantly Oriel continued, 'Colin tells me that you threatened Marcus Flaviel. How much do you know about his disappearance?'

There was a momentary pause and then Piers said, 'I know nothing about it. But it is perfectly obvious to me that the man has returned to Gascony.'

'And why would he do that?'

The black pearl eyes looked slowly up and down Oriel's swollen shape. 'Why indeed, dear sister? Did he have something to hide, perhaps? Something that he could not conceal much longer?'

Oriel's heart began to thud but she maintained a calm exterior. 'Piers, I believe Marcus is dead.'

'Then if that is a fact, good riddance. But let me tell you one thing. If he *is* finished – and I personally do not believe he is – I can assure you that I am not responsible. Much as I would have loved to strike the death-blow I can swear that somebody else robbed me of the pleasure.'

She believed him. Detestable though Piers was there was a certain look on the handsome face – now growing somewhat debauched and bloated – that she knew from childhood. It meant he was telling the truth.

She sat down hard, 'Then who did?'

Piers stood up, gesturing abruptly for Crispin to leave them. 'I repeat, I do not accept he has been killed. I think he has run away. And do you know why ...' Piers lowered his voice to a whisper, 'because he is the father of your child, Oriel. I have never believed your story that it was sired by the half-wit.'

She could not bring herself to answer and turning silently, Oriel left the hall, trembling while her attendants lifted her clumsily into the litter, to take her back to the palace and the imminent birth that she awaited.

The wood at Bayndenn had been a lake of foaming blue earlier in the year, but now its triumph was over and there was only the glow of late summer to reflect in the dreamy waters of the dew-pond that lay so still beneath the drooping branches of a golden beech.

In all that place no bird sang, or so it seemed to Isabel de Bayndenn where she sat by the edge of the water, staring joylessly at her reflection in the mirrorlike surface. No birds to sing, no hope to grasp, no pleasure left in her entire life. Everything destroyed by her certain and sure discovery that Adam – poor sad Adam whom she had tried to transform into something he could never hope to be – had finally slipped out of reality and into madness.

With the knowledge she had grown suddenly old. The flesh of her beautiful and shapely thighs had begun to sag, lines and wrinkles had appeared like a mushroom crop upon her face and her lively eyes had lost their lustre and grown glazed, peering out at the world from above two unsightly bags.

Then had come the final blow. Exactly seven days ago, sitting in the very spot in which she was now and staring at her reflection with just the same despair, she had seen something glint beneath the water's surface. Putting in her hand she had drawn out a corroded ring which, at first, had meant nothing to her, but which, when she had taken it home to clean, she had recognised with a thrill of fear. It had been the property of Marcus de Flaviel.

That it had been thrown into the water to escape discovery she had no doubt. And the more she stared at the ring, the more she had become convinced that Flaviel had been murdered on her land and his body subsequently removed; the ring, which had probably come off during a struggle, hurled hurriedly into the pond to be hidden for ever. But that event had not come about for now she had found it and had guessed its secret.

Isabel remembered the night of the great snowfall. Remembered how she and Adam had watched the valley transform to a crystal fairyland; remembered seeing the purity of the landscape and contrasting it with the blackness of Adam's heart as he had spoken of Oriel and the Gascon squire.

And now Isabel sat alone, turning Marcus's ring in her hand, and staring into the waters of the dew-pond, seeming hardly to breathe.

The day began to fade, shadows falling over the valley and a mist coming up from the sparkling river and lying over the lowland in little fingers of grey, and the dew-pond turned, first, the colour of jade and then the deeper, more mysterious, shade of green jasper.

With a last sad sigh Isabel, without moving more than her arm, threw Marcus's ring back into the silent waters. A great ripple formed, then slowly died away until nothing was left at all, and the pond returned to its former glassy state.

Very slowly she got to her feet and climbed laboriously up the incline beyond the wood. Very much as she had suspected, Adam, a shadow long as a giant's before him, was plodding up from the river valley. She watched him in silence, thinking how perfect he was, how beautiful still. How, as if to compensate for the deterioration of his brain, his physique continued splendid, devoid of fat and packed hard with muscle.

He looked up and saw her. Years before, when they were first married, he would have hurried to be with her. Now he continued to trudge forward, his head lowered like that of a sheep on its way to slaughter.

He began to climb the hill, his face set hard as stone, and as he drew nearer, Isabel saw that he silently wept.

'Adam, don't,' she called out. 'Do not punish yourself like that. What is done, is done.'

He drew close to her. 'I could not help loving her,' he said. 'Yet she betrayed me so often. My pure little girl was really a whore.'

Very gently, Isabel answered, 'Oriel was no whore, Adam. She loved Marcus.'

'But I saw them together last winter. He rode her like a stallion. I could not bear to watch.'

'Is that why you killed him?' said Isabel softly.

Adam's great blank face turned to her in astonishment. '*I* killed him ...?'

But the fact that it was a question was lost on Isabel as she took a sickle from behind her back and brought down its moon-shaped blade upon the artery that pulsed in Adam's neck. He stood staring at her, amazed, watching his life's blood course down his shirt and into the mossy earth below.

'Isabel...' he said, 'I...'

And then he dropped, quite silently, his sad eyes staring up to the treetops and the great sky beyond, his gigantic body as still and calm as if he had just gone to sleep.

Isabel said nothing at all, merely shaking her head a little sadly as she would at a child who had been naughty in her presence. Then, the dripping blade still in her hand, she made her way down the slope towards the river.

As she came to the banks the sun began its final descent in a blaze of crimson, the Rother taking on the colour of fire and amber as it reflected the fiercesome light. Without a word Isabel raised the sickle above her head and watched the blood on it mingle with the brilliant waters as she threw it in. Then she stripped herself quite naked, gazing down at her ageing flesh without love.

'Make me beautiful again,' she cried to the flowing river.

A heron, startled, rose from his evening nest as she waded into the fast-flowing water and felt the coolness of it close over her luxuriant dark head.

SEVENTEEN

Harvest time, and the villeins and tenants hearty and hale as they wielded scythe and sickle, jug and ale. In the air the first crisp apple smell of autumn and over the land an intangible haze; a haze that spoke of summer but was really the very first sign of the end of the year.

In a glow of scarlet against the golden wheat, vividly bright next to the rich dark earth, noisy as it hurried through towns and villages, the archbishop's retinue, gleaming cross in the morning, prayers and wine cups at night, set forth from the hallowed town of York, through the long green stretches of middle England until the primate was, at last, once more within the boundaries of the ancient and mystical land of Sussex. After almost a year serving his king as chancellor and principal adviser for a second period of office, the archbishop ended the journey from York and came once more to his ancient palace.

'How good,' he thought, 'to sniff the raw bright scents of Maghefeld in the autumn time.' And then he thought of his sister-in-law Oriel, and of the child that she was to bear, and of all the love and all the hate he felt for his sad, mad brother Colin, and of everything he would do and had done to appease his guilt and assure his brother's happiness.

Wafting from the kitchens of the palace came the smells of meat upon the spit, of herbs being thrown into hot dark soups, of vegetables grown beneath warm and roseate walls. Stratford relished them all and felt that he had come home. He smiled to himself as he called out, 'Wevere, who is about? Where are you?'

There was an instant hustle and bustle as every servant in the place scurried to receive the Lord Archbishop of Canterbury. Horses' heads were held, legs swung out of stirrups, the wizened cleric who still, despite his eighty years, acted as Stratford's secretary, was lifted bodily down to the cobbles below. Everything was right in the great Palace of Maghefeld: the Primate of all England was once more in residence.

As soon as they heard his voice, Colin and Oriel came from

their apartments to greet him, his brother running and calling out, 'John, John,' the girl walking more slowly behind. She was heavy with child now, almost at full term and longing to be free of her burden and hold Marcus's baby in her arms.

With these guilty thoughts she descended the stone staircase and found herself, after so many months and so many stirring events, staring into the frozen face and glittering eyes of her mighty brother-in-law.

Oriel dropped a difficult curtsey and felt Stratford's hand take her elbow to raise her up.

'You are well, my child?' he said.

'Yes, my Lord.'

'And the babe?'

'It moves within, my Lord. The midwife tells me it will be here very soon.'

He looked at her dispassionately and Oriel found herself wondering whether he guessed the secret of its paternity.

As if he read her thoughts, the archbishop said, 'I hear that Flaviel has left the palace and is presumed by many to be dead.'

Oriel said nothing, certain that a trap was being set, and Stratford went on, 'Wevere has kept me informed of events. There is little that escapes him and he is an excellent correspondent.'

Though his face had not altered at all, Oriel became convinced that he was giving her a secret message.

'I am glad, my Lord.'

She could see that he was about to speak again, was about to delve more deeply, but was saved by the return of Colin who had bounded off to search for Paul d'Estrange.

'My Lord,' said the knight, bending his knee and kissing Canterbury's ring.

'I hear that you have kept the palace safe in my absence, d'Estrange. I also hear that you have lost Flaviel in mysterious circumstances. Is there any hope that he might still be alive?'

Paul stood up. 'No body has yet been found, my Lord, so there is always hope. But knowing him as well as I do I cannot bring myself to believe that he would have gone of his own choosing without a word of farewell.'

The archbishop nodded and said, 'I would speak of this further. Come to my chamber. Let the younger people rest before the evening's repast.'

He swept past the three of them, his cloak rippling, and mounted the great staircase at speed, the heavier-built man panting behind him. And so far ahead was he that by the time Paul caught him up in the antechamber above the staircase, the archbishop had already let the cloak slip to the ground where it lay like a scarlet pool, and stood, a sombre black-clad figure, staring out of the window, his back averted.

'Sir Paul,' he said, without turning round, 'you must deal with me honestly if you value your future. Is there any chance of my brother being the father of his wife's child?'

In an agony the knight shifted from foot to foot, his fieldmouse eyes dark.

'Speak out! I must know the truth. You have been here all these months while I have served our Sovereign Lord in York. And though no man can be privy to the bedchamber of another, there is a way of knowing these things. Tell me the truth.'

He wheeled round and for a moment Paul thought that the second most powerful man in England had taken leave of his senses. The archbishop's skin had blanched to the colour of snow, his eyes turned glassy, while a beating vein throbbed snakelike at his temple.

'Speak up man, It *was* Flaviel, wasn't it? He fulfilled the role that Colin could never take?'

'My Lord,' answered Paul in distress, 'it is not right that you should ask me these things.'

'It *is* right,' hissed the primate. 'Some deeds are done as a result of others. It is essential that I know the facts.'

'Then to the best of my knowledge the child that your sister-in-law carries is that of Marcus de Flaviel.'

The most curious expression crossed the face of the archbishop, an expression that seemed to carry in its depths triumph, despair and a strange kind of relief.

'As I thought,' he said. 'God's will be done. You will not speak of this again. Let Colin be accepted as the father in the eyes of the world.'

For two men with the same objective there seemed a strange disharmony between them. There was a coldness in the room and Paul caught himself shivering. Much as his natural son had done before him he caught something, then, of the essence of Stratford. Saw him like a black rook, plotting the downfall of kings and the raising up of princes; saw him signing his name to documents of which surely God, in His infinite love and mercy, would not have approved. Saw him as a whisperer in corners and yet at the same time, confusingly, saw him as a man of vision, a man who would stop at nothing in order ultimately to achieve the good of all.

'My Lord, what can I say?' he replied. 'I would not wish Marcus's name to be slurred – nor yet that of your brother and Oriel. I learned many years ago the power of keeping a still tongue.'

'Does anyone else know?'

'Only Oriel's mother, and she is sworn to secrecy for love of her daughter.'

'Then so be it. We must forget Flaviel, and look to the future.' An obvious elation now held Stratford in its grip.

'I shall certainly do so, my Lord. But as to forgetting Marcus – that is a different matter. I shall always remember him with the greatest affection.'

'Of course, of course,' the archbishop shrugged a thin shoulder. 'Thank you, d'Estrange.'

In one stroke he had ended the conversation and Paul was left with no choice but to bow his way out, wondering all the while about the strange facets that went to form the character of God's foremost servant in England.

But an hour later in the splendour of the great hall a different side of the primate was on display. Before his temporal subjects a gorgeously gowned actor now appeared, magnificent of speech and easy of laugh. The great voice, intoning thanks for the repast, was telling all those bowing their heads and clasping their hands that no distant saint was amongst them but a man of flesh and blood; that a sympathetic and worldly ear would listen to their little misdeeds with compassion and understanding. And as he swirled from his place on the dais to feed the poor of Maghefeld with his own pale hands there were few present who did not consider him a great man, a visionary, a true Vicar of Christ walking amongst and loving them all.

Only Oriel felt bemused by his display; felt after her early rush of courage she no longer had the strength to deceive her mighty brother-in-law. She sat, like a flower about to burst its seeds – in a gown full as a tent yet which still felt tight – eating scarcely nothing. And the smell from the floor, clean at first for

172

the archbishop's arrival but now giving off odours of spit, vomit and urine, assailed her nostrils like poison.

Beside her Colin watched like an anxious pup, gazing earnestly into her face and occasionally leaning forward to wipe her brow and the place above her upper lip. He was the only one who noticed her distress and she turned on him a faint yet grateful smile as he took her hand in his.

'Presently we shall go to our room,' he said, and she thought of their cool, quiet chamber where she occupied the bed and he lay, like a servant, on a trussing mattress at its foot. Last winter they had occupied it together, cuddling like children, but now that she was so large he had moved out to make way for her.

'Let it be soon,' she answered, and as she did so a wave of sensation, starting in her womb and building up like an arch, seized her entire body. Her breathing quickened in response and Paul d'Estrange heard her from where he stood behind the archbishop.

She saw him step forward and whisper in Stratford's ear and she felt the crystal eyes turn assessingly in her direction. 'Oriel, are you not well?' The full voice was lowered to a whisper.

'If I might retire, my Lord. I am in discomfort.'

'Is it the child?'

She could not answer but heard Paul murmur and then saw Stratford turn to her once more. 'You may withdraw discreetly. I will have word sent to your mother to attend you in your chamber. A servant will fetch Joan the midwife.'

As she got to her feet so, too, did Colin, and Stratford added abruptly, 'Stay where you are brother. This is not your affair.'

Like a child, Colin said pugnaciously, 'If my wife is leaving, so am I.'

Oriel felt everyone at the table stiffen but particularly Stratford. Caring nothing for any of them as her womb tightened hard once more, she gasped, 'Colin, please come with me.'

He thrust out his lower lip and glared at his elder brother, 'Yes I shall.' Then he announced at the top of his voice, 'I put the babe there with my love, you know.'

At any other time Oriel would have hidden her head in shame but now all she could think of was walking through the screens at the back of the dais and making her way somehow – anyhow – to the top of the staircase. Water began to trickle down her legs.

'What is happening?' she called out fearfully.

'The baby is leaving its caul,' said the voice of Paul, surprisingly close behind her. 'Come Oriel, we must put you to bed.'

'Am I in labour?'

'Yes, but don't be afraid. The women will be here shortly.'

As the next wave of contraction came Oriel reached the door of her room and she fell forward upon her bed as the impact struck. Someone took off her shoes and someone else removed her flowing robe and replaced it with a shift. She opened her eyes to see her mother leaning over her, her face anxious and, turning her head slightly, Oriel saw Colin struggling in the doorway, wrenching at the arm of the midwife as she tried to put him from the room.

'Oh let him stay,' she gasped. 'He is so harmless and I draw comfort from his company.'

Margaret and Joan exchanged a glance but eventually Madam Sharndene weakened and said, 'Very well, he may sit outside the door. But he must go even from there when your labour advances.'

Oriel could not answer as a huge wave dashed against her, leaving her broken and trembling. Then she cried, 'Colin, play for me. Play to help me, my little love.'

She saw his worried face as he snatched up his gittern a moment before he was shown outside and the door locked against him. In it Oriel read so much love, so much compassion, that she marvelled she should have known such tenderness in her short life; that two men should have cared for her so much. Then all thought was gone as another wave came upon her unannounced, throwing her fragile body into the air and breaking her against the rocky shore before it died away.

The music began, soft and insinuating, and Oriel realised dimly that Colin was playing as he never had before. That from his poor blunt hands was pouring forth a lullaby composed for the child of a lost dead friend, the infant of a well-beloved wife. From beneath her closed lids tears began to trickle as the tempest hit her without mercy.

Oriel had never realised that a human being could be subjected to so much suffering. She was in a lashing sea without a spar; she was in the depths, sucked beneath icy waters; she was helpless, shot towards heaven on the crest of monstrous waves. A siren began to sing from the deep, a merchild joined its voice with Colin's gittern, a girl began to scream as she fell down and down into the vortex.

Somewhere, Margaret's voice said, 'For God's sake fetch Sir Paul. Maybe he can help her.'

Out of the darkness, Joan answered. 'There is something wrong with this labour. It is women's curse to suffer but never like this.'

In the far corner of reality the chamber door was unlocked. 'Oriel,' said Colin, 'I am here. They won't put me out again. I shall stay with you until the infant comes.'

Now he played a requiem, but for whom who could tell? Distantly Sir Paul said, 'The child is too big. It is taking the mother with it.'

'Save her,' said a voice that resembled Margaret's. 'Sacrifice the baby. Kill it if you must.'

'I can't,' said Paul. 'She is too small and it has won.'

The voice of the gittern rose high, drowning all, then, as the thin cry of a new-born child rang out, Oriel smiled as her hand fell into that of a sad little simpleton who wept beside the bed as if his heart would break.

Midnight in the palace; candles and whispering; and in the two chapels, two brothers about their different affairs. In the room above the porch where Oriel lay at peace, only the sound of Colin's sobs. In Becket's tiny praying place, the muttered words of baptism as John de Stratford held Marcus's son in his arms and acknowledged him into the Christian faith.

She had died quietly, her cries stilled as the baby was assisted into the world by Paul d'Estrange. She had suffered very little at the end, full of some potion the Gascon knight had given to ease her passing. But, as if her agony had gone in to him, Colin had fallen to the floor, crumpled and beaten, and had had to be carried to the chapel where, later, he kept lone vigil beside the slight body of his young wife.

From his great chamber the archbishop had come, vestments rustling as he walked, and had administered the last rites before he had gathered the infant up and taken it away from the midwife to where he might be alone with his thoughts. Looking down at the sleeping child, John Stratford's face had taken on the odd frozen expression that was so very much part of him.

Then he had made the sign of the cross and dipping his fingers in holy water had repeated it on the forehead of Marcus's son.

'God forgive me for the destruction of your father,' he prayed. 'It was too dangerous to let him live. He might not have been able to hold his tongue when you were born. But a small evil is sometimes necessary to achieve ultimate good.'

And how easy it had been for the hired assassin to waylay the unsuspecting squire in the darkness and afterwards hide his body by concealing it within the wall of a cottage still under construction.

The child did not stir and laying it down on his bed, Stratford went to kneel where Thomas à Becket had before him.

'Absolve me of guilt,' he said, 'the future is better thus. God grant that Oriel – and Marcus – find peace.'

Then he rose up and went on his way to offer public prayer, not only for all those that had gone but for everyone left behind to suffer.

PART TWO

The Magic Valley

EIGHTEEN

From the slopes beneath Baynden a figure could be seen walking towards the house, swinging a basket on its arm, and singing. It was tall, bony, and from a distance not recognisable as that of man or woman. But then, as it suddenly moved its head, the thick dark hair that fell to its waist revealed that it was a young female who strode up the hill, her black skirt tucked up that she might walk more freely and her long fingers snatching at the early spring flowers and placing them in her basket.

As the girl drew level with the house she waved but when nobody responded did not halt her progress, merely passing by and taking the track that led up towards Maighfield. She began to slow her pace slightly as the incline grew acute but still went steadily on, not pausing to gossip with the woman who called, 'Good day, Jenna,' who stood, rocking a baby, outside one of the few cottages that straggled beyond the confines of the village.

Eventually, breathing faster, the girl reached the top of the steep hill that led to the village street, and paused for a moment looking about. Before her the broad track that ran through the centre of the village stretched away; the fine house built for Sir Thomas Gresham thirty-four years earlier, in 1575, by far the most imposing dwelling, other than Maighfield Palace itself, which lay back from the track in its own grounds.

It was through the archway in the palace gatehouse that Jenna now went, making her way round the side of the great building towards the kitchens. There was a morning smell everywhere; freshly baked bread combining with the raw sharpness of newly killed meat and the salty tang of fish, brought to the steward for his approval. Going inside, Jenna picked up a sharp knife and began to attack the mound of vegetables that lay on the wooden trestle before her. Instantly the atmosphere of the kitchens consumed her and she was happy.

She had always felt like that about the palace, her earliest recollection being of sitting upon her father's shoulders and tilting her head back to see the shadow cast by the arch of the gatehouse as he walked beneath it. After that she could recall her burst of intense emotion as she had cast her eyes for the first time upon the graceful stone walls and flowing lines of what had once been the palace of the archbishops of Canterbury. She had never been able to explain it then or since; the great feeling of oneness with the building.

It had been something of a family joke and they had laughed about it and other strange ways of Jenna's until her mother, on her death-bed, had whispered to Jenna's father, 'Do not repeat what the girl says. Remember Alice.' And this mention of his aunt had silenced Daniel Casselowe from then on.

Jenna had often been told how her father, as a little boy, had stood with the other villagers on the dusty track and watched the queen arrive at the palace to visit its owner, her courtier Thomas Gresham. How he had shouted and cheered as the glittering figure – tall, with pearl-decked red hair in startling contrast to her pale enamelled face – had turned to look at her humble subjects of Maighfield. Daniel had always sworn that the queen's deep blue eyes had singled him out and that he had seen in their depths the fierceness and fanaticism that had let her rule England so powerfully for so long. But now the glorious creature was gone and King James had come from Scotland and had occupied the throne of England for the last six years.

A noise of crashing kitchen irons broke the train of Jenna's thoughts – of a great queen sleeping in a chamber which had once been the private domain of celibate archbishops – and she ran to help the hapless girl kneeling on the stone floor, picking up the scattered implements.

'You've broken the jointed stool by dropping the great pan on it,' said the master cook accusingly. 'I've a mind to thrash you.'

But another voice spoke up saying, 'Benjamin Mist is in the palace mending one of my lady's chairs. Take it to him before he leaves.'

At the very mention of the name, Jenna's hand began to shake and her heart quickened its beat. Her cheeks went bright and she bent her head forward over the floor, pretending it was the effort that made her suddenly colour. Even to be under the same roof as the carpenter was enough to arouse emotions in her that were too disturbing to contemplate, for Jenna could not remember a time when she had not been in love with Benjamin Mist.

Even as a child she had been drawn to him and then when womanhood had come upon her some years later she had realised that she was frantically in love. So frantically that a wild and unpredictable streak in her nature had flared when he had escorted Debora Weston to the fair, and she had lain in wait for the girl and thrown her bodily into the stream that ran by Cokyngs Mill.

The incident had not been serious, Debora suffering no more than a chill and Jenna, Daniel's belt, but from then on Benjamin had grown distant. His dreamy eyes had hardened whenever Jenna had come near and she had, on several occasions, seen him deliberately side-step rather than have to speak to her.

Now she said, too eagerly, 'Shall I take it to him to be sure he gets it? Where is he working?'

'In the stables. But don't waste time talking. There's a great deal to do and my lady will be furious if all is not ready when Sir Thomas comes home.'

'I'll only be a moment,' said Jenna, snatching up the broken stool and hastening into the courtyard before the cook could change his mind.

The early morning freshness had gone and now the bright spring sun was turning the old walls from stone to rose. Pennants of smoke ascended from the family apartments towards the fluffy clouds that chased one another across the mazarine March sky. Jenna paused for a moment, listening carefully. From the far stable came the steady tapping of a hammer, and even knowing that the noise had been made by Benjamin Mist was enough to set her heart pounding again, and make her palms go moist. Jenna walked steadily enough though, pausing in the stable doorway to watch him unobserved.

Benjamin was on his knees by Lady May's farthingale chair, which lay in three separate pieces before him, his back turned, so that he was completely unaware of Jenna's presence. She remained where she was, relishing the moment, admiring his small capable hands, the wiry frame, the delicious way in which his hair – the warm bright brown of a Spanish nutmeg – curled about his neck.

She felt such a sudden rush of love that she let out a cry, and Benjamin glanced up. Just for a moment, before he had had time to register who it was, she saw a welcoming look in his blue eyes, then they clouded over.

'Oh, it's you, Jenna,' he said.

'Yes.' She felt herself flushing awkwardly and could just picture herself, tall and bony, her black hair falling forward over her eyes, and her skin the colour of beets. 'I'm sorry to disturb you, Benjamin. It is just that this stool has broken and the master cook wondered if you could mend it.'

He stood up, brushing his hands against his breeches. 'Let me look.'

She advanced towards him and handed him the stool, only too cruelly aware that her unusual tallness must make her seem like a giant to a man of only average height.

'Oh yes, I can easily repair this,' he said, turning the splintered wood in his fingers.

She hesitated, knowing that the carpenter was regarding her in a dismissive manner, but determined to remain where she was. 'My father remarked only the other day that he had not seen you for an age. He wondered if you might like to come and sup with us.'

Benjamin paused, and if she had not cared for him so much Jenna would have been angry that anyone should waver over an invitation from Daniel.

'Yes,' he said eventually, 'thank Daniel from me. I will come soon.'

'Tomorrow?' Jenna answered, refusing to be put off. 'Or the next day? Which?'

'The next.'

'Then we shall expect you.'

'Yes,' he said. He turned away, 'Farewell Jenna.'

She ran back to the kitchens without daring to look over her shoulder, afraid that Benjamin might call out to her that he had changed his mind. But once inside the high-ceilinged room, now full of delicious smells – the great rotating joints mixed with the comforting aroma of pastry and fresh quivering custards – her confidence returned.

The girl who had broken the stool looked at her slyly. 'Did Benjamin say he could mend it?'

Jenna remained blank, lost in her thoughts.

'Benjamin. Your friend. Did he think the stool could be mended?'

'Oh...yes. I have given it to him.'

'They say he'll be taking a wife soon.'

'What?' Jenna turned an expression of such horror on the girl that her companion laughed.

'My sister saw him walking in Byvelham Woods with Debora Weston. She said they were kissing one another.'

'Lucy, are you saying this to annoy me?'

The girl's face softened. 'No, it's true enough. I think he has always had a fancy for her. Jenna, if you want him you will have to act fast.'

'What do you mean?'

'That you will have to snatch Benjamin away from her.'

'But how can I do that?'

'Surely there must be ways?' Lucy lowered her voice to a whisper. 'Couldn't you witch him?'

'Don't even say it. You know the penalties as well as I do.'

'Aye, but with your great aunt being that way I thought they might not find you out.'

Jenna looked away. 'My aunt died in gaol for her sins. I have no mind to follow her.'

'Then you will have to think of something else. Otherwise you'll lose him to the sweetest little meat of them all.'

'Is that how men talk of her?'

'Aye. My brothers say she looks good enough to eat.'

Jenna pulled a face. 'Don't! I wish the horrid creature at the bottom of a pit.'

Lucy chuckled. 'Perhaps you could witch her too.'

'Oh stop it,' said Jenna, hiding the solitary tear that had begun to trickle down her nose.

Having finished his work at the palace, Benjamin Mist carefully placed in a bag those pieces of wood that he needed to take home with him and walked briskly out through the arch of the gatehouse, pausing for a moment to look about.

To his right lay the cottages that stood close to Maighfield's main track, while on his left a well-trodden path went steeply downhill, passing a few dwellings, on its way to Cokyngs Mill. Benjamin frowned with indecision. If he called on Debora Weston without previous arrangement, might he be given supper? Or, as his stomach was rumbling furiously, would it be better to go home and eat first? Deciding that a meal was a small sacrifice to make for love, Benjamin finally shouldered his carpenter's bag and took the track to the left.

Behind him lay the descending sun, while the sky was luminous, a pinkness merging with the deepening blue. Every bird seemed to be giving full throat as above Benjamin's head a thrush suddenly began a strange and exotic chant to the day's end. From the slopes above the river a sweet, clean wind carried in it the scent of wild flowers. It was an evening that held in its heart the sweet essence of spring, and, there, ahead of him, he could see Debora Weston running up the path to meet him.

She was as pretty as a snowdrop and as delicate: tiny in both height and figure with a mass of golden hair, while her eyes were the colour of spring violets. The whole impression was flower-like even down to the petal fairness of her skin.

As she came nearer, Benjamin took both her hands in his, pulling her close to him. But the sound of her mother's voice from the cottage doorway interrupted them. 'Debora, who's there? Is it Benjamin?' and Goodwife Weston darted into view, a little dark, shrewish woman, quite the opposite of her delicate daughter.

Benjamin gave a polite salute and she smiled broadly, her face wrinkling into what seemed a thousand lines, her blackberry eyes gleaming. They stood for a moment smiling at one another: she thinking what a good catch Benjamin Mist would be, with his own cottage inherited from his father; he, remembering the old saying that girls grow like their mothers with the passing years, and wondering if it would happen to Debora.

But, undeterred, he whispered to the girl as her mother disappeared indoors. 'You are sure you want to marry me?'

Debora's face changed. 'You know I do. But there is someone who will want to kill me for it.'

'What do you mean? Who?'

'That evil Jenna Casselowe. She was so jealous when you took me to the fair she pushed me into the river.'

'I know. I've despised her ever since.'

'I think she has a passion for you, Benjamin. I hope she will do nothing to get her revenge.'

'How could she?'

'Her great aunt was a witch and died in gaol.'

'But that does not mean Jenna takes after her.'

184

'My mother says it runs in families, like madness. Oh Benjamin, I feel so afraid.'

He put his hands firmly on her shoulders. 'You can leave Jenna Casselowe to me. She will not dare lay a finger on you.'

'But are *you* not terrified of her?'

'Of that great horse?' answered Benjamin angrily. 'Why, she is nothing but a joke. She wouldn't be capable of bewitching a mouse.'

'I am not so sure,' answered Debora slowly, as hand in hand they went in to supper.

NINETEEN

Crouching so that she would not hit her head on the bedroom beams, Jenna Casselowe stared solemnly into the mirror, given her by Lady May, her finger tracing the bones of her countenance as if feeling them for the very first time. An unusual face looked back: long and angular with high arched cheeks and slanting green-gold eyes, surrounded by a mass of heavy black hair, silken and straight as a rod.

The hand that reached for the crude hairbrush was also bony. Yet, in its way, it too was beautiful, the fingers long and delicate and at the same time strong and capable. In fact the person who now left the mirror and crossed to her truckle bed was unquestionably striking, the kind of woman that a man of perception would be unable to forget.

But Jenna thought none of this as she doubled her long body and drew from beneath her bed a large, locked wooden box, the key to which hung on a chain about her neck. After glancing over her shoulder, she unlocked the heavy clasp and putting her hand within, drew out a leatherbound book and turned the pages, each filled with cramped, dark writing, until eventually she found what she sought. Then she swiftly started to read, her hands reaching for her basket of herbs as she did so.

Unlike many of her contemporaries, Jenna was literate, tutored by her father who had learned from his aunt, Alice Casselowe, who had been taught, in her turn, by Lady Gresham in return for mixing beautifying potions. This was the aunt who had been accused of bewitching her neighbours' oxen and pigs and who had been found guilty and died in Horsham Gaol before her sentence was served.

Holding her great aunt's book and seeing the writing leap from the pages as if it had been inscribed yesterday, Jenna shivered. On the throne of England sat a Scots king so conscious of the Prince of Darkness that he had written a book in three volumes entitled *Daemonologie*. And in the first year of his reign King James's parliament had passed an act giving the death

186

sentence to all those who used witchcraft to kill or injure another, and imprisonment to those who bewitched cattle, gave love potions or used their powers to discover the whereabouts of treasure. The very possession of Alice's book was a danger in itself.

Yet Jenna knew every page of it almost by heart: innocent herbal remedies, potions, salves, cures lay at the beginning, followed by other things more dangerous. Lists of herbs that could bend a man to one's will, bring him to one's bed, keep him there forever. And darker things too: poisons to kill, paralyse and madden, and spells to achieve one's heart's desire.

Jenna had hardly ever dared glance at this part of the book, and now she looked only at the content which dealt with beautifying the face and body, rubbing into her skin and lips the crushed leaves which her great aunt recommended for colouring the cheeks and mouth and brightening the eyes.

Then she turned back to the mirror questioningly, thinking that, perhaps, she did look a little more handsome than formerly. But before she put the book back in its box she could not resist one final touch. Following the instructions given, Jenna had previously prepared a heady mixture of herbs and flowers which she had left to stand overnight in a fairy-ring beneath the light of a day-old moon. Now she took the bottle from the bottom of the chest and splashed the liquid liberally on to her neck, her hair and finally her breasts. The smell was overpowering. She locked the book away and descended the ladder to the room below.

Jenna had left the palace early, saying that she must return home to tend the animals, but really hurrying back to prepare supper for Benjamin Mist. Too poor to eat meat more than once a week, she had persuaded Daniel that this afternoon should be the occasion for a truly grand meal: a roasted chine of beef, served together with a neat's tongue, and – by begging items from the master cook – Jenna had also contrived a Tansy: a dish of eggs, cream and spinach mixed with the juice of wheat blades, and violet and strawberry leaves, topped with grated bread, cinnamon and nutmeg. This noble repast would end with a custard and would be quite unlike anything normally eaten by the family.

Pleased with her preparations, Jenna began to sing as she set the table with wooden platters and knives, and was startled and surprised when a voice behind her said, 'Very pretty, you have a tuneful note.' She turned rapidly, thinking, just for a moment, that Benjamin had come early and that she was to be allowed the pleasure of being alone with him. But the man who stood in the doorway eyeing her was not the carpenter, nor even one of her friends. His elegant dress – a short velvet cloak hanging from one shoulder complete with standing collar – denoted him at once to be a gentleman of means.

'Don't be startled,' he went on, looking at her with an appraising gaze. 'I have come to see Master Casselowe and was told that I would find him here.'

Jenna bobbed a curtsey, painfully aware that she was taller than he was.

'He's out, Sir, but will be home soon. Do you want to wait for him?'

Her heart sank as the man took a step forward into the room. 'You are his daughter, I take it.'

'Yes, Sir.'

The man bowed and Jenna wondered if he was making fun of her. But he said quite simply, 'I am Robert Morley of Glynde,' and took another step inside. 'That jug of ale looks very good, may I have some?' he added.

How could she refuse in view of who he was? Though she had never actually met him, tales of Harbert Morley's younger half-brother – and the heir to the Glynde estates as Harbert had only fathered daughters – ran wild in the valley, and had often been recounted to Jenna. Some said that more bastards in Byvelham and Maighfield had been fathered by Robert than could ever be counted on a clear day, and others claimed that he had brought one of the Pelham ladies to bed of a son when he had been a mere twelve and she forty-one! Whatever the truth, Jenna had to admit that he had a scamp's grin and eyes and looked ready for merriment.

'I'll pour you some,' she answered reluctantly.

The man sauntered to the table and sat on the edge, one leg wearing a close fitting and thigh length boot, swinging. 'And what is your name?' he asked.

'Jenna, Sir. Jenna Casselowe.'

'How very unusual. I can't recall having heard that before.'

'I was to have been Jenet, Sir, but my mother changed her mind, thinking Jenna more musical.'

Master Morley downed his ale, then stood up.

'Will you tell your father I called on him and that I will return tomorrow at this time? My brother has asked me to see that all is well in the valley.'

Jenna dropped a respectful curtsey. 'I will, Sir, thank you.'

'Farewell until then. I hope you will be here when I come, musical Jenna.'

'Oh, I'm not the musical one, Sir,' she answered. 'That gift belongs to my sister Agnes.'

A tiny drop of blood ran down Benjamin's chin, falling, like a crimson raindrop, into the bowl of water before him. He stood in the downstairs room of his cottage, bare to the waist, washing and scraping his chin in preparation for his supper with Daniel, but dreading the ordeal that lay before him. For this evening he was duty-bound to tell the Casselowes of his betrothal to Debora, and something of her unease about Jenna had conveyed itself to him.

Benjamin paused reflectively, his razor in his hand, gazing out of the cottage window to the land that lay beyond. In the far distance the slopes of the Rother valley rolled away softly, covered by patterns of densely growing trees, while from his bedroom, if he gazed to the left, the fields belonging to Baynden appeared as slashes of emerald.

Immediately before him, Benjamin could see the top of the deep well which provided his water and behind that the shelter for his animals. In common with most of the other villagers he had a smallholding which he worked to supplement his main occupation of carpentry.

Benjamin had inherited the cottage, which lay a quarter of a mile away from the palace near iron-master Aynscombe's house, Aylwins. In this matter of possession he was better off than Daniel Casselowe, who rented his cottage from the Lord of Glynde, and something of the quality of Benjamin's furniture reflected this. For Benjamin had a cup-board and his other wooden movables were jointed. Though not affluent, the carpenter's home bore the sign of someone making a respectable living for himself.

Realising that his preparations were not yet complete, Benjamin resumed his shaving, contorting his features before his wood-framed and home-made mirror. As he did so he thought he saw another face reflected behind his, an elfin face with a pointed chin, but when he whirled round to see who was there, there was nothing, only a trick of the light – a shadow thrown by the afternoon sun. Nonetheless, it was unnerving and the carpenter hurried through the last of his tasks, pulling on his clean woollen shirt and stockings and buttoning his good breeches below the knee. Then he left the house, locking the door behind him, and mounting the old nag who plodded him round the countryside in pursuit of his occupation.

The afternoon was so fine that Benjamin decided to make his way through the woods and fields to Baynden. Plunging into the dense trees he stopped short as the sound of a lute burst out so suddenly that his horse shied. For a moment or two Benjamin did not move, listening to the rapturous sound. Then he walked the nag over and looked down at the player. It was Jenna's sister Agnes, as fat and unappetising as ever. Yet when she played she looked strangely changed. Unaware that he was watching her, even now she bore an entirely different expression from that of the podgy, noisily-breathing girl that was her usual self.

She heard him and looked up, and just for a second held his gaze. Benjamin had the strange impression that somebody else was looking at him; that out of Agnes's round grey eyes someone else was peeping. Then the moment was gone.

'Good-day,' he said.

She flushed and scrambled to her feet, her hands clutching the lute as if it was a lifeline. 'I did not hear you approach, Benjamin. Are you on your way to see us?'

'Yes.' He hoped his apprehension did not show on his face. 'I'll go ahead and warn Jenna.'

Then without another word the girl turned and ran off through the trees, the carpenter leading his old nag by the reins behind her.

As he approached he saw that Baynden lay peacefully in the light of the setting sun, its far windows diamond-bright as they picked up and reflected the sinking rays. The house had always been the property of the Lords of Glynde and at one time had been a manor house in which courts were held. Now it was simply a farm leased to the yeoman Richard Maynard by Harbert Morley, though a farm in which Harbert still reserved the right to hold courts should he so wish.

As he walked down the slope beyond the house, Benjamin

wondered who had been the tenants centuries ago and what sort of life they had led; whether they had known joy or sadness, hope or despair. For no reason he gave a violent shiver.

In the distance lay Daniel's little cottage, the smoke rising from its chimney, and the pond, beside which it had been built, a sheet of gold dancing with lights. It seemed so peaceful and picturesque that it was difficult to believe a woman had once been taken from there to answer charges of witchcraft; that, as the sun had set like this one evening some thirty years ago, an elfin creature had been dragged out, screaming, to go to her eventual death.

Benjamin crossed the few remaining yards to the cottage door. It lay open and in the room beyond he could see Daniel, his sleeves rolled up, pouring out a goodly measure of ale. Behind him, busy with her cooking pots, was Jenna, her dark hair clean and silky and tied back beneath a lace cap that had once belonged to her mother.

'Good evening,' said Benjamin from the doorway, and they both looked up. Jenna's eyes promptly slid away from his, and he felt certain that Debora was right and that the girl was in love with him.

'Benjamin,' said Daniel heartily. 'Welcome. Come in and sit down. I was about to have something to drink. Will you join me?'

'Indeed I will,' answered the carpenter, taking a seat at the wooden table and removing his hat. 'Your brew is the best for miles, Daniel, or so it is said.'

He was being over-enthusiastic in his attempt to avoid the bright, golden gaze that Jenna had now fixed on him. But poor Jenna, watching as her father and her beloved chatted together, wept inwardly that he would not return her glance.

'... delicious smell.'

He was looking at her at last, saying complimentary things about her cooking, but only doing so because he felt obliged. Unbidden, a page from Alice Casselowe's book came to Jenna's mind. She saw the close, dark writing as if it was in front of her: Crush all together dittany, pennyroyal and verbena and mix with a woman's most secret blood. Then, when blessed by a waxing moon, let the potion be given.

The consequences were clearly detailed: no man born could resist – within the passing of a day and a night he would be begging for one's love, one's bed, for the most private parts of one's body.

'I hope you will enjoy the meal, Benjamin,' said Jenna slowly. 'And indeed any refreshment you may take within this house.'

Good food, strong ale and a warm fire had taken their effect on Benjamin Mist. He sat grinning comfortably, his legs stuck out before him and his hands folded over his stomach, looking benignly at his host, who was talking of folklore. Or at least Benjamin thought he was, only lending half an ear to the conversation, the rest of his concentration being given to Agnes, who sat in the shadows playing her lute. Tonight she seemed inspired, the notes sobbing out a song of both love and despair.

'... famous local name,' Daniel was saying. 'Do you know about your forebears, Benjamin?'

'All connected with this area, I believe,' the carpenter answered slowly, his mind on the music, wishing Daniel would stop talking.

'Much as I thought. I believe at one time your family name was le Mist. Did you know that?'

'No.' The carpenter wished more than ever that Daniel would be quiet. Agnes had begun to play a lilting air to which she was singing, her odd, hoarse voice filling the room.

In the half-dark of the doorway, Jenna stood watching the scene: Daniel silent at last, the hiss of the wood on the fire the only other sound besides that of the song. Her eyes, dark in the scant light, went first to her father, then to her sister, seeing how her head bent forward over the strings, the barley-coloured hair hanging like a concealing veil. Finally they came to rest on Benjamin. She wondered, as she had a hundred times, why he should arouse so much feeling in her, when he obviously cared nothing at all in return.

'There's a full moon outside. Will you look at it with me, Benjamin?' she said very softly.

He gazed at her startled, not wanting to go, and then said abruptly, 'Oh very well. When Agnes stops playing.'

'She won't,' Jenna whispered. 'She will either go on till we take the lute from her or go upstairs and play it in bed. That is her way.'

Benjamin rose reluctantly to his feet, knowing that this must be the moment to tell Jenna he was to marry. 'Then I'll come,' he said.

Outside the tiny cottage a night so infinite in its proportions dwarfed not only the little building but the entire world. A black sky riven with mysterious stars soared above Jenna and Benjamin, in the midst of the glistening canopy an enormous moon, full of faces and shapes, shining down on them so clearly that they could see each other distinctly.

In the strange light, Jenna's hair was full of little gleamings and shades of blue, while her eyes were green, slanting beneath the curve of her dark brows. Benjamin, on the other hand, looked pale, his skin and hair bleached of colour, only his eyes vivid and strangely penetrating.

'What is it you want to say to me?' she asked.

'What do you mean?'

'You have avoided me even more than usual. What have I done?'

He tried to smile but found himself unable to speak.

'You are going to marry Debora Weston,' Jenna went on flatly.

Benjamin was astonished. 'How did you know?'

'There have been rumours. But you have been more eloquent than any of them. Your very silence told me everything.'

He tried a laugh which fell flat as lead. 'Aren't you going to wish me joy?'

The unpredictable side of Jenna's nature suddenly flared. 'No, Benjamin, I am not. If that pretty sop is your choice I have nothing further to say to you.'

She turned on her heel and strode off in the direction of the river and though Benjamin tried calling her name once or twice, the only answer was the cry of a fox, out hunting and sporting in the excitement of the silver night.

TWENTY

The night and Jenna's wretchedness of spirit became one – stretching on endlessly, with no sign of the life-giving dawn.

'Surely', she thought, 'this must be hell. To lie here in such a gawdy setting – all stars and moon and nightingales – and feel myself begin to die.'

There was such an ache in her, such a pain, such a hurt where there had once been a heart, that she did not know how she could bear another second of life. She had plummeted to the nadir of existence. And now, lying in their suffocatingly tiny room, staring out of the window at the whorish moon parading in all her finery, she must listen to Agnes sobbing as if she was the one who was in love with him.

The moon began to dip and at last came the moment that Jenna had been dreading. Soon daylight would come and though the night's ordeal would be ended, another trial would begin with the first pennants of red. Life must continue; meals must be cooked, work must be done, a face for the world must be decided upon and worn. She must bear the derision of those who knew where her love lay and who would soon be hearing for themselves of Benjamin's betrothal.

Suddenly Jenna knew what she must do. She did not even have to struggle with her conscience before deciding. The answer was so simple; she even had the means at her fingertips. Earlier that evening she had looked at the first part of Alice Casselowe's book. Now she would consult those other pages, the pages that gave power over people and events, and would use them ruthlessly.

Jenna sat up in bed, collecting her thoughts. The penalty for bewitching another to unlawful love was imprisonment, not death. Surely the risk would be worth it, for who could prove a thing? Without further hesitation, Jenna lit a spluttering candle, feeling a cold thrill of elation as she took the book from its hiding place and turned to the part she wanted. It was just as she had remembered – the dark writing listing the ingredients for the charm; herbs that she grew herself in the garden that lay beside the cottage. Those and her most private blood must be mixed to give the potion its full power.

Something had been written underneath the spell and, in the poor light, Jenna strained to see what it was: 'Let the moon be new or, at most, a day old for the enchantment to be at its strongest. Let the consummation take place before the moon has had time to die.'

So she had six weeks: two to see this moon gone and for her own secret flow to come and go, and another four before the magic wore off. But need it ever wear off? Turning to another page, her face hard and secretive, Jenna found what she knew to be there: 'Jessamine gathered at full moon and crushed to liquid, will keep love alive for ever.'

All the answers were here. Her great aunt's legacy to the niece she had never lived to know. She had put the key to happiness – and perhaps also death – into the girl's hand.

Jenna pushed all other considerations away and in the candlelight her eyes gleamed green fire. Then a voice startled her so violently that she dropped the precious book to the floor. 'What are you doing?' Agnes said.

'Reading. I thought you were asleep,' Jenna answered sharply.

'It was the light. It woke me up.'

'Well go back to sleep and leave me in peace.'

Agnes looked suspicious. 'Are you going to witch Benjamin Mist?' she said.

Jenna's fury was instant and ice-white. She leapt over to their shared bed and shook the hapless girl violently. As she did so, Jenna had the extraordinarily vivid feeling that this moment had happened before; that she had stood, just like this, with murderous intent towards Agnes, and that the victim's eyes had rolled up to look at their attacker just as piteously as they did now.

'Jenna, why are you so angry?' gasped Agnes, 'Do not hurt me. Please! You know how much I love you.'

With a cry, Jenna let her sister go and stumbled to the edge of the bed where she sat down, her head in her hands.

'Forgive me,' she said. 'Oh Agnes, forgive me. I love you too. It is just that I am so desperately sad tonight I would wound anyone to be avenged.'

Agnes got out of bed, her plump form trembling in its white shift as her feet touched the cold floor.

'Jenna, there is no need to explain to me. Benjamin is going to marry Debora Weston and it is not right. *You* must marry him even if you have to witch him.'

'But you know the punishment.'

'That could only happen if you were accused. And who would there be to accuse you?'

'His bride.'

Agnes looked thoughtful. 'Supposing she were to fall in love with another?'

'It might be possible,' answered Jenna slowly.

'Then that's the way to do it. Make her lose interest in Benjamin. There must be someone to take her fancy.'

'Yes,' said Jenna. 'I believe you might be right.'

The great moon waned and, when she was nearly spent, the silent mystery of her cycle mirrored within a woman's body came to Jenna. She caught some of the crimson drops in a phial and mixed them with the volatile oil secreted by the aromatic plant known as dittany, adding to this that species of mint called pennyroyal and finally the pale and delicate petals of hedgerow verbena. Then she locked the mixture away to await the night when the moon started her life again as a timorous crescent. When that time came, Jenna would cross the Rother in the darkness and climb the hill beyond to the ring of trees that grew on the summit almost opposite the little cottage. There she would keep vigil until the dawn came up.

Without being quite aware of what she was doing, Jenna went to Alice Casselowe's book again. It was two days since she had made the love potion and as she scanned the pages it occurred to her that she was turning to witchcraft once again to achieve her ends. In a moment of clarity she saw that the situation was feeding upon itself, that one twisted action was leading to another.

'This final time,' she murmured, as she raised the candle and read, 'To bring a person to your bidding take the bladebone of a lamb's shoulder and for nine nights stick a knife through it in varying places, saying, "Tis not the bone I mean to stick but —'s heart I mean to prick; wishing him neither rest nor sleep, till he comes to me to speak".'

It had to be done. She would fetch a bone from the palace the next day. If Debora Weston were to lose interest in Benjamin, it was essential that Robert Morley of Glynde should come to visit Baynden and the little cottage once more.

TWENTY-ONE

The silver candlestick flew through the air, mercifully missing the beautiful fourteenth-century window, the pride and joy of Sir Thomas May, but denting the wall beside.

'Hell!' shouted the young man responsible, wiping his eyes with the sleeve of his doublet. 'Hell, hell, hell!' Then he subsided into a chair and started to weep silently. Yet despite his tears he was as handsome as a summer day, in a dark Romany way, having a mass of curling black hair and vivid grape eyes.

In looks the youth favoured his mother, Jane, a member of an old Essex family with a great estate at Horndon-on-the-Hill. The Riches of Horndon had been swarthy since the Crusades when, so legend went, Saracen blood had been introduced into their strain. Yet the beautiful diamond hid a terrible flaw, for on certain days the boy was rendered almost speechless by an impediment which made him incomprehensible. And it was this fault which led him to moments of bleak depression like the one in which he was presently submerged.

Tom May – son and heir of Sir Thomas – considered himself especially unfortunate for he loved words, writing poetry and plays which he subsequently burned considering them to be unworthy. Truly he would like to have been an actor, to have joined William Shakespeare's company and acted with them, first at the Globe in Southwark and now at their private theatre in Blackfriars. But three years ago Tom had seen *Macbeth*, written at the special request of King James himself, and had known then that though he would never deliver lines upon the stage, at least he could write them. His ambition to be a poet and playwright of note had been born. Yet now, sitting in his father's ancient palace in Maighfield, he wept, unable to utter the words that were bursting to come out of his head.

With a sigh Tom stood up, wiping his face on a silken kerchief, resolutely straightening his doublet and brushing his trunk hose into careful pleats. Then he made for the door, descending first a small spiral staircase then the grand stairs before turning right towards the domestic offices where he ran straight into Agnes Casselowe.

The girl bobbed a curtsey and said, 'How are you, Master?'

Tom pointed to his mouth and shook his head.

Agnes's round grey eyes looked sympathetic. 'Would you like me to play for you before I go home?'

Tom nodded.

'Shall I come to your room?'

He nodded again and Agnes said, 'I'll be there in an hour. But not for long, mind. Jenna likes me in before dark.'

Tom flashed her his glorious smile, making her wish that he was more interested in women and not destined to be a rum bawd as the other servants whispered.

'Farewell for the moment then.'

Agnes bobbed another curtsey and turning round, hurried through the buttery to the kitchen, just in time to see her sister take a large meat bone from the spit and slip it beneath her apron.

'Jenna, what are you doing?'

The girl turned a frantic face towards her. 'Be quiet for the love of God. If I am caught, questions could be asked.'

Agnes lowered her voice to a whisper. 'Is it for a spell?'

Jenna nodded but said, 'Don't speak of it here. Agnes, I am running such risks for him. Is he worth it?'

'Of course he is. He belongs to you – and to me too, in a way. If he marries anyone else everything will go wrong.'

'What do you mean?'

Agnes's face lost its customary stupid expression and she said, 'He was born to be our friend. Do you not think so?'

'Yes . . . no. I don't know.' Jenna frowned. 'I used to believe that when I was small.' She turned away, looking out through the kitchen window to where the shadow of the palace had turned the quadrangle into a shaft of twilight.

'I often think that the courtyard reflects the pattern of our lives.'

'What do you mean?' answered Agnes.

'Sometimes the place is warm and full of sunlight and sometimes it is dim, as now.'

'So . . .?'

'So some people have sunny lives and others shadowy – and others still have a combination of both. Why?'

'Because that is the way of things.'

'Is it?' said Jenna questioningly.

'Who's there?' shouted Robert Morley, starting up so suddenly that his sword, lying beside his bed in its scabbard, was in his hand before he knew it.

There was no answer, the room so still and dark, that it took all Robert's courage to leap out of bed and make a search, thrusting his weapon beneath the bed's broadsilk draperies, convinced that he had seen a tall, dark figure stand in the room and call his name. But there was no one hiding and, much relieved, Robert crossed to the windows, drawing back the curtains to let in the early morning light.

It was a glorious April dawning and an early shower had already drenched the stone and flint walls of Glynde Place, built some forty years earlier by his father, William Morley. Relishing the air, Robert opened the window and leaned out, his thudding heart resuming its normal beat.

The marriage of Robert's ancestor Nicholas Morley to Joan Waleys – great-granddaughter of Sir John Waleis who had been alive in the reign of Edward III – had been one of great advancement for the Morley family. They had acquired the Waleis estates at Glynde and Maighfield as a result, and their consequent involvement in the iron industry which had boomed in the Weald during the last sixty years had made them a fortune.

Thinking about his inheritance, Robert leaned out further to look at the house and parkland that would one day be his, and noticed that his sister-in-law, Ann, was already up and about and walking in the knot garden with her two young daughters, Margaret and Chrisogon. It was the births of these two girls that had finally put Robert in line for the Glynde inheritance, for up till then his older half-brother had hoped for a son. But now Harbert had devised his vast estate to Robert in the event of his death.

A sudden compulsion to look over the lands that would one day be his sent Robert to the stables, after snatching a venison pasty to break his fast. There he ordered his speediest horse to be saddled up and, whistling cheerfully, clattered off over the cobbled stableyard.

It was a glorious morning and as Morley turned away from the downs he saw signs of spring everywhere: thrusting green buds were opening and wild flowers already carpeted the woods, while in the heavens the sky was a soft rain-washed blue, and the shafts of sunlight heightened the fine pale gold of the primroses.

Overhead a bird sang, seeming to call out his name and reminding him of his dream. Without knowing quite why, Robert found that he was turning his horse towards Maighfield, towards Baynden and to the adventure that he felt sure was about to begin.

A new moon. But not the clear, dark night Jenna had hoped for; instead an overcast sky with no sign of the new-born goddess, and a wicked wind lashing from the Channel. Yet, despite the threatening storm, Jenna rose from her bed shortly before midnight and, taking the phial containing the potion from its hiding place, made her way from the cottage in the pitch darkness, her only light a small and ineffective lantern.

The night was fathomless, the crescent moon obscured by the menacing clouds and the wind driving the stinging rain hard in the girl's face. Jenna peered into the downpour, her eyes searching for the distant line of hills beyond the Rother but they were lost in the low-lying cloud. And the river, too, seemed wide and deep, reflecting the ink-black of the sky and gurgling at its banks like a drowning child. It was frightening, and Jenna made her way through the thick clumps of bending trees with a fast-beating heart.

'How can I love like this?' she thought. 'To walk in this terrible night and put myself in danger for a man who cares nothing for my life.'

Yet nothing would have made her turn back. She would have journeyed on through fire and flood to achieve her objective.

The ground began to climb and Jenna's pace slowed as she toiled up through the fields and woods to the summit of the Rother valley where, beside a well-worn footpath, grew a circle of trees. That magic rings had long been associated with witchcraft, Jenna knew as part of country folklore – it was said that Chanctonbury Ring was a place where rites were performed – but she did not know if that was true.

As she entered the spinney the wind, howling bleakly in this exposed spot, tore at Jenna's cloak, raising it from her shoulders and streaming it out behind like a fantastic pair of wings. Just for a moment, for one clear-sighted moment, she stopped short and saw herself as if she had stepped outside her own body.

The girl she looked at, her black hair wind-blown and wild, her eyes glittering and strange, her long-fingered hands clutching a small phial of liquid, was still innocent. She might already have mixed a love potion, and stabbed a lamb bone nine times to bring Robert Morley from Glynde to Maighfield, but she had never really summoned up the full might of nature's power. But now, in this rain-lashed and isolated place, she was about to step over the brink, knowing she could never return to what she had been before. And yet what choice had she? She must have Benjamin; it was not part of the scheme of things that they should be separated.

A frenzy engulfed her and, not caring about the consequences, Jenna placed the phial in the centre of the ring. Then, partly because she was drenched through and partly because she believed nudity to be essential to the ritual, she threw her garments to the ground and stood long and lean and naked in the pouring rain. Then, very slowly, she started to dance.

The fact that the Lord of the Manor's half-brother had arrived unexpectedly that morning and now, by ancient right, was occupying the room set aside for the Lord or his steward at Baynden, did not please Richard Maynard, tenant of the great house. Indeed, it was an irritant, breaking into his orderly life and making annoying demands on him in the way of food and shelter.

He had been forced to have a meal prepared – while he on his own would have eaten little, preferring to sit before his hearth and drink himself to sleep. For Richard did not care to go to bed too soon, fearing the long night's watches when he would be vulnerable to the Dark Lady.

He had first seen the ghost on the day he had taken up residence in Baynden, eleven years ago now, in 1598. He had leased the house originally for seven years but had extended his tenancy with Harbert Morley when that period had lapsed. For by that time Richard's unhealthy preoccupation with the place had him completely in its grip. There was something about the house that he found utterly fascinating and yet quite terrible.

The first thing to strike him as odd had been that, though Baynden itself was unfamiliar, the land seemed recognisable;

even that strangely silent bluebell wood. The very quiet of the place, the fact that not a breath of breeze seemed to move the trees, had set his heart pounding with fright. And after that, if Richard had gone there at all, it had been with at least two dogs panting at his heels, throwing sticks to make them bark and be rowdy.

But the ghost was a different matter. On the day he moved in he had seen her at an upstairs window, quite immobile, and thought her to be one of the servants. Then he had passed her on the stairs and made way, again thinking it a serving woman he had yet to meet. She had walked right by him and he had seen a beautiful face stricken with grief, a lock of lustrous, dark hair escaping from a white wimple. The rush of intense cold as she had come close, and the fact that she made no sound as she moved, had set every hair of Richard's head on end. Then he had watched her glide straight through a wall and heard the closing of a door that was no longer there.

He had been so shocked that he had almost fainted. He, Richard Maynard, yeoman farmer, had had to sit on the stairs with his head between his knees in order to clear his reeling senses. But the strange thing was that when he had mentioned, over-casually, that he thought Baynden to be haunted, the servants had stared at him with blank faces.

'How could that be, Goodman Maynard?' one had said. 'The house is new.'

'No, but built on the site of something more ancient surely?'

'Yes, reckon. There's been a house at Baynden since way back.'

After that Richard met the sad-faced ghost everywhere, even watching her come to his bedroom to gaze unhappily around. He realised then that nobody else *did* see her; that she appeared exclusively to him.

Sometimes, in the loneliest part of the night, he would hear her sobbing, the sound going on so long and with a pitifully desperate note. On those occasions he would light as many candles as he could find and go downstairs to doze by the fire, fearing to be alone in the stillness. And now, as he sipped his home-brewed beer, aware of the sounds of the sleeping household, Richard hoped that the Dark Lady, as he had named her long ago, would rest quiet tonight and not disturb Robert Morley.

As he finally slept in the chair, Richard dreamed of her; dreamed that he followed the Dark Lady out of Baynden and through the fields towards the wood. But there he grew frightened and looked round for his dogs, only to find they were not there but that, instead, Jenna Casselowe's cat stropped itself about his ankles, arching its back and rubbing against his legs. Even in his dream Richard thought how extraordinary a creature it was – pure white, with eyes that he would not have believed possible in an animal; clear crystal blue with not a trace of green.

Richard woke up abruptly, every nerve taut, but there was silence in Baynden, not even a distant snore breaking the quiet. Stiffly, he got to his feet knowing instinctively, though it was dark as the grave outside, that within an hour it would be dawn and that life on his farm must begin. Without even stopping to take a bite of food, Richard pulled a roughspun cloak around him and stepped out into the raw and bitter morning.

The rain had ceased but the wind was wilder than ever, booming with a great voice down the valley and hurling against the yeoman like a physical force. He thought of going back for a moment but was too strict an employer for that, liking nothing better than to be visible to his labourers as they came through the darkness to work.

With his head down, Richard started to make his way across the fields known as the Five Acres – and then stopped in amazement. Coming towards him out of the blackness, concealed in an all enveloping cloak, was a woman. Just for a second he wondered who it was and then that familiar height gave it away. The Casselowe creature was wandering about on her own, before the sun was even up.

Silently Richard stepped behind a tree, though there was little need in such poor light, and Jenna walked right past him, totally unaware of his presence. As she did so her cloak blew back on the wind – and Richard's eyes started from his head. He saw high, full breasts and long, lean legs. The slut was naked beneath her mantle.

Just as he was preparing to ride through the early evening to William Weston's cottage a knock came on Benjamin Mist's door. Answering it with none too good a grace, he felt his face grow even longer on seeing Jenna Casselowe standing in the

204

twilight. He had not cast eyes on her since the night she had walked off in a fury, and now the memory of that hung in the air between them as she said, shuffling her feet, 'I am sorry to disturb you, Benjamin, but my father's milking stool broke this morning and it is difficult for him to manage without it. Would it be too much trouble for you to look at it?'

Her tone was conciliatory, apologetic almost, and relenting a little Benjamin said, 'You had better step inside. I can tell you now whether it can be repaired.'

It was a curious split he thought; the leg fractured off so neatly that it looked almost as if it had been done deliberately.

'How did this happen?'

'Very simply. I sat on it and it gave beneath me.'

'It's a very clean break. I can do it tomorrow. I'm afraid I can't start now. I am going out.' He did not like to mention Debora in Jenna's presence.

The girl went rather white and Benjamin noticed for the first time how strained she seemed, but she said with a smile, 'Then I must leave at once. I would not like to make you late.' She turned as if to go and then her hand reached inside her basket and she said, almost carelessly, 'Oh, I nearly forgot. Daniel sent you some beer remembering how much you enjoyed it the other night. Here it is.'

She produced a stone bottle and put it down on the table.

'How kind. I shall enjoy that later.'

'You'll drink it tonight?'

'Yes, when I get back from Debora's. But first let me take you home.'

Despite the fact he had mentioned her rival, a smile – so vivid and so beautiful that it quite startled Benjamin – flashed across Jenna's face. But thinking no more of it Benjamin turned away, pulling on his cloak and securing the doors as he led her outside.

TWENTY-TWO

Maighfield at dusk and lights beginning to appear at the windows of the dwellings which stood on either side of the track that ran through the village's heart. The glow of candles illuminating Aylwins, Master Aynscombe the iron-master's house; the cottages round the churchyard lit by economical tapers; the palace blazing with every kind of light, for Sir Thomas did not care for stint in anything; the dark timbers of the house built for Sir Thomas Gresham and now occupied by the Houghton family, reflecting the light of candles which suddenly appeared in one of the rooms in the upper storey.

As Debora Weston came out of the house next to the walnut tree, she turned with some speed down the track, the track that led from the village to the heights above Sharnden, passing through the cluster of cottages which formed the hamlet of Cokyngs Mill. For home to Debora meant protection and security; a place where the dreadful thoughts that sometimes beset her could be shut away in the privacy of her tiny bedroom; a sanctuary where no one could see how she wept and cried. For Debora could not remember a time since childhood when she had been truly happy.

Every since the change had come about in her body and womanhood had come upon her, a terrifying fear had taken hold, a fear which, she knew, if it grew any worse, could threaten her sanity. For Debora sometimes felt that she had another side to her character, an evil side that lurked just below the surface yet might one day gain the upper hand.

Timorous, flowerlike Debora would, by choice, have picked her way through life without ever having to see, or hear, or think anything that was ugly, dirty, or revolting. Delicate Debora would have disregarded nature's functions, never have been visited by the flux, never wished to see a man's nude body or, worse, felt that part of him that was so horrible, enter her inviolate flesh. But then, beneath the surface, lurked the other

206

one. The one who would grin at lewd passages read from the family bible; the one who would stare at her naked self with a knowing smile; the one who would take over in the dream state and let terrible things roam through the mind of the innocent sleeper.

Before Benjamin Mist had begun to court her, Debora had been called upon by both John Cosham and Michael Baker, handsome young men born in the same year as she, and had once snatched the hand of Michael and run her lips over it, not so much kissing as drawing out his flesh so that he had been appalled and had visited the cottage no more.

It had been beyond bearing and Debora felt now, as she fastened her woollen cloak to her neck and hurried down the path past Pound Farm, that her only hope was marriage to a respectable man like Benjamin Mist. Perhaps, if she endured his lovemaking, the other Debora would be satisfied and go away for good.

Even as Benjamin came into her mind the girl heard hooves on the track and, turning, was amazed to see the carpenter, astride his nag with Jenna Casselowe sitting behind, heading in the direction of Baynden and not even noticing that they had passed Benjamin's betrothed, standing alone and forlorn in the dusk.

'Benjamin,' she called, but he did not hear and Debora was left with the dismal prospect of staring at the retreating back of Jenna Casselowe, the girl she disliked more than any other, riding with the man Debora was soon to marry.

She knew it was weak of her but she started to cry, not loudly or enough to make Mother Maud, the village gossip, peer out of her cottage window, but copiously and miserably.

She felt so alone and frightened that, when a voice behind her said, 'May I escort you home, Mistress?' she turned with a smile, realising that she had not heard anyone approach because of the noise of Benjamin's mount. However, her welcome faded to an icy stare as she saw, leaning down from his saddle so that he might look better into her face, the heir to the Glynde estates, Robert Morley, a man she had never met but whose reputation preceded him.

Instantly Debora was in a quandary. It was not politic to be rude to a member of the landed gentry but on the other hand she shrank from him. He was so obviously a womaniser, all swagger, fingers and winks, not at all the kind of man with whom she felt at ease.

'I . . . er . . .'

'Come now, Mistress, don't hesitate. I can have you home in an instant.'

Debora went scarlet, realising he must be aware of what a shrinking creature she really was.

With a faint touch of defiance she said, 'Thank you, Master Morley. I'd be obliged if you could take me to Cokygns Mill.'

Without answering, Robert dismounted, lifted her to the front of the saddle then swung himself up behind.

She thought she was going to suffocate. In a fashion that Debora could only think of as lunatic, every nerve in her body became taut, and her heart doubled its pace. Without wanting to, her mind began to dwell on the muscle and sinew that she could feel through Robert's clothing.

As the horse moved into a steady trot, Debora thought she was going to be sick; frenzied and ill with all the terrible thoughts that were going through her mind. And then quite suddenly, and quite frighteningly, a feeling stirred within her, a feeling base and vile which would not go away. Her head spun and she believed she would faint.

'Is anything wrong?' said Robert's voice, almost at her ear.

'No, nothing,' she answered breathlessly.

There was a pause and then he said, 'I hope I can remember the way. I am not really familiar with this area.'

Debora peered into the darkness. 'We seem to have left the track. I think you are heading towards Baynden.'

Robert did not answer and an unreasonable fear beat down every other emotion in Debora's breast. A shiver that ran from her shoulders to her heels shook her, and Robert said, 'You're cold. I have wine in my saddle bag. Drink some.'

Without thinking, Debora took the leather bottle and raised it to her lips. As the strong warming liquid reached her stomach she realised that she had not eaten for hours, that every mouthful she took would only serve to make her heady. Yet she drank again, deeply, without knowing why.

'I must be home soon,' she said slowly.

'I'm afraid you were right,' answered Robert with a note of apology. 'I must have taken the wrong track. We are almost at Baynden.'

She wanted to say: 'Then turn back,' but instead she put the bottle to her mouth and again drank her fill, not answering.

'I must call in for a moment to collect a warmer cloak. It is getting very cold,' Robert said, without looking at her.

Still Debora remained silent, fighting with every ounce of her strength all the hideous thoughts that were flooding into her brain.

'Well?' They had come almost to a halt and Debora realised that she must answer in some way or another.

'We'll go to Baynden,' she said slowly, and felt herself grow weak as Robert's arms tightened around her, and he spurred his horse on towards the house.

'No, Benjamin, I'm sorry, I don't know where she is.' Goodwife Weston stood in the doorway of her little cottage and looked at the carpenter from narrowed, curranty eyes. 'I thought she might be with you.'

Benjamin shook his head. 'I said I would come here as soon as I had finished working. I'm late only because someone called unexpectedly. Has Debora been home at all?'

A fearful look came into the little eyes as Debora's mother answered, 'No, she hasn't. I do hope no ill has befallen her. Perhaps her brothers should go searching as soon as they come home.'

'I'm sure she's safe,' answered Benjamin. 'She has probably stayed talking longer than she intended.'

He did not know why but he had a sudden compulsion to get away from the cottage, overpowering with its smoking fire and smell of constant cooking, to say nothing of escaping Goody Weston's close dark scrutiny. All he could think of was returning to the quietness of his own home where he could sit alone, his old wheezing cat at his feet, gazing into the fire and drinking the beer that Daniel Casselowe had sent for him.

'Benjamin?'

'I'm sorry, I . . .'

'I said shall I tell Debora that you will be here tomorrow?'

'Yes, please do.'

He bowed his way out – a politeness not called for – and then, having mounted the nag, paused for a moment. It was terrible to admit it but he did not want to come across Debora tonight. Vaguely, Benjamin wondered what was the matter with him;

209

why his desire to think things out should be strong enough for him to take a route through the woods that ensured he would meet nobody, even the girl he intended to marry. Almost hastily, almost furtively, he turned his horse's head in a direction that would take him across country and went at a good speed, not stopping for anything until he had crossed his threshold and closed the door behind him.

Once inside, he went through his usual routine, throwing sticks on the wood ash that held the embers of last night's fire and, when the tongues of flame began to leap, blowing them with a pair of bellows till they blazed.

Benjamin suddenly found himself beyond eating, his one thought to sit down in his favourite chair and stare at the flames. With the grumpy old cat sitting on his lap, he put his head back and in a moment was asleep.

He dreamed that he was wandering in a wood white with snow; the valley in the distance a patchwork of sombre trees and milky fields. Only a woodcutter's hut stood out like a blot of ink in the virgin purity. Coming from a hole in the roof he saw that a thread of smoke rose up like a pointing finger, and Benjamin, his feet leaving the frost unmarked, felt himself drawn closer to see who dwelt within the heart of the deserted forest.

He pushed the door slightly and, to his horror, realised that he had come across two lovers, caught in a secret act. He would have averted his eyes but something about the long, lean back of the man reminded him of someone he knew well. As he stared the man jumped up and came towards the door as if he had heard something.

Just for a moment, before he turned to run, Benjamin saw his face; saw the shock of shoulder-length hair, the hawklike features, the lively eyes. Then Benjamin was hurrying over the snow to escape and the dream ended.

Benjamin woke suddenly and stood up, the old cat sliding to the floor and glaring at him, and thought of his gift of beer. Pouring himself a pint, Benjamin sat down and raised it to his lips, thinking it a delicious taste, quite the best brew he had had in a long time. He finished it almost in one and poured out the remainder, drinking it all before he went upstairs. There he fell into a deep and entirely dreamless sleep.

'I shall wait outside,' said Debora. 'Master Morley, it would be better if you went in for your cloak and left me here. I would be embarrassed to meet Goodman Maynard in these circumstances.'

She was afraid again, her true nature asserting itself over the wicked feelings that had possessed her a moment ago.

'Nonsense,' answered Robert briskly. 'Come in and warm yourself before your journey. The servants are already abed and there's no one about. You need only stay a moment.'

Without another word, he lifted her down from the saddle, keeping his body tantalisingly apart from hers.

As they went inside, the fire in Baynden's great hearth sent out a welcoming heat and, ignoring Robert, Debora hurried to it, holding out her hands. She realised that she was alone with a man whose reputation was worse than any she had ever known. To her horror, she heard herself say, 'How warm it is here. What a pity we must venture out again, Master Morley,' and almost seemed to see herself give a slow smile and walk towards him.

Inside, a voice screamed, 'Help me. I cannot allow this.' But the evil part of her held sway and was pressing itself against the Master's brother seductively. Small wonder that Robert Morley swept her into his arms and without a word headed purposefully for his chamber.

TWENTY-THREE

The new play that had begun to form itself in the mind of Tom May woke him shortly after midnight. At once, without having to wait for nebulous outlines to form, he knew the character of the heroine; and this was followed shortly before first light by an insight into the hero's motive for his wicked acts. After this there was no alternative but to rise from his bed and, by the light of as many candles as he could muster, first write down the development of the comedy and then the compelling opening lines. So it was, with the reedy signs of dawn forcing themselves through his curtains, that Tom finally laid down his pen, throwing back the drapery to look on the morning that lay beyond the palace.

Rain hung over the hills, not a heavy dulling rain that put the spirits low but instead a lively spray, leaping down over the earth and throwing up vast rainbows in its wake: it was a rain that brought on bracken, that washed the face of the earth with gentle freshness, turning the slopes green and pattering amongst the daffodils. It was a rain that wetted the coats of lambs and made the sweet harsh smell of wool pervade the woods and valleys of Sussex.

For a poet, standing at the window and looking out at the birth of such a morning, there was no decision to be made. With a pleasant compulsion, Tom put on his roughest clothes and headed for the stables before anyone but the bakehouse servants, filling the air already with the seductive smell of hot bread, was stirring. And then what more sweet than to swing his leg up over a bay horse and hear the sharp clatter of hooves as he headed out over the cobbles to investigate the day?

As Tom left Maighfield behind him and headed for the valley of Byvelham – that magic place which still belonged to the Rape of Hastings and which was quite separate from Sir Thomas May's manorial rights – the young man's artistic soul bounded within, assuring him yet again that he was rather a special person; capable of feeling the raw contrasts of pain and pleasure as intensely as a poet should.

He was in a green and gold morning; the fields stretching before him like an emerald shawl, the sky the light, clear colour of newly-minted coins and all the earth in that capricious mood which, at a fingersnap, could roll down thunder and wind and lightning to soak the unwary.

Yet Tom, expansive as only a writer who has put a new idea safely beneath his belt can be, only saw the fine things: the undulating line from hill to hill, the glinting vastness of the never-ceasing sky, the coldness of the sparkling air to the naked cheek, the warmth of it to the heart.

He felt himself absorbed by the personality of Sussex; by its lack of sentimentality, its cruelty disguised beneath the sweetly rolling hills, the whole huge canopy from brilliant sea to flat dark fields, spread before him.

Yet, as his horse went forward, nosing and nuzzling amongst the grasses, he became aware of a disturbance in the atmosphere; was aware of a sadness in that morning of hope and inspiration even before he had actually heard a thing. So Tom was not at all surprised as his horse climbed up and stood looking down the slopes that led to Baynden, to see a girl – a pale and ravaged girl at that – come towards him as if her life had just been cast into ruins.

Tom did not recognise her, bothering little with those who did not work at the palace. Yet he had to agree that for a peasant – which her dress revealed her to be at once – she was exceptionally charming, quite flowerlike and sweet, in fact.

'Good morning,' he said.

She paled and drew back, but managed a faint 'Good-day, Sir,' before bursting into a flood of weeping.

Tom looked at her awkwardly, wishing she would go away. But the girl held her ground and continued to gaze at him through a storm of tears.

Feeling an idiot, Tom eventually said, 'Is anything wrong?' He supposed it beholden on him as the Lord of the Manor's son to enquire, while fearing desperately that she might actually tell him. To his horror she nodded her head even while the tears continued to course.

'In that case do you want to see my mother?' he asked hopefully, but the swift, sad look in her eye dashed any idea he might have had of getting rid of her.

'Then what can I do to help?' he went on lamely, wishing that he was more than fourteen years old and had even the vaguest semblance of liking women's company.

'A great deal,' she gasped, through terrible sobs. 'Oh Master Tom, if my father has ever served yours, then please help me now.'

Much to his dismay she grabbed hold of him, her fingers dangerously close to rending his sleeve.

'Please,' he said, brushing her off. 'If you could calm yourself, and tell me quietly what is amiss.'

She gazed at him from pretty damp eyes, looking like a daffodil after a storm.

'That I never can,' she answered. 'I would not dare to. Instead, Master, I am going to ask you to grant me the greatest favour of your life.'

Tom gulped in horror, sure that she was going to beg for money, a commodity which – despite his father's legendary extravagance – rarely came his way.

'I'm afraid I ...' he started but she cut across with, 'Sir, it is terrible to ask a gentleman in your position to lie, but I beg you please to tell my father I spent last night at the palace.'

Relieved, Tom said, 'Well, really I would not like to ...'

But the girl began to weep again. 'If you do not help me, Sir, my life will be ruined. I cannot tell you where I was but be assured I must never confess the truth. Sir, I implore you.'

Longing to say no and have done with the girl's sordid little intrigue, as he now suspected it was, Tom reluctantly answered, 'Well, I ...'

She gave him such a piteous glance that he stopped again, filled with the thought that he ought to be kind, that really he ought to try and help his fellows if he was to develop into a true personality, a personality that one day might rival that of William Shakespeare.

'What do you want me to say?'

'That I called round to the kitchens having injured myself, and that it was thought I should stay at the palace rather than walk.'

'Do you think it will be believed?'

'If *you* tell my mother so, yes.'

Very reluctantly, Tom said, 'I'll help you on to my horse. If you go back riding it will appear that you are still injured.'

Despite the risk, Tom was beginning to be amused by the

situation and he said in a low voice, glancing to right and left though there was not another soul visible for miles, 'I take it there was a man involved?'

To his horror the girl's skin became livid. 'I cannot bear to think about it. Please do not ask.'

With a look of consternation he said, 'Surely you were not raped?'

'No, it was all my fault,' she answered slowly. 'I cannot soil my lips by speaking of it.'

The girl would say no more and in silence Tom led his horse back towards Cokyngs Mill and Debora's parents.

The knock on the door was so loud that as Robert Morley woke he had automatically shouted, 'Enter,' before he remembered that a naked woman was lying in the bed for all the world to see. Yet a rapid glance at the place beside his showed it to be empty, with no sign of the wicked little wanton who had filled his night with never-ending passion and left him exhausted.

'What is it?' he asked, as Richard Maynard, his strangely pale skin glowing white, stepped boldly into the room.

'There's a messenger from Glynde, Sir. He thought he might find you here. Master Harbert has been taken ill and they are requesting that you return immediately.'

Robert leapt out of bed, contriving to pull the covers off as he did so and thus conceal its disarray.

'Is it serious? What has happened?'

'The messenger is downstairs, Master. He simply said to me that Master Harbert was ill.'

Throwing on his clothes, Robert said, 'Thank you, Goodman Maynard. I shall be ready in a moment,' relieved when the fellow withdrew his strangely staring gaze and went out.

What could be amiss, Robert wondered? Though considerably older than he, his half-brother was still only in the later part of his forties and up to now had suffered little more than a day's illness. But the servant knew nothing more than that Master Harbert had collapsed with pains in his chest the night before, and the physician had been sent for from Lewes. Robert had to be content with this as he urged forward to Glynde.

Yet despite the seriousness of the occasion and despite the fact that he loved and respected Harbert – even though they did not share the same mother – Robert found his mind going back again and again to Debora Weston. What an inspired lover. He had never come across a woman like her. Yet it was strange that she had not woken him with a word of farewell. Strange, too, that she had been intact, untouched by another. He would not have believed that possible if he had not proved it for himself. For she seemed to be totally knowledgeable of all the things that delighted, of all the thousand and one wicked little acts that could set a man alight and leave him gasping. It was as if she were born wanton, needing no tuition in the art of love.

Robert was still thinking about the strangeness of it all as he crossed the courtyard of Glynde Place and was brought abruptly back to earth by the sight of Dr Bulmer of Lewes, followed by a boy carrying a box of equipment, mounting his horse in preparation to go.

Swinging from the saddle, Master Morley hurried over on foot and said, 'Sir, what news of my brother?'

Knowing that it was almost obligatory for physicians to pull long faces, he was not altogether surprised when Dr Bulmer looked grave and replied, 'Ah Sir, there's the tease.'

'You do not know?' Robert answered anxiously.

'I do, Sir, and then again I don't.'

'Meaning ...?'

'Meaning, Sir, that though I have seen many such cases in men of Master Morley's age, I am still not sure what exactly the contributory factor might be.'

'Perhaps if you could spare me a few moments we might step into the house and you could explain it to me in layman's terms.'

With a sigh Dr Bulmer swung a stiff leg over his horse's back and allowed Robert to usher him forward. And once again he spoke rapidly, as if even this intrusion into his time was a nuisance.

'What I am trying to say, Master Robert, is that men of your brother's years are prone to mysterious pains in their chest which I personally believe to emanate from the heart. An idea with which many of my colleagues might not agree.'

'And the prognosis?'

'Reasonable – if they survive this initial attack. And with care and comfort they usually do, Sir. Yes, my patients usually do.'

He paused to let the words sink in and Robert looked at him, slightly amused. The doctor was a little bantam of a fellow, pink

216

of face and round of stomach and defying the world to disagree with his ideas. In common with many men short of stature, he had a slightly defensive air which manifested in a show of truculence.

Robert smiled. 'Then he is not in danger?'

The bantam ceased to strut. 'If he lives through another day and night, Master Robert, then he is safe. But after that he must always be careful. I have seen these things recur after a gap of several years. What I am saying is that your brother will never dare to be so active again.'

Robert's amusement faded. 'In short I should take over some of his duties?'

'Indeed you must, Sir, if there is to be a happy outcome. I think it only fair to warn you that in future you will have to spend more time at Glynde and less involved in your other pursuits –' The doctor allowed himself a wintery smile. '– if Master Harbert is to retain his good health.'

'Then so be it,' answered Robert. 'The welfare of my brother and the future of Glynde must always come first.'

The moated manor house of Sharnden had always been something which had, for no reason he could pinpoint, both delighted and intrigued Benjamin Mist. His very first glimpse of it as a child – seeing the house where it lay in its naturally protected basin – had him running in excitement down the slope, longing to get near the cool, green water of the moat and the two swans who drifted, with their family of cygnets, on its glasslike surface.

But when Benjamin had arrived at the house he had received a shock. It had not been what the boy had expected at all. He had thought there would be a stately building there, a grandiose dwelling comprising a great hall and other graceful chambers, but instead the child had seen a yeoman farmhouse, large admittedly, but nonetheless austere.

When he had asked his father about it, Ralph Mist had told him that there had once been an older house on the site – or so it was said – but that the present Sharnden had been built in the fifteenth century by the Vicars Choral, into whose hands the manor had passed after the deaths of Robert de Sharndene and, later, his son Hamon.

Now it was leased to Stephen Penkhurst and it was the fact

217

that Master Penkhurst's favourite bed had broken a leg that necessitated Benjamin's presence there on this rainbow-filled afternoon, bright with little showers splashing into the moat and diamond drops falling from the glistening feathers of the graceful swans.

Standing in a top chamber at the eastern end of the house, and looking out at the moat's sweep round the island, Benjamin wondered again why he liked the place so much, why it had such a reassuring atmosphere. Perhaps because that view had changed very little in the last few centuries, giving the impression that he was looking at a vista seen by the original builder all that time ago.

Benjamin gave a start as, without warning, a long dark figure glided into his sight, stopping at the moat's far edge and gazing up to where he stood. Despite the fact that it was daylight, he felt terrified. For though he could plainly see that it was Jenna Casselowe, there seemed something strange about her. She stood utterly motionless, as if she were sleepwalking, and even from this distance he could see that her eyes stared ahead unblinkingly.

He felt unnerved and he called out, 'Jenna! What are you doing?'

She made absolutely no response and it was then that the oddest thing of all took place. As he watched her, it seemed to him that she changed. Instead of seeing a gawky beanpole, he suddenly realised that she was beautiful. He saw her height as graceful, a thing to be admired; he noticed that her hair flowed like a torrent of silk, and the colour of her skin was the ripe gold of summer. At that moment Benjamin realised, for the first time, Jenna was a very beautiful young woman.

A sound behind him made the carpenter turn round, but it was only the creak of a floorboard settling, and he turned immediately back to the window. But there was no longer any sign of Jenna. Benjamin felt his spine begin to tingle as he realised that he could not really have seen her at all – no one could have vanished so rapidly in the brief moment he had averted his gaze.

Mystified, Benjamin began to pack up his tools, his repair of Master Penkhurst's bed complete, but his mind too full of the extraordinary vision to concentrate on anything else. Then suddenly he was filled with such a longing to see Jenna and find out for himself if she had been at Sharnden that afternoon, that he decided he must go to her immediately. Another thought struck him. If it had been a trick of his imagination, did it, by any chance, mean that Jenna was in some sort of trouble, that she had been sending him a message through her thoughts?

Anxious now, the carpenter collected his dues from the master of the house and crossed the causeway to the slopes beyond the moat. Then he followed the course of the river to the lands that belonged to Baynden, and on a caprice climbed up the valley through the bluebell wood. As always the silence of the place disturbed him and he felt, with the trees bending together above to form a ceiling, that he had entered not so much a church as a vault.

Passing beyond the house, Benjamin went down towards Daniel's cottage, pleased to see that the door was open. Jenna's cat Rutterkin was sitting on the step, cleaning her face and whiskers, and knowing that this meant her mistress was at home, Benjamin went straight through the open door without knocking.

The girl he had come to see stood in the entrance arrayed in a golden gown, complete with a curving farthingale on her hips and a high, white falling collar at her neck, just as if she had been expecting him. Though Benjamin knew at once that it must be a hand-down from Lady May, the gown could have been made for Jenna, for the cut and sweep of the skirt was exactly right for her height, and the boned bodice enhanced the curve of her breasts.

Benjamin stood transfixed, gazing at Jenna as if he had never seen her before; noticing how her eyes tilted upwards at the far corners; how her hair smelled of wild, rare perfume; how her mouth was full, with a slightly drooping underlip that spoke of passion and tenderness and all the great gifts that a woman could bestow on a man.

He could hardly trust himself to speak but eventually managed to whisper, 'You are beautiful. I never knew.'

He realised he sounded ridiculous, a total fool, but she seemed to understand and smiled a sweet, strange smile before she said, 'I had hoped you might one day.'

He wanted to ask her whether she had been at Sharnden or whether it had been an illusion, but suddenly it seemed unimportant. All Benjamin wanted to do was touch the exquisite

creature that stood before him, lay his fingers, gentle as butter-
flies, on the curve of her cheekbone, the sweep of her lashes, the
delicate pattern of her ear.

'I must have been blind,' he said. 'Jenna, you are perfect.'

Again she smiled that sweet, odd smile and answered, 'My
father and Agnes will be in soon. Would you like to stay and
sup?'

He knew quite definitely that he would not; that it would not
be possible for him to share with anyone the fairy-being into
which Jenna had suddenly turned; that this evening must be for
the two of them alone even if, in time to come, they must mix
again with ordinary mortals.

At the back of Benjamin's mind came the thought that this
must be enchantment, that this wonderful sensation of floating
into glory must be an illusion – but he dismissed it. He was too
happy to care as he took Jenna's long fingers, tapering and fine
as the stamens of a flower, between his own and then raised
them to his lips.

'No, I do not wish to sup,' he said, wondering why his voice
sounded so strange. 'I want to talk to *you*, Jenna. I want to be
alone with you. I feel as if we have years that we must suddenly
catch up.'

She laughed for the first time. 'But this house will shortly be
filled with my family.'

'Then we must go to my cottage. We must be alone together
this evening. Will you come with me, Jenna?'

As if she had been high born, Jenna curtsied, the silk of her
gown rippling about her knees as she did so.

'Then let us go now, before they come. Will you leave them a
message?'

He watched her write, wondering at her many skills, and then
read the words she had put. They were, 'Agnes – Benjamin has
called for me.'

'But Agnes cannot read.'

'My father will tell her what is there.'

He did not question further and they walked out together into
the April evening, an evening soft with the death of rainbows
and the mad, mad call of birds. It seemed then that they must
not speak as he lifted her on to the nag who, this twilight, looked
younger and more like the fast chestnut mare she once had been.
They rode together along the way through the woods, where the

horse's feet fell softly on turf that sprung beneath their touch.

Nor was speech possible until they had come to Benjamin's cottage, painted pink with the setting sun. They walked together through its welcoming door, Jenna bending her head low in order to enter. Then, secure in the fact they would be alone, they stood looking in silence, one at the other.

'How could I have been so foolish?' Benjamin said finally but Jenna did not answer.

They were standing without touching, merely exchanging glances. It was then that, just for a fleeting moment, Benjamin felt all this had happened before. That – whether it had been a dream or reality – he had stood gazing at Jenna like this, and felt his body and mind fill with emotion.

Eventually he said, 'You know that we must never separate – now that I have at last found you.'

Still with her beautiful smile, Jenna replied, 'Benjamin, do not be afraid of what we are about to do. The consummation of our love is part of what must be enacted.'

He never remembered afterwards the way in which they found themselves standing in his little room, recalling only the glory of her body as it slowly revealed itself to him; seeing the high, full breasts, the curve of her waist, the dark hair from which he could hardly take his eyes. It was then that they, at last, kissed one another. From that kiss they slid downwards, quite slowly, until they lay upon his bed.

They did not speak at all after that and as he took her for his own, she gave with such joy, such happiness to have a part of him within her, leading her to womanhood, that he felt as if they had been lovers for ever.

The climax of their passion was so perfect that she, still unsure of herself, thought she had leapt over the moon, so intense was her pleasure. And Benjamin at last knew what it was to burst forth in glory, to fill the woman he loved with something of himself and give his heart for evermore.

'Jenna,' he said, 'Jenna, I love you so much.'

In her mind's eye the girl saw pages of dark writing and read the words, 'Dittany, verbena and pennyroyal will bring any man you wish to your bed – but jessamine will make him *stay forever*.'

221

TWENTY-FOUR

It was on her way home from her workplace that Agnes decided to call on Mother Maud, knowing that if news of Jenna's absence from the kitchens that day – an absence that Agnes had covered with an excuse of illness – had reached the gossip's ears, it would by now be common knowledge. And if this were the case, Daniel's rage would be too terrible to contemplate, furious as he already was that Jenna had stayed out all night.

Dreading the interview, the girl nonetheless left the palace and set off in the direction of Maud's cottage. Even as she approached, Agnes could see that the old woman stood on her doorstep, deep in conversation with a neighbour, their heads wagging like mops at a fair.

As Agnes drew nearer they both looked up and Maud called out at once, 'Oh Agnes, my dear. How nice to see you. Would you like some ale to refresh you for the rest of your walk?'

Disguising the fact that her heart had just lurched with anxiety, Agnes smiled and said, 'How kind, Goody Maud. But I am surely disturbing you?'

'No, I must go,' replied the other woman rapidly. 'The men will be in soon. I'll see you tomorrow Maud. Farewell.'

She hurried away, giving a meaningful glance in Agnes's direction, and the next moment the girl found herself in Maud's cottage, a jug of ale in one hand and a cake in the other.

'Now, my dear, sit down,' said the gossip, 'and tell me how you are. And your sister too. In fact, how are all who dwell at the palace?'

'Well,' said Agnes, through a mouthful of cake, 'Sir Thomas is back and entertaining friends and Lady May is concerned about the food, as always. And the master cook wants to argue with her and dares not – and we are all working harder than ever.'

She laughed over-merrily, wishing that Maud would take her beady little eyes from her face.

'And what of young Tom?'

'Oh, he is very well too. I believe he is writing something new.'

'I heard a very strange thing about Master Tom today,' said Maud, narrowing her gaze.

Surprised, Agnes said, 'What?' thinking that the conversation should have turned to Jenna by now, and wondering if word of her sister's absence had escaped Maud's ears.

'That yesterday morning he escorted home young Debora Weston after she had had an accident at the palace.'

'An accident at the palace?' repeated Agnes, astonished.

'You were not there when it happened, then?'

Sensing a trap, Agnes answered hastily, 'Sometimes I leave early. When my cleaning is done, Lady May says there is little point in my staying unless an extra pair of hands is needed in the kitchens.'

Maud nodded wisely. 'Of course, my dear. Well, as you do not know the story I will tell you. It seems that the night before last Debora injured her ankle while visiting the palace and was advised to stay there and be taken home in the morning.'

Thinking it very odd that nobody had mentioned it, Agnes said, 'And Master Tom took her back?'

'Yes, but had such a bad attack of stammering that he could hardly utter a word of explanation. Goody Weston was most perturbed, I hear.'

'And is Debora better now?'

'On the contrary. She has taken to her bed and refuses to speak to anyone and, even odder, though one of the Weston boys went up to fetch Benjamin, he could get no answer. Though he swore that two people were in the cottage, for he heard the low murmur of voices.'

Agnes stared aghast, unable to think of a thing to say, suddenly full of an inexplicable fear.

Without waiting for her to answer, Maud continued, 'I believe Benjamin has another sweetheart, Agnes. I believe he is playing Debora false and that is why she has taken to her bed.'

Gulping a mouthful of ale, Agnes said, 'Oh surely not. How could that be?'

'Very easily. He is a good catch and quite handsome. I believe some heartless wretch has set her cap at him and taken him away from poor Debora.'

Very boldly, Agnes said, 'Who do you suspect, Maud?'

The old woman hesitated, her beady eyes turning to slits. 'I thought you might know, Agnes. You are in touch with every-one, working at the palace.'

Agnes stood up, wondering if Jenna's absence was being saved for Maud's final attack.

'I have heard nothing, Maud. I am sure you are mistaken.'

'We shall see.' She paused. 'I hear that Jenna has an ague. How very unfortunate. Debora in her sick bed and your sister also. Let us hope they are not suffering from the same complaint.'

The double meaning hung in the air between them.

'I shouldn't think so for a moment,' answered Agnes, briskly. 'There is a considerable difference between an injured ankle and a chill, you know. Good evening Maud. Thank you for the ale.'

'Good evening, Agnes. My kind wishes to Jenna and Daniel.'

'Thank you.'

She hurried through the door and down the track towards Baynden but, as soon as she was out of the cottage's line of vision, Agnes turned back and cut through the woods towards the village.

It was only Agnes calling to warn her that made Jenna realise she had been away - not only from her home but also from her workplace - for an inexcusable day and night. Yet even the thought of Daniel's belt could no longer frighten her. She had achieved her heart's desire and won the love of the man she had always longed for, and, in the uniting of their bodies, had achieved a completeness she had not imagined could exist.

As she looked at herself in Benjamin's mirror, Jenna Casse-lowe felt that she now had an expression like summer; of mellowness, warmth and burgeoning. She saw that she had become serene and beautiful in the great fulfilment of her love. With enormous gratitude she bent her head as she thought of her aunt and the potion, and all that had been achieved through Alice's magic.

'Thank you,' she whispered. 'Thank you, thank you, thank you.'

'Do you always speak to your reflection?' called out Benjamin from behind her.

She turned to look at him with a smile. He had just woken from sleep and seemed boyish and a little vulnerable. Another rush of love swept over Jenna. She crossed to him and, sitting down, bent over to kiss him. Her hand brushed against his and their fingers locked together.

'That is how I want the future to be,' said Benjamin, 'like our hands. Entwined always. Jenna, there *is* no future without you. I must be your husband.'

'But what of Debora?' she asked softly.

'I will tell her we cannot marry – and thereby earn the contempt of the Westons. But I care nothing. If life is made too unpleasant we can always leave Maighfield and set up home somewhere else. Nothing else matters as long as I have you.'

'*Pennyroyal to bring a man, jessamine to keep him.*' The words danced before Jenna's eyes again, and she knew what she must do. She could not risk losing the glory of this happiness now. Every week Benjamin must be given a special draught and so be kept within her thrall for ever.

Just for a moment – a moment that she rapidly thrust away – Jenna felt a thrill of resentment, resentment that she could not win Benjamin without resorting to such means, that it was Debora's beauty that had attracted him when he had still been master of his destiny. But she conquered the feeling. Love had come for her and Benjamin, and that was all that was important.

'Then, if you think we can survive William Weston's anger, I will marry you, Benjamin. I can think of nothing I want more.'

He drew her into the bed beside him.

'You fascinate me,' he said. 'You are so mysterious. Sometimes I think some of your great aunt's power has been passed down to you.'

Jenna flushed angrily. 'My great aunt had no power. She was the subject of malicious gossip, that is all. She was just a harmless woman who knew something of herbalism.'

Benjamin regarded her closely. 'You are vehement! Have you something to hide, Jenna?'

He spoke lightheartedly but Jenna's expression grew dark and for a moment he felt nervous. Then the feeling passed and Benjamin was himself again, his body aware of the long, lean shape next to his, the brush of her breast against his arm, the feel of her legs beside him. Very slowly he bent his head and kissed her.

'I will never speak of it again,' he said, 'yet know that as long as your magic lasts I will be yours. Only death can separate us now – Jenna, my sweet enchantress.'

TWENTY-FIVE

The dream was absolutely terrifying because it was so real. It was a sharp, fine morning and Jenna was walking from the door of the cottage to pick the herbs and flowers that grew in the shallows of the little lake. Each one of her senses seemed heightened: the light of the midday sun on the water throwing a million glancing, dancing reflections, so bright that a host of fairies appeared to leap upon the pond's unruffled surface; the sound of the spinning wheel from within echoing the rhythmic heartbeat of life; the feel of Rutterkin's fur as Jenna bent to stroke it, soft and sensual. The smell of the day, too, was as clear and clean as crystal, bearing in its depths the first seductive scent of blossom.

As Jenna stooped to gather the water-plants, she saw two people also breathing in that fine air, one skimming stones upon the pond, the other sitting beneath a tree and looking straight at her. The smaller of the two was misted, vague, yet Jenna had the strong impression it was Agnes, despite the fact she could still hear the clack of her sister's spindle from within the cottage. But the tall one was a stranger and somehow frightening. She saw long hair and hawkish features and beautiful, brilliant eyes; she saw savagery and kindness and unpredictability. She saw tragedy and sweetness – and she saw herself.

In her dream Jenna thought that this must be death. That her soul had taken fleshly covering to meet her face to face, and that this gaunt, young man was here to take her out of life. She felt then that she had always been expecting him, that all her days she had been preparing for something as odd as this.

'You've come then,' she said, and the effort was so great that she sat down on the stone step and closed her eyes.

When she opened them again the man had gone, and the funny little Agnes figure as well. But the frightening thing was that she *was* outside the cottage and was holding flowers in her hand. Where had reality ended and illusion begun? Afraid and trembling, Jenna went indoors.

It was Sunday and the Casselowes, clean and in their best clothes, had already walked to Maighfield's church and heard divine service. Jenna had found it difficult to concentrate sitting in its shadowy interior, seeing Benjamin there and exchanging with him the kind of smile that only lovers know. For everything was still secret, Benjamin having yet to ask Daniel's permission for Jenna's hand in marriage, thwarted by the extraordinary events taking place at Cokyngs Mill. Three times he had gone to see Debora and three times she had refused to receive him. Three times he had wanted to tell her that he had made an unforgiveable mistake, that a marriage between them was no longer possible, and three times William Weston and his wife, apologetic and embarrassed, had told him their daughter was too unwell to see him, that he must call again another day.

'I swear she knows,' he had told Jenna. 'I believe she already knows.'

And now, idly watching Agnes breaking God's holy law and spinning on the Sabbath, Jenna wondered if he was right. For everyone was gossiping about Debora Weston's malady and what could possibly have caused a beautiful young girl to go to bed and refuse to get up again. No twisted ankle could account for such strange behaviour, nor for the fact that Debora also refused to address a soul, not even Goody Weston. Some went so far as to rumour that Master Thomas May had interfered with the girl, but the young man seemed just as usual and even the most eager gossip found it difficult to believe he could have a guilty conscience while maintaining such an innocent air. The whole affair was a mystery.

Realising they were alone, Agnes looked up from her spinning and whispered, 'When is Benjamin coming to call on Father?'

Jenna whispered back, 'As soon as he has ended his betrothal to Debora. But that is so difficult because of her illness.'

Agnes snorted. 'She's not ill. I don't believe it.' She looked up suddenly as a thought struck her. 'Jenna, you haven't ...?'

'No, I have not,' answered Jenna firmly. 'It's not as simple as that.'

'Then what can be the cause?'

'I believe that it is Master Robert Morley whom I summoned to Maighfield for that purpose.'

Agnes's eyes widened. 'You think she is pining for him?'

'Either that or hiding from him.'

'Hiding! Whatever could he have done to make her do that?'

'Or she to him,' answered Jenna with a slow smile.

The little room which served Debora Weston as a bedchamber was scarcely more than a cupboard, a room at the top of the house partitioned off from the sleeping quarters of her five large and hearty brothers. Yet it gave her privacy of a sort, and it was here that she had chosen to withdraw from the world, after that night when the other wretched side of herself had succumbed to Robert Morley.

She turned her face into her pillow and began to cry for what must have been the millionth time. Her life had been ruined. For though Debora might refuse to eat and grow even thinner and see the flesh drop from her bones, there was one place destined to grow larger. There had been no flux from the girl's body since the evil of three weeks ago and she now knew, quite certainly, that she carried Robert Morley's child.

Innocent though she was, Debora realised that there were ways out of the situation. She could tumble into Benjamin's bed and then name him as the father; she could claim that she had been molested by a stranger on the way home; or she could ask Jenna Casselowe for one of her aunt's aborting potions. But Debora knew that she would do none of these things. She knew that she would never allow Benjamin to be saddled with another man's bastard; that no one would believe a story of rape; that she could no more ask Jenna Casselowe a favour than fly through the air.

The only solution would be to go to Glynde and beg Master Robert for his help. But the memory of their night together was too degrading and terrible. She could never look him in the eye after such an experience, remembering how he had made free with her body, running his lips over it and making it his own.

Shuddering, Debora tensed as if her very rigidity might shoot the child straight from her. And she was locked like this, in a minor catalepsy, when her door flung suddenly open and her mother said crossly, 'Benjamin is downstairs to see you, my girl. And I insist – as does your father – that you come at once.'

Debora did not answer, turning her face away, but to her horror a stinging slap on her cheek brought her, gasping, to a sitting position.

229

'I've had enough of you,' said William Weston. 'Either you behave yourself or I'll put you from this house. You are no more ill than I am, and you'll lose your chance of a husband if you're not very careful. You will see Benjamin now or suffer the consequences.'

And before she could object her mother was bundling her into her clothes like a helpless child, and her father was propelling her downstairs by the simple method of pushing her sharply at every step.

For the first time in three weeks, Debora found herself in the lower room, and there stood Benjamin, rather pink in the face, and turning his hat in his hands with every sign of discomfort.

'There you are,' said Goodman Weston, with alarming heartiness. 'There is your betrothed, dressed and ready to receive you.'

Benjamin looked agonised. 'Sir, with your permission ... in view of the circumstances ... Please Sir, may I speak with Debora alone?'

William and his wife exchanged a glance and then he nodded.

'This has been a difficult time for you, I know. We shall stay outside for ten minutes. Debora, you are to talk to Benjamin, do you hear me?'

She did not respond, her face merely growing paler and her pretty eyes, almost unrecognisable with weeping, lowering their glance to the floor.

There was a fraught silence for a moment, and then Benjamin said, 'Debora, what ails you? Why are you so disturbed? What has happened?'

She did not answer, wondering if, after her self-imposed silence, any sound would come out. But eventually she whispered, 'Nothing.'

'And that means everything. Debora, you must tell me what is wrong.'

The look she turned on him frightened him. He had not realised the girl to have so much ferocity.

'I have nothing to say, Benjamin. Except that I will not marry you; can never marry you; no longer have any wish to do so.'

The relief was so stunning that Benjamin stood open-mouthed, hardly believing that he had been released from his obligation so easily, yet knowing that he should ask why, that if he was any sort of a man he could not let the anguished creature who stood before him suffer so much. Yet he was afraid that if he asked too many questions she might change her mind.

Eventually, rather warily, he said, 'Nobody has hurt you, have they Debora? Have I, or has anyone else, done anything to bring about this change?'

The bitterness in her tone surprised him as she replied, 'There is no one to blame but myself. It is just that I have seen too much too clearly and know that we can never make a match.'

'And no outside agency has influenced you in this?'

'No, nothing *outside*,' she answered, strangely accenting the word. 'Only those secret things that dwell within.'

'She's mad, of course,' he thought. 'Debora Weston has gone mad.'

Aloud Benjamin said, 'Then the understanding between us is over?'

'Yes it is. I am sorry, Benjamin, but I really do not think I am the kind of woman who would make you a good wife.'

'Then I'll take my leave,' he said. 'Shall I inform your father? Would it be easier for you?'

For a moment she looked like her old sweet self. 'Indeed it would. He is angry enough with me as it is. Can you say that we decided jointly. Don't blame it all on me.'

Benjamin knew that he should try and wring the truth from her. But he hesitated for fear of the consequences.

'I'll do my best. Farewell.'

She cried then, instantly and copiously, and Benjamin was left with the alternative of taking her in his arms to comfort her or leaving discreetly. Ever afterwards he blamed himself for a coward, but he took the easier course.

Outside the cottage William Weston, his face a stormcloud, tried an encouraging smile. 'Well, well, Benjamin,' he said, rubbing his hands together. 'Is everything resolved? Did my little girl speak to you?'

Benjamin fingered his hat. 'Goodman Weston, I am sorry but it has been mutually agreed by Debora and myself that a marriage between us is no longer possible. Our betrothal is at an end.'

William went purple. 'But why? What is amiss? What is this

231

mysterious ailment of my daughter's that seems to bring madness in its train?'

Benjamin shuffled from foot to foot. 'I do not think it is her illness, Goodman. I think it is merely that she no longer loves me.'

'What! We'll see about that. Benjamin, hold fast. I may yet turn events in your favour.'

Benjamin lost colour but stood his ground. 'Sir, I do not want that. Debora and I have agreed. We no longer wish to marry.'

'Then you had best be gone, Mist. If you cannot take the swings in a maiden's fancy you will never make a husband. Good-day to you.'

Benjamin felt himself to be less than the dust. He should have stayed and told William Weston the truth – that he had fallen in love with another woman and was intent on marriage to Jenna Casselowe. But yet again he chose discretion.

'Good-day, Goodman Weston. Try to forgive me.'

But Debora's father was no longer listening; he was staring at the door of his cottage as if he was about to kick it down. Then he strode inside and Benjamin heard him shout, 'Debora, what have you done? I want an explanation from you, my girl, and I want it now!'

The carpenter lingered for a moment to see if there was any cry from the hapless creature but all was quiet and, wanting only to put the whole incident behind him and return to Jenna, Benjamin hurried the nag on towards the cottage at Baynden.

Just as the carpenter left Cokyngs Mill, Richard Maynard whistled to his dogs and set off for a walk towards the River Rother, wishing that he was not so tired; that the Dark Lady would lie quiet; that his life would alter direction.

Recently, it had seemed every twist and turn of fate had been against him. His sighting of Jenna Casselowe, naked and beautiful, making her way back from some Satanic ritual – for nothing would convince him otherwise – had disturbed him. The glimpse of that firm, bare flesh had started a torment in him that he could not dispel, however hard he tried. He had become horribly aware of his celibacy, of his fixation with a ghost, of his need for the companionship of a woman who was flesh and blood. Night after night he had tossed sleepless in his bed, running his hands over his own body, calling out in despair.

As if she had known his anguish, the Dark Lady had manifested herself more and more. Richard had heard her sobbing, had seen her glide sorrowfully past, had sensed her cold rushing presence almost every day. He had felt he could go on no longer, yet could think of no means of escape. He was the tenant of Baynden; his livelihood lay amongst its fields and pastures; he was tied to the place.

Now, even without realising it, the yeoman found his feet turning towards the part of his property that he both feared and dreaded: the wood which, in this month of high spring, rippled wave upon wave of vivid blue. Its beauty was extraordinary, even he had to admit; drawing him there against his will, leading him to sit down for a moment beside the dew-pond over which the willows bent so caressingly.

Richard closed his eyes and must have dozed off, for he dreamt that he saw the Dark Lady sit beside the pond's edge and draw from its shallow waters a bronze ring with a strange design upon it.

He woke abruptly, full of fright, and then gasped. Before him stood no ghost but a girl, watching him intently. Richard stared aghast as he recognised Debora Weston, though this was hardly the respectable woman he knew, for her face was twisted with desire.

'God's life, what are you doing here?' he said, startled.

She did not answer but sat down beside him, then said shockingly, 'I've come to give myself to you, now. And if you like what you discover you can marry me. I don't care. My father threw me out of doors for being a fool. Now let's see who wins in the end.'

Despite his fear, Richard felt aroused and his mouth suddenly went dry.

'But Debora ...'

'Don't give me buts, Richard. Give me yourself.'

His thoughts came in a horrifying welter: that the girl was obviously deranged, that she was cheap as the lowest doxie, that she was as fierce as fire, and that he would die if he did not enter her at once.

'Oh God, God,' he gasped. 'I never knew it could be like this. You glorious, beautiful slut. What am I to do?'

'Make me your own,' she answered, laughing huskily. 'I am no longer betrothed to Benjamin Mist. If you marry me,

Richard Maynard, every night of your life will be like this.'

And as she pleasured him again unbelievably, he knew that he could no longer live without her.

The double calling of banns by Mr Whitfield the Vicar – Jenna Casselowe and Benjamin Mist, spinster and bachelor of this parish, and Debora Weston and Richard Maynard, likewise – caused a sensation in Maighfield. What could have occurred, everyone asked, to bring this sudden change about? What could have persuaded Benjamin Mist to give up the prettiest girl for miles and take as a bride a dark, gawky creature, taller than he was?

Goodman and Goody Weston were saying little, merely hinting, without directly saying so, that Debora had tired of the carpenter and formed a love match with the tenant of Baynden. But this had not altogether been believed, and when Mother Maud's opinion had been sought it had seemed to many that she had found the right solution. She had winked a hard eye, formed a tight mouth and whispered, 'Perhaps there have been dark doings. Do you remember Alice Casselowe . . .?'

That witchery was the cause of the upset seemed a likely explanation, and though no one had given public voice to the theory, it was repeated again and again behind the closed doors of Maighfield. It was said that Jenna had followed in her great aunt's footsteps, yet there seemed no case to bring against her. No child or adult had died, no ox or ass had fallen sick. Her only crime seemed to be that of enchanting Benjamin – and he was lodging no complaint.

In fact, standing in the cool of Maighfield church and watching him as he awaited his bride at the altar, wearing his very best clothes, Maud thought spitefully that she had never seen the carpenter look better. It was patently obvious to all that the man was glowing with love. The gossip experienced a curious moment, remembering a dream in which she had taken a bridegroom, dark and handsome, with black pearl eyes, vaguely reminiscent of young Master Tom. But as she sought to recall more of it, it faded, leaving her with just a moment's excitement as she thought of the wedding night that she had never, in reality, experienced.

She looked round the church. Debora Weston, the next bride, was there with her parents, her eyes cast to the floor, meek as a

234

harvest mouse. Beside her sat Richard Maynard, his blond hair curling tightly about his head, his pale face gleaming above the brown of his clothes.

'No doubt he is keeping his best till his own wedding,' thought Maud with a malicious grin.

But even she, cruel as she was, had to admire the bride who appeared a moment later in the doorway. Jenna wore white – one of the two bridal colours – in a material given by the ever-generous Lady May, the cut and swathe of the gown and bodice so fine that there was general surprise at the beauty of Jenna's figure, not usually so noticeable in practical working clothes. On her sleeves she had stitched favours in the form of ribboned lovers' knots, which would later be fought over by the young men at the wedding feast.

Though only a country girl, Jenna had made every effort to look beautiful and had woven a garland of fresh flowers to circle her brow, while others tumbled in the long black hair which hung loose to her waist. Beside the bride walked two sweet boys, Daniel's nephews, with bride's laces and rosemary about their sleeves, and behind came Agnes, radiantly happy, carrying a bridecake and a gilded garland of leaves.

It was the grandest wedding for years, and the obvious patronage of Lady May, who swept into the church late and took her place in her private pew, set everyone wondering what particular beauty potion had been so successful that Jenna Casselowe had earned these many favours. But conjecture ceased as the ring was slipped on the bride's thumb and the couple exchanged a kiss and a look that spoke of love – raw and sweet, wild and gentle, tender and fierce.

After this happy moment the bride and groom walked from the church, hand in hand, and all those present followed them, marching along in bright procession amidst the clamour of bells: children running, old dames waddling, husbandsmen and labourers striding out, till they reached the barn where the feast had been spread, enough for all the village. Once again the hand of Lady May could be seen as the people gazed in delight and astonishment at beef sides, mutton, venison pasties, and barley and rye bread with great hunks of cheese. There was beer and ale; sack and Rhenish – a spread fit for the gentry, of whom Jane May, joined late by a panting Master Tom, were the sole members.

235

'Do you reckon Jenna has witched her too?' said one unkind soul to Maud, nodding her head in the direction of the Lady of the Manor.

But for once the gossip was in a good mood as the unaccustomed warmth of wine glowed in the pit of her stomach. 'No, she mixes my lady's beauty lotions. And Jenna's cured her ailments. That's all it will be.'

But Lady May, smiling graciously, did not stay to dance, though Tom – a little drunk and utterly incoherent – remained to whirl with the village girls. As Benjamin and Jenna took to the floor, everyone rose to their feet, and so it was that Richard Maynard found himself with Debora in his arms and felt her shudder as she drew away from him.

It was incomprehensible to him. Ever since the frenzied episode amongst the bluebells she had treated Richard so coldly, bearing his kisses with such scarcely concealed dislike, that sometimes he wondered if he had imagined the whole abandoned scene.

Feeling utterly confused, he offered a tentative, 'In a week's time we will be bride and groom.'

'Yes,' came the stony reply.

Richard's pale cheeks whitened further. 'But, sweetheart, are you not pleased at the prospect?' He pulled her hard against him. 'Remember what you said, "Do you want every night to be like this?" Why are you so distant?'

The flowerlike face hardened. 'That was another side of me that spoke. A base side which I do not admire.'

Richard's fingers tightened around her. 'Be that as it may, I intend to marry you. I've tasted your sweets once – and I swear that I will taste them again. Make no mistake, Debora Weston, next week you will be my bride.'

She raised miserable eyes. 'And if I refuse?'

'Your father will turn you out for good. He tolerated your broken betrothal to Mist merely because you told him you loved me – and a yeoman is a better prospect than a carpenter! Make no mistake, you'll have nowhere to go if you rid yourself of me.'

In a way he regretted his harshness, for the girl trembled in his arms, but in another way he did not care. His obsession with his house and the woman who haunted it was too strong to allow a great deal of other emotion. Almost cruelly, he whirled Debora so fast that she had to hold him tightly to stay on her feet. 'That's better,' he said, 'press close against me.'

She did not answer, excused from speaking by the sudden hush that fell on the company as Agnes Casselowe began to play her lute. And though one or two drunken voices went on babbling, these, too, were quickly silenced by the glory of sound that burst forth. Sitting on the floor of the barn or perched on bales of hay, the villagers of Maighfield listened to the soaring notes that seemed to speak of birth and death – and birth again.

Without knowing why, Richard began to shake, thinking how wrong it was that a dull-wit like Agnes should have that glorious gift, and how terrible to see Jenna Casselowe happy, when all she deserved was anguish. Even as he thought these things he wondered why, searched his soul for the key to his inexplicable hatred of the girls. But no answer came, only the nonsensical belief that the sisters in some way represented his rivals.

Eventually, as candles were lit, the feasting and dancing resumed until that long awaited moment, the time when, with teasing and jesting, rudery and japes, they must escort the bridal couple to their marriage bed. Though not everyone present liked Jenna; Benjamin was popular. So, for his sake, the couple were raised shoulder high and carried through the village and down the track to the cluster of dwellings beneath the shadow of Aylwins. Then the carpenter's cottage was besieged as Jenna was taken up the ladder by the women while, in the room below, Benjamin was stripped amidst ribald comments; after which, dressed in a nightshirt, he was taken to where his bride sat awaiting him in bed.

As he got in with her the villagers cheered and, while a last toast was drunk and some sang a marriage song, the bride and groom kissed one another. This gave rise to wild shouts and improper jests but had the desired effect. Slowly, the guests began to descend the ladder to make their way home.

Jenna laughed in the candlelight. 'So . . .'

'So we are alone.'

She laughed again, producing from beside the bed a flagon and two mugs. 'I have made a special loving cup. Will you drink it, Benjamin?'

'I will. I shall drink to our love and happiness, and to our lives together.'

'Dittany, pennyroyal and verbena will bring him to your bed, jessamine will keep him there.'

As Benjamin downed the draught and blew out the candle, Jenna smiled in the darkness.

June, a glorious morning in Sussex; and Robert Morley riding out from Glynde with a scarlet feather in his hat, all about him rolling downs, and a crystal-bright sea on the horizon. A glorious day and glorious thoughts to match – for he was, at last, on his way to Debora, the beautiful, wanton girl who had stolen the heart of that cynic and seducer, the heir to Glynde.

Everything appeared more intense than usual, an ice-blue lake, glimpsed through the trees, shot here and there with splinters of argent, so calm beneath the peacock sky that Robert felt a mere breath would shatter its stillness to a million fragments.

Everywhere he looked he saw an array of colours: emerald fields rose to hills that changed from amber to purple beneath sealskin shadows and a gilded sun. So, too, the air was shot with specks of gold, so fresh and alive was the atmosphere. And, like strips of ebony, flowing forests smudged darkly against a vista that glistened dew drops in the early light.

Robert left the downs and started towards Maighfield, bending low over his horse's neck and urging it on. He could already imagine a lifetime spent with Debora as his mistress, and her fragile beauty was so much on his mind that when he saw a woman in the Five Acres, Robert did not – just for a moment – realise who it was. For here was a drab thing, bent over the earth tending the soil, her clothes dull brown, her finespun hair tucked in a sensible cap.

'Debora?' he called uncertainly, and saw her hand fly to her mouth in shock. But before she could hurry away, he had crossed the short distance between them and leapt out of the saddle to stand before her, realising only then who she really was.

She looked so distraught that the smile died on his lips. 'Sweetheart, what's wrong?' he said. 'I came back as quickly as I could. But you left me that morning without a word. I was not sure what to do.'

The very sight of her aroused in him instant longing,

238

remembering – as he had done every night since they had been apart – all the lovely lines of her body.

'Debora, don't look at me so angrily. I mean no harm. I want to regularise our position,' he said, as it slowly dawned on him that she seemed a different person, regarding him with a cold and unfriendly stare.

'Go away,' she hissed through clenched teeth.

'Why? What have I done? That night I thought you loved me.'

Her hands flew over her ears and she shrieked, 'Don't ever speak of it. It was disgusting. We were base as animals.'

He gazed at her in horror, seeing for the first time the ring that glinted on her thumb. He snatched her hand, then held it up between them.

'What's this? What have you done? This is a wedding ring.'

'Yes, yes it is. I married last week to give your bastard a name.'

'My bastard? You mean I left you with child?'

'Yes, I have had to pay for my sins. That is what happens when one's baser side dominates.'

Robert grasped Debora by the shoulders.

'What are you talking about? What baser side?'

'The side of me that allowed you to seduce and despoil me. I believe my soul once belonged to a whore.'

'That makes no sense, you wanted it,' answered Robert savagely, shaking her until her teeth chattered. Debora struggled free and burst into tears, weeping with rasping sobs and only controlling herself as Richard Maynard appeared from the far field.

'Good day, Master Morley,' he called, then shouted to Debora, 'wife, make your curtsey to Master Robert. We owe him respect.'

But ignoring him, Debora turned on her heel and ran, crying, towards the manor house.

TWENTY-SIX

The flow of the seasons, one into the other, could not be better
observed than from the little vantage point beside Benjamin's
well. It was from there, as she drew their daily water, that the
carpenter's bride watched the stainless blue sky, the wine-grape
hills, the vivid fields, give way to the first fine fingers of scarlet,
the russet threads, the blaze of spice that suffused the trees
beneath a hunter' moon.

Then she saw follow the whole rich panoply of autumn:
villagers dancing in the fields when the harvest was gathered in,
clapping hands and jugs of ale, and the old fiddler working till
he dropped. And then blackberry time and stained fingers and
flying dark hair as Benjamin chased his dear love until they fell,
laughing, beneath the haystack.

Finally there came winter, and the hills glittering white,
every pond sparkling diamonds, and a great silence lying over
the land as out of the sky fell that soft and gentle blanket that
brought death and sickness in its wake.

Most unusually, for she was strong as she was tall, Jenna fell
victim to quinsy and no sooner was Christmas out and the end of
the year but a day or two away, than she took to her bed, unable
to raise her dark head from the pillow. And it was then, for the
first time since her marriage, that she found she no longer had
the strength to mix the posset of jessamine which, every week
without fail, she had poured into Benjamin's ale.

It was then that old thoughts came to torment the carpenter,
as he sat by the fire, his wife asleep in the room above. Thoughts
of his affection for Debora before Jenna burst upon the scene, of
the strange twist of fate which had brought Benjamin's former
love to marry Richard Maynard.

Angry with himself for his disloyalty, Benjamin stood up and
walked about the room. But still his mind wandered down
dangerous paths and as he thought of how close he had been to
marrying Debora, he wondered what would have happened if
the revelation about Jenna had not come to him.

As if she sensed something was amiss, Benjamin heard his wife call his name from upstairs and, hurrying up, found her leaning against the pillows, her face white and drawn.

'Benjamin,' her voice was weak. 'I heard you pacing about. Is anything wrong?'

'Nothing, my sweetheart,' he lied. 'But how are you? Is there anything I can get you?'

'Only a drink containing herbs. But I would rather prepare that myself.' As if she could read his mind, Jenna added, 'What news of Debora? Have you seen her about the village?'

'No, her child is due in February and Richard is keeping her indoors, at least so I am told.'

Jenna got out of bed. 'I must mix her some potions to ease the birth. Agnes can take them to Baynden. I doubt Debora would receive them from my hands.'

Benjamin shook his head. 'I never thought you to have any liking for Debora Maynard – and now here you are struggling up to compound possets for her sake.'

His wife looked slightly guilty. 'Sometimes I feel that I took you from her, that I owe her a debt.'

'How could you think that? I came of my own free will.'

'Yes,' answered Jenna, with a little laugh. 'Of course you did. It was only a figure of speech.'

The hunters were out from Glynde, pursuing a white hart through the winter forest, anxious for fresh meat for their board and glad to breathe in cold crisp air, leaving behind the stifling atmosphere of smoking fires and unaired rooms.

They had travelled far that day, crossing fields iridescent beneath the crimson sun, and fording streams running at full spate. So far had they come, in fact, following the clamouring hounds, that now they found themselves drawing near Harbert Morley's territories at Byvelham and, even before they were aware of it, entering the confines of Hawkesden Park, Sir John Waleis's old hunting ground.

Below them lay the moated site, the timber-framed hunting lodge surrounded by the more recent addition of an impressive wall, clearly visible. Beyond it the hart, running as if possessed, had plunged into the dense trees.

'Come on,' shouted Harbert, raising his gloved hand. 'We've come too far to let it outrun us. Follow me.'

Like a human stream the dark-clad hunters and the panting dogs flowed down the hill towards the lake, splashing through the icy water, the dogs swimming where it grew too deep for them.

'Robert!' shouted Harbert, over his shoulder. 'Where are you, man?' And his brother, coming up hard behind him, thought it difficult to believe that earlier in the year Harbert had lain upon his sick bed, dangerously ill.

Urging his mount on, Robert drew alongside and the two of them raced side by side, stooping in their saddles to avoid the snow-filled branches. It would seem that the hart had vanished, almost by magic, because as they drew into an unexpected clearing there was no sign of it.

'Damn the creature,' shouted Harbert, and then wheeled his horse as behind him there was a flash of white. He was off instantly and Robert, close behind, wondered how much longer they could keep this up, pursuing a beast that seemed to have the power of ten.

He saw that ahead of him, Harbert had halted once more, peering through the trees at a building outlined black against the whiteness all around it. Robert saw it was a forge and though this was nothing unusual in an area of iron workings, realised he had never been aware of its existence until now.

'Whose place is that?' said Harbert, just ahead of him.

'It's a smithy, not an iron forge,' said Robert, coming up beside his brother.

'And there's the smith, by God,' answered Harbert. 'What a strange fellow!'

It seemed to the brothers that a monk was working the furnace and beating the glowing metal. A monk in a roughspun habit, his hair close cropped about an ascetic and bony face.

'Ho there!' called Harbert. 'Where are you from?'

Startled by the unexpected shout in the silence of the frozen woods, Robert's horse reared suddenly, taking him by surprise so that he lost his seat and found himself crunching on to his buttocks, a blow made all the more painful by the fact that the ground was iron-hard with ice. Harbert leaned from his saddle and proffered his hand and Robert hauled himself up again.

'Who is he?' asked Robert.

'I don't know.' Harbert appeared thoughtful. 'He did not answer my call, merely turning to look at me. His eyes were like glowing suns. It was the most frightening thing I have ever seen.'

'I didn't see him,' answered Robert. 'The horse threw me before I had a chance. What do you mean – he had eyes like glowing suns?'

'Just that. The light from them was blinding. If I believed in such things I would have thought it an apparition.'

Both men shivered and turned to look at the forge again – but it had vanished. From nowhere at all an unseasonable mist, one they could only suppose was caused by the extreme frost, had come swirling through the trees towards them, catching them in its fingerlike vapours and obscuring the smithy from view.

'Well, that's put paid to hunting for today,' said Harbert. 'We'll go back empty-handed.'

But he was wrong. As they picked their way back to the hunting party, guided mainly by the sound of voices, they saw that the hart lay upon the ground, jets of scarlet pumping from its long white neck.

'It bolted out of the forest,' said the steward, 'and came straight towards us. It didn't have a chance.'

Robert turned away. Something of the creature's sad, dead eye reminded him of Debora's cowed expression when he had last seen her; that bright day when he had ridden from Glynde wearing a red feather in his hat, only to find her married to Richard Maynard, and all his hopes of her dashed for ever.

Thinking of her like that, Robert could not believe his ears when Harbert announced to the company, 'We'll sleep at Baynden tonight. It can only be a mile away and I've no stomach to ride back through this fog.'

Robert nodded in reluctant agreement. He had no wish to see Debora ever again. In fact, as he set his shoulders and followed his brother towards Baynden, Robert Morley felt desperately sad and cheated.

The January night grew even colder and the wind whistled round the house as if it were a human voice. Pulling her shawl tightly around her swollen body, Debora went to check that every window was closed.

She had always hated the wind, thinking of it as a beast that rent and tore at houses, sitting upon the roof and clawing off the thatch and sometimes descending into the chimney breast where, because it was caged, it would spit and snarl and fill the rooms with choking smoke.

Debora moved closer to the hearth, resting for a moment before she continued her inspection of the rooms. Beneath her breasts the baby that was due any day now kicked and jumped in its eagerness to see the world beyond its dark dwelling place.

Debora wondered what it would be: a boy, dashing and naughty as his father, or a girl who might take after either of the two Deboras whose body sheltered the unborn life within.

Outside, the gale took up a note like a song. Debora pictured a girl sitting upon a rock, her gown misty, filled with a million diamond lights as it swirled outwards and upwards upon the air, concealing a great fish's tail thrashing beneath.

'Oh God,' she said, beneath her breath, 'don't let the wind whistle down this house any more.'

Heedless, the song continued and Debora rose to her feet again and climbed to the Master of Glynde's room to see that all was secure. Peeping round, she saw herself reflected in the great carved mirror that Harbert Morley had placed there. A frightened creature looked back, a creature haunted by the fact that smouldering beneath the surface lay another being who might at any time break forth.

'I am the mother of this child,' said Debora defiantly, running her hands over her mighty womb.

Her features changed and a leering expression came upon them. 'I wouldn't be too sure of that,' said a voice which Debora barely recognised as hers. 'I had more to do with it than you did, you silly, whimpering milksop.'

With a scream, she ran from the room and descended the stairs, suddenly noticing how the temperature of the house had dropped below freezing point. She came to a halt on the landing, looking down to the place below, barely realising that a woman servant – a servant who wore an old-fashioned white wimple from which a lock of black hair was bursting forth – was about to push past her.

'Where are you going?' Debora said. 'Everything is secure above stairs.'

The servant did not reply, merely bestowing upon her a strange, sad smile; a smile that made Debora freeze with fear.

'Who are you?' Her voice was sharp with terror.

Still silence – and then Debora found herself unable to move.

The woman vanished even as she watched her; there was nothing there but the smoke-filled chamber and the shout of voices from below. A shout that, as Debora listened to it, filled her with even greater unease.

'. . . been hunting and then a mist came up,' said someone. 'We'll stay the night here, Maynard, and move on tomorrow. The men can sleep in the hall. My brother and I will have the Master's rooms.'

Debora's baby heaved as she realised that she was walking down the stairs towards its father. That below, in the hall of Baynden, stood Robert Morley, his hat in his hands and his face tight with nervousness as he looked around for her, the mother of his bastard.

There was a fraught silence felt by everybody, even though they were quite unaware of its cause. Then the general noise made by the party from Glynde covered it up, and Debora found herself hurrying around, giving orders to servants and personally supervising the airing of beds, the lighting of candles and the preparation of extra food.

It was not until the hunters were gathered round the table for supper that she found herself catching the eye of the man who had taken away her virginity.

Robert said nothing, merely raising his glass to her, and then looking away. There was something about his whole manner that filled Debora's heart with misery. She knew that though he had only met her twice, she had captured his affection, and that she could still – gross with child as she was – ask him any favour she wished.

With a shock, Debora realised that Richard was staring fiercely at the two of them.

'. . . bad day's hunting,' Harbert's voice broke into the sudden silence. 'Only a hart to show for all the miles we travelled.' His voice changed. 'Maynard, I came across a curious thing. Can you enlighten me? In Hawkesden Park, with the mist coming up and nobody else about, my brother and I stumbled across a forge, apparently worked by a monk. Do you know anything about it?'

'There have been no monks in England for seventy years,' answered Richard. 'Not since the monasteries were dissolved.'

'That is what I believed – and so was much surprised. But I saw the man distinctly. He turned his head and looked at me.'

'Very strange,' Richard replied. He paused, then said, 'Perhaps it was the forge of St Dunstan.'

Somebody gave a nervous laugh as Harbert said, 'What forge is that?'

Richard's pale skin glowed white. 'It is only a legend, of course. They say that the valley of Byvelham is magic and that a vision of St Dunstan, working in his smithy, appears there from time to time.' He paused as if considering his next few words and finally said, 'Naturally, it isn't true. You must have come across one of the others and not recognised it in the snow, Master Harbert.'

'I suppose so,' answered the Master of Glynde slowly. 'Yet the man looked so odd. His eyes seemed to glow in his head.'

'You saw his face?' asked Richard, his voice very soft.

'Yes. Why? Are you hiding something, Maynard?'

'No, Master Harbert.'

But later on when he and his half-brother had retired, Morley said gloomily, 'I am sure Maynard could have told us more than he did about that forge. I am sure it bodes no good to look on the monk's features.'

Half-listening, his brother answered cheerily, 'Nonsense. It was Hawkesden Park forge, and that was one of the Istead family at work. It is just that everything looks so different in the snow.'

Harbert shook his head in disbelief and lay down wearily upon the bed, falling asleep at once as did Robert. But in the morning, after dreaming of her all night, he was a little dashed by Debora's absence and when Maynard told the departing hunting party that his wife had taken to her bed, wondered immediately if she was in labour.

'Perhaps it is the babe,' he ventured, only to be met with a cold glance and the information that the child was not due for another month. So she had lied and hidden the fact she was pregnant when Maynard married her.

'Of course, of course,' Robert answered evenly. 'But I am told that sometimes they come early into the world.'

Richard turned down his mouth, obviously not wanting to discuss the matter further, giving Robert the impression that the yeoman was guilty. So Debora had seduced him before the wedding and blamed the child on him. A clever woman as well as beautiful. A broad smile crossed Robert's face and he wrung Maynard warmly by the hand. 'Whenever it is born I wish you joy of your child, Goodman. I shall return in the spring and bring it a gift, if that is agreeable to you.'

Richard's features were waxen as he answered grudgingly, 'Of course, Master Robert. You are always welcome at Baynden, you know that.'

But his face contorted as he watched the hunters depart, then hurried up the stairs to where Debora lay.

'What have you been saying to Morley?' he shouted. 'I saw the way you looked at each other last night!'

Her only reply was a moan and, drawing nearer the bed, he saw that she was lying in a ball of pain.

'Debora,' he said in a different voice. 'What is it? Are you ill?'

'It's the babe,' she gasped. 'It is coming before time. You must fetch the midwife.'

To his shame, Richard felt himself grow faint and instead of rushing out sat down weakly upon the bed, his head in his hands.

'Richard, help me.' His wife's voice was distant, and he could think of nothing but that the temperature in the room had suddenly dropped to freezing and there was a strange rushing of currents. Much as Richard suspected, the Dark Lady stood in the doorway staring straight at Debora and shaking her head. Then she raised her hand and pointed straight at the girl, before melting silently into the wall behind.

Just after midnight, Robert woke with the strong conviction that Debora had borne him a son. In fact, he was so certain of it that he lit the candles in his chamber and sat up in bed, then decided to venture downstairs for wine to celebrate. But no sooner had he set foot on the top step than the sound of somebody running brought him to a stop. His sister-in-law, Ann, dressed only in her night clothes, appeared before him breathlessly.

'Robert, you must come at once,' she said. 'Harbert has been taken ill.'

Clutching Ann's fingers he raced towards the master's bedroom and as soon as he went through the doorway, knew his brother was dying.

It seemed to him that he covered the distance between the

entrance and the bed in a single jump, and that he gathered Harbert into his arms in the same movement. But one glance at his half-brother's face told him that his beloved Harbert – the stern elder of the family and respected father-figure – was beyond speech, beyond even seeing. The grey eyes were already glazing over and there were snowdrop patches on either cheek.

Believing that hearing was the last of the senses to be given up, Robert whispered, 'I love you, Harbert.'

But his half-brother could not answer. His lips parted silently, his eye set firmly on the distance, and the snowdrops in his cheeks came finally to bloom.

'Our Father ...' Robert began, but the words died in his mouth. How could he speak of daily bread at the moment when all was lost?

It was left to Ann to say, 'Lord, receive this Christian soul in Thy infinite mercy.'

And it was with the sound of her weeping prayers in the background that Robert kissed his brother and then turned away towards the window knowing, with a leaden heart, that all he looked out on was finally his. That he had at last become the Master of Glynde.

TWENTY-SEVEN

Bluebell time again, and Richard Maynard ventured into the place he feared most, to pick posies for his wife and baby. For though Debora might not love him she had given him the greatest gift of all in a son to call his own. Armfuls of flowers were the least he could bring her.

Ankle-deep in the glorious lake of blue, Richard thought of the child's conception in this very place – a conception full of fire and passion which he had never found again with a wife grown cold. For some reason Jenna Mist came into his mind and he thought of the night he had seen her naked beneath her cloak and of the long, lean lines of her body. It was then, right at the back of his mind, that Richard realised that she excited him.

Picking the last of his flowers he was turning to go when – just as if she had been summoned – he saw Jenna coming through the trees towards him, her basket over her arm. Why he panicked, Richard did not know, but he nervously scrambled off towards Baynden, pretending that he had not seen her, all the while conscious of her presence behind him. As she knelt to fill her basket with blooms, Richard heard her sing, and his usual feeling of dislike for her was completely swamped by a desire to see her naked again. He had grudgingly to admit that he envied the carpenter his tall, dark bride.

Watching his retreating back, Jenna breathed a sigh of relief. He was one person she had no wish to converse with, clearly so wild and unhappy these days. It was perfectly obvious to her, if to no one else, that his marriage to Debora was a failure and, as she often had of late, Jenna thought again about the identity of the father of Debora's child. She dismissed the thought that it was Benjamin's, but that it was Master Morley's was a different matter. She had drawn him to Maighfield by stabbing a lamb-bone. Had her spell been wholly successful? Had he seduced the innocent girl as she had hoped?

It was a line of thought she had no wish to pursue and, over-briskly, Jenna concentrated on gathering flowers, going to the dew-pond and pulling at the soft moss that grew at its very edge. Through the trees above golden shafts of light lit the cool darkness of the place and it was in one of these that she saw something reflected in the water. Slowly she put her hand into the shallows and drew the object out.

It was barely recognisable as a ring, so corroded was it; yet, as Jenna slipped it on to her finger, it seemed to her that it pulsed with power. She had a mental picture of the hawk-faced man who had stared at her across the waters of her own little pond at home. And then everything grew frighteningly still as she saw the man again, quite dead, and lying only a yard or two away from her.

As she knelt, stiff with fear, Jenna heard the sound of hooves approaching, and saw a man ride towards her, apparently unaware of her presence. For, uncaringly, he roughly threw the body over his saddle and passed quite close beside her as he led his horse down the slope towards Daniel's cottage. She watched horrified until he had vanished from view. Then everything returned to normal.

Puzzled, Jenna stood up, pulling at the ring. Annoyingly, for it was too large, it had stuck on her knuckle, and the more she wrenched at it – terrified of its power to conjure up visions – the harder it seemed to stick. Eventually she was forced to run towards her father's cottage, where she might find grease to ease the ring off, rather than return home to Benjamin.

The instant he crossed the threshold of Baynden, Richard, by now in a towering rage caused entirely by his own hateful thoughts about Jenna, called out, 'Debora, where are you? Come here at once!' And was thrown into a fury when there was no reply. But the sight of her sitting outside, staring at the beautiful view and rocking her child gently in her arms, quietened him a little.

'I've brought you some flowers,' he said, more kindly.

She looked up, a ghost of a smile her only greeting, and he felt all his anger return. She had tricked him into marriage by pretending to want him and now all she did was fob him off with distant looks and icy manners.

'Debora!' he said in a low voice. 'Give the child to a servant. I want to speak to you privately – now!'

She gave him a look that withered his heart; so full of

repugnance and fear that, had he not been so angry, he could have wept.

'Why do I repel you?' he thundered, not caring who heard. 'You were willing enough once. Do you remember – or is it something you would prefer to forget?' He caught hold of her arm, pulling her close to him and disregarding the fact that the baby had started to cry. 'Well?'

She wriggled free. 'That was a moment's madness, Robert. I am a respectable wife, not a whore!'

And with that Debora thrust the baby into Richard's arms and ran off so fast that for a moment he stood transfixed. Then he collected himself and hurried into the house to deposit the frightened infant on an equally startled woman servant, before he sprinted through the trees and down the slope after her.

As he ran, he thought, 'I'll rape the bitch. I cannot stand this a moment longer.'

And all the time his heart was pounding with anger and misery, the turmoil of every emotion he had endured for the past few months.

'If Debora won't have me I'll kill her,' his thoughts ran wildly on. 'Or else I will take a mistress and never put my hands on the slut again.'

Richard stopped short, his mind suffused once more with sudden and unwelcome thoughts of Jenna. He could not think why he had hated her all these years, when really she was so beautiful and desirable.

He must make amends to her, he thought. Perhaps take the odd gift of food and other produce. Surely he had an ornate comb somewhere that had once belonged to his mother? How well it would look with those lustrous black tresses looped about it.

Richard started to run again, but with less enthusiasm than a moment before. If his frigid wife wished to elude him, then so be it. He knew a dark-haired witch girl with more charm in her little finger than insipid Debora Weston could aspire to in a lifetime.

That evening the valley was green and gold, the river water cool and clear, as it tumbled over little falls of rock, then skimmed like cream above pebbles the colour of milk. In its depths the

251

calm, white clouds that passed overhead as gently as brides to an altar, were reflected like snowflakes.

Benjamin, crossing the moat at Sharnden and wondering, as always, why this particular place gave him so much pleasure, decided to take the high track to Maighfield, where he could look down upon the Valley of Byvelham and marvel, yet again, at its unique beauty.

Beneath him fields, every soft colour from jasper to emerald, swept away to hills that possessed at one moment the shade of plums and, at another, the sombre hues of ink and indigo. It was a marvellous evening; every scent, every sight, quite perfect, and somewhere a lark chanted a song of rapture to complete it all.

Benjamin reined in his horse and looked about, glad that he must plunge down into the valley's lovely heart as part of his journey home. From this vantage point, with the sheep little white dots and the cattle mere round brown stones, he saw that one dot, larger than the rest, was moving rapidly in his direction. As it drew nearer he saw it was a woman panting up the hill.

With a lurch of his heart Benjamin recognised Debora and realised that, for the first time since their parting, he was alone with her. Full of misgivings, he walked his horse forward.

As soon as she got within reasonable distance he noticed that she was not only out of breath but crying, her hair hanging in disarray down her back and the skirt of her dress ripped to festoons.

'What is it?' he called, urging the nag to the trot. 'Debora, what has happened? Have you been attacked?'

At the sound of his voice she stopped her frantic progress and stood, gasping for breath, watching his approach. Then answered, without so much as a greeting, 'I'm running away from Richard,' and burst into another flood of tears.

The carpenter's heart sank even further. He had no wish to be involved in Debora's matrimonial difficulties. Not knowing quite what to say he remained silent, dismounting slowly and standing beside his horse.

'Take me home with you,' the girl continued hysterically. 'Benjamin, you must protect me.'

'I can't,' he answered, aware of his own abruptness. 'Debora, you are Goodman Maynard's *wife*. If he is being cruel to you, only your family can intervene.'

She gave him a bitter glance, smearing the back of her hand across her face.

'How typical of you,' she said. 'Benjamin Mist the dreamer. Always so kind and good – but prepared to do nothing.'

He smarted beneath the insult, aware, perhaps, that there was a grain of truth in it.

'What do you want of me?' he asked grudgingly.

'That you take me to my brothers. My father may have turned me out but they still care for me. They will not stand by and see their sister abused in her own home.'

'I do not want to interfere between man and wife.'

She gave him a withering glance. 'Then leave me. I shall walk alone to Cokyngs Mill.'

Benjamin hesitated, then said reluctantly, 'No, as you are obviously distressed, I will take you on the nag. But Debora ...'

'Yes?'

'That is all I dare do. You understand?'

She laughed bitterly. 'Yes, I understand only too well. We were once betrothed – and you said you loved me. Now you have married the witch's niece and everything has changed. The situation is perfectly clear.'

'What exactly do you mean by that?'

'You will find out in time, no doubt,' Debora answered as he lifted her on to his horse.

'It won't come off,' said Agnes, larding the ring with even more goose grease, and tugging at Jenna's finger. 'It seems to have settled on your knuckle.'

'It *must* come off,' answered her sister, with a note of desperation. 'It frightens me. I'm sure it isn't lucky.'

'Where did you find it?'

'In the bluebell wood. It was lying in the dew-pond. It must have been there for centuries, hidden by water or leaves.'

'I wonder who it belonged to.'

'I know,' answered Jenna softly. 'I have seen the owner.'

'You mean he is still alive?'

'No. He is long since dead. But he comes to me sometimes. Once he stood outside here, Agnes, and looked at me across the pond. It was a daydream but I had the feeling that *you* were with him and when he looked at me, his eyes were mine.'

Agnes looked confused, her mouth dropping a little. 'I don't understand. How could I have been with him, when he is a ghost?'

'I don't know. It is very difficult to comprehend. All of what happens beyond this life is a mystery.'

The sisters regarded one another silently, until eventually Agnes said, 'I don't understand you but I love you, Jenna. You have always been good to me. Would you like me to play just for you?'

Jenna glanced at the sinking sun and then said, 'Very quickly, then. Benjamin will be home soon.'

Agnes picked her lute from the table and began to play but, for once, it was an angry air, full of fire and fury, drowning any sound that Richard Maynard – walking silently from the river and out of the girls' line of vision – could possibly have made.

'What's the matter?' said Jenna, looking curiously at her sister.

'I'm thinking about Debora. I believe she saddled Goodman Maynard with a bastard.'

'I have never thought the child to be his,' Jenna answered thoughtfully.

'Poor Richard,' said Agnes, and as if it were part of her, the lute's song became sad. 'I have never liked the man but I would not wish that on him.'

'Nor I.'

Agnes stopped playing and both girls turned round as from outside came a curious sound like a muffled shriek.

'What was that?'

'I don't know.'

Jenna got to her feet and walked round the cottage but there was nobody there, only the wildfowl on the pond and the clumps of trees swaying in the evening breeze.

'It must have been one of the creatures,' she said uncertainly.

'Not your ghost come for you?'

'I hope not.' Jenna kissed Agnes on the cheek. 'I must go. Give my love to father.'

'You will not stay and see him?'

'No, Benjamin will worry if I am late.'

And she was gone into the twilight, her black hair floating out on the cold little breeze that had suddenly come up from the river.

The bluebells that Richard had gathered for his wife drooped in their vase, and the child that she had given to him cried in its sleep. For two days the baby had had neither mother nor father to comfort him. The servants of Baynden, speaking in whispers, could only conjecture that there had been a mighty argument between the tenant and his wife, for some had seen the mistress running off towards the river, and others the master going after her in furious pursuit. After which Goodwife Maynard had never returned and was presently hiding out, so it was said, with her eldest married brother. A situation which, curiously, the master chose to ignore. If the word ignore could be used to describe such behaviour as drinking himself unconscious every night, speaking to nobody, and refusing to eat so much as a crumb.

The atmosphere in the house was such that the youngest servant girl was in tears most of the day. And the baby's nurse, not to be outdone, fainted with shock when the master shouted, 'Take that bastard away from me. I don't want it anywhere near, do you hear!'

Excitement supplanted misery at this unguarded remark and it was only a matter of hours before the opinion of Maud was sought.

'I would have thought the facts spoke for themselves,' she said, nodding wisely and putting her finger to the side of her nose.

'You mean that the baby is *not* Goodman Maynard's child?'

By way of answer Maud asked another question. 'Was not the Goodwife betrothed to another? And did not that betrothal end suddenly and strangely?'

'Yes.'

'And did not Debora marry Richard Maynard in what seemed indecent haste and wasn't a child born seven months later?'

'You mean . . .?' The nurse clapped her hand over her mouth in delight. 'You mean it's . . . *Benjamin's*?'

Maud's brown eyes snapped with triumph. There had not been such a good scandal in the village since Master Tom was

255

seen holding hands with a fellow university student whom he had brought to the palace last Christmas.

'I wonder what Jenna will say when she gets to hear of it?'

Maud looked very knowing and lowered her voice. 'I don't think Jenna is in a position to say anything at all.'

'What do you mean?'

'Years ago I had a nephew that died.'

Had the servant imagined it or did Maud hesitate minutely over the word nephew?

'Yes?'

'I always thought that Jenna's great-aunt put the eye on him.'

'What did you do?'

Maud looked slightly flustered as she answered, 'It was not my affair. But I believed then that I saw the face of evil. And I believe that evil lives on in Alice Casselowe's niece, and that she has cast a spell of unlawful love on Benjamin Mist.'

'So Debora was forced to marry the master when Benjamin deserted her and left her pregnant?'

Maud looked triumphant. 'Of course. But it won't take long for the truth to come out now. Now that Goodman Maynard has discovered the deception.'

'Well God have mercy on them all.'

'Amen,' answered Maud piously.

The carpenter, going about his rounds on the nag, wondered why he suddenly seemed the object of so much interest and presumed it was because he had been seen taking Debora to her brother's home. Not that he cared what people said, as long as Jenna believed none of it, though he was greatly embarrassed when Debora came to his door in broad daylight.

He had returned home early to carve a table and, as far as he was aware, no one knew he was there. But Debora obviously did for there she stood, looking more than beautiful in the sunshine, her lips curling strangely as she smiled at him.

'I have come to thank you for helping me the other day.'

Her voice did not sound quite as usual, he thought, having in its depth a throaty – and somehow suggestive – quality.

'Come in. How did you know I was here?'

'I saw you take the short-cut through the woods. I thought I would follow you and pass the time of day.'

Something about the girl's manner seemed different to

Benjamin, but she came in and sat demurely enough in his favourite chair, looking up at him with a face transformed from the last time he had seen it, so frantic and tear-stained.

'You are still with your brother?' he ventured.

'Of course,' came the reply, in that odd low voice. 'I would not go home to be defiled.'

'Defiled? By your own husband?'

'I do not love him,' she said, standing up impatiently. 'In fact I love another, who is far closer to me than he has ever been. But love does not interfere with wanting, does it Benjamin? You of all people should know that. You, who were bewitched into marriage, should know the difference between love and lust.'

He was aghast, partly because the girl who stood before him had put into words the idea that had been worrying him for months.

'What do you mean, I was bewitched? I love Jenna.'

Debora laughed, putting her head back so that her throat arched like a swan's before Benjamin's unbelieving gaze.

'Naturally. That is all part of the spell under which you have laboured these twelve months past. But, really, it is me you still love, Benjamin. It is me you still want with all your body and mind. It is me who will take you to a paradise that you do not even know exists.'

She looked up at him and he saw, with a horrified fascination, that her hand had gone to the fastenings of her dress. He realised then that Debora – quiet, innocent Debora – was about to strip naked before him.

'Don't . . .' he said. But the words died on his lips as his eyes feasted on the curve of her high, tight breasts; the hand-span waist, unchanged by childbirth; the delicate hips and legs.

'Debora,' he said, then added stupidly, 'You are very beautiful.'

'Beautiful for you,' she said, still in that strange deep voice, then without another word sank to the floor. Before he could stop himself, Benjamin, fully dressed, was upon her where she lay, knowing it was madness, lunacy, folly, but unable to resist her. Thus they were, entwined one about the other, moving in relentless rhythm, when Jenna walked through the door and stood gazing down at them in horror.

'I'll kill you both,' she said quietly. 'Do not think that either of you can betray me like this and live.'

Benjamin had never known greater despair. He was at the climax of lovemaking and for several moments could not move. But when at last he collected himself, it was to see a Jenna transformed. Her features those of another, fierce and hawklike, as she hissed at him, 'How could you have done this to me? How could you cheapen a love so splendid?'

At once he felt base, a shoddy thing scrambling to do up its breeches and hanging its head in shame.

'And as for you, you wretched harlot,' snarled his wife, turning her attention to Debora. 'You shall leave this house as you stand. Let you run naked through the village and let all turn their eyes upon you and know you for the whore that you are.'

As she caught the girl by the throat, Benjamin seemed to see Jenna as a tall, young man, a man whose fingers were choking the life from the girl Benjamin had just loved. It was an illusion, of course, for the next second Jenna had abruptly released her and thrown Debora bodily into the street, slamming the door behind her.

'And now, Benjamin Mist,' she said, white to her throat, 'it is your turn. I wish you ill luck. I wish you no happiness. I wish you nothing but misery until your days are over.'

Without being able to look at her, Benjamin heard her run up the ladder and throw her few clothes into a basket. Then he heard her come down again and take her pestle and mortar. He looked up at last.

Jenna stood in the doorway, brimming with hatred. 'So magic served me ill in the end,' she said. 'Then so be it. I will never indulge in it again. Be damned to you, Benjamin Mist, for you have brought me down so low that I doubt I will ever raise up again. Let vengeance be wreaked upon you.'

Benjamin never knew how long he lay on the floor sobbing, hour upon hour after she had gone. Over and over again he repeated, 'Jenna, come back. Please come back to me. You are all I was born for, we cannot be separated now that I have found you again.'

TWENTY-EIGHT

To ride out beneath the gentle slopes of the Downs cradling the manor house of Glynde was always pleasurable to Robert Morley. And at no time more so than on a gentle June evening, when the sun caressed the hills as it dipped behind them, throwing patches of colour on to the fields. For here was England at its best. Gone the ugliness and smell of town, the raucous cry of trouble-makers and the thrust of thieves. Here was splendour and sweet scents, the high bleat of native sheep, the freedom to ride forth without fear in the heart of the land.

The Master of Glynde thought back on all that had passed before this moment. The shortcomings in his life, his wasted years, the women who had been and gone. But most of all he thought of his inheritance, and how proud he was now to bear the title; how inspired to tread in the footsteps of those extraordinary men who had gone before.

Reining his horse in and looking down on his house – a mere dot in the valley's depths – Robert felt a pride of possession, a pride of place, a pride in the very Englishness of both himself and the scene that lay spread beneath him. He would, at that moment, have laid down his life to preserve the peace and beauty of that little part of England of which he was lucky enough to be Lord of the Manor.

His thoughts turned to the future, and away from the splendour of his inheritance. As Master it was now his responsibility to marry and produce a legitimate heir, by a respectable wife. Rather reluctantly, Robert's mind wandered over the eligible women in his circle and then settled on Susanna Hodgson of Framfield, a considerable heiress and at fifteen years old, obviously a good match to make in a year or so.

Excited by all that lay ahead, Robert hurried his horse home. But as soon as he walked into the hall and saw his steward's face, knew that something had happened in his absence.

'Well?' he said.

'There's a person to see you, Master. A female person.'

'Who is she?'

'She says that she has ridden from Maighfield and that her business is urgent.'

'Then I'll receive her. Show her into the library.'

It had to be Debora! Nobody else would dare call at this hour of the evening. Hardly able to believe this latest twist of fate, Robert went to stand before the fire, adopting a masterful pose, and wondering which side of her strange personality would present itself to him.

She came into the room almost meekly, her gaze cast to the floor, and it was impossible to read from her face which role she had chosen to play.

Rather uncertainly, Robert said, 'What can I do to help you, Goodwife?'

She raised her eyes and he was shocked to see that they were swollen with weeping.

'I have come to throw myself on your mercy, Master. I have run away from Richard and my father has forbidden me to show my face in Maighfield again. I am wondering if you would give me work at Glynde, that I might at least have a roof over my head.'

He surveyed her somewhat coldly. 'Goodwife, I have not had good treatment at your hands. The first time we met we became lovers and I believed this was because there was an attraction between us. But when I saw you again you had married another to give our son a name, and you treated me with contempt. Yet last time we spoke you gave me a look in which I read strange thoughts but not those of love. Why should I help you now?'

'Because I am the mother of your child.'

'It is true I should make provision for him but he is not even with you.'

Debora turned away, staring out of the window at the dusky parkland.

'There is another reason.'

'What is that?'

'That a part of me loves you still.'

He stood wavering, not really wanting further involvement with such an extraordinary woman, and then the transformation took place. He saw the delicate sad face, so close to his, harden, he saw the lips part and the eyes widen and grow dark.

260

'You want me, don't you, you mad creature?' he said.

She did not answer but instead swept her hands over his body without any shame or sense of decency. Robert was outraged that here, in his own library at Glynde, he should be subjected to such an attack.

'Debora ...' he began, but she would not let him speak, kissing him as only she was able to.

In an atmosphere of mounting excitement the girl whispered, 'Let me stay tonight at least, Robert.'

He knew that she was probably crazed; that she was certainly dangerous; that he was a fool; but as Robert took her into his arms he heard himself say, 'You can stay as long as you like. It would take very little to make me fall in love with you.'

Then they spoke no more as Robert entered a sinister paradise, yet a paradise that he never wanted to leave again.

With an important clip-clop of her shoes, Maud crossed the cobbles of the palace quadrangle and made her way to the kitchens, smiling with malice. The master cook had sent for her to hear the latest gossip, for what a remarkable year it had been! As if the discovery that Debora's child had been fathered by Benjamin Mist had not been enough, there had come the revelation that the affair was still going on, that Jenna had come home and caught them in the very act of coupling. And this had led to an extraordinary scene in which Debora had run stark naked through the village, men whistling, women calling 'Whore', and little boys throwing stones.

Of course that had been the end of her. She had never dared show her face in Maighfield again. That very evening Debora had disappeared and no one had had sight nor sound of her since. Some even went so far as to say she was dead, while others held that she had gone to London to take up prostitution. It was all most intriguing and delightful.

And that had not been the end of the story by any means. As a result of the scandal, Richard Maynard had turned to drink and these days was scarcely fit to conduct his business; while the deserted baby was being brought up by a servant who said the master never even looked at it. Jenna, in her turn, had returned to Daniel's cottage and left her work at the palace, going instead to Baynden to help out. Yet most exciting of all was Benjamin's reaction.

It was Maud's opinion that Jenna's spell on him was still at work, for he had grown thin and haggard and unkempt, his dreamy eyes bloodshot with lack of sleep. This had given rise to a question: why had he continued to make love to Debora if under Jenna's thrall? Maud thought she knew the answer. Debora had used an even stronger spell on him, probably purchased from a descendant of Mabel Briggs, who had practised witchcraft in Maighfield long before Alice Casselowe was even born.

And this day, as Maud took her seat in the kitchens before an eager audience, someone called, 'Have you seen aught of Jenna?' and she was able to reply, 'Aye, I called on Daniel the other evening. She is keeping well and often plays with Debora's baby, poor motherless little thing. But be it Benjamin's or be it not, Daniel has threatened to kill the carpenter if he does not leave his daughter alone.'

This was a new piece of information and there was an appreciative murmur.

'Has he been pestering her?'

'He has been outside Daniel's cottage, begging to see Jenna, every minute that he is not working or sleeping. But she will have no dealings with him. And the other night saw the end of it. Daniel and some of the lads threw him in the river and threatened him with worse if he ever showed his face again.'

'So she'll never go back to him?'

Maud opened her mouth to reply but the master cook got in before her. 'Jenna is a kind-hearted girl. I think he might get round her yet.'

'Perhaps he should put a spell on *her*!' said a wit, and there was a burst of laughter in which Maud eventually joined.

'Enough of this,' said the master cook. 'It's time you all got back to work. Now Maud, may I offer you a jug of ale?'

'Oh most gladly,' she said, settling down, and hoping that she might glean some information about Master Tom's latest exploits. 'It is always a pleasure to drink here at the palace.'

At harvest time that year all the village seemed to be at work in the fields gathering the golden crop that would feed them for another winter. In the fierce, fine air the sickles flashed until the sun went down and then, when it was too dark to see, the harvesters plodded home in the gloaming, talking quietly, too tired to hurry or shout.

At Baynden everyone turned out, even the baby being brought along to the fields to sit in his sun bonnet and watch the proceedings, wide-eyed. From the little cottage, Daniel and his two daughters came to help; Agnes, as always, carrying her lute, and their food wrapped in a handkerchief.

It was the custom to stop briefly when the sun was at its highest and spread the bread and cheese out on a cloth. Then everyone would eat and drink before continuing with the afternoon's work. But this day Jenna ate scarcely nothing and Agnes, wondering what was wrong, saw her sister's hand go briefly to her stomach.

'Have you a pain?' she asked, but Jenna shook her head, not meeting her glance. Puzzled, Agnes picked up the lute, playing while the others ate, totally unaware that her sister was experiencing the most incredible sensation known to woman. Within Jenna's womb it seemed a butterfly had woken from its chrysalis; wings stretched and fluttered; a soul found a dwelling place. The babe, the very existence of which was a secret known only to its mother, was quickening into life.

She had wanted to be rid of it when she had first discovered its presence. And the formula was there, in Alice Casselowe's book, amongst all the other potions and cure-alls. Jenna had mixed it up and stood alone before her mirror, the cup in her hand, and had remained like that for an age, her green-gold eyes going from the cup to her stomach, flat and lean as ever, revealing nothing.

She had known then that she was deceiving herself, that she could never destroy a life put there by Benjamin, that she still loved him and would continue to do so until she died. With a crash she had dropped the cup to the floor, watching the dark red contents spread like blood. Then she had gone to bed and wept herself into sleep. Now here, in the field at Baynden, Benjamin's child fluttered inside her.

Jenna looked up and caught Richard's eye, seeing in it the strangely speculative expression he had worn of late.

Yet again she had the uncomfortable feeling he lusted for her and this, coupled with the eagerness with which he had given her work and his many calls bearing gifts, led her to the conclusion that his attitude had gone from one extreme to the other – his old feelings of dislike had given way to desire.

As if he knew what she was thinking he stood up and crossed over, sitting down beside her. His voice was drowned by the sound of Agnes's lute so nobody heard when he murmured, 'How beautiful you are, Jenna. It would give me pleasure if you were to sup with me at Baynden when the work is done.'

'I don't think . . .' she began, but he interrupted with, 'Please. It would be a kindness. Besides, I want to tell you something in confidence, something I cannot say here.'

'What about?'

Richard answered intriguingly, 'Debora. She has been seen. Will you come?'

Jenna's natural curiosity overcame her better judgement. 'Yes. I'll visit for a while.'

His pale features lit up and his mouth curved into a smile. 'Then I shall expect you.'

Before she had time to change her mind, Richard stood and picked up his sickle, indicating to the others that their midday break was over.

Despite the fact that it was only an hour after sunset, Benjamin was asleep; stretched out, fully dressed, on his bed, his face flushed with drink. He was dreaming a vaguely familiar dream in which he raced on horseback across bright sands, two tunicked boys beside him. As he shot into the lead, his horse seemed to bolt, and with a start Benjamin woke up and in a panic reached out for Jenna. There was no one there, no lean body next to his, no dark musky-scented hair lying on the bolster beside him. He was completely alone.

'Oh God have mercy,' he said aloud. 'I must get her back. I *must*.'

He sat up straight, realising something for the first time. If Jenna had been giving him love potions, as he had suspected and the wretched Debora confirmed, then there was no question that she could be doing so now. And yet he loved her more, if that was possible.

Lighting a candle, Benjamin sat with his head in his hands, trying to clear his ale-befuddled brain, and eventually, in the darkest hours of the night the answer came to him. Jenna was his soulmate, but it had taken their parting to make him realise it.

With a wild shout, Benjamin leapt out of bed and went down

the ladder. He had to see her again, make one last desperate attempt to get her back. Nothing could stop him – and even death at the hands of Jenna's father would be better than continuing a life without her.

Pouring himself another glass of wine, Richard Maynard said, 'I am so glad you came tonight, my dear. It is a long time since I have dined in the company of a beautiful woman.'

He was not yet drunk but had had enough liquor to loosen his tongue, and his companion was already wishing that she had not come. However, remembering why she was there, Jenna said, 'You have news of Debora, I believe. Where is she?'

'At Glynde,' Richard said shortly. 'Working as a servant in Glynde Place. And being serviced by the Master, no doubt.'

So it was true! Robert Morley had responded to Jenna's spell and had bedded the girl.

Mistaking her expression, Richard said, 'A terrible thought I agree. She has cast us both into the abyss, Jenna. But there is a way in which we can be avenged, the pair of us, if you are agreeable.'

'And what is that?'

He smiled unpleasantly. 'I'll tell you when we have eaten.'

He had prepared a good board for her; mutton flavoured with sauce, a crisp brown goose, Rhenish, a cake of sweetened spiced bread, and several types of English fruit. Jenna, eating hungrily now that her babe was quiet, was grudgingly grateful to him. Yet no quantity of good food could allay the disquiet that the tenant of Baynden aroused in her.

Richard, however, ate little, contenting himself with wine, whilst staring fixedly at his guest and waiting until Jenna had finished before saying in a slightly slurred voice, 'I'm going to be direct with you, my dear. I overheard a conversation you once had with Agnes. I believe you think young Richard is not mine.'

'Yes,' she answered slowly. 'That's true. It is very charitable of you to keep him here, in my opinion.'

'Oh it's not charity.' Maynard stood up. 'It is to lure Debora home.'

'You want her back?'

'Yes. Not because I love her, believe me. No, I want to get my revenge. I want to teach her to be a dutiful wife if it is the last thing I do.'

Jenna shivered, aware that he had come to stand behind her and wondering what move he was going to make next.

'I spoke earlier of how we could both be avenged. I'll tell you my thoughts, Jenna. Let you and I become lovers and turn the wheel full circle. Every time we pleasure ourselves we will be mocking the adulterers, paying them back in their own coin.'

Jenna turned to look at him and saw that the pale skin had two high spots of colour in either cheek. It occurred to her then that Richard was slightly crazed.

She stood up also. 'Goodman Maynard, please stop. I have no wish to be your lover – or anyone else's. Please don't speak like this.'

'Why not?' he said, lunging for her. 'Don't you find me attractive, is that it? Or are you just playing coy like that bitch Debora?'

His hands were pawing at Jenna's breasts and his mouth came down on hers in a hard, horrible kiss. With his foot she realised he was raising the hem of her skirt and, before she could stop him, he had pulled the material into his hand and was dragging it upwards. She felt his fingers on her thigh.

'Let me have you,' he said. 'No one will come in.'

'No,' she shouted, pushing helplessly at him. 'I don't want it. Leave me alone.'

He began to laugh, enjoying her struggling.

'I'll scream so loudly someone *will* come,' she said.

For answer he put one hand over her mouth, bending her back over the chair. She could feel him trying to enter her. With an enormous effort she pulled her knees up and kicked him hard in the stomach, the chair toppling over as she did so. He lay on the floor, winded, and seizing her moment, Jenna ran past him and out of the room, then out through the door and down towards Daniel's cottage, gasping for breath as she went.

In her panic she did not see the tree root in her way and, as her foot caught in it, would have gone flying had it not been for a strong pair of arms that caught her.

'Oh my darling,' said a voice. 'Why are you running like that? What has happened?'

Gratefully she turned – and saw that it was Benjamin.

Hours later, lying in her husband's arms, Jenna thought how strange it was that the same act could be both beautiful and hideous. If Richard had raped her she would have felt corrupted and debased, but within hours of his attack she and Benjamin had made love. She had felt his hands on her, felt him, hard and demanding, and it had been both glorious and exciting.

He had been so tender to her, had walked so caringly with her back to Daniel's, that she had not been able to tell him about Richard then or later. Nor had she told her father. It was best that neither of them knew.

But when Benjamin had turned to go, leaving her at the cottage door, the droop of his shoulders, the quiver of his lips, had been so tragic that all her resolve had vanished on the instant.

'I love you,' she had said without meaning to, the words tumbling out on their own.

'Oh Jenna.' She had never seen him weep before but now he broke down, sobbing desperately and hiding his face in shame. She could see that he was wrecked by all that had happened, and this left her no choice. She had walked into the cottage and said to her father, 'Curse me for a weak-willed fool but I cannot help myself. I still love Benjamin.'

'Thank God,' was all he said, and he had embraced her.

'But I thought you wanted to kill him.'

'He has been punished enough for what he did. Go back to him and live in peace.'

They had returned to the carpenter's cottage as a family, for, no sooner were they inside the door than she had told him about the babe. He had knelt to kiss the place where it grew in a way that somehow gave Jenna the idea it had happened before.

And now as she lay in her marriage bed, feeling the mysterious ring still on her finger, she thought about the future, wondering if she would have many children. Beside her Benjamin slept peacefully. Jenna knew then that he truly loved her, even though no spell or potion had been involved. Her heart rose with joy and she finally fell asleep resolving that the very next day she would burn Alice Casselowe's book.

TWENTY-NINE

Seeing spring come again to the magic valley, Jenna and Benjamin walked hand in hand by the river. Benjamin's touch was firm on Jenna's long fingers, there was gentleness in it and love.

Though the winter had been long and hard, holding back the flowers and buds, the earth had now relentlessly burgeoned forth and everything trembled on the brink. Lambs, born into snowdrifts, suckled by their mothers, wobbled about on woolly legs, raising their frail voices in the anthem of regeneration.

'Soon we will have our own child,' Jenna said, and Benjamin answered, putting his hand on her distended belly, 'It can't be too soon for me.'

They were enormously happy, as if their coming together again, putting the past and the bad memories behind them, had sealed their companionship for ever. In fact Jenna sometimes felt that the splendour of their love was too great, that neither of them could taste such sweetness and live. When she thought like this she would shiver with apprehension and wonder what she could do to ward off disaster.

She had not found herself able to destroy her great aunt's book, had stood with the dark pages in her hand for an age before she had locked it back in its box, unable to commit a lifetime's work to the flames. Yet in a way Jenna had kept her word. She had never consulted it from the day she and Benjamin had been reunited to this, even making the raspberry leaf potion to ease childbirth from memory.

And now, walking by the river, she felt suddenly in need of a draught of it, for a low, dull pain had started in her back and she was anxious to get home. Sensing her change of mood, Benjamin said, 'Are you all right, sweetheart?' and she answered, 'A little tired, that is all. I do not think we should call on Agnes today.'

But there fate interceded, for as they drew level with the little cottage, looking with pleasure at the lights on the pond as the sun dipped overhead, Jenna felt a great rush of water course down her legs and knew that the baby would wait no longer.

'We must go in,' she said, 'the child is on the way.'

What a fussing and rushing ensued: Agnes helping Jenna up the ladder, laying her on the bed they had shared until recently; Benjamin hurrying to the village to fetch the midwife and the raspberry leaf potion; young Richard's nurse coming down from Baynden and Daniel going out to find some cronies and drink ale. Then, in the way babies have, nothing more.

But during the hours of waiting, soothed by the herbal remedy, Jenna day-dreamed, thinking that she could see the hawkish young man, the owner of the ring that remained wedged upon her finger. She thought that she stood outside and watched his poor hapless body being hidden in the wall of her own home, that Daniel's cottage held the key to the mystery. Then she woke up and found herself lying on the bed, with Benjamin leaning over her and saying anxiously, 'Oh, my darling, you were so still and pale, I thought you to be near death.'

'Not I,' replied Jenna, 'I have too much to do delivering your babe.'

Afraid, Benjamin would have stayed with her then, wanting only to share her experience and be part of the child's birth, but the shocked faces of the midwife and the others drove him out to find Daniel. Yet, as he finally stepped from the inn in Maighfield, having drunk his fill, Benjamin shivered. There was a wind blowing hard from the coast, clean and strong and stinging with salt. It was a raw March night for his child to be born, and he felt a shudder of apprehension.

'I must go back,' he said to Daniel. 'I will not leave Jenna any longer.'

Something was amiss, he felt sure. Some cruel force had started its inexorable progress. Making the sign of the cross, Benjamin galloped his horse off into the darkness.

It was as he entered the trees above Baynden that he first saw the glimmer of a lantern and, thinking it a messenger from the cottage, hurried his horse forward. But there were two riders out and he realised, even at that distance, that one of them was a woman. At once something about her seemed frighteningly familiar and as the lantern moved in the wind, Benjamin saw the gleam of fair hair. It was Debora Maynard, come back to Maighfield on the very night his child was to be born.

His immediate instinct was to avoid her and he crouched low in the saddle, guiding his horse into a thick patch of trees. But then he heard a whinny of alarm and, peering cautiously, saw that Debora and her escort had drawn to a halt before a low-roofed building, her mount stamping in panic.

Why he went to help her he never afterwards knew, but go he did, catching her horse by the reins and bidding it be still. Debora did not even look at him, peering instead at the building in front of them.

It was a forge and as Benjamin did not recognise it, he immediately lost his sense of direction and thought he had taken the wrong turning.

'Where are we?' he said.

No one answered and very much to his surprise, Benjamin heard Debora's escort, a servant from Glynde, give a shout of alarm and gallop off. There was silence, except for the cry of that harsh salt wind; then every other sound of the night became magnified a hundred times. Benjamin's ears were full of the noise of tiny nestling creatures, the sniff, snort and stamp of horses, the cry of a distant owl.

He turned to look at the forge. A monk bent over the furnace, his tonsured head revealing the gaunt sweeping lines of a bony face.

'Where are we?' repeated Benjamin, but Debora did not answer and a brief look at her frozen profile revealed her to be in a trancelike state, gazing at the monk quite petrified.

Very slowly the smith turned his head and Benjamin found himself gazing into his eyes. Molten orbs of brilliance stared into his, everything of light and power reflected in them.

'Who are you?' shouted Benjamin. There was no answer as the monk turned away again and bent once more over the furnace. From nowhere possible in such a sharp hard wind, a mist came up and blew over all, hiding the forge from the gaze of the onlookers.

'Christ's mercy!' said Benjamin. 'Was that an apparition?'

Debora turned to him and he saw that she was looking at him, seeing who it actually was for the first time.

'Perhaps it was the fatal vision?' she whispered.

Suddenly realising that the last time they had been together they had been engaged upon the most intimate business of all, Benjamin hurriedly said, 'My marriage is mended, Debora.'

She gave him a look of scorn. 'I was ill when that happened. I am no longer interested in men. I have banished the evil one at last and so been banished in my turn. My only concern now is for my child. Do you know where he is?'

'He spends much time with Sarah Steven, his nurse. I'm afraid your husband is totally disinterested in him.'

'And does she still go home each night from Baynden?'

'Aye, and takes the child with her on occasion. You'd best seek her out, Debora.' Benjamin laid a hand on her arm. 'Forgive me for what I did.'

Her face was ashen beneath the lantern. 'No, forgive me. Sometimes I get a – wildness. That was what you saw. It will never be repeated.'

'Indeed it won't,' he answered bitterly.

'Benjamin, a final favour. Will you ride with me to Master Steven's house? I am too frightened to go there alone.'

He hesitated, longing to be with Jenna but knowing he could not leave Debora defenceless in the darkness.

'Quickly then, my wife is in labour and I must go to her.'

She made no reply, merely nodding her head, and they cantered off together towards the village. Entering on the eastern track they started to climb up the hill and were almost half way up when the bobbing light of a lantern revealed Maud, making her way to her cottage.

'Good evening to you both,' she called, her face a pudding in the flickering light. 'Why, it's Debora ...' Her voice died away. '... and Benjamin! So you are still together!'

The carpenter would have liked to tell her that he had not seen Goodwife Maynard for nearly a year, that Maud was a wretched old gossip and should mind her own affairs, and that his one thought was to go to Jenna, but he was too short of time to explain.

'We met again this evening,' he said abruptly and rode on, leaving Maud staring after them, her face going from a pudding to a walnut as an evil smile spread over it and crinkled every one of her deep-creased lines.

The labour had been hard and, at first, the mother had moaned in agony, calling out again and again for her husband to come. Then, at the moment when she had seemed in greatest pain, a look of determination had suddenly crossed her face and she had muttered, 'I'll cry out no more, no matter what. I shall ride this sea alone if I have to.'

For it had seemed to Jenna then that she was drowning in an ocean of pain and only by forcing herself to swim could she get the cruel sensation to stop. So, to help herself, she imagined that she was riding the waves with two tunicked boys. At first it had been difficult and she had fallen off into pain again and again but then, somehow, she had brought her labour under control and together Jenna and the boys had scaled the sides of monstrous white-tipped breakers that would have frightened them if they had dared to look.

The height and sheer raw power of the sea had grown ever fiercer, but the strange little trio had still plunged bravely on and scaled even the tidal waves with which that beautiful forcing ocean finally challenged them. They had triumphed. The water had calmed and then there was nothing left but a great and uncontrollable urge to growl like an animal and push the babe, strangely quiet now that the walls of his world had fallen in, out into the light.

The boys were gone and suddenly Jenna was alone, lying on skins in a great dark cave, outside the roar of vast and monstrous beasts. As the midwife said, 'Easy now, hold your breath,' the sides of the cavern vanished and she saw that she had been in her father's cottage throughout. She gave a shout and a gasp as the baby slid in to the world and no sooner had he been wiped and handed to her, wrapped in a cloth, than the gasp turned to a cry of greeting. A son lay in her arms.

She dropped a kiss on his brow and said, 'Can Benjamin come up now? He will want to see him so much.'

'Benjamin is not here,' answered Agnes from below. 'He is not back from Maighfield.'

'Is father still with him?'

'No,' came the slow reply. 'Father has been here some while.'

Jenna felt tears sting her eyes, but there was no sign of them when, an hour later, her husband walked in without explanation. Almost angrily she held out the baby.

'Here! Here is your boy. What do you think of him?'

Benjamin kissed the infant brow. 'He is the most beautiful thing I have ever seen – apart from you.'

*   *   *

The next morning, before he had had time to get drunk, two pieces of information were passed on to Richard Maynard by his servants. One was that Jenna Mist had gone into labour in Daniel's cottage and had given birth to a son. The other, that Debora had returned to the village and had stayed the night at the house of Thomas Steven.

The yeoman turned away, retching, as soon as the door closed, feeling as bitter as the taste in his throat. The two women he hated most in the world had triumphed, or so it seemed to him. The black-haired bitch who had rejected his advances had been reunited with her husband and given birth; and the biggest whore in the land had returned to the village, after consorting openly with the Master of Glynde, to rub his nose in shame. He felt he would like to kill them both.

Richard slumped down at the table, his hand automatically reaching out for the ale jug, regardless of the early hour of the morning. He drank a pint without pausing for breath and felt a little better. He poured another and the wonderful elation that only drink could bring swept over him. He felt human again, ready to plan.

Another draught and Richard could see everything clearly. Debora must return to him so that he could inflict on her a life of misery to make her pay for her crimes. She would die of a broken heart and no blame would be attached to him. After that he would take another wife and, when he was settled again, set about the destruction of Jenna Mist.

He stood up, reaching for his hat and whip, and walked a little unsteadily to the door.

'Going to church, Goodman?' a servant asked.

'Later, later. First I have business in the village. And Joan . . .'

'Yes, master?'

'Prepare the house. I think the mistress might be coming home.'

'Very good, master,' said the startled girl, wondering what could be going through Goodman Maynard's mind now.

The cold, salt-filled wind dropped during the night and Debora, looking out of the tiny window of Master Steven's house, could see that it was a fine March, a Sabbath day, with a high, bright sun already out and lighting the village to the colour of buttercups. She wished that she had more heart to enjoy the scene – so gentle and pastoral – but could feel nothing but apprehension as to what her future might hold. Today she might be a calm and sober woman, searching for her child, but at any time the other part of her could gain dominance once more, forcing her to flaunt herself at Robert, at Benjamin – at any man who might cross her path. It occurred to Debora that her only possible hope was to cross the Channel and enter a religious house, where, even if the wicked side of her took over completely, there was not a man to be seen. Or, failing that, simply to die.

Sighing deeply, she started to dress and was almost finished when she heard the sound of banging on Thomas Steven's front door and then Richard's voice raised in anger. Hurriedly she pulled on the last of her clothes and went down the ladder.

Her husband was standing with his back to her, drinking a measure, but turned as he heard her approach. Debora saw with horror that though his pale skin was flushed and mottled and his hair clung damply to his forehead, he was attempting a smile. The effect was dreadful; he looked like something stepped straight from hell.

'My dear,' he said, 'I had forgotten how beautiful you are.'

His speech was slightly slurred and Debora realised that he had been drinking since he rose.

'Richard, what do you want?' she asked. 'Everything is over between us.'

'Want?' Again that ghastly smile. 'Why, nothing but to settle our differences. I realise now that I upset you with my demands. Debora, I am here to ask you to come back to me. For the sake of the child, if nothing else.'

She did not trust him. His eyes were staring wildly and in his cheek a muscle had started to twitch.

'But Richard, I don't want to come back. I don't love you. All I want is to take my child and live out the rest of my days in peace.'

Once again he spoke in that terrible placatory voice. 'But, Debora, you are my wife. *I* can give you peace and love and joy. Please say you will return.'

For a second she hesitated, believing that perhaps he really meant it, that she might attain a semblance of happiness with him. Then she saw behind the veneer and shuddered.

'No,' she said, 'we could never be happy.'

The smile erupted into a snarl and his hand shot out and delivered a stinging blow on her cheek.

'You slut,' he hissed. 'You are my wife and must do my bidding – all of my bidding. I'll drag you back to Baynden by the hair if necessary, and there you shall stay for the rest of your days.'

She turned to run past him and out through the door, but he blocked her flight, pushing her to the floor and throwing himself on top of her. Shuddering beneath his heaving, sweating weight, Debora felt him push cruelly into her.

'Master Steven,' she screamed, 'help me.'

'He's gone to church,' came the growled reply. 'There is no one here to save you – and I intend to have what is rightly mine, even if it kills us both.'

'Richard, I beg you...' she gasped. Only to lose consciousness as the pain he inflicted on her became too great to bear.

That evening, Daniel and Benjamin carried Jenna down the ladder and, wrapped in warm coverlets, laid her on the floor of a cart and took her back to the carpenter's cottage, the baby – in tight swaddling – beside her.

There she was put to bed, and the child placed in the cradle carved for him by his father. They were both fast asleep by the time Benjamin went up to see to them.

He went below again, smiling, and took his usual place by the fire, watching Rutterkin eye the grumpy cat who had, inevitably, jumped heavily onto his knee. Benjamin stared into the flames, thinking how good it was to be indoors on such a night, for the salt wind had come up again and was howling about the house as if trying to enter.

His thoughts turned to Debora, not far away in Thomas Steven's house, and he hoped fervently that she would either go back to Richard, who strangely had not been in church this morning, or leave Maighfield for good.

Benjamin stood up, crossing to the window, and looked out. The sky was lit with a faint pinkish glow, just as if it were dawning, and the scattered stars seemed to be tinged with the same colour. Wondering what was causing the extraordinary light, Benjamin went to his door and opened it.

The wind hit him like a physical force and he smelt on its breath not only the tang of the sea but something else as well.

Benjamin sniffed and the acrid smell of burning filled his nostrils. A fire was raging somewhere in the village.

As he ran out he found that others were doing the same, and with the crowd he rushed up the lane and into the village. 'What's burning?' he asked.

'It's Thomas Steven's house and the blaze has caught the cottage adjoining as well.'

'Is Thomas safe?'

'There's no sign of him. I think they're all in there.'

'All?'

'He and Sarah – and Debora Maynard.'

'My God!' said Benjamin, and started to sprint towards the cottage. But as he turned the corner he saw that the situation was hopeless. The flames had turned the two cottages into an inferno, while the wind was fanning tongues of fire towards another nearby house and barn.

'They won't have a chance,' he said.

'Some say the baby's in there too. That Sarah brought him home for Goody Maynard to see.'

Benjamin shook his head but could say no more as he was pushed into a line of people forming part of a human chain, and set to work with the others to put out the blaze.

'If we don't get it under control the whole village might go up,' said an educated voice beside him, and Benjamin saw that Sir Thomas May had left the palace, and had set to work in his shirt-sleeves with the ordinary folk.

As the witching hour came to Maighfield, their luck turned. The wind dropped a little as the fire lost fury and finally was put out. And some hours later, when the worst of the heat had gone from the buildings, the men were able to go into what was left of the cottages and look for bodies. They were all there: Thomas and Sarah, recognisable only because they could be no other, and Debora by the wedding ring that Richard Maynard had given her. The baby beside her was nothing more than a charred heap of little bones.

Despite the fact that the girl had been branded as a whore, there were many who wept. And more tears were shed when the remains of Mother Beeny, a kindly old widow woman, were discovered in the house next door.

It wasn't until dawn that someone thought to ride to Baynden to fetch Richard Maynard, and it was over an hour before the yeoman appeared, heavy-lidded and smelling of drink.

'Who started this?' was all he could say. 'Who started it?'

'No one started it. It was an act of God. The violence of the wind simply fanned the flames to a frenzy. There was nothing anyone could do.'

'You should have sent for me earlier. I would have got my wife out of there. She was coming back to me, you know. Our quarrel had been resolved and all was sweetness between us. And now she's dead.'

Richard's head sunk into his hands and his body racked with sobs. Despite the tragedy of the situation, Benjamin felt he had never seen anything more revolting. The yeoman looked as if he had slept in his clothes, so stained and crumpled were they. In fact he smelt as if he had not washed himself in a month.

Sir Thomas May had returned to the palace and it was left to Mr Luck, the vicar, to speak with the voice of authority.

'The whole thing has been a tragic accident, Goodman Maynard. Be assured of our heartfelt sympathy and our prayers.'

Richard's head rose and it seemed to Benjamin that he appeared quite mad.

'Aye, prayers will be needed before this day is out. And prayers will be needed for the months to come. I know who killed my wife and son and I intend to have my revenge.'

'What do you mean? What are you saying?'

'That this is Devil's work.'

There was an audible silence and then, for the first time, the constable spoke. He was new to the post, having only been elected and sworn at the last quarter sessions, and he was taking his unpaid honour more than seriously.

'Are you accusing someone, Goodman Maynard?'

'Indeed I am.' Richard turned to look at Benjamin, who stood on the edge of the crowd, watching with a kind of terrible fascination. 'I am accusing the wife of that creature there; that creature who raped *my* poor wife and let her be shamed before you all. I am accusing Jenna Mist of starting this fire by witchcraft, knowing full well that my family would perish.'

Into the murmur Maud spoke. 'I say the Goodman speaks true. Why, Benjamin could not leave Goodwife Maynard alone. He was with her on the very night his wife gave birth. No wonder Jenna wanted revenge.'

'These are very serious charges,' said the constable. 'How say you, Benjamin?'

'That it is a monstrous tissue of lies. Jenna is still in her childbed. How could she have done this thing?'

'It would not be difficult for the niece of Alice Casselowe,' said Maud. 'She had the evil eye. Besides, Benjamin, were you not yourself bewitched into unlawful love?'

He stared at her in horror, his mouth dropping open, unable to speak for the fury that was rising inside him. Finally he stuttered out, 'My wife's no witch. You are all liars. I was not spellbound. I married Jenna out of love, not magic.'

'A strange love that allows you to commit adultery with the original object of your affections. I think there is a case to answer.'

Afterward Benjamin knew that he did the stupidest thing of his life, but he rushed past the constable and threw himself headlong at Maynard shouting, 'You bastard. You evil bastard. This is some kind of plot, I know it.' Then he smashed his fist into Richard's face and had the great satisfaction of hearing one of the yeoman's teeth dislodge.

Hard hands pulled him away and as Richard got up, cursing and spitting blood, there was a cry of 'Look!' and every head turned. Benjamin turned with them to see what was causing the stir and saw, to his horror, that Rutterkin had walked up the lane and now sat on the main track, cleaning her face with a long white paw.

'And there's the proof,' cried Maud in triumph. 'She has sent her familiar out to do her bidding.'

With a roar the crowd began to shout, 'Witch! Witch!' and there was a sudden rush away from the scene of the fire and towards the carpenter's cottage.

THIRTY

The first day of April, 1611, and already sweet, clean showers drenching the land: the village fresh and washed, the grass verges of the track glistening, the houses white, dark timbers fine as fingers; and through the village a witch-girl – black hair and golden skin and tall, lean body – being led by the constable to attend the presence of Sir Thomas May, Justice of the Peace.

In that April morning, the girl who walked to the palace, the girl full of love and kindness, the girl whose sweet babe lay wide-eyed in his cot, knew that she was about to be plunged into an abyss of darkness.

Jenna stood before Sir Thomas – neat-bearded, small, spend-thrift, foolish – and said, 'Sir, I know I stand accused, but pray tell me of what fault.' And he answered, 'Jenna Mist, if you deal plainly and confess the truth, then will you find favour.'

To which she replied, standing very dark and straight, 'Sir, there is nothing on my conscience concerning the deaths of Debora Maynard and young Richard. Sir Thomas, tell me my fault.'

Then, very directly, he answered, 'Jenna Mist, a book has been found. Even while you came here the constable's man searched your house and, breaking the lock on a box, discovered this.'

Sir Thomas put his hand beneath his desk and drew out Alice Casselowe's journal, thrusting it under Jenna's nose.

'Now what say you?'

'That it is a book written by my great aunt who died in Horsham Gaol for her crimes.'

'And you kept such a monstrous thing? Why did you not commit it directly to the flames?'

'It was her life's work, Sir Thomas. I could not bring myself to destroy it.'

There was a silence and they stared at one another, until Sir Thomas said, 'And tell me, Jenna Mist, have you ever made any of the potions listed here?'

'Yes, Sir. I have mixed the preparations for beauty especially at your wife's request.'

It was the wrong thing to say and Jenna knew it at once. Sir Thomas's brow darkened and he said, 'Don't try to be clever with me, girl. You know very well what I mean. Have you ever used the spells for bending the will of others? Remember, if you confess the truth you will be treated fairly.'

Jenna hesitated and Sir Thomas pounced. 'Yesterday I examined both Goodman Maynard and Mother Maud. Both say that you bewitched Benjamin Mist to unlawful love, and the Goodman bore witness that he saw you return naked from a Satanic rite. The case against you is strong, Jenna. *Did* you bewitch your husband?'

A million thoughts went through the girl's mind and she began to feel terribly afraid. If she persisted in remaining silent she could be punished just as severely as if she spoke. Whichever course she took she knew herself to be in great danger. Eventually she said slowly, 'I did give Benjamin a love potion, Sir Thomas. Yes.'

'More than one?'

'I... I... can't remember.'

Sir Thomas bristled with impatience. 'You are making things very difficult for yourself, my dear. I have told you all along to deal straightly with me. How many potions did you give him?'

'One a week.'

The Lord of the Manor leaned back in his chair and put his fingertips together, nodding. When he next spoke his voice held a soft, purring quality.

'I am glad that you are beginning to see sense. Now let us speak of your familiar. From where do you give it suck?'

Jenna stared at him in horror. 'What do you mean? I have no familiar.'

'Oh I think you have. Is it not a white cat called Rutterkin?'

'I have such a cat but it is a pet, a harmless creature.'

'We shall see. You shall be examined for such marks, Jenna. And if they be found then further questions must be asked.'

If they be found! Jenna knew that any scratch on her body, any tiny pimple, mark or spot would be pounced upon as the place from which the spirit drank her blood.

'Oh God help me, Sir Thomas,' she cried out violently. 'I am 'no witch. It is true I used herbs to win Benjamin's love but this talk of familiars and such is hideous and untrue.'

'We shall see,' he answered again. 'Now what do you have to say to me about the deaths of Debora Maynard and her child?'

'Nothing. I was at home in childbed. How could I have had anything to do with it when I could not move?'

'Quite easily, if you sent your familiar forth to do your bidding. And there are many who will swear that the creature appeared the next morning to see what results it had achieved.'

Jenna burst into tears, falling to her knees in distress.

'Sir Thomas, I beg you to believe me. I am innocent of Debora's death. Why should I want to kill her?'

'Because you caught your husband with her in the act of adultery.'

'But I have forgiven him that. He and I are reunited.'

'According to the testimony of Mother Maud, Benjamin and Goodwife Maynard were still lovers. She saw them together on the very night you gave birth.'

Jenna hid her face in her hands. 'They will not rest till they see me done for, will they? Sir Thomas, you must believe that I am innocent of causing the fire and its resulting deaths.'

His voice was frighteningly quiet as he answered, '*Must* believe? Why? Jenna Mist, by your own confession you practised witchcraft to procure an unlawful love. Why should I believe that you are not capable of far more serious crimes? I am not satisfied with your reply and I commit you to the ward and keeping of the constable for the rest of this day and night. Tomorrow, when I have spoken to other witnesses, I shall examine you further.'

Through her tears Jenna stared at him in anguish. 'But what about my babe? Who will care for him?'

'He shall be made provision for, never fear.'

'But I *do* fear. I fear the web of false accusations that is being woven around me. I fear for my life if my enemies have their way.'

Sir Thomas stood up. 'If you deal fairly and confess your crimes it will go better for you. Remember that when I examine you again tomorrow. Now, constable, take her away.'

Benjamin cried out when he saw Jenna leave the palace, walking between the constable and his man. He had waited outside, thinking she would be free to come home even if things should go badly for her. He had not suspected for a moment that she would be put in charge and taken away as a prisoner.

He had run forward to speak, only to be met with an abrupt, 'Benjamin Mist, you are not permitted to talk to the examinee.'

'But she is my wife!'

'All the more reason.'

He walked along beside the trio, shouting, 'But her babe needs feeding. She is suckling him. At least let me bring him to her breast.'

The constable and the deputy exchanged a look. 'Very well, but just this once. After today you must find him a wet-nurse.'

'Why? How long will she be in custody?'

'That is up to Sir Thomas May.'

In a frenzy, Benjamin ran all the way home, picking his son up from the arms of a neighbour and hurrying back to the constable's house. And it was by this quick thinking that he managed to get a few moments private conversation with his wife.

As she sat, her full and beautiful breasts naked as the baby took each in turn, the constable's wife briefly left the room, and Jenna and Benjamin were alone.

'My God, what's happening?' he whispered hoarsely.

'Sir Thomas accused me of bewitching you to unlawful love – as well as causing the deaths of Debora and her child.'

'What did you say?'

'That I did bewitch you. Which is true! Oh Benjamin, forgive me for that sin.'

He shook his head impatiently. 'I forgave you long ago.'

'You knew?'

'Of course I did – but that is not important. You should have said nothing. You should have stayed mute.'

'But then I could be imprisoned for not allowing myself to be tried. Sir Thomas told me I would be dealt with fairly if I confessed. So I did.'

In the passageway the feet of the constable's wife could be heard.

'Oh Benjamin, what am I going to do?'

The door was opening and they could say no more. Very gently, Jenna took her nipple from the now sleeping infant.

'Who will you find to feed him?'

The constable's wife, a kindly enough woman, said, 'Try Euphorix Hoodsby. She's given birth – again.'

'And who will look after him?'

'I'll take him to Daniel and Agnes. They will help us.'

Jenna smiled faintly. 'Give them my love. All that is left, after my love for you.'

As Benjamin stooped to take the child from her, he bent his head – regardless of the beady eyes observing him – and kissed Jenna full on the lips.

'I love you,' he said. 'And I shall stay close to you, have no fear.'

Just for a second they clung to each other and then the constable came in and they were forced to separate.

'You must leave now, Mist,' he said, 'and I want no trouble.'

'There'll be trouble,' Benjamin answered. 'There'll be trouble every minute of the day until my wife walks free again.'

Then he went from the room, carrying his baby, suddenly looking small and defenceless and as if he had no idea what to do at all.

As soon as Tom May broke the seal on his mother's letter, he knew that he must return to Maighfield. Pleading a family bereavement he left Cambridge and came back to a Sussex village seething with unpleasant excitement. Villagers stood in whispering huddles, and as he rode up the main track and turned into the palace beneath the arch, he felt every eye on him. Defiantly muttering, 'Whoresons!' Tom waved his flamboyantly feathered hat and disappeared from their gaze.

The palace was strangely quiet and the young man guessed at once that his parents were quarrelling; and, as soon as he saw his mother, he knew the argument to be even worse than he had imagined. Jane May's eyes were swollen with weeping and her normally ivory skin was flushed and mottled.

She flew to embrace him, holding him at arm's length and thinking, in a proud and motherly way, that her son could not be more handsome if he tried. Then she said, 'Tom, the news is so grim. Your father has examined Jenna Mist three times and she has confessed to bewitching Benjamin, though not to causing the fire and the subsequent deaths. He found, therefore, that she should be sent for trial and she has been taken to Horsham Gaol.'

'My God,' said Tom, sitting down, the idea that he must expunge some previous guilt by getting Jenna released so powerful that he could scarcely credit it. 'What shall we do?'

'Tom, I thought that you, of all people, might persuade Maud to change her statement. The old wretch has always had a soft spot for you and I do believe you could make her retract.'

'You really think so?'

'It is worth trying. Anything is! Why, I am so anxious to save Jenna Mist that I even thought of enlisting the help of Robert Morley.'

Tom looked at his mother thoughtfully, putting his head first on one side and then on the other. 'I am not so sure that he would be the right person to go to.'

'Why do you say that?'

'Mother, the woman who died – Debora Maynard – I have a feeling that she was evil. I do not believe that she would hide at Glynde as long as she did without attending Master Morley in his bed.'

'Tom, to say such things is slanderous!'

'Nonetheless, I once had to lie for that girl. She begged me to say to her parents that an accident had caused her to spend the night at the palace. I was never more embarrassed in my life. So much so I could not find my tongue and Goody Weston stared at me as if *I* had interfered with her wretched daughter.'

At the very memory of it Tom's speech defect became more apparent and his mother found herself having to strain to understand him.

'Yes, but the Maynards are Master Morley's tenants, as are the Casselowes. I think he should be informed.'

'Very well. I'll go to him if you wish.'

'Oh, dearest Tom, if you would.'

'And what of Goodman Maynard? You have not mentioned him.'

Lady May shivered, her flush disappearing and her skin ivory again at the mention of the name. 'Don't go near that man, there is something terrible about him. It is my belief, Tom, that he started the fire himself and then blamed it upon Jenna. I think he is a madman.'

'But not so mad that he has not managed to destroy two women, if what you say is true.'

Lady May sat down, looking suddenly drained. 'The fates are

ranged against Jenna, Tom. I doubt that we will succeed in this venture.'

'And what does her husband think?'

'Benjamin? I do not know. Since Jenna was taken to Horsham he has vanished.'

'Oh dear,' said Tom, seating himself by his mother and sighing deeply. 'I wonder what he is up to.'

'Who knows?' answered Jane May. 'Who knows?'

With his mouth dropping open, Richard Maynard dozed before the hearth, the cup of wine he held in his hand tilting in his loosening fingers and spilling in a thin stream down his leg. He was almost unrecognisable from the man he had been a year before when, had he but had more colour in his cheeks and less in his lips, he might have passed for handsome. Now his half-closed eyes were glassy and bulging, his red lips slack and wet, his fair hair a filthy mat about his head. He smelt rankly of a mixture of stale perspiration, urine and sour feet, and his clothes looked as if he had slept in them.

The fire burned low and Richard slept more deeply, dreaming that he was married to the Dark Lady, but loved another; another whose beauty was a dazzling combination of white-gold hair and eyes vivid as forest bluebells. In the dream Richard was running, speeding through the woods and dales of the magic valley, following the fleeting figure that ran before him. In his ears was the sound of an instrument like a lute and Richard found himself saying, 'Curse the half-wit. Why is he always here?' There was no response, the music continuing to play a bizarre accompaniment to the movement of his limbs, as Richard sped deeper into the wood to catch the object of his love.

Before him lay a golden glade, full of sunshine and light bright trees, which seemed to be the only place into which the girl could have vanished. He hurried in after her. She stood there, smiling, her features half hidden by leafy shadows and Richard advanced towards her with his arms outstretched. 'I love you,' he said, and bent to kiss her. The face that looked up at his was Benjamin Mist's and Richard started back in horror. The running girl and the carpenter had become one person. The dream had turned into a nightmare.

With a groan, Richard woke up, dragging himself back to

reality and seeing the dogs, which had been asleep at his feet, stirring, the hackles on their backs starting to rise. Richard moaned in despair. The chill and the reaction of the animals could mean only one thing. Somewhere in the quiet of that sleeping house the Dark Lady was walking.

In sympathy with the yeoman's jagged nerves his bladder shot him an urgent message and, opening the front door, he stepped outside to deal with it. Thus he was caught completely unawares when a man flew at him out of the darkness, knocking him to the ground even as his water continued to flow.

'Whore's pox!' screamed Richard. 'Who's there?'

For reply his assailant leapt on him, punching and kicking and being none too careful where he directed his blows. Doubled in agony Maynard shouted, 'You bastard, Mist. I'll kill you for this.'

The answer was two savage kicks from which Maynard felt he would never recover. 'You're ... ruining ... me,' he gasped.

'Good,' said a rough gruff voice and, as the moon peeped for a second, Richard saw that his attacker was unknown to him.

'Who ... are ... you?' he said, as consciousness drifted away.

'No one you'll ever meet again. I'm here on behalf of your wife, that's all you have to remember.'

Everything went black and the yeoman lay still as the sound of retreating hooves filled the night with echoes.

From the outside Maud's cottage always reminded Tom May of a ship. It seemed to lean slightly, like a vessel coming into port, and with its wooden boarding painted white and its structure so untypically large, the illusion was complete for him. It lay back from the track, on the incline to the east of the village, only a slight distance from the walls of the palace itself, and he thought it far too pretty to house such a repellant old beldam.

Though he could easily have walked there, this day Tom made the journey on horseback, tricked out very finely as befitted the Lord of the Manor's son. He was amazed, therefore, when he arrived to find Maud, as if fighting fire with fire, grandly bedecked in bright clothes – which Tom recognised at once as cast-offs of his mother's – and sporting an overpowering hat.

'You look very festive,' he said, in some astonishment. 'What a magnificent *chapeau*.'

'I wore that to Jenna's wedding,' she answered, simpering, 'and to Debora's too. That all seems so long ago now. How sad is the way of the world.'

This gave Tom the very opening gambit he required and as, at her invitation, he sat down at her rough wooden table and took a draught of ale, he said, 'Sad indeed that such rejoicings should have led to this – Debora dead and Jenna in gaol on such flimsy charges.'

She took him up on his words at once, her eyes suddenly hard as pebbles. 'Flimsy, Master Tom. Why say you that?'

Praying that his speech defect would not spoil his burst of confidence, Tom answered roundly, 'Because I do not believe Jenna started that fire. I believe it was started by a human agency and she is having to bear the blame for it.'

'But she is a self-confessed witch.'

'For using love potions? Why, if all the women who had secretly resorted to them were put on trial, I believe that half of Sussex would be in gaol.'

Maud said, 'It is a good thing your father cannot hear you say that.'

'My father has a duty to do,' Tom answered. 'I am a poet and see things differently.'

Maud did not reply and there was no sound except for the swigging of ale and the bark of a dog outside. Eventually she said, 'It may be unguarded of me to tell you but I had a son once. He was born out of wedlock, and to most people I pretended the child was my nephew.'

'Did he die?'

'Yes, he was witched. It was Alice Casselowe who killed him. But, of course, I could prove nothing. She was already in Horsham Gaol by then, serving sentence. And by the time I was sure of her guilt and would have made complaint, she had perished in prison.'

'So you are no lover of the Casselowes,' said Tom reflectively. 'Tell me, how did she bewitch him?'

'I called her in to help me when he was sick and lay in his crib in the chimney corner. And though she gave him possets and said to him, "Ah, good child, how thou art burdened" – and did this three times, Master Tom, each time taking him by the hand – he died that night.'

'I see,' answered Tom. A strange certainty was coming to him

287

and he stood up, leaning over Maud until their eyes were level. 'Are you sure that it is not your grudge against Alice that has affected your judgement of her niece?'

'No,' the gossip answered vehemently. 'I saw Benjamin Mist and Debora on the night Jenna was in labour. The witch's niece killed Goody Maynard for revenge.'

'You saw the couple making love? Is that it?'

'No.' Maud suddenly sounded less sure. 'He was riding along with her.'

'I see,' said Tom again. He put his hands on her shoulders, very gently. 'I am sorry for the death of your son but you should not let that cloud your judgement. It seems to me that all the evidence against Jenna is based on the hearsay of those who bear her ill will.'

Maud's face contorted. 'Get out,' she screamed, 'get out of my house. You cannot speak to me like this, Master Tom. Though you may have seduced me with fine words in the past, you have now turned traitor...'

And without further explanation she snatched up her broom and beat Tom May out of doors.

THIRTY-ONE

The sun came up dripping with blood; no gentle rose or amber to soften the eastern sky, no first deep shards of nutmeg, no faint gleam of gold to banish the starshot night. Instead a furious eye, glaring down on the world with loathing, ready to scorch and hurt and wound those who dared fall beneath its violent and malevolent stare. Could any good, Benjamin thought, come on a day starting with so ill an omen? Shaking his head fearfully, he went inside.

He had followed the cart that took Jenna – her hands manacled behind her, her long hair hiding her face – out of Maighfield and on her journey to Horsham. At first he had walked behind it, only a yard or two away from where his wife sat slumped, her head bowed forward, a stain forming on her bodice where her heavy breasts leaked out milk. But after a few miles the constable, who sat in the cart with his prisoner while his deputy drove the horse, started to shout at him.

'Mist, be off with you. You must not follow like this. Go home or I'll put you on a charge.' Then, when he had looked at the carpenter's dust-streaked, defiant face, he had said in a more moderate tone, 'See reason, man. It will do neither of you any good if you are both in trouble.'

Yet how could he ever leave her, now that at last he knew her for his soulmate? Knowing that he must appear to give in, Benjamin had turned round and headed back to Maighfield, realising that Jenna was too exhausted even to raise her head and see him go. But as soon as he was safely within his cottage walls, he had collected together all their money and a few pathetic valuables and put everything he had into his saddle-bag. Then, praying he would meet no highway robbers, he had set off on the nag as night fell.

He had been lucky, and had arrived at Horsham before dawn, going straight to the George Inn, which stood immediately opposite the gaol. The inn was the gaoler's tap, the place where he bought drink which he subsequently supplied to prisoners at his own price. In fact all their needs were supplied by the gaoler in return for cash, and it was he who took charge of any money allotted for support of the felons, either by statute or charity. Benjamin thought bitterly that though some inmates lived on the brink of starvation, the gaoler's purse was never empty.

He had not slept after his ride, preferring to stand in front of the fire and dry his sodden clothes, before sitting in a chair and waiting until the moment when the evil red-eyed sun had risen in the heavens. When it had come at last, poor Benjamin had gone to the doorway and thought it the most cruel dawning he had ever seen. A shiver which seemed to rise from the depths of his soul had sent him scurrying back to the embers, praying for Jenna's welfare.

Immediately opposite the George, its grey walls deceptively rosy in the early light, stood the gaol, separated from the inn by Gaol Green and a track called Carfax, nicknamed the Scarefolks by the prisoners. The place had originally been built as a religious house but in 1539, after the dissolution of the monasteries, it had become the prison for both debtors and felons. Within that limited space were herded indiscriminately males and females, old and young, the dying and the new-born, the healthy and the sick. It was the common meeting ground for murderers and those whose only crime was penury; for pimps, whores and parsons; for gentlemen and vagabonds; for women, and men too, accused of consorting with Satan to achieve their heart's desire.

So it was with halting steps that Benjamin knocked on the door of the gaoler's house, built on the northern corner of the Scarefolks, and asked to visit Jenna Mist, his hand holding out a purse of money as he spoke. Yet prepared as he was for the worst, he found it difficult to believe the sight that greeted his eyes.

The communal cell in which his wife sat on the floor, her back turned away from him, was filthy, the only places for relief being a pile of straw and a pail shared between all the inmates. Needless to say very few bothered with such niceties, and the cell smelt like an open sewer. Not only that but it was overcrowded to the point of suffocation, and the air, foul with ordure and unclean bodies, was scarcely breathable.

Some of the prisoners sat on the floor, their knees drawn to their chins to make more room, while others leant on the walls, pressed against the damp stones. In the middle of the area, regardless of the crowd around them and watched by a dirty, wide-eyed child, a couple were fornicating, as much to relieve themselves of boredom as for gratification.

Benjamin was sickened to the heart; sickened that such degradation should be forced upon the innocent as well as the guilty, sickened that children should be forced to witness all that was worst in humanity's nature, sickened that his wife should have been brought to the place where Alice Casselowe had suffered so much and now, in her turn, must follow suit.

Kicking the jerking couple as he passed, Benjamin pushed his way over to Jenna. At the sound of footsteps she turned, her face lighting with a smile that made Benjamin feel he could weep.

'You've come,' she said. 'I thought you would.'

He took her in his arms and held her without speaking, staying like that for several minutes. It was she who finally broke the embrace, saying urgently, 'Benjamin, I know I will never escape from here and I truly believe my life is drawing to a close. Promise me that our son will be cared for.'

Her words filled him with dread, a dread made all the more acute because she had put into words what he had been denying to himself for several days.

'There is no question of that,' he answered, almost angrily. 'You will be coming home to look after your son yourself. You will be acquitted of the charge. I know it.'

She smiled, despairingly, but instead of answering him asked, 'Have you brought any food? I have not eaten since I arrived here.'

Cursing himself, Benjamin brought out a basket prepared for him at the George and containing a cooked chicken, a loaf of bread, cheese, apples and cakes, together with several jugs of ale. Jenna drank deeply and he saw the potent liquid take effect on her, empty as she was. Her colour heightened, her eyes sparkled, and her smile brightened.

'I feel better,' she said.

Watching her, Benjamin was not surprised that those prisoners who could afford it spent most of their days in a state of total drunkenness.

'Better enough for me to leave you?'

Her face fell. 'You are going home?'

'No,' said Benjamin. 'I am going to see the Master of Glynde. Something has to be done to help you.'

'But I am sure he was the father of Debora's child, the child that died in the fire. Surely he'll want to see me hang?'

'Only if he believes you started it. Is he a sensible man?'

Jenna drank again then answered, 'He is something of a profligate but, for all that, no fool. I think you will like him.'

'I would like the Devil himself if he could help you,' answered Benjamin, then, realising what he had said, went white to the lips.

The bloodied sun had drained of colour and now soared high in the heavens as golden and fine as king's plate. April was everywhere, smiling one minute, crying the next and Benjamin rode from Horshan to Glynde through showers that fell in sunshine, shattering the prisms and sending huge rainbows towering over the Downs like magic arches. The shades of the fields, fresh from the rain, were brilliant, the colours of flowers: pansy, columbine, golden brook and the dark sombre blue of monkshood were everywhere. At any other time Benjamin's spirits would have lifted with the beauty of the sight, would have sung with the call of the cuckoo, but today he had no heart for splendour. Like an omen, as he entered the woods above Glynde, directly in his path a dead hawk silently swung from an oaktree's branch, its wasted eye regarding him sorrowfully, its tail feathers starting to rot. With a muffled exclamation, Benjamin hurried the nag on towards the great house.

Yet if the hawk had been a sign of ill luck its malevolence had not yet begun, for Benjamin just caught the Master of Glynde mounting his horse in the stable yard and obviously preparing to be away some days.

'Yes?' said Morley, rather crossly.

'It's about Jenna Mist,' answered Benjamin with no pre-amble. 'I am her husband. May I speak to you privately?'

His desperation made him abrupt but he saw the Master's eyes change as Robert said, 'You'd better come in.'

Benjamin shuffled his feet wretchedly. Standing in the beautiful library of Glynde Place he could still feel the stench of prison hanging about his clothes.

He fought back his discomfort for Jenna's sake. 'You know what has happened, Master Morley? That Debora Maynard who worked here as your servant, has died in a fire in Maighfield?' Benjamin omitted to mention the baby supposedly sired by the Master, and went on, 'And that as a result my wife has been accused by Goodman Maynard of starting the fire through witchcraft and has been sent to Horsham Gaol pending trial?'

At the mention of Richard's name a curious expression crossed the Master's face. 'Aye, I know all that,' he said.

Benjamin at once guessed the connection between the attack on the yeoman by a mysterious assailant – an attack that had almost emasculated Richard, or so it was said – and Robert Morley. Chancing everything, he said, 'I gather from your look that you do not like Maynard, Sir.'

'Dislike is too strong a word,' answered Robert, pouring out two glasses of Rhenish and handing one to Benjamin. 'Despise describes my attitude to him more accurately.'

'So you do not believe my wife started the fire in which Debora died?'

Waving Benjamin to a chair, Robert sat down, crossing one leg over the knee of the other. 'No,' he answered slowly. 'I do not believe that Jenna did that.' He paused then added, 'Though she is probably capable of it.'

Benjamin stared angrily, half rising from his seat.

'Sit down, Mist. I meant no harm. It is simply that I believe her to be... powerful.'

Controlling his annoyance, Benjamin said, 'Can you help her, Master Morley? The case against her is very strong. I believe Richard Maynard wants to see her dead.'

Robert looked thoughtful. 'They have a great deal of evidence against her. They say the motive was jealousy and that she had already practised the black arts on you.'

Despite the terrible circumstances and the grim nature of the conversation, Benjamin felt his cheeks grow hot. 'Yes ... well. I believe she once gave me a harmless concoction.'

Morley raised his brows.

'... but a spell of unlawful love only means imprisonment. What am I saying? If Jenna was sentenced to a year in that stinking hole, it would surely kill her, just as it did her great aunt.'

293

'But that sentence would be better than the death penalty, Mist.'

'Yes it would. Master Morley, is it possible that she will be found not guilty of the other charge?'

Robert fingered his chin thoughtfully, saying nothing. It was not the reaction Benjamin had been looking for and he stood up impatiently.

'Well, I shall continue to fight for her.'

Master Morley stood up also, signifying that the interview was at an end. 'I will do all that I can, Mist. Be assured of that.'

'Do you have a plan, Sir?'

'I'm afraid not. The most I can do is to give assurances that she and her father were model tenants. But mud sticks. The name Casselowe will always be associated with witchcraft in the minds of many.' His voice changed. 'And now I must hurry you. Go to the kitchens on your way out and my steward will see that you are given food for Jenna. Farewell, Mist.'

'Farewell, Master,' said Benjamin, bowing.

They were not to meet again until the day of the trial itself.

In the darkness just before dawn the gaoler's key rattled ominously in the lock of the crowded cell shared by so many wretched people and, by the light of a guttering candle, he began to read names from a list that he held in his hand.

'Richard Moyse, Andrew Waters, Thomas Doggett, Margaret Langridge, John Langridge, Agnes Swift, Jenna Mist, John Valentyne, Elizabeth Valentyne . . .' The voice droned on.

Those prisoners who were not already awake were shaken by the others and Jenna came suddenly to consciousness, aroused by a hand on her shoulder, to see Elizabeth Valentyne leaning over her.

'What is it?' she said, fearfully.

'The call to trial. Come on. The assizes begin tomorrow.'

'Is it June already? I've lost count of time now that Benjamin has returned home.'

'It must be. Hurry up.'

They began to file out, a thin line of dirty humanity, their clothes sticking to them, their hair hanging in filthy locks about their ears.

'God help me,' said Jenna, 'that I should go anywhere looking like this.'

But once outside the prison wall she forgot her appearance and sniffed the morning air, the first freshness she had smelt for three months. The scent of roses from the gaoler's garden made her want to weep. Already, despite the fact that a mere finger of crimson was in the sky, the air was warm and she knew for certain that it was a fine summer. Something only assumed till now from the stifling atmosphere in the cells and the flies buzzing constantly about the heaps of human excrement.

Jenna's heart leapt. She was outdoors again and her eyes, unstrained by the kind dawn light, were taking in her surroundings – even the outline of the grim prison – with a kind of love. Everything, the grass of Gaol Green, the wisp of smoke climbing up from the chimney of the George, seemed new and beautiful. She felt then that she could never bear further incarceration, that if she was found guilty of bewitching Benjamin she could not tolerate another term of imprisonment, that it would be almost preferable to hang and let her soul fly free than bear the filth and indignity of a cell any further.

The rumble of wheels brought her thoughts back to the present and she saw that two big carts, each pulled by a hefty carthorse, were making their way towards the group. The journey was about to begin. It was time for the Judge of the Assizes to clear the prison of felons – as he did twice a year – by hanging, burning or pressing them to death, or even setting a few of them free.

'Hands behind backs,' shouted the gaoler and manacles were put on so that there was no chance of escape during the day-long journey. Then they were climbing up, nine prisoners and two warders to each cart. There was a crack of whips, the gaoler's shout of farewell, and they were off to meet their fate.

In the first golden flush of dawn Sir Thomas Walmsley, Judge of the Common Pleas, woke in the lavender-sweet sheets of his bed, situated in the finest inn in Sevenoaks, and stretched his long arms above his head, yawning. He had been dreaming; a strange haunting dream in which he rode in the centre of a huge cavalcade of monks, part of a crowd and yet quite alone. A feeling constantly familiar to him in waking life.

He had left London early on the previous morning, travelling with his fellow lawyer, Serjeant John Dodderidge, in the relative comfort of a coach drawn by two fast horses, and boasting a well padded interior to minimise the agonising process of bumping over the evil tracks of southern England. Stopping regularly for relief and refreshment and to change horses, they had still arrived at the village of Sevenoaks, with its comfortable inn, in good time to dine both well and leisurely. It was little wonder that both Dodderidge and Judge Walmsley preferred the assizes at East Grinstead to those held at Lewes.

After dinner, Serjeant Dodderidge had yawned his way to bed, leaving Sir Thomas sitting alone, gazing into the flames, his light eyes reflecting the glow and his long fingers twirling the stem of a wineglass. He had been none too pleased when a noise in the doorway announced the arrival of a traveller, spoiling his solitary contemplation, and had frowned when the man had said, 'Sir, there is no room to sit elsewhere. May I join you?'

Sir Thomas would have refused had the person not bowed his way in and immediately taken a chair, calling for a good wine to be served. Then they had stared at one another, the frosty-faced judge and the intruder, until finally the newcomer had looked away, his gaze falling beneath Sir Thomas's light, unblinking eyes.

After a long silent pause, during which the stranger had consumed several glasses of vintage Gascony, he had plucked up the courage to speak once more and asked politely, 'What brings you to Kent, Sir? I imagine from the fine cut of your clothes that you must have journeyed from London.'

'Business,' Sir Thomas had replied shortly, but the other had persisted. 'I too, travel on business, Sir. My home being in Sussex. At Maighfield to be precise. Do you know Maighfield, Sir? It is not far from Lewes.'

As Sir Thomas knew all the villages and towns on the home circuit extremely well, he nodded his head in assent.

The other went on, 'Pray allow me to introduce myself, Sir. I am Tom May, a student at Cambridge and son of Sir Thomas May.'

Sir Thomas had thawed visibly. 'Thomas May? Why, I know him well. An estimable man and an excellent Justice of the Peace. Pray remember me to him.'

'Indeed I will, Sir. May I know your name?'

'Thomas Walmsley.'

'Not Sir Thomas Walmsley, the famous judge?' Sir Thomas nodded assent and the younger man rose to his feet and bowed deeply. 'I am honoured to make your acquaintance, Sir Thomas. Your reputation precedes you. How well I remember reports of the Essex Assizes last year, and the one before that too, when you sentenced four witches to death.'

Sir Thomas's face did not change nor did his eyes alter expression as he answered, 'One pleaded pregnancy, you know. But she was turned off as soon as the child was born. A strange business that, for no man would admit to having known her. I wonder if Satan himself was the infant's father.'

Tom shivered violently. 'What a terrible thought.' He paused, then drank deeply, his dark eyes suddenly intense. 'But surely you must occasionally come across people who are innocent? Against whom there is some kind of plot?'

Sir Thomas smiled thinly, his pale eyes unblinking as he regarded Tom coldly. 'It has been known, of course. But such things are a rarity. Remember that the women who come to the Assize Court have already been examined by a Justice of the Peace such as your father, and found guilty enough to be sent for trial. It is not very likely that we would all be fooled.'

'But it must happen,' Tom persisted. 'To a victim of a whispering campaign for example.'

Sir Thomas sipped his wine. 'I think it is a far cry from whispers to open accusations.' He paused. 'You are interested in the subject, obviously.'

'Yes.'

'For any particular reason?'

Tom longed to beg help for Jenna Mist but quailed before the cold, grey gaze regarding him, sure that at any moment his speech impediment would become noticeable. It struck him that Judge Walmsley believed himself an avenging angel, a force for stamping out evil, and seeing that right prevailed. The man had the air of an fanatic.

Changing his ploy, Tom said somewhat incoherently, 'A girl from the village is accused of causing deaths by witchery. But she is innocent of the crime, I am sure.'

'Is she coming up before me for, if so, I am not at liberty to discuss the case with you?'

'Oh no, I don't believe so,' mumbled Tom, lying in his teeth. 'No, I am sure that her trial is set for the Lent Assizes.'

'In that case I would be interested to know why you think her innocent.'

'Because I believe her a victim of circumstance. Her great aunt was indicted for witchcraft and died while serving sentence. Then, by her own confession, Jenna admitted giving a potion, that her love might wed her and not another. But now it is said that she sent her familiar to start a fire in which people died.'

'People of whom she was not fond?'

'One of them, yes.'

'I see,' said Sir Thomas, leaning back in his chair and putting his fingertips together. 'It seems to me to be an obvious case, Master May.'

'On the face of it, perhaps. But the husband of the dead woman bears a grudge against the girl.'

'I am hardly surprised in view of his wife's death.'

'But...' started Tom and then stopped, his stammer suddenly so pronounced that he found himself unable to speak at all. The judge stared at him politely, waiting for him to say something but the poet could do no more than utter a series of sounds, his heart shrinking beneath the gaze of the merciless being who sat staring at him. Of all ill luck, Jenna was to appear before the famous Hanging Judge, the scourge of the assizes, the destroyer of four Essex women convicted of witchcraft and sorcery.

Tom's plans began to fall apart. Knowing full well the corruption that existed in every strata of society, he had intended to offer a bribe. But face to face with this ice-cold man, whose eyes seemed to be seeing into his secret thoughts, Tom knew surely that to do so would be to put the death sentence on Jenna Mist, that Sir Thomas would turn on her in a fury of righteous indignation and send her to hang.

As he sat there, still silent, Tom May had the strangest sensation. He imagined himself sitting in a great hall, at a wedding feast, a bride and groom on a raised platform above him. With them sat Judge Walmsley, dressed in a gorgeous mantle, his hair close cropped beneath an archbishop's mitre. He was looking at Tom in the very way he was looking at him now, thinking him effeminate and barely tolerating his presence.

The daydream faded and the poet shook his head. He realised that Sir Thomas was speaking.

'... be assured that justice is always done. Master May?'

'I'm sorry,' Tom mouthed, recovering himself.

'I said that your village girl will be treated fairly when her case finally comes to court.'

Unable to make a reply, Tom merely rolled his beautiful eyes, turning away his head and realising finally that his plan to help Jenna Mist had totally failed.

Jenna was taken from the cage in which she sat with her fellow prisoners until, one by one, they were led into the Sessions House to face trial, and brought into a courtroom. On the bench above her, wigged and gowned, sat a man with light piercing eyes who stared at her unblinkingly. At the back of the court in the public seats, amongst that ocean of gawping faces, Jenna saw – in a blur – Benjamin and Agnes, and Robert Morley too. She was put to face the jury, who looked at her sullenly, and a clerk of the court rose to read the indictment. As he spoke, Jenna could smell hot, stale breath.

'The Jurors for the King,' he said, 'do present that Jenna Mist, late of Maighfield, in the County of Sussex aforesaid, wife of Benjamin Mist, not having God before her eyes, but seduced by the instigation of the Devil, being a common witch and enchantress, on 15 March, 8 James, did exercise magic and enchantment by which means a house belonging to Thomas Steven, the house adjoining, another house and a barn valued at £30 did with fire and flame then become kindled and burned from within, and that a certain Debora Maynard, wife of Richard Maynard, did die in the blaze of the aforesaid enchantment and witchcraft.'

There was more but Jenna no longer listened. She knew that her cause was hopeless, that her confession to Sir Thomas May that she had indeed enchanted Benjamin to unlawful love, had finished her. She ceased to care, gazing at the ceiling, letting her thoughts soar free.

She thought of the eternal beauty of the magic valley. Of how the great hills and sparkling river, the woods and fields and incomparable views, would be there long after she had gone; she thought of the continuity of life and of how everything would go on as before even though she had been removed from the world.

Without meaning to, Jenna began to cry. Not because she was afraid, but because she was going to be separated from Benjamin and Agnes; because she must take flight before they

299

did; because she would no longer be able to smile on their dear familiar faces.

A black cap was being placed on the judge's head and Jenna, at last, looked up into those cold, crystal eyes. All in the court drew breath as the dark-haired girl who had just heard she was to be hanged by the neck until she was dead, gave the judge a strange, fierce smile before she was taken below, while Sir Thomas Walmsley, looking strangely shaken, rose to dismiss the court.

It was over. A self-confessed witch was to die. The world would be a safer place for those left behind to live out their lives.

He had done it! With one stroke Richard Maynard had rid himself of the two women he hated most. He had triumphed over both the bitches who had rejected him and ultimately shown them who was true master.

He sat before the hearth at Baynden, not lit on this warm June night, and thought back over recent events. How much he had enjoyed forcing himself on Debora, the memory of it making him tremble with delight even now. He had left her almost dead of course, but that did not matter in itself, the only important thing that he should silence her before she recovered consciousness and spoke the name of her attacker.

Richard grinned with pleasure and reached for the bottle. It had been so easy to light the fire. Almost too easy! In fact he could never remember Maighfield being quite so dark and deserted. But then, when it was blazing and he had been sent for, had come his most brilliant stroke. He had not originally planned to accuse Jenna but standing there, staring at the carpenter, full of drink and with his brain working all the better for it, the idea had come in a flash. And then what luck that the silly whore's cat should walk up. She had been as good as dead then.

Richard drained his glass and refilled it, laughing at the thought of it all. This morning he had given evidence at the assizes, followed by Maud and some of the other villagers, and had had to struggle to stop himself jeering openly at Jenna. She would never know what she had missed in refusing him. If only he could have told her what a powerful lover he was and that in passing over such pleasure she had brought about her downfall. But, obviously, it was not possible and the annoying thing had been that on the one occasion he had caught her eye she seemed in a trance, as if she no longer cared what happened to her and had ceased to listen to the court's proceedings. He could have hit her smug face for that!

The yeoman stood up, picking up another bottle to take to bed. He could lie warm in there, drinking and planning whom he should marry next. Then he shivered again, realising that the house had grown cold while he sat so still.

'Curse you, Dark Lady,' he called out. 'I'm in no mood for you tonight. Leave me alone.'

Almost defiantly he began to climb the stairway, the one on which he had first encountered her when he had newly become the tenant of Baynden.

'To hell with you,' he called again.

Without warning she was suddenly standing before him, one lock of dark hair escaping from her wimple and he noticed, yet again, her beauty and her terrible sadness.

'Get out of my way,' he mumbled.

She did not move and Richard felt the first prickle of fear attack his spine.

'Be gone,' he shouted, more loudly.

Without taking her mournful eyes from his face the ghost raised its arm, and it seemed to Richard that she held a sickle in her hand. He knew that she could not harm him, that she was not of the mortal world as he was, but he was irrationally and immensely afraid. He turned to run from her and his unsteady legs gave way.

With a cry Richard fell the entire length of the stairs, landing on his head with a tremendous impact. There was a sickening crunch as his neck broke, and after that nothing but silence as the Dark Lady glided down the stairs weeping, then went away from Baynden for ever.

THIRTY-TWO

Morning, the mist lifting slowly from behind Horsham Gaol to burnish it with garish sunlight, so at odds with the scene that must shortly be enacted. Already a huge gaping crowd, jostling and scuffling, and in high good humour at the day's sport. Pedlars selling their wares, children playing and women sucking sweetmeats, the sight and smell of them filling Benjamin's nostrils with disgust. The occasion as merry as a May Fair, in fact someone had even brought a performing monkey on a silver chain, and one stall was busy selling rag dolls labelled 'The Witch' complete with long black hair and a rope around the neck. Benjamin would gladly have killed them all had he had the means to do so.

Unable to bear being part of such a mob he had hurried into the George to dull his senses with drink, and was not actually outside when the 'Ooh!' of the crowd told him that the gates of the gaol were opening. So he was at the back of the throng as Jenna came out and was forced, quite literally, to fight his way to the front, where he stood, breathing fast and bleeding, as the cart bearing the prisoners passed slowly through the waiting people.

There were four of them, Jenna and three men – Thomas Gerney of Henfield, found guilty of taking a hat, a purse and two silver rings; and Richard Moyse and Andrew Waters of Buxted, guilty of stealing a sorrel horse, two cheeses, a crock of butter, a petticoat, a carpet and two flitches of bacon. All four of them sat on the floor of the cart, their hands manacled behind them, and Benjamin saw that Jenna's dark hair had been swept up into a grey cap so that the rope could be put around her neck. He called her name but she would not look at him, frightened, he supposed, that she might weep and publicly shame herself.

The cart rumbled past and on towards the common beyond the town, the crowd starting to follow in a jeering, pushing procession, some shouting out obscenities and others calling, 'Whore of Satan'. Then the noise changed to another cheer as the plodding old horse rounded a bend in the track and the public gibbet loomed in the distance, a long beam with four nooses already attached to it, a ladder leaning against one of the two upright poles. Standing beside the gibbet, talking to the hangman, the carpenter saw Sir Edward Bellingham, Sheriff of Sussex, with his escort of javelin men, ready to keep public order by force should it be necessary to do so.

With a huge effort, Benjamin thrust himself on to one of the cart's wheels, trying to hang on to the hub, calling again and again, 'Jenna, I'm here. Be brave, my sweetheart. I'm here with you.' But one of the javelin men knocked him off and he had to fight to keep his balance, terrified of being trampled by the crowd and disappearing from Jenna's view. She smiled at him very faintly as the vehicle came to a standstill beneath the nooses.

'The woman to be turned off first,' said the Sheriff, and the mob, swollen in number by those who had been waiting at the foot of the gibbet itself, let out an almighty cheer. Then there was a sudden silence as the bellman began to ring the clapper to denote the time of execution had arrived.

Benjamin closed his eyes for a moment, and when he opened them again, Jenna, the rope being placed around her neck by the hangman, was frantically searching the crowd. Then she saw him. His darling saw him. And as the hangman kicked the old horse's rump and the cart moved forward, she smiled one long last sad smile before, very slowly, she began to dance.

The valley grew quiet as night fell. Over to the west, beyond the little cottage and the dancing silver pond, the sun lowered in the sky amidst a crimson tournament, tents and flags and devices clearly visible in the clouds. A round moon, pale as milk, appeared nervously and a thin persistent wind moaned round, taking away the last bright heat of the day.

Agnes, the baby in her arms, said at last, 'Do you think Benjamin will come back tonight? Perhaps he intends to stay with Jenna, keeping watch.'

'I'll go and look for him,' answered Daniel. 'He's bound to take the high track above Sharnden. Get some hot food ready, Agnes, I feel this might be a long night.'

Putting on his hat and taking a lantern, he left the cottage and Agnes was alone to throw more wood on the fire and see to the cooking. But when all her chores were done and there was still no sign of the men, she grew anxious and, taking a shawl, stepped outside to peer into the darkness.

High above, the silver goddess gleamed faintly, for the wind had dropped again and the heavens were misty and starless. There was no noise anywhere except, unexpectedly, a fox suddenly barking near at hand. Agnes, turning her head in the direction of the sound, saw that Jenna stood in the doorway, her black hair flowing outward like a veil. With a cry she spun round to look properly but saw only the shadow of the porch and the cloud of roses that rambled over it.

Shivering, she went inside and threw all the wood she could find on to the dying flames. The fire flared up and Agnes, crouching by the hearth, thought of another fire, a fire that had culminated in the grim scene at Horsham today, and brought them all to grief.

There was the unexpected sound of voices outside – men's voices. She ran to the door and threw it open in welcome, thinking that her father had met Benjamin and invited others in from Baynden to comfort him. But the greeting died on her lips. Her brother-in-law lay across the shoulders of Daniel and three others, his head hanging backwards and his bright blue eyes staring straight into hers. He was as dead as a slaughtered lamb.

Too shocked to speak, Agnes gave a choking cry and her father said, 'Rob Collyns found him in Hawkesden Park. He had hanged himself. He died by his own hand in the same way as Jenna.'

'Put him on the table,' answered Rob. 'Then one of us best go for the constable.'

But Agnes was no longer listening to them, nor even thinking of poor dead Benjamin. From his wooden crib beside the hearth, the baby had given a sudden cry. She bent over and picked him up and he opened his eyes and smiled at her; a small sweet milky smile.

Then he fell asleep again but Agnes, taking her place before the hearth, stayed awake and stared for a long time into the ever-deepening shadows.

PART THREE

The Midnight Maze

THIRTY-THREE

In the dense blackness that followed the hour after nightfall, the horse and rider, waiting in the copse beside the track, seemed to merge into the landscape, their breathing muted and the jangle of harness as the horse moved his feet very slightly, little above a murmur. The night had absorbed the man and his mount into its mysterious quiet.

Then came a change. The horse's ears went forward and the man moved in his saddle, leaning over his mount as he strained to hear a distant sound. It came again and he tensed even more: at the top of the hill a coach had started its lumbering progress down the steep incline of Pennybridge. The moment had arrived.

Like shadows, the two glided through the trees to the side of the track – well worn with the marks of wheels – and once more melted into their surroundings. Though the man could not see the coach, he could hear the driver calling to the horses to slow down as they started the steepest part of the descent of the main London to Mayfield coaching road.

He was ready. Pulling his neckerchief up over the lower part of his face, the highwayman stepped from the shadows, drew out his pistols, and, calling, 'Stand fast,' was at the coach door before any inside had had a moment to draw a weapon. Again he ordered, 'Stand fast,' and then, as the vehicle drew shudderingly to a halt, stared through the window at the people within.

At first he could see nothing but a large wig and a hand nervously turning a silver snuff box in its grasp, but then a movement drew his attention to a girl sitting beside the male passenger, a girl who leaned forward and gave the highwayman a curious look from eyes as clear as jade, before she leant back once more against the upholstery. There were also two servants, one young and frightened, obviously the girl's maid; the other a great hulking fellow who stared at the robber as if he would like to kill him.

A movement from the coachman's box caught the highwayman's eye, and he had shot the pistol from the man's hand and wounded him in the shoulder before he had more than half turned. As the coachman gave a cry of pain there was a shout of, 'You bastard,' and he saw that the servant was leaning out of the window, observing him.

'Come on,' he called roughly. 'Get out all of you. And you get down from the box. A shoulder wound won't kill you.'

The passengers began to dismount, first the wig, followed by the girl and her maid, finally the hefty servant. As they drew to eye level, the big man said, 'Who are you? There's been no highwayman at Pennybridge these six months past.'

'Don't ask questions,' came the growled reply, followed by the instruction, 'You men, lie on the ground, face down. And you . . .' He gestured to the frightened serving girl. '. . . tie them with this.' Throwing a rope from his saddle he turned his attention to the owner of the jade-green eyes. 'Where's the money-box?'

'We carried none,' she answered quickly.

'Really? Unusual for a gentleman returning from London to be without funds. Now where is it?'

'Tell him, Henrietta,' said the muffled voice of the bewigged man.

Shooting her questioner a dark look, the girl gestured inside. 'It's on the seat. The steward was carrying it.'

The highwayman smiled beneath his masking kerchief. 'Then fetch it, my girl.'

'You insolent poxer,' said the wig, still in muffled tones. 'You are addressing Miss Henrietta Trevor of Glynde and will show some courtesy, damme.'

Now it was her turn to smile. 'Oh Squire Baker, this is no time to teach him a lesson in manners. Let us give the ruffian what he wants and be on our way.' And with that she stepped up into the coach and returned a moment later with a heavy, securely locked box.

'Thank you, Miss Trevor,' said the robber, 'most kind, damme.' He was mocking the squire in his growling voice with its marked accent of some county in England foreign to Sussex. 'Now put it on the ground.'

She did so and, gesturing her to stand back, the highwayman shot off the lock, then dismounted, taking his saddle bags and flinging them to the servant-girl.

'What's your name?' he said, not unkindly.

'Sarah, Sir.'

'Then fill the bags, Sarah, while I take the gentleman's jewellery. I'll deal with Miss Trevor in a moment.'

He bent down, briskly searching the vigorously protesting Squire Baker – whose wig had now slipped to one side making the shape of a ridiculous spaniel ear – and removing his jewels, snuff-boxes and sovereigns. Then he turned back to Henrietta. 'Now what do you have, Miss Trevor?'

He leant close to her, his eyes smiling, and at that moment his loosened neckerchief suddenly slipped and they were face to face to face in the darkness. In what light there was, Henrietta looked at him, and in the brief second before he pulled the mask back into place, glimpsed a face that seemed hewn out of granite. She saw a broad, strong nose, a hard mouth, a determined chin and eyes of a deep sea-blue. She looked at his hair and spied, from beneath the black hat, a curl of fiery red. It was the colour of a fox.

'Forget you saw me,' he said fiercely, 'do you understand?'

For the first time Henrietta Trevor felt a tinge of fear. 'Yes,' she whispered, 'I'll forget.'

Apparently satisfied, the highwayman turned his attention to the struggling Sarah but it seemed to Henrietta that his manner had changed; that he was anxious to be away now that his disguise had been penetrated.

'Make haste,' he said abruptly. 'There can't be many more bags to fill.'

'There's only one, Sir.'

He looked back at Henrietta. 'Then there is nothing left but to have your jewels.'

She began to remove them, taking off the necklace and earrings given as a present for her eighteenth birthday, three weeks earlier, by her beautiful widowed mother, Lucy Trevor, all precious heirlooms of the Montague family.

'You seem reluctant,' he said, as she handed them to him slowly.

'They were a birthday gift from my mother. They have been in her family many years.'

Henrietta saw the deep eyes look at her gravely before he kissed her hand and gave them back.

'Keep them and remember me.'

'A gentleman robber!' she said, and dropped a small curtsey.

'No, not that,' he answered, scooping up the bulging bags and securing them to his saddle. 'Just as rough as all the others. Now, when I'm gone untie your companions and be on your way. And get the coachman to a surgeon before he loses too much blood.'

He swung up onto his horse. 'Farewell Henrietta.'

'Farewell,' she called, and stood for a second watching the departing figure before she turned back to help the others.

As was her custom every night of her life, Lucy Baker, eldest surviving daughter of old Squire Baker and, alas, the only spinster female left at home, began her ritual tour of the palace, making her way up the ancient spiral staircase, knowing that as she reached the top the chiming clock in the withdrawing-room would strike ten. This always gave her satisfaction, the very punctuality of her nightly inspection of the household imbuing her with a sense of stability in a world fraught with irritations and tests of patience.

And tonight was no exception. Lucy stood at the top of the spiral, looking towards what had once been the solar of the archbishops, and heard the gentle chime tell her that the time was near when the whole family would settle down for the night.

With a small sigh, Lucy swished her hooped dress through the door of the solar and, holding her candle high, stood looking about her. Despite the enormous size of her father's family – twelve children in all, and seven of them still alive – they had never, even when at full complement, used this room as a bedroom. Lucy's mother, dead these twenty-six years now, had always said, 'It was a place where great men sat to think. I do not believe it should be subjected to noisy children,' and the family had continued this tradition ever since.

Now it was serene in the darkness and Lucy walked happily through it and out to the small chambers beyond in which the children of the household had always slept. Nowadays, with Charity and Ruth married, and Peter the Vicar of Mayfield and resident in the Middle House, only Thomas and Nizel – Lucy's bachelor brothers – occupied this west wing of the palace, so that her brother George and his wife Philadelphia had the south wing to themselves.

310

Lucy listened for the sound of her brothers but concluded that they must still be downstairs. Yet someone was abed, for as she turned the corner to the south wing a petulant voice called out, 'Lucy, is that you?' and, after knocking politely on the door, she went in to her sister-in-law's apartments to see Philadelphia Baker sitting up in bed, clutching her hand to her breast and saying, wild-eyed, ' Oh, I cannot sleep for worry. George should have been home hours since. Why, Lucy, he was due to leave London this morning. I am certain that the coach has over-turned or been set upon by cut-throats. Oh, oh, my heart is fluttering like a bird.'

Philadelphia sat up straighter with those words, gasping hard and apparently having to fight for breath. With a shake of her head, Lucy sat down on the bed beside her, gathering her sister-in-law into her arms. 'Now, now, Delphie dearest,' she said, 'there is nothing to worry about. Both George and Sam Briggs are armed. None of them can possibly come to any harm.'

Two frightened eyes peered at Lucy from behind a cloud of dark hair. 'But I *am* worried. Oh Lucy, may I get up and wait downstairs for them? I should so like to.'

Normally this request from one sister-in-law to another would have seemed odd, but as Philadelphia was only twenty-six years old and a bride of less than a year, while Lucy was forty-six and had acted as the female head of the house ever since her mother's death, there was nothing strange about it.

'Well, dearest Delphie, if it would make you happy.'

'Oh it would, Lucy, it would. I shall get dressed again so that George will not think me foolish when he comes in.'

'Very well, as long as you don't become over-tired.'

Lucy kissed Philadelphia, who was small and childlike and what was known as 'delicate', and left the room to continue her tour. Passing her own large bedroom in the east wing, Lucy descended the spiral to the next floor, having now completely walked the square quadrangle around which the palace was built.

To her left on the floor below was the family withdrawing-room – once the archbishops' reception room and later the dining-room of both Sir Thomas Gresham and Sir Thomas May. It was Sir Thomas's son Tom, the celebrated poet and historian, who had sold the palace to Lucy's grandfather, John Baker the iron master, when Tom's father had died leaving the estate so impoverished that his son had had no choice but to dispose of it. The Baker family had lived there ever since, needing a place the size of the Archbishops' Palace to accommodate their vast horde.

Without entering the withdrawing-room, Lucy went through the door facing her into her favourite part of the building. This was the bedchamber in which the archbishops had slept; in which were the remains of a tiny thirteenth-century praying place supposedly used by Becket; where Queen Elizabeth had slumbered, for which special occasion Sir Thomas Gresham had commissioned a tower containing a staircase to be built so that she might enter it directly from outside.

The Bakers had always used it as the master bedroom and it was in this room that Lucy's mother had died giving birth to her twelfth child, Lucy's younger sister, Ruth. Now old Squire Baker, in his seventy-seventh year and with no sign at all of departing this life, slept there in solitary state.

As she came through the door, Lucy smiled at the reverberating snores. But the smile had an edge to it. It had not been easy for a girl of eleven to suddenly find herself the eldest surviving female and the one to whom everybody, even her father, suddenly seemed to turn. Nor was it easy to sacrifice everything to bringing up the family, only to see two brothers die early and her two younger sisters marry, leaving her to cope with the old squire, her hearty brother George, silly Philadelphia, languid Thomas, and Nizel, who could not look a woman in the eye without going scarlet.

Lucy crossed over to the window and, twitching back the curtains, stood looking out. A fitful moon had just come through the clouds, lighting the palace gardens and, in the distance, the church spire. Lucy stared at the building moodily. What chance had she of ever entering it as a bride? Sadly she turned back to look at the mighty bed which dwarfed the night-capped figure that lay in the centre. Even from this distance her father's bright red face seemed to glow in the gloom.

Lucy stared at the floor. If only she could feel genuine love for him instead of resentment that he should go on living, keeping her a prisoner of conscience. If only she were free to leave the palace, to become a wife before it was all too late. If only ...

A loud noise from the stairs broke her train of thought and she

312

hurried through what had been the archbishop's private room – now her father's dressing-room – and through her mother's saloon, now her own little sanctum, to the broad stone staircase known as the grand staircase, down which some of the most famous feet in the history of the Church had trodden. In the entrance-hall below, Lucy could hear a commotion, generally drowned by Philadelphia's screams and her brother George's voice saying, 'Damned cut-throat took everything. Everything we had on us. The only one to get away with her jewels was Henrietta.' He cursed, then bellowed, 'Lucy, Lucy, where are you? We've been robbed by a poxy highwayman and Henrietta is in a state of shock. Come along, my dear, there, there! Lucy, where the devil are you?'

'Here, George, here,' she called, hurrying down the great stone sweep and stopping on the bottom step to take in the scene before her.

Far from being in a state of shock, Henrietta Trevor, eldest daughter of the late John Morley Trevor, Squire of Glynde, appeared to be the calmest present, other than Sam Briggs the Baker steward, who stood, taciturn as usual, staring at the ceiling and obviously furious that he had not had the opportunity to shoot the highwayman dead. For Miss Trevor stood, with the slightest suggestion of a smile playing about her lips, watching George blustering and Philadelphia having hysterics, and looking scarcely ruffled at all.

Unobserved, Lucy studied her, envying the splendid little face, with its two dimples running in opposite directions, and the honey-bright hair that framed it. For though Henrietta was not a beauty she had an endearing quality that men adored. Quite unconsciously, Lucy sighed.

She went forward with her arms outstretched. 'My dear, what a terrible ordeal for you. Are you quite safe? Did the villain lay hands on you?'

Henrietta turned to her with a smile, the warring dimples appearing amusingly. 'No, not at all. He even let me keep my jewels.'

Philadelphia stopped shrieking and squeaked, 'How romantic! Did he steal a kiss, Henrietta?'

'No.'

'So you didn't see his face?'

Henrietta hesitated. 'Well, I ...'

George was suddenly all attention. 'Did you, Henrietta? Zounds, if you could identify the fellow, he could be caught yet.' He grinned at her hopefully, his large wig quivering in excitement.

Yet again, Henrietta hesitated, reluctant, for no reason, to admit the truth. Then her innate sense of honesty made her say, 'His neckerchief slipped for a moment and I *did* get a glimpse of him.'

'Was he handsome?' This from Philadelphia.

'No, hard looking. A villain really.'

'Would you know him again if you saw him?' said George, excitedly.

Again that odd reluctance before Henrietta answered, 'Yes, I think so.'

She was saved further questioning by the arrival of the Baker Bachelors, as they were nicknamed by their intimates in the county. Yet, though they bore the same sobriquet, two greater contrasts there could never have been, for Thomas, though now quite middle-aged, still dressed in the height of fashion, just as if he lived in London and not a remote Sussex village; while Nizel hid himself away in a low-necked coat with dark buttons, and an old pair of knee-breeches, as if he belonged on a farm. These were not the only differences, for where Thomas still regarded hiself as a rake and a lady's man, Nizel would have spent every day painting his watercolours and speaking to no female other than his sisters.

Now, on seeing Henrietta Trevor, Thomas hurried forward to kiss her hand, bowing and saying, 'My dear Henrietta,' while Nizel shuffled his feet and blushed violently, muttering something incoherent.

For once Lucy had no patience with either of them and she swept Thomas aside, declaring, 'Henrietta is tired and has had a frightening experience. Let us all go to the withdrawing-room for some light refreshment and then, I think, we should retire. You shall stay in Ruth's old room, Henrietta dear.'

She took Miss Trevor's hand and would have led her up the stairs without further ado had not George called out, 'One moment, Lucy. Sayer has been shot in the shoulder and is losing a lot of blood. Late though it is, someone must go and fetch John Langham.'

Henrietta felt the hand holding hers give an involuntary

twitch and, looking at Lucy closely, saw that her hostess had lost a little colour. But her voice was perfectly even as she said, 'Then I shall wait up for him. There is no need for you to bother, George.'

'There's every need,' answered her brother, as he started up the stairs. 'Dammit Lucy, he is my coachman and was shot by the man who robbed me. I have every need to be present.'

They continued to argue between themselves and Henrietta suddenly found herself left behind, mounting the grand staircase beside Philadelphia.

'I would have fainted,' said the silly little creature, her long dark hair escaping from the ribbon with which she had hastily tied it. 'I would have fainted because he must have been so *manly*.'

Henrietta laughed. 'He was fiery, all red hair and blue eyes, not handsome at all.'

'So you *did* see him clearly?' said Philadelphia, with more acuity than Henrietta would have given her credit for.

Miss Trevor had the grace to blush. 'Well . . . yes. I did notice his colouring.'

Philadelphia giggled but said no more and Henrietta was glad to enter the beautiful withdrawing-room which she always, on every occasion she visited the palace, greeted with pleasure. Almost as if she had once known every stick and stone of the place.

An hour later Henrietta Trevor sat before the mirror in Ruth Baker's – now Mrs William Fuller's – old room, slowly brushing her hair. She had dispensed with the services of Sarah, whose hand still shook so much that she had hardly been able to get the brush to her mistress's head, and was alone, revelling in the silence which had fallen since the Bakers had retired. Dearly as she loved the whole eccentric crowd of them, this night they had overpowered her. She put down her brush and stared at her reflection. Cool green eyes regarded a serious face with no sign of the unruly dimples.

Henrietta rose from her chair and slowly walked over to the window, throwing the curtains aside to look out at the night. The moon was fully risen now and the clouds had dispersed so that the gardens and the church beyond were clearly visible. There was not a soul to be seen.

Her thoughts went straight to the robbery and she considered where the highwayman had gone – and where he had come from. He was obviously not a Sussex man and she wonderd what could have brought him to Mayfield.

Henrietta turned away again but as she did so a movement in the churchyard caught her eye. She drew back. The night was not so peaceful after all; apparently someone was out and about and up to no good, for no one other than smugglers would walk about near midnight unafraid. Almost too timid to look, Henrietta gave one last glance before drawing the curtains tightly shut, and saw a vaguely familiar figure standing by one of the crypts. Then it had vanished, gone to earth – and she was left to go tremblingly to bed and pull the covers up over her head.

THIRTY-FOUR

Rolling slumberously across the vivid spring sky came a chain of enormous clouds: some like daisies with petalled edges, others as dark blue as the heart of a hyacinth, and others still resembling the white roses that would soon bloom in the gardens of the great house Wenbans, that stood at the very head of the valley of Bivelham beneath the dark and mysterious spread of Snape Wood.

Reflected in the stream that ran down to the farm on Wenbans land, the image of the clouds became distorted as the ripples turned their fluffy edges into wavering lines, to be banished altogether by a stone that was hurled into the stream, breaking the mirror completely.

The man who had thrown it, after lifting his head and scowling at those same beautiful clouds, proceeded into the farm, banging the door behind him and shouting, 'Kit, Kit for God's sake wake up. I've strange news.' He then made for the kitchen and poured himself a jug of ale, which he proceeded to drink, even at that hour of the morning.

He was an intriguing young man; quite small and dark with a day's growth of beard about his chin which served to accentuate the fact that his eyes were of a very light blue, ringed with a darker shade. In one ear he wore a gold ring from France.

As no sound answered him from the upper room, he went to the bottom of the staircase and called again, 'Kit, have you died up there? Come down for the love of God.'

There was a mumbled response and a moment or two later a bleary-eyed figure appeared at the top saying, 'What the devil's amiss? Edward, is that you?'

'Of course it is,' came the answer. 'I've been in Mayfield and seen Dash. There's trouble.'

Kit seemed to suddenly awaken, coming down the stairs quickly, though still yawning.

'What's up?' he said, seating himself at the rough wooden table and pouring out another jug.

317

'A gentleman outer held up Squire Baker's coach at Penny-bridge last night.'

Kit sat upright. 'There's been no one there since they hanged Sixteen Strings. Who is he?'

'Nobody knows. Dash says he had a strange accent. He's not from hereabouts.'

'Well he'd better get back to wherever he comes from. I'll have no strangers on my patch. Find out who he is, Ted – and quickly.'

Edward nodded, saying, 'There's a brandy run at Seaford tomorrow. It's said a hundred tubs will be landed.'

'And some letters for London. I think I'll make my way there this morning.' Kit stood. 'But I want you to stay here, Ted. I need to know about the new cove fast. I'll have no gentleman outer spoiling things for the rest of us. Curse the bastard!'

Edward looked disappointed but answered, 'I'll have him tracked down by the time you return.' He laughed suddenly and added, 'Dash says that one of the Miss Trevors was in the coach, being escorted back from London by the Squire. The outer didn't rob her.'

Kit fingered his chin thoughtfully. 'A dolly lover, eh. That won't do him much good.'

'No, it certainly won't!' answered his brother.

There was no window in the room beneath the eaves, the only light trickling through the thatched roof. Yet the room itself was large and had in it a bed, a wooden chest, a chair, a chamber pot and a basin. Clothes were scattered everywhere: breeches, a shirt, a plain riding coat, a pair of boots and a black hat. Tumbling over the chair were female garments: a scarlet petticoat, stockings and a pair of buckled shoes, together with a dress and mob cap sporting satin ribbons. In the narrow bed by the wall lay the owners of the clothes, asleep.

The man awoke, stretching his arms over his head, and this movement also wakened the girl, who yawned noisily and then fixed her lover with an accusing eye.

'So you're home, Jacob Challice. I didn't hear you come in. Where did you get to?'

He laughed. 'To Pennybridge – and back again. It was successful, Emmie. My first time out in Mayfield and I bag the local Squire.'

'Had he much on him?'

'His money-box and jewellery and some snuff-boxes. Sovereigns as well.'

'Was there anyone else aboard?'

He hesitated. 'There was a woman with him but she only had baubles. I think her name was Henrietta Trevor.'

'Oh she must be one of the Trevors of Glynde. Probably the eldest girl if she was travelling back from town. She has a very beautiful mother but her father died two years ago. The little boy is Squire now.'

'The little boy?'

'Henrietta's brother. Mrs Trevor had nine girls and then produced a son at the very last knocking. I think the shock of it must have killed the old Squire, because he was dead three years later.'

Jacob got out of bed, obviously interested, for as he started to dress he said, 'I like this place. The pickings seem excellent.'

Emily gave him a long stare before answering, 'As long as you don't fall foul of Kit Jarvis.'

Jacob turned to look at her. 'And who is he?'

'The leader of the free-traders. He's famous throughout Sussex. His real name is Gabriel Tomkins but Kit is his favourite alias. He used to be a brick-layer but started owling some years ago.'

'Owling?'

'The illegal lifting of wool. But he lands spirits and tea now. To say nothing of silks and laces. He supports the Pretender as well. He publicly drank his health when Jamie landed in 1715.'

Jacob pulled a face. 'He sounds quite a man.'

'Oh he is,' answered Emily softly. 'Quite a man.'

Pulling on his boots he turned away from her. 'I think I'll go out for a little. Just to get the lie of the land.'

'Be careful no one recognises you.'

'No one saw me.'

With uncanny perception, Emily said, 'Not even Miss Trevor?'

'Not even Miss Trevor. Now hurry and get dressed. I'm hungry as a wolf.'

Leaving her, Jacob went down the ladder and then down again to the kitchen, sniffing the smell of freshly baking bread as he went. And sure enough, there, pulling a loaf from the oven with a long-handled scoop, was Emily's mother, Lizzie.

She turned at hearing footsteps and gave Jacob a brown-toothed smile. She had been as pretty as her daughter once, but those looks had long since gone. Now she was a small, dark-eyed lump with greying black hair, one straggle of which hung unattractively from a greasy cap. For no good reason she filled the highwayman with a strange sense of foreboding.

Lizzie's smile deepened as he approached. 'I heard you come in. Was it good pickings?'

'Very. I happened on Squire Baker returning from London.'

'But no one saw you get away to here?'

'No. I vanished from sight.'

She smiled again. 'Good.'

As Lizzie turned her attention to the oven, Challice stepped outside and away from her, looking with pleasure at the prospect which lay before him.

Just beyond the cottage the land dipped in a flow of emerald green, and beyond that lay the darkly wooded hills which concealed Pennybridge and the steep descent down which coaches must go at snail's pace if they were to keep their balance. Other than a house at the summit, there was not a building to be seen. It was perfect territory in which a gentleman of the road might secretly pursue his business.

Jacob breathed in deeply, the smell of hot bread mingling with all the scents of April. He suddenly felt happy, as if he had come home after a journey, and wondered at the chance of fate which had brought him to the magic county of Sussex. Yet he knew he had made the right decision. Already he loved the place; already he had got a good haul; already he had cast eyes on one of the most intriguing young women he had ever seen. Jacob's heart started to thump at the memory of those crooked dimples. Sighing a little, he turned and went into the cottage and the prospect of a loaf of hot and delicious bread.

Henrietta woke slowly, stretching and yawning and looking about her at the pretty lines of Ruth's old room, wondering why she always felt such a comforting sense of familiarity whenever she visited the palace. Much as she loved Glynde Place, adored the long gallery, its crimson dining room, it could never hold such a place in Henrietta's affections as did the old palace at Mayfield.

She got out of bed, slipping a gown about her shoulders.

Sarah had rather snivellingly unpacked her night things on the previous evening and Henrietta's green hooped petticoat and emerald open robe lay on a nearby press. Ringing a little bell in the hope that her maid had recovered and would come to tend her, Henrietta started to dress. Fortunately the girl, looking quite her old self, appeared and within thirty minutes Miss Trevor was attired, her headdress with fine, looped lace fixed into place, and she was ready to descend to the floor below.

The palace seemed unusually deserted, only old Squire Baker sitting noisily breaking his fast in what had once been the archbishops' ante-room, now the dining-room. On very special occasions the Bakers dined in the great hall, but it was little used these days and was beginning to fall into a state of disrepair.

Dropping a curtsey, Henrietta went to greet him. The old man's florid face turned in her direction and, just for a moment he stared at her, his gimlet eyes suspicious, until he realised who she was and gave a wintery smile.

'Good morning Squire Baker. I was looking for Lucy. Do you know where she is?'

His chest rumbled and he began to speak. 'In the servants' quarters, tending the coachman. He was shot you know. They say there's some damnable highwayman down at Pennybridge. I'd string him up if I caught him. In chains! Vermin, the lot of them. Don't deserve to live!'

Henrietta shivered, imagining vividly the terrible agonising kicks of the dance of death.

'Then I'll join her there.'

The old man, his mouth crammed with food, flapped a hand in acknowledgement, and Henrietta left the room, descending the grand staircase and going across the central courtyard to the kitchens, then round to the tower where the servants were housed. Following the sound of Lucy's voice she came to a small bedchamber, furnished only by a bed and a chest, to find the wounded servant lying asleep and Lucy and a man engaged in earnest conversation. They jumped apart as Henrietta tapped on the door and entered.

'Why,' said her hostess, flushing a little, 'Henrietta dear! I did not know you were about. I have been keeping watch over poor Sayer with Mr Langham the surgeon, who last night extracted a bullet from his shoulder. May I introduce you? Henrietta, this is

321

Mr John Langham of Luckhurst Hall. John, this is Miss Henrietta Trevor of Glynde.'

'How do you do, Miss Trevor?' said the surgeon, rising and executing a polite bow. Henrietta curtsied and murmured a greeting, covertly watching him as she did so.

She took her new acquaintance to be about fifty years old and, though not at all handsome, having a tendency to be plump and moon-faced beneath his wig, she saw that he had a pair of magnificent eyes, deep and penetrating. Henrietta felt drawn to him at once. And so too, she thought, was Lucy Baker, whose very manner spoke volumes of the depths of her feelings. Henrietta found herself hoping for her dear friend's sake that the surgeon was not a married man.

Lucy said now, 'Have you breakfasted yet?' and when Henrietta shook her head, went on, 'Perhaps we could all take a light repast together. John, I do believe that you should have something to eat after such a long night's vigil.'

'Gladly,' he said, giving another courteous bow. 'And then before I leave perhaps I should look in on Philadelphia.'

'I wish you would. She has taken to her bed this morning.' In response to Henrietta's slightly puzzled look Lucy went on, 'She is so prone to nervous disorders, you know. She should have gone to Aylwins as a bride, but George wished that she would stay with me for a while in order to feel her feet.'

Henrietta smiled. The prosperous Bakers owned not only the palace but the house built for Sir Thomas Gresham, which they had renamed the Middle House, together with Aylwins, once the dwelling of Thomas Aynscombe, the iron master. It was the custom for the heir to live in the old Gresham residence, and, indeed, there dwelt Peter Baker, the eldest surviving son, and also the Vicar of Mayfield. Henrietta could not help but think that the Bakers had an almost octopuslike hold on the village.

Now she said, 'I will see Philadelphia before I leave.'

'Must you go so soon?' answered Lucy, and that one sentence spoke eloquently of her troubles.

'I am afraid I must. My mother was expecting me last night. She has come to rely on me rather a good deal since my father died.'

'Oh I *do* understand,' sighed Lucy with feeling.

And she sighed all the more when, an hour later, Mr

Langham's horse and the Baker coach which was to carry Henrietta home, were brought to the front of the palace.

'I shall miss you,' she said, and Henrietta could not help but notice that the surgeon's fingers gripped the maiden lady's hand tightly as he bent to kiss it. Feeling an intruder, Henrietta looked away. When she glanced up again, John Langham had mounted his horse and was riding off.

'Come to see us soon, dearest Henrietta,' said Lucy. 'And give my warmest regards to your dear mother, and all your sisters and little brother.'

Henrietta hugged her, momentarily feeling the sadness which always swept her when she had to leave the palace.

'I will try.'

'It may be sooner than you think. If they catch that robber, you'll have to identify him.'

'I hope not,' answered Henrietta, before she could stop herself. Lucy looked astounded but, unwilling to explain, Miss Trevor climbed into the coach, Sarah clambered up behind, and they were off to Glynde with a quick wave and a blown kiss.

But Lucy's words played on Henrietta's mind. If the high-wayman were caught and she was sent for, it would be her duty to tell the truth. For all he had returned her jewels, it was a fact that he and his fellows were a scourge to the countryside, the worst kind of criminal who attacked the innocent and defence-less under cover of darkness. Yet how loath she would be to condemn a man to die. She abominated hanging and even now still had to avert her eyes from a gibbet lest she faint. She feared that death so much yet, cruelly, thoughts of it came to plague her at night. Time and again she dreamed that she was being forced to witness an execution, an execution of someone she loved and yet was powerless to help. Always she would wake up crying and sweating, her hands on her neck, and now the very thought of it made her choke.

Sarah looked at her curiously.

'Are you all right, mistress?'

'A tickle in my throat, that is all. Where are we?'

'At Cross in Hand. Shall we stop before we reach Glynde?'

'Yes, we shall.' Henrietta put her head out of the window and called to the coachman, 'I would like to rest at the Blackboys Inn for a while.'

'Very good, Miss Trevor.'

Sarah grinned, wriggling in her seat in a most uncomfortable manner, and it was with some relief that Miss Trevor drew up before the ancient coaching inn and saw her servant dive off into the bushes. With the Baker coachman preceding her as escort, Henrietta went inside.

The inn was fairly empty and she was shown to a small snug with only one other occupant. He stood up politely as she came in, seeing that she was a woman of position, and asked, 'Does my presence embarrass you, Madam? Would you prefer me to go?'

Very charmingly Henrietta smiled and said, 'No. Do stay. I shall not be here long.'

The man bowed, sweeping off his hat. Henrietta noticed that, a little unfashionably, he wore a tie wig, the queue woven with a black ribbon. She wondered at once who he was, for this was a wig that though considered undress was worn by every social class.

Curious, she asked, 'Are you travelling far?' and when he replied, 'To Mayfield,' was all attention.

'I have just come from there,' she volunteered, studying him closely.

He was reasonably tall, rather slender in build, his features mobile and expressive. Predominant in his face were a serious pair of eyes, pewter in shade and very well shaped. Henrietta noticed, too, that he had beautiful hands, long-fingered, almost feminine looking.

He was speaking. '. . . and don't know the area at all. I am going there to visit.'

'The Bakers?'

The man suddenly looked cautious. 'No. To renew acquaintance with an elderly aunt.'

'I see.'

There was silence as they stared at one another. Right at the back of Henrietta's brain came the thought that she had met him before. Much to her surprise he said at that exact moment, 'Forgive me, but do I know you?'

She laughed. 'I was thinking the same thing.'

'Hastings? Could it be there? I have lived in the vicinity some while.'

'I doubt it. I very rarely go there.'

'Then it is a mystery.' He stood up again and bowed. 'Allow

me to introduce myself. Nicholas Grey. Lieutenant Nicholas Grey.'

'Henrietta Trevor of Glynde.' She inclined her head. 'So you are an army man, Lieutenant?'

Grey hesitated and a shadow crossed his face. Then his eyes became even graver as he said in a lowered tone, 'No, actually not. I am attached to the Excise Service.'

'You are a Riding Officer?' asked Henrietta wide-eyed.

'Yes.'

'And bound for Mayfield? May I ask for what purpose?'

'To catch Kit Jarvis.'

'Kit Jarvis!' said Henrietta, swamped with relief. 'Then I wish you luck, sir.'

'I shall need it,' said Nicholas Grey grimly, 'because I swear to God I'll have him before this year is out – or die.' He straightened himself. 'I must take my leave. I have said too much already. I do trust that you will keep my confidence, Miss Trevor.'

'You may rely on that.'

'Thank you.' He picked up his things and went to the door, then turned to give her a smile. Henrietta noticed that, of all the inappropriate things, the Riding Officer carried a lute.

THIRTY-FIVE

A spring night with a fine light breeze blowing the racing clouds over the face of a high young moon. Everything still, and then a faint whistle in the darkness, followed by a low chuckle. From the secret pathway through the fields and woods, coming out at Coggins Mill, two figures detached themselves from the dense shadows. Kit and Edward Jarvis had left the smugglers' road and were calmly walking towards the public highway.

In silence, Edward mounted the horse that had been left tethered to a tree; while Kit went on foot to the three attached cottages overlooking the sweep of countryside leading to the twisting road at Pennybridge. He knocked on the door of the central one, smiling to himself, then when Lizzie Pearce answered it, candle held high, an anxious expression on her face, he broke into a laugh.

'Lizzie, you old witch. How are you?'

She quailed before him. 'Kit! I never thought to see you here.'

'I'm sure you didn't,' he answered, still grinning. 'May I step inside?'

Reluctantly she drew back, allowing him just enough room to walk past her, watching while Kit went straight to the fire in the inglenook, holding his hands out to it.

'It's still cold for all it's the end of April.'

'Aye, it is. Will you stay for a jug of ale?'

'I'll stay longer than that. I believe you have certain information for me, Lizzie.'

The woman went pale and said feebly, 'What information would that be, Kit?'

'What indeed?' He turned from the fire to look at her. 'I'm told that Emmy is back.'

Lizzie hesitated, wondering whether to tell the truth or feign ignorance. Finally she said, 'She's visiting, yes.'

'Visiting is it? That's not what I was told. I heard she was back from London with a fancy man. A gentleman outer who lives here as well. So you're harbouring criminals now, eh Lizzie?'

The woman rallied a little. 'Who are you to talk, Kit Jarvis? Why, if the names of all who give you safe house and whose cellars you stock were to be revealed, then most of Mayfield is harbouring a criminal.'

He laughed more gently. 'Don't be riled. I spoke in jest. But you know how it was with me and Emmy.'

'I know that she found you in bed with a London doxie and left you flat.'

'That was just another female. But I had feelings for Emmy. Always did, from the moment I set eyes on her. I dare say in time I would have married her.'

The atmosphere between them had relaxed and now they sat down on either side of the fire, smiling at each other.

'So who is her new lover? What's his name?'

Lizzie looked cautious again. 'Why do you want to know?'

'Because he's on my patch, that's why.'

'But he's not doing you any harm. You're not in the same line of trade.'

'He'll attract attention to Mayfield.'

Lizzie laughed scornfully. 'Mayfield is the centre of attention already. It is hardly likely to gain more through him. What's the real reason, Kit? Are you jealous?'

He looked uncomfortable. 'A little, yes. I'll brook no challenge to my leadership.'

There was a companionable silence while the two listened to the song of the fire; the spit of logs and the lick of flames, and the puff of the blackened kettle that stood on the grate. Kit, following an obvious line of thought, asked 'Are you all right for tea?'

'I could do with some more.'

'Then you shall have it. Anything else?'

'I can't afford it.'

Kit leaned forward, putting his elbows on his knees and cupping his face in his hands. 'Then you shall have a gift. Perhaps some lace. If you will give me one piece of information.'

'The gentleman's outer name, I suppose.'

'Correct. Who is he?'

'Jacob,' answered Lizzie slowly, suddenly relishing the betrayal. 'Jacob Challice from Norfolk.'

When Edward left Kit at Coggins Mill, he rode swiftly up the eastern track to the village, passing a cottage that looked like a ship on his right and, amongst others, one of his safe houses with a concealed cellar. But tonight he had no wish to stop and instead hurried to the brow of the hill and, as always, cast his eyes in the direction of the palace.

He loved the place; loved its old warm lines and glorious history. In fact he liked nothing better than to dwell on its past; on archbishops strong and weak, pious and plotting; and on the private citizens who had owned it – Sir Thomas Gresham, courtier to Queen Elizabeth; Sir Henry Neville; Sir Thomas May and his brilliant son Tom, who had become both poet and historian and who, after losing favour with Charles I, had turned against the king and taken the side of the Commonwealth in the Civil War.

Edward thought of Tom's death, alone and unmarried, strangled by his nightcap. It was said that from being a handsome youth, Tom had gained weight in middle life and on going 'well to bed' was found dead next morning, the tragedy apparently caused by Tom tying the strings of his nightcap too tightly beneath his fat cheeks and chin. Edward had once discovered a little rhyme about his hero which read, 'As one put drunk into the packet-boat, Tom May was hurried hence and did not know't.'

Thinking about it always made him smile and he wondered why he should have such a soft spot for this tragicomic figure from history. He thought that possibly it was they had something in common. Deep down in Edward, though he would rather have died than let it be found out by anyone – particularly Kit – was a yearning for handsome young men.

The thought made him shudder and he hurried on, passing the Middle House and the Star Inn and all the many cottages that huddled on either side of the track and about the church, until he came to the Royal Oak, where he tethered his horse to a post and went inside.

He was greeted with enthusiasm – the Oak being not only a safe house but a local distribution point – for rubbing shoulders with the agricultural workers were several members of Kit's gang, and some present were both. These were hard times and men could receive more for a single night's work with the free-traders than they had a hope of earning during a week's labouring.

Detaching himself from the others, a man came to join the new arrival. It was the infamous Francis Hammond, recounting with glee the story of how he had been arrested by the Jaretts – a father and son still swearing revenge against the smugglers for a beating they had once received – and of how Justice Selby, the magistrate, had refused to commit him and had, instead, ordered the Jarretts to accept Hammond's fine as recompense.

'It was a triumph,' he said now, rubbing his hands in glee. 'You should have seen their stupid faces, like a pair of cheeses on the sweat, Edward.'

He was a jolly little man, round as a ball and quite as bouncy; his principal preoccupation, other than his function as a free-trader and Jacobite, being women, a fact that Edward found faintly distasteful and Kit amusing.

'Oh, I met a lovely dolly-mop in London last run. Oh, oh, oh could she jig Moll Peatley's,' said Francis now.

Edward pulled a face. 'I have no wish to hear the details of your sordid life, thank you.'

'Not a rum puff are you?' asked Hammond, and then screamed with laughter.

The question hit Edward's weak spot and he answered angrily, 'No. Nor a rum dell lover either. Be off!'

Their voices had risen without them knowing and there was a sudden hush in the long room, its walls and beams blackened with pipe-smoke and its stone floor worn with the centuries of feet that had trodden it. Into this silence, rather as if he was making an entrance in a play, a newcomer walked in from outside and, as every head wheeled round to look at him, gave a nervous smile.

The landlord, a swarthy pock-marked man known as Unkle to free-traders and villagers alike, hissed, 'Now lads,' and then stepped forward. 'Can I help you, Sir?' he asked in a different voice.

'Er, yes,' the man answered diffidently. 'I was hoping to find a room for the night. I am here visiting relations but discover there is no place for me to stay at the moment.'

'Well, it might be possible,' Unkle said slowly, aware of every eye upon him and not wanting to make a mistake before Kit Jarvis's brother.

'I'll pay well,' put in the other.

'Perhaps for one night. We're a busy coaching inn and I don't like to fill the rooms for too long.'

'I'd be most grateful. Perhaps I should introduce myself. I am Nicholas Grey from London. A student of flora.'

'Who's she?' asked someone – and there was a general rumbling laugh.

'Wild flowers,' answered Grey, blushing a little. 'I hope to compile and illustrate a book.'

There was another snigger and then attention turned away from the stranger, who was considered by those present to be a regular pinkum and not worth looking at. Edward was the only one who went forward, knowing that his reason for joining the slender young man was not entirely to glean information.

Saying, 'Can I sit with you?' he did so, adding, 'I'm quite interested in wild flowers myself and could show you where a few rare species grow.'

The stranger's arresting eyes looked at him gratefully. 'Would you really? How very kind. Please do join me. May I get you some ale?'

'I'll take a jug,' said Edward, wondering which of his many aliases he should use. He decided on Rawlins, a pseudonym the brothers had often adopted in the past.

'I'm Rawlins,' he said. 'Roger Rawlins.'

Was it his imagination or was there a momentary flicker of interest on Grey's face? But if so, the explanation came at once for Nicholas said, 'That was my mother's maiden name, you know. Do you come from round here? We might be connected.'

Edward blundered on, his guard somewhat lowered by the stranger's manner.

'Well, I do and I don't. I was born in Tunbridge Wells but moved to Mayfield some years ago.'

'Really? I wonder if I have any connections in Tunbridge Wells. I cannot recall my mother mentioning any. But it is possible I suppose.'

'And your relatives in Mayfield. Are they Rawlins?'

This was Edward's attempt at a trap. However, Nicholas Grey answered smoothly, 'No, they are the Medleys of Sharnden.'

'And they had no room for you to stay?'

'Not tonight,' continued Nicholas, unruffled. 'They were not expecting me. All will be prepared by tomorrow.'

Satisfied, Edward leaned back and consumed his ale in a single draught, allowing Nicholas to replenish it for him. And it was at this precise moment that Kit walked in and came straight to the table where his brother sat.

Instinctively, the smuggler knew at once that the man with whom Edward was so obviously entranced was a Riding Officer, despite his slender appearance and attractive face. For Kit knew better than most that the Excise were not without cunning, that the men they employed to listen to rumours, yet keep their own identity secret, were often the most unlikely. He also knew poor Edward's weakness, suppressed and supposedly secret for so many years, and thought to himself, 'If he continues like this, he'll have to go.'

Taking the only remaining seat on the settle, right beside Grey, Kit said, 'I don't know you, Sir, but would like to make your acquaintance. I'm John Gibb of Coggins Mill, a fish hawker by trade. And you?'

'Nicholas Grey, Master Gibb. An author – or hopefully to be so when my book on flowers is complete.'

'Flowers, eh? Well, if you're roaming the woods in search of your subject I'd advise you to be in before dusk.'

Grey looked nonplussed and then his brow cleared. 'Because of the smugglers, you mean?'

Kit roared with laughter. 'Smugglers? Dear me no. They'd not harm an innocent gentleman like yourself. No, there's a far greater menace in Mayfield nowadays.'

'And what would that be?'

'A rum-padder, sir. A highwayman, properly equipped with pistols and horse. He held up the Baker coach last week and got away with the money-box, to say nothing of Squire Baker's personal effects. And since then he's been on the same road, higher up, and taken another picking.'

Again Grey's expressive features registered more than a passing interest and Kit could not resist a grin.

'I shall have to be very careful, I can see. But surely the villain is not residing in Mayfield?'

'Ah, that is where you're wrong, sir. He's lodging not a stone's throw from where I live. Why, I could point out the very place to you.'

'I should be very interested to see it, Mr Gibb,' said Lieutenant Grey, this time with admirable facial control. 'And do you also know his name?'

'Aye, that I do, sir. It's Challice. Jacob Challice.'

'Well, well, well! Surely he must be new on the scene. I've never heard him mentioned before.'

'Oh, he's new all right,' said Kit Jarvis, 'but I reckon it won't be long before he's history. If a Riding Officer should get onto his trail ...'

'Quite so,' said Nicholas Grey.

'Why, dearest Grace,' said Mrs Trevor, slitting open the seal of the letter just handed to her by a footman, 'this is from Miss Baker, hoping that you are well.' She scanned the contents and drew in her breath sharply, then went on, 'She says that six dragoons have arrived in Mayfield and that there is to be an imminent arrest but no one knows quite of whom. Oh, my love, do you think they are going to apprehend that dreadful cut-throat who robbed Mr Baker?'

Mrs Trevor prided herself on using names correctly and insisted that George Baker was not really the squire, as his elder brother the Reverend Peter Baker was the heir, and in any event their father was still alive. She also liked to call Henrietta by her given name of Grace, though she had to admit with the rest of the family that it really did not suit her.

But for once her eldest daughter did not demur, simply rising to her feet and saying, 'If they are, they will call me back to Mayfield to identify him and I should hate that. I would not like to be responsible for seeing a man hang.'

'But he is a robber and a villain and the gallows is where he belongs.'

'I know you are right, Mother. It is simply the thought I cannot abide.'

Henrietta stood up restlessly and crossed over to her mother's bedroom window. The room was situated in the east wing of the manor house and was one of the few family rooms in that wing. As far as her eye could see the grounds beyond the ha-ha stretched away to a magnificent parkland while in the fore-ground, sweet brown cows grazed contentedly beside a flock of sheep and lambs. It was all so beautiful and so alive beneath the butterfly blue late April sky, that she could not bear to think that a mere word from her might condemn a man never to see such a sight again.

Reading everything in her daughter's averted back, the beautiful Widow Trevor also rose to her feet and crossed to Henrietta's side, slipping her arm about her waist.

'Perhaps Mr Baker will identify him instead.'

'He couldn't, Mother. At least he couldn't without lying. I was the only one to see his face.'

'And what sort of face was it?'

'Ugly. No, not really. Handsome in some ways. Very rugged. Do you know what I mean?'

'No,' said Mrs Trevor. 'To be honest, no. Yet he must have held some fascination.'

Henrietta shot her a quick glance. Sometimes her mother, despite all the difficulties put upon her through bringing up a family of ten children alone, was strangely perceptive.

Mrs Trevor kissed her daughter at the point where the luxuriant honey-rich hair sprang from the forehead, noticing that her crooked dimples had vanished. 'My dearest, if you are called upon to do your duty and identify this fascinating rogue, then you must do so. Otherwise innocent people might suffer. People who cannot afford to be robbed as well as Mr Baker can.'

With an impulsive gesture, Henrietta threw her arms around her mother's neck. 'You are right, Lucy Trevor,' she said, using the form of address that had started when she was a child and had now grown into a private joke between them. 'I shall do what I must.'

'Then come, my love, let us take the air.'

And with that the older woman and the younger entwined fingers and went out into the large cherry garden in front of Glynde Place.

THIRTY-SIX

Leaning his head out of a first-floor window, Nicholas Grey thought he had never seen anything more beautiful than first light over the moated site of Sharnden. For though this house was not the original dwelling, having been built in the fifteenth century, still the lines of the moat were quite distinct, and on the clear green water two proud swans greeted the dawn, while Sharnden itself was lit with a burnished glow.

He leant in again, feeling light with a strange unfamiliar excitement, and left his room quietly, anxious not to wake his hosts, the Medleys, who were lodging him because he did, indeed, have a remote family connection with them. Then, not even stopping to break his fast, Nicholas left the house and crossed over the causeway and up to the heights of Rushurst Cross.

Now he was in true valley country, seeing before and beneath him the majestic sweep of Bivelham, covered with contented, grazing beasts. And as Nicholas plunged down the hill and headed towards Coggins Mill, through the sweet green trees of Hole Wood, where bluebells were raised ready to burst forth, he decided that one day he must traverse the whole of the magic valley's length, from Bainden across to dark Snape Wood.

As he entered the hamlet, pretty and tree-filled, Nicholas found his eyes turning to the three attached cottages from which two nights before, accompanied by six dragoons, he had arrested Jacob Challice.

To have also arrested Kit and Edward, who had not fooled him for a moment, would have been easy. But Lieutenant Grey had not wanted that. Hoping, instead, that by waiting he could break the entire organisation, bring charges that no magistrate, bribed or otherwise, could refuse to listen to, and finally smash the Mayfield Gang, with all its radical leanings towards Jacobitism.

Nicholas reached the top of the steep hill leading into Mayfield and, crossing the track, passed the porter's lodge and went

334

into the palace grounds, following the drive put down by the Bakers.

And then he saw the old palace for the first time. Never in his life had he had such an extraordinary experience. As he approached the door, his wonderment grew with every step, for he realised he could have found his way round with no one to guide him at all. It was like coming home.

Almost instinctively, Lieutenant Grey found himself turning his horse towards the great hall and was horrified to see that it had been allowed to grow a little shabby, that one of the windows was broken and a bird swooped in and out.

As he looked, a door to his right opened and, turning round, Nicholas saw a tall man with a flowing wig, large nose and beady eyes.

'Lieutenant Grey?' he called loudly, and at Nicholas's nod said, 'This way, this way, that's the unlived-in part. Miss Trevor has arrived and now all we need is the prisoner.'

Nicholas dismounted and extended his hand. 'Squire Baker?'

'My father is officially the squire, but I'm known by the name. Where's Challice?'

'Being marched up by the dragoons, sir. I thought it as well to call in their assistance with so many criminals at large.'

'So many ...? Oh, you mean the smugglers. Yes, well ... Anyway, come in do. Let's get this sorry business over.'

It was just as Nicholas knew it would be. The great stone flight of steps leading off to his right, the door to the buttery beyond.

'My father, the Justice, is waiting in the ante-room. I must warn you that he is now very elderly, but still able to give a fair hearing for all that.'

Nicholas nodded, too overwhelmed to speak, and followed the squire's large legs up the stone staircase. By the time he reached the first-floor chamber overlooking the palace's front lawn, and saw the beautiful Miss Trevor standing waiting, eyes widening in recognition as he came in, he felt that he was moving through a dream.

'Lieutenant Grey! So it *is* you. I thought it must be,' she said.

'You've met?' asked George, in a surprised tone.

'Only briefly and by chance, Squire Baker. It was in the Blackboys Inn on my journey from Mayfield.'

The squire seemed about to comment but the noise of marching feet from outside silenced him.

'They're here,' said someone, and Grey distantly heard the sergeant tell the arresting party to wait below as he took the prisoner up. Then the door opened and Jacob Challice, his hands in chains behind him, stood in the entrance, staring round the room as if he was receiving a group of petitioners.

Briefly, his eyes met those of Grey and, seeing him in these surroundings, Nicholas suddenly realised what it was about the man that was so compulsive. He was one of those people that one felt one knew, even at first meeting.

Remembering his duty, he said firmly to Henrietta, 'Miss Trevor, I would like you to come with me and stand a little closer to the prisoner. Then I would like you to say whether or not this is the man you saw robbing Squire Baker's coach. You need have no fear of him. His hands are bound and if you declare that he is the guilty party he will never leave custody again. Now will you come with me?'

She nodded, giving him such a sweet look of gratitude that Nicholas felt himself growing a little flushed.

'Don't be afraid, my dear,' said the squire in a loud voice. 'The villain can't harm you.' While from the back of the room old Squire Baker, who was seated in a chair before a desk, wrapped in several shawls, said, 'String 'em up. It's the only way. Hang 'em in chains for all the world to see.'

Nicholas offered his arm and Henrietta took it, the feel of her so close to him making him go hotter than ever, so that he scarcely knew how to conduct himself. But his years of rigid training stood him in good stead and he marched, military style, to a few feet away from Challice and then turned to Henrietta.

'Is this the man?'

She knew what she must do, knew that everything her mother said had been right and that she must protect the innocent. Henrietta opened her mouth and then closed it again, aware that every eye in the room was upon her.

'Well?'

'No,' she said. 'I have never seen this man before in my life. It was not he who robbed Squire Baker.'

'But Henrietta,' screamed George furiously, 'he is of the same height and build. Are you sure?'

'I am positive,' she answered in a low but clear voice. 'This is not the man.'

All Nicholas could feel was inexplicable relief, and for a

moment this must have shown on his face, for he saw Henrietta give him a curious sideways glance. Then, turning to old Squire Baker – still the local Justice of the Peace despite his great age – he said, 'Sir, I feel there is insufficient evidence for a committal.'

'Of course there's insufficient evidence,' answered the old man furiously. 'If the girl can't identify him, that is the end of it. Release him, Grey. You have no choice.'

'Sergeant,' ordered Nicholas to the dragoon, 'release the prisoner.'

Challice stood for a moment, rubbing his wrists, then turned to look at Henrietta. 'Thank you for treating me so fairly, Miss Trevor.' He addressed Nicholas, George and the old squire. 'Thank you too, gentlemen. good day,' he said, and sweeping off his hat, he gave a low bow and rapidly left the room.

'Villain!' shouted the old man, going red in the face. 'I'll swear he's a villain. If he didn't rob George he must have robbed somebody else. I feel it in my water.'

'Father!' said George reprovingly. 'Be calm, pray. You know how a choleric mood brings on choking.'

And indeed the old squire was beginning to cough and splutter. 'I'll get the arrogant rogue one day,' he gasped. 'Grey, keep on the watch, d'you hear?'

'Indeed I do, sir. And now I must take my leave. I bid you farewell, gentlemen, and am only sorry that you were put to trouble for nothing.' He turned to Henrietta saying, 'May I escort you back to Glynde, Miss Trevor?'

Avoiding his eyes, she answered, 'No, I am staying on at the palace for a few days, Lieutenant Grey.'

'Then perhaps I will have the pleasure of seeing you before your return. I will call on Miss Baker and present my compliments.'

Henrietta curtsied but said nothing, still keeping her gaze firmly on the floor. In a very low voice, Nicholas added, 'Challice has a great deal to be grateful for, Miss Trevor. You have given him his life.'

At last she looked up, her clear eyes troubled. 'I would be loath to commit a fellow creature to hang, Lieutenant. It was most fortunate that Challice was not the right man.'

'Most fortunate indeed,' he said – and with a slightly mocking bow was gone.

* * *

Just as Jacob Challice walked from the palace a free man, a cart – borrowed from a neighbour and bearing Emily Pearce – began the rough descent through the wooded hills at the top of the valley of Bivelham. To Emily's left was the great dark cluster of Snape, brooding in ebony anger, the trees dense and unrelenting, while on her right she could glimpse Wenbans, the fifteenth-century house, now much altered and owned by the Maunser family, who also held an iron foundry on the estate's eastern boundary.

Skirting the mansion, Emily guided the plodding old horse downhill to the fresh brook that gurgled by Stream Farm, the remote and hidden house in which the Jarvis brothers lay low, paying newly minted silver shillings to the farmer and his wife in return for silence.

Here she pulled the horse to a stop, securing the reins to the trunk of a tree and, removing her best shoes, bought in London, tucked up her skirt and waded across, creeping silently over the grass at the far side. Gently, Emily tried the handle of the back door. It swung open and she stepped inside, directly into the kitchen.

The sudden coldness of a pistol against her neck frightened her so much that she froze where she stood, her eyes bolting in her head, trying to see who menaced her.

'Kit, is that you?' she gasped.

'Who else, you bitch?' he said, turning her round roughly. 'What do you want with me?'

'Revenge, that's what,' she shouted furiously. 'Revenge for peaching Jacob Challice. He's under arrest and they've brought the Trevor girl from Glynde to identify him. He's as good as hanged.'

'And damn good riddance. I'll brook no rum-padder on my patch – and you know it, you two-faced doxie.'

She flew at him, fists beating against his chest and feet flying about his shins. 'You loathsome bastard. How I could ever have borne you near me, I'll never know.'

Jarvis grinned, lifting her up off her feet by the elbows and holding her suspended in the air, still punching and kicking. Then happened something so natural, so joyous, that all fighting ceased. Kit lowered Emily to the floor, where they stood straining together, lip upon lip, like lovers that had been parted for an age.

* * *

It was as the Baker coach, bearing Miss Lucy and Miss Henrietta Trevor, slowed down at the end of the drive beside the porter's lodge, that the note was handed up. A grubby child, his feet bare, dashed from nowhere, risking life and limb beneath the wheels and, jumping precariously on the coach's small step, stuck his dirty face through the open window and said, 'Please Miss Baker, a gentleman gave me this for Miss Trevor. Would that be her?'

'Yes,' the two ladies chorused, startled, and Henrietta went on, 'I am Miss Trevor. What is it?'

Meanwhile Lucy was calling to the coachman to stop so that imminent threat of injury to the boy might be averted.

'I don't know, Miss,' the child said, a look of relief on his face as the coach jerked to a standstill. 'A gentleman give it me and told me to deliver it to Miss Trevor at the palace.'

Puzzled, Henrietta gave him a coin and the boy jumped down from the step, pulling his forelock enthusiastically as the coach trundled forward once more.

'Aren't you going to open it?' said Lucy, agog with curiosity.

Henrietta turned the roughly sealed paper in her gloved hands, noticing the firm manner in which the words, 'Miss Trevor' were written. 'I would rather do so later unless you cannot wait to know from whom it came.'

'Of course I can wait, dearest Henrietta,' answered Lucy, somewhat chastened. 'Keep it until we have returned from taking tea.' Henrietta gave her a grateful smile and hid the letter in her glove.

The coach took the eastern track out of Mayfield, going down the steep hill but not bearing left to Coggins Mill, instead going straight on passing, on its right, the track that led down to Bainden, and then climbing until it drew up finally before a pair of handsome gates that opened onto the circular drive – a lawn in its midst – of Luckhurst Hall, the home of John Langham, the surgeon.

Henrietta thought it quite the most extraordinary house she had ever seen, for the back was old, built in Tudor times, with sloping roofs and mellow old brick; while the front was modern, put on four years ago in 1717. She had never observed two more contrasting styles, the elegant facade with its colonnaded porch and the flagstoned farmhouse behind.

But her attention was drawn away by the great fluttering to-do that Lucy was making as she descended from the coach and saw the front door being opened by a liveried servant. Any suspicion that Henrietta might have had that Miss Baker loved Mr Langham was now confirmed. Her middle-aged spinster friend was in a positive flurry of emotion.

The two ladies were shown into a cool and elegant hall, from which a gracious staircase rose to a landing above. Coming to meet them down these stairs was their host himself, dressed most elegantly in a deep blue coat, gold threaded waistcoat, a Steinkirk cravat and full-bottomed wig. He had made a great effort to cut a dash and Lucy, equally elegant in a green gown, open on either side to reveal a yellow petticoat, and stretched over a bell hoop, curtsied deeply to show her appreciation. John Langham raised her up and kissed her hand, his eyes looking deeply into hers. Poor Henrietta immediately felt *de trop* and wished she had not come.

But it was only a moment before Mr Langham remembered himself. 'My dear Miss Trevor, how very kind of you to call on me. And on the very day of your ordeal too. Come into the salon and have some tea.'

He ushered the ladies in, making small talk about the weather, and it wasn't until Henrietta was comfortably seated that she remarked, 'The ordeal was not too great, Mr Langham, after all.'

'I'm glad to hear it. He was the guilty party, of course?'

'On the contrary,' Lucy put in. 'Henrietta found they had arrested the wrong man.'

'Good gracious.' John looked thoroughly surprised. 'Then the real villain is still at large.'

'It would appear so, yes.'

There was a pause during which Miss Trevor found herself the subject of scrutiny from two pairs of eyes, the more disturbing of which were those belonging to John Langham. For they had in them something she had never come across before, a force-fulness which made her, reluctant as she was to do so, unable to look away.

'How very interesting,' he said. But whether he was talking about Jacob Challice or something he had observed about Henrietta, it was difficult to tell.

The moment was broken by the arrival of the silver tea-tray and the ritualistic serving and drinking of this highly-taxed commodity. So highly-taxed, in fact, that Henrietta did not like to enquire too closely as to where Mr Langham had obtained this particularly delicious consignment. But he said quite openly, 'I found this in my cellar two nights ago. The rooms connect with the smugglers' road that runs just beside the house.'

'And did you keep it?' asked Henrietta, surprised.

'Keep it, I ordered it!' answered John, and burst out laughing, while Lucy pretended to look shocked.

'So the smugglers have many local purchasers?'

'Indeed they do. With the import taxes imposed by our German king, what can you expect?'

Miss Trevor thought it wise to change the subject and said, 'Have you studied surgery for many years, Mr Langham?'

'It seems almost always. I was born with a liking for it. But though I am a surgeon it is in the more unusual branches of medicine that I am most interested.'

'And what are they?'

'Herbalism and the relationship between mind and body, to name but two.'

'I did not know that the mind and body were related.'

'Very much so,' said John, warming to his theme and leaning forward earnestly, while Lucy looked on so lovingly that Henrietta, glancing at her, felt her own heart lurch at the pathos of this thwarted couple.

'Pray go on.'

'I made a very interesting discovery some years ago. I was about to perform an operation on a young sailor to amputate his leg, and before the surgery began was talking to him calmly, telling him to have no fear and so on. I noticed at the time that he was gazing at my watch, which I was swinging in my hand without realising what I was doing. It used to be a silly habit, now put to a better use I might add. However, I saw that the poor lad had passed into a dreamlike state, neither awake nor yet asleep, and the extraordinary thing was that I was able to operate on him without his feeling any pain at all. Even stranger, he continued in that state for hours, until I grew worried and begged him to wake up. Then he did so.'

Henrietta shook her head. 'I have never heard anything quite like that.'

Lucy broke in. 'John believes it to be a great discovery. He

341

has subsequently used the method many times to soothe patients.'

'And this can be done to anyone?'

'To anyone who does not fight against it, Miss Trevor.'

'Then I should like so much to try.'

'Well, not now,' said Lucy rising. 'We must return home to see to the evening's preparations.'

John stood up too. 'Alas Miss Trevor, you have been summoned. But I do assure you that at some time in the future we will try the experiment. It really is most fascinating.'

'I can hardly wait,' she said, looking childlike in her excitement.

The older two smiled indulgently. 'Well, you must for a while longer.'

'Have you ever been in this dream state, Lucy?' asked Henrietta.

'With John I am in it all the time,' she answered, indiscreetly but most romantically, and making her curtsey Henrietta withdrew to the coach to give them a few moments alone together.

It was not until she got into bed, the evening's card games finally at an end, that Henrietta opened the note which she had taken to her bedroom and hidden. Now, sitting up, her nightgown slipping about her shoulders, she broke the seal, looking straight for the signature which she was sure would read, 'Nicholas Grey'. Much to her astonishment she saw written there one word, 'Challice'. She went back to the beginning and read in full.

My dear Miss Trevor

No words can express the gratitude I feel to you. Out of the goodness of your heart you have saved the life of a stranger. A stranger who menaced you, moreover.

I would deem it the greatest favour you can bestow if I might be allowed to thank you personally. I will wait in the high wood beyond the house known as Bainden, at ten of the clock tomorrow, and hope that you will have the kindness to come.

My salutations and greetings to the remarkable Miss Trevor.

Challice

342

Henrietta put the letter down, her principal feeling one of surprise; surprise that the highwayman could even write, let alone produce a note of such eloquence. Blowing out the candle, she tried to sleep but could not do so, her mind full of thoughts of tomorrow's meeting and whether it was safe for her to go alone. Eventually she fell asleep, planning how she would set off on an early morning ride and thus escape the attention of the ever-protective Lucy.

Accordingly, Henrietta rose early and breakfasted alone, avoiding the family and leaving a message that she would return before midday. Then she went to the stables and chose a fast, dark horse to be saddled up, refusing the company of a groom and cantering away from Mayfield down the eastern track.

It was a fine, bright morning but over the distant hills, Henrietta could see falling showers. The air was full of the sweet, strong smell of newly washed earth and the heady scent of rain-damp flowers. For a moment Miss Trevor reined in, looking about her, seeing the harsh green of the woods mould against the soft slopes of the fields, and the vivid blue of the April sky lift the colour of everything to the brilliant shades of a childhood paintbox. She felt suddenly excited, as if all her life she had been preparing for something, and that shortly the secret of what it was would be revealed.

Turning right away from the track, Henrietta galloped through the woods, emerging above the manor house, still owned by the Squire of Glynde who was, in this case, her four-year-old brother, John. Cautiously, Henrietta hurried her horse beyond, aware that the tenants of Bainden knew her face and might wonder what she was doing riding alone towards the high wood. But she saw no one and entered the shadow of the green-gold trees quite unobserved.

The bluebells, that in a month's time would turn the place into a lake of colour, stood in regiments, their heads closed and dark. And dark too was the coat of the man who stood awaiting her, his horse tethered to a branch, his face breaking into a smile as she approached.

'So you came?' he said, holding up his arms to lift her down.

'Yes,' she said, sliding from the saddle and taking care not to brush against him.

'I'm glad.'

Once again, Henrietta studied the hacked-out features of that granite face, its one redeeming feature the deep blue eyes that were now staring at her.

'I was not sure whether I should.'

'Why? Surely you are not afraid of me? I would not like to think that, Miss Trevor.'

Henrietta did not reply, merely shaking her head, and the two of them stood looking at one another in silence.

'Have we met before?' Jacob said finally. 'A long time ago?'

'No, I don't think so.'

Yet, even as she answered, Henrietta could not help but feel that he *was* familiar.

'Why did you do it?' Challice asked. 'Why did you deny you knew me? Why should you bother to save me?'

Henrietta looked at him gravely. 'I don't know. I meant to betray you, had opened my mouth to do so, but the words refused to come out. It was extraordinary. I was compelled to give you your life.'

'Thank you for it,' he said, equally grave. 'I wish I could make recompense.'

Before she could stop him he had raised her fingers and brushed them with his lips. Henrietta felt as if a lightning flash had run through her.

'I don't want your gratitude,' she said abruptly. 'I could not help what I did. You should not be humble towards me.'

Jacob Challice smiled. 'Most men are humbled by beauty, Miss Trevor. And you have that in plenty.'

She wanted to be aloof; proud, as if she was used to receiving compliments. But, perversely, her funny dimples sprang into life, and they stood smiling at one another, like children. Then, suddenly the spell that held them was shattered and, hastily mounting her horse, Henrietta wheeled round and cantered away towards Mayfield, without pausing once to look back over her shoulder.

THIRTY-SEVEN

The visit, all too short for Henrietta's liking, was over. At precisely four o'clock the next day, she stood on the drive outside the main door of the palace, the coach bearing the Trevor coat of arms ready and waiting, and the family lined up to say farewell. Even old Squire Baker was present, wrapped in a mountain of shawls and leaning heavily on Lucy, who had a slightly despairing look on her face.

'Pity she wasn't sure of the villain,' he kept saying in a loud voice. 'Perhaps next time, eh Miss Trevor?'

'Perhaps,' she answered politely and kissed the bulging old cheek in farewell.

'Pretty gal,' he said suddenly, his little eyes narrowing. 'Very pretty, what, what, Nizel?' He nudged his youngest son, who had been called away from his easel set beneath the sturdy holm oak which, so legend had it, had been planted long ago by Tom May the poet and, as expected, Nizel went crimson.

'Very pretty,' he repeated uncomfortably as Henrietta dropped him a curtsey, followed by a peck on the cheek.

Now it was George and Philadelphia's turn, the latter moist-eyed with the strain of parting. 'You'll come back soon, won't you dearest Henrietta?' she gasped breathlessly as they embraced. 'The palace is so much gayer when you are here.'

'Perhaps next time Henrietta calls we will entertain her in Aylwins,' said George cheerfully, and was rewarded by Philadelphia giving a tremulous little sob and saying, 'I hope not. The house is so *old*, George.'

'Not as old as the palace.'

'That's different,' answered his wife illogically, and they stood frowning at one another while Henrietta went to embrace Lucy.

'You will remember me to Mr Langham,' said Miss Trevor, as they hugged each other.

Rather wistfully, Lucy answered, 'When I see him next,

which may not be soon. It is very difficult to get out with father so frail.'

'Frail? Who's frail?' bellowed the old man, cupping his hand round his ear.

'No one, dearest,' said Lucy, patting his head resignedly.

The departing guest could not help but smile as Thomas, dressed in a pink and violet embroidered coat, with flared skirt and hip buttons, to say nothing of silk stockings and lace cravat, arrived to say farewell.

'You look splendid,' she whispered as they embraced.

His eyes twinkled. 'One must attempt to keep up, my dear. I would not like it to be said that we country people do not move with the times.' He handed her in to the coach, bowing again as he did so.

Henrietta put her head out of the window, holding her wide-brimmed hat with one hand and waving with the other until they had turned the bend in the drive and the Baker family was out of sight. Then she settled back against the cushions, glad that Sarah her maid was following behind in another convey-ance to watch over the luggage.

Without her chatter, Henrietta had almost nodded off to sleep, as the coach drew up before the great gates of Glynde Place. She woke and looked out of the window, seeing a dark figure on horseback separate itself from a copse. She knew at once who it was. Challice had obviously followed all the way and now stood, silently watching her departure.

She half got up, gazing out at him, but neither of them made any move to wave a hand or raise an arm. They just remained staring until the gates opened and they were lost to each other's view.

Henrietta sat down again, her heart racing. The thief, the robber, the gentleman outer, had come to take his farewell of her. And that very action told her that he would not let it rest at that, that he would make it his business at some time in the future to seek her out once again.

By the time Jacob reluctantly returned to Mayfield, the evening had become a silver midnight, with a full moon over the valley of Bivelham. From the dark mass of sleeping Snape Wood to the little pond beneath Bainden next to the ruined cottage, all was changed by the wild, bright light. It was as if a second world lay just beneath that of the daylight hours, a world in which shapes and dimensions were subtly altered. The black and indigo hills took on softer lines beneath their silver-bright crowns, and the rivers and lakes sparkled. The deepest part of the valley was now a great mysterious sea in which there were islands of brilliant light where the moon caught a barrel of water or the surface of a duck pond.

But Jacob was in no mood to appreciate such delicate beauty, his mind too full of recent events. With a sigh he let himself into Lizzie's cottage and climbed to the stifling room beneath the eaves.

It looked empty now that Emily's gawdy belongings had vanished. She had gone back to Kit Jarvis, of course, as he should have guessed she would all along.

He had come back early on the previous day, still bemused from his encounter in the woods with Henrietta Trevor, to find Lizzie waiting for him, a grim expression on her face.

'She's gone to Kit,' had been her opening gambit. 'The bitch has flown the nest. She was always after him, ever since he came to Mayfield to go owling on Romney Marsh. I reckon he first had her when she was little more than a child.'

'Then I'm well rid of her,' answered Jacob tersely. 'And my only concern now must be where I lodge.'

Lizzie's face had taken on a placatory expression and a wheedling tone had crept into her voice. 'There is no need for us to be enemies, Jacob. What Emmy chooses to do is her concern. Besides, there's something strange between her and Kit. They are hopelessly drawn to one another. I say we forget them and you continue to lodge here.'

'Very well. But Lizzie ...' His hand had shot out and taken her hard by the shoulder. '... no betrayals. I have escaped justice once, I doubt I should be so lucky next time.'

'There'll be no betrayals from me, Jacob.'

Now, lying here sleepless upon his bed, Jacob's thoughts turned, yet again, to Henrietta Trevor. He could no longer imagine a future without seeing her, without being close to her, without watching those crooked dimples appear. Wild schemes in which he abducted her and married and reformed, pursued one another, as Jacob Challice realised he was in love for the first time in his life.

He rose from his bed, tired of the airless attic on a night when

347

all the earth was bathed in moonshine, and creeping down the ladder and past Lizzie's room went down some further stairs and out into the open air, smiling to himself. It had suddenly occurred to him that Kit Jarvis could do with a lesson and Jacob was just in the mood, full of pent-up emotion and energy as he was, to give it. Quietly whistling to his horse, he mounted, and in the glory of all that mad moonlight, headed off towards Snape Wood.

On that silver night, the moat at Sharnden had become a crescent, a brooch for a fairy's gown, but the sleeping Lieutenant Grey saw none of this splendour for he had been removed to his own world of fantasy. In his dream, Nicholas saw the palace at Mayfield and a vast, merry crowd thronging into the great hall. Through the open door he could see that a fire roared in a central brazier and the room was set with many tables.

'You can't go in,' said a voice, and Nicholas turned away, disappointed. After that, he slept fitfully, constantly waking and thinking, not about the Jarvis brothers, but of Henrietta Trevor and her eyes and dimples and hair, and of how much in love with her he already was.

Nicholas suddenly sat up in bed, wondering if Challice appealed to the romantic streak in the girl's nature. Had she denied she knew him because in her eyes he was a dashing figure? If so, the highwayman was a bigger menace than he thought.

He lay back on his pillows again, knowing that a plan must be found – a plan, which, with any luck, might rid him of the smugglers and Challice in one stroke. Before he slept again, Nicholas determined that the very next day he would call on Kit Jarvis.

It was not usual for the smugglers to make a run when the moon was full, and this night was no exception. It was quiet along Mayfield's track, no muffled hooves heading from the road towards the safe houses or the Royal Oak and, consequently, every noise seemed overloud. In fact, as Dash touched the mechanism, hidden in a gargoyle on the wall, that moved aside a floor-stone in the great hall, it creaked so loudly that he feared he might wake every sleeping occupant of the palace. He slipped into the shadows for a moment, standing motionless as he listened, but there was no sound either in the archbishops' dining-room or the dwelling beyond. Reassured, he quietly proceeded down the steep flight of steps revealed and pulled the lever at the bottom, closing the entrance behind him. Then he ducked his head as he entered the tunnel that lay ahead.

After a few yards it bore round to the left, coming out in the cellar of the Royal Oak, and Dash pushed open the heavy door at the far end and stepped out into the Oak's cellar, climbing another flight of stone steps and leaving the building by a side-door, unseen. In a second he was in the stables where a horse, already saddled, waited for him, its feet tied with sacking to deaden the sound. With a quick glance about, Dash swung into the saddle and headed off towards the valley of Bivelham and the secret farm that lay beside the stream running beneath the shadows of Wenbans, to give instructions to the gang's figure-head – Kit Jarvis.

The night was so bright that the sun had to battle for dominance in order that daylight might come. But finally the silver goddess conceded and as the sky turned mauve, Nicholas Grey left Sharnden and made his way on horseback to the place where he believed the Jarvis brothers hid out.

To remain unobserved, he went the hidden way through Combe Wood and then, crossing Tide Brook, through Ashett's, finally coming out into open country above Wenbans.

The sun was just beginning to light the great house – considerably enlarged and extended some forty years earlier – and Nicholas thought it magnificent, its huge chimney and jutting wing already beginning to glow as the morning came. He found himself wishing that something other than his duties as Riding Officer had brought him to a place where the dawn gleamed crystal, and the evenings were alight with amethyst and gold.

As he began the descent to the track below, Nicholas's horse stopped short, neighing at an obstacle lying in its path. Reining in, Lieutenant Grey saw that it was the body of a man; a man lying horribly still. Dismounting, he ran forward and knelt beside the prostrate form, lifting it slightly so that he could see the face. He was not altogether surprised to find it was Jacob Challice.

Lifting the body higher, Nicholas put his ear to Jacob's

chest and there, sure enough, was the beat of his heart, not as weak as Grey had feared. Yet a cursory examination revealed that Challice had sustained a severe beating and was losing blood, and it was with a groan that the injured man opened his eyes, focusing them with difficulty on the face of the Riding Officer.

'Lieutenant Grey?' The voice was little above a whisper.

'Yes. Who did this to you? Jarvis's gang?'

Jacob nodded. 'It was a fair rumble. I was sworn to shoot off his culls in revenge for stealing Emily Pearce.'

'I thought she no longer concerned you. I thought you had eyes for no one but Miss Trevor since she lied to save your neck,' answered Nicholas harshly.

'That's as may be. But I still had a score to settle. It was a matter of pride.'

Nicholas smiled grimly. 'Honour amongst thieves, eh?'

'If you say so. But, Lieutenant, there was one there who was no common robber. Jarvis is leader in name only. Their financier was present.'

'What!' Grey could not believe his ears.

'It's true. I heard his voice. He is a gentleman.'

'Did you get a look at him?'

'No, he wore a mask, yet he had a familiar air. I've seen him somewhere before – and recently.'

'Could you identify him?' asked Nicholas, the irony of the situation not altogether escaping him.

But Challice did not answer and the lieutenant saw that the man had lost consciousness. He toyed momentarily with the thought of leaving him to die, then his better nature won and he bundled the highwayman onto a horse and headed off in the direction of the village and the home of John Langham the surgeon, his idea of a dawn raid on Kit Jarvis laid aside as another plan formed itself in his mind.

THIRTY-EIGHT

In the dark, salt-filled night there was a sudden flash of light, followed rapidly by another; from a ship riding at anchor came a responding signal. After that everything was black for a moment and then a steady beam from a spout lantern was directed out to the open sea. In its pale gold glow several large rowing boats pulling towards the beach became visible, and on the shore Kit Jarvis laughed in the darkness. The run was on!

Tonight the nucleus of the Mayfield gang – the Jarvis brothers, Francis Hammond, Thomas Bigg, John Humphrey, Francis Norwood – were supplemented by a force of fifty men, mostly local labourers anxious to earn well. For this was a big haul. One thousand tubs of spirit were to come in, to say nothing of chests of tea. It had cost Dash dearly to finance such an enterprise and now it was Kit's responsibility to see that the operation went smoothly.

His narrowed eyes scanned the beach and cliffs for any sign of Excise men or Riding Officers but all was apparently quiet, and as the first of the rowing boats drew onto the shingle, its wooden base crunching against the pebbles, he called out 'Now.' In one silent swoop his entire company of men came out of their hiding places and swarmed down to the sea, hands grabbing for the end of the rope brought in by the rowing party, attached to which were the tubs of spirit.

The Mayfield gang prided themselves on speed. It was Kit's boast that he could beach five hundred tubs in twenty minutes and now his minions began to haul in the casks, each one of which held half an anker or four gallons of spirit. The barrels were roped in pairs making it easier for the free-traders to carry them on their shoulders to where pack animals and carts stood waiting.

In key position where they could see all and turn to fight the Excise men should it be necessary were Edward and Kit, armed with wooden staves which they referred to as bats, and hangers, their nickname for swords. The similarity between the brothers

– even though they had not shared the same mother – was very marked when they were tense, and tonight even Francis Hammond, bouncing like a ball about the beach as he supervised the unloading of tea chests, mistook them.

'Has Grey really vanished, Kit?' he asked, only to realise his mistake as Edward answered, 'They say he left Mayfield several days ago.'

'Does anyone know where?'

'No. He's just gone.'

'Well I don't trust the bastard,' said Francis.

'I quite like him,' Edward answered, looking out to sea.

But there was no time for further talk. The race was on to get the goods ashore and Kit was shouting to them to hurry. Half an hour was up and only a quarter of the tubs were loaded on to the packhorses who would take them through the night to a secret depot, where the horses would be changed. If all went to plan, the cargo would reach the southern fringe of London during the following day, then be taken on to the hamlet of Stockwell, three and a half miles from the city and lying discreetly hidden between the commons of Clapham and Kennington.

It was at Stockwell that Kit would drive his final bargains, getting the maximum price he could from the London merchants who would come to the hamlet to buy. Dash had leased a house there which was used partly as a warehouse, along with barns and storerooms. When the purchases were made the contraband would be handed over to carriers, who owned teams of horses and worked on a commission basis. Their convoys would proceed into London by night, crossing the Thames on the ferries at Lambeth or Battersea, and be out again before daybreak. Ten days later they would return with a new consignment, while Kit and his men would go back to Mayfield and plan the next run.

But now the first stage of this one was complete. Edward and Francis were checking that all the items had come ashore. The great rope which had landed the barrels was being hauled back to the lugger, which still rode at anchor waiting for the return of the galleys – the large open boats propelled by oars.

All was safely in and the elder Jarvis was counting out the payment to the leader of the sea-smugglers. The initial part of the exercise was successfully over and as the galleys began to row out to the waiting ship, Kit turned his convoy inland and, riding at the head, began the trek that would finally deposit the smuggled goods in London.

'You've healed well,' said John Langham. 'You must be a strong man, Challice.'

'Aye, it's true enough. I've had to be, Mr Langham.'

'I'm sure,' answered the surgeon drily, removing the last of Jacob's dressings and feeling a certain pride in his own skills at mixing ancient remedies from herbs and achieving such success as now stood before him.

Lieutenant Grey had brought John Langham a battered and bleeding wreck to attend to and now, a week later, Challice had little more to show for his beating than some rapidly healing cuts and a few yellowing bruises.

'You've left me free to fight another day, Sir,' he added now.

'I wouldn't do too much of that if I were you,' answered Langham with a grim smile. 'Next time you might not be so lucky.'

'Next time I'll move more quickly.'

'You say it was the smugglers who did this to you?'

'Yes. There was a score to settle. But it's over now.'

It was on the tip of John's tongue to say, 'So you *are* the highwayman of Pennybridge' but he kept his counsel. He was as convinced as Nicholas Grey that the culprit and Challice were the same man; that Henrietta Trevor had lied for reasons best known to herself.

On an impulse, John drew his watch from his pocket as if to look at the time. Then, as if he hardly knew what he did, he began to sway it back and forth saying, 'Sit down, Jacob. You look tired. Sit in that chair and rest. Close your eyes if you want to.'

Challice's attention had been caught by the swaying watch and as he reluctantly took a seat, John could see that the man's lids were already beginning to blink heavily.

'Yes, you look very tired,' the surgeon went on. 'Just close your eyes and rest. We can continue to talk. Can you hear me, Jacob?' Langham continued.

'Yes,' came the answer, and John knew by the tone of the man's voice that he had passed quite easily into the dream state.

'Now Jacob,' he said, 'I want you to tell me the truth. Do you understand?'

There was a strange flat-voiced, 'Yes.'

'Did Miss Trevor tell a lie to protect you? Did you rob Squire Baker's coach?'

'Yes.'

'And why did she lie?'

'She said she felt compelled to help me. She could not understand it herself.'

John Langham paused, feeling guilty. He was using his power to extract information of the most confidential nature. But the scientist in him could not resist continuing the experiment. Without compunction, John went on, 'Jacob. I want you to go back in time to when you were fourteen years old. Do you remember that? Tell me where you are.'

Challice gave a chuckle and said, 'With the rum coves in London. Learning how to filch. Good times these are. Not that we get a lot to eat.'

John sat down opposite the highwayman and wondered at the miracle that always took place when he played this game with his patients. The hard granite face had taken on childish features and the grin that spread over Challice's face was that of a naughty boy.

'And now go back to when you were five, Jacob. Tell me where you are now?'

The robber began to grub at his eyes with his knuckles. 'I am in Norfolk with my mother. She is very cross with me because I have stolen some cakes. She hit me with her hands on my buttocks.'

'So you knew then that it was wrong to steal?'

It was said so quietly that Jacob did no more than nod his head in reply. 'I have been a bad child,' he said.

It was then that John Langham had the notion to take him even further back, wondering if, as he had seen grown men do twice before, Challice would draw his knees to his chin in the foetal position.

'I want you to go back before your birth,' he said. 'I want you to remember how you were.'

The hard face grimaced and, just for split second, John felt a strangely paternal emotion, as if the man in the chair meant more to him than simply a patient on whom he was conducting an experiment.

'Go on, Jacob,' he said. 'Try to remember what it was like.'

Challice remained quite still and then suddenly and without warning let out a horrifying gurgling sound, as if he were choking to death. The blood froze in Langham's veins as he watched the highwayman's legs jerk and the whole of his body go into a series of convulsions. Then, as his tongue began to loll from his mouth, Jacob's hands tore at his neck as if he were fighting to remove something from it.

'My God!' exclaimed the surgeon. 'Jacob, be calm, be calm.'

But the writhing figure seemed not to have heard as it continued to dance and convulse where it lay in the chair. Then it suddenly grew stiff and Langham watched with horror as Challice sat bolt upright and rasped out a ghastly cry that seemed, somehow, to be a name '...en..a..min'. Then he went limp.

In a second the surgeon was on his feet, raising Challice in his arms and putting his ear to his chest to listen for his heart. There was nothing.

'Oh God's mercy,' whispered John, fighting to stay in control of himself and the situation. In a commanding voice he said as calmly as he could, 'That memory is finished, Jacob. I want you to come back from that time and move forward. I want you to be yourself again. You are Jacob Challice, aged about thirty. You are in good health and you are to come out of the dream state. Can you hear me, Jacob?'

There was silence and John caught himself praying, 'God, don't let the man be dead. If these experiments can kill I must ...'

But Jacob had let out a great sigh and colour was beginning to return to the dead white face. Listening again, John could hear the strong firm beat of his heart.

'May the Lord be praised,' he said. Then, more loudly, 'Jacob, I am going to count from ten to one. You will feel yourself grow less and less tired and when I reach one you will wake up refreshed and well. The memory of that terrible moment will be gone from you. Do you understand?'

There was no response but John saw the highwayman's lids flutter and as the count of one was reached, his eyes slowly opened and Jacob Challice was staring at him with a puzzled expression on his face.

'I must have slept for a moment,' he said.

'You did,' said John hastily. 'The herbal preparations I use sometimes have that effect.'

'Strange,' said Challice, standing up. 'I must apologise. Now, how much do I owe you, Sir?'

'One guinea. And keep out of trouble in future.'

Jacob smiled, the deep eyes creasing at the corners. 'I am a stormy petrel, Mr Langham. Sometimes trouble comes looking for me. But I thank you for your concern and your remedies.'

John held out his hand wondering why he should like the villain so much, particularly in view of what he had learned. And long after Challice had gone the surgeon sat in silence, staring out of the window, thinking of all that had happened while the highwayman had been in a dream and what could be the significance of that terrible enactment of death by strangulation.

As darkness fell over his gardens, John finally rose and went to his desk where he penned a brief letter. Then he rang for a servant, saying, 'Deliver this to Miss Baker at the palace at once. Tell her the matter is urgent and that a reply by tonight would be appreciated.'

As the man went out, John sat down again and poured himself a glass of wine and sat quite still, occasionally sipping, until darkness fell.

As always when he sought solace, Nicholas Grey picked up his lute and, in the lengthening shadows of his room, started to play. The tune stole out of its own accord, not planned or prepared, but simply singing its own song. He bent his head over the instrument, unaware that his expressive features had changed, that he had become transformed by the glory of the sound, that he looked like a different person.

His father had once joked that Nicholas had been born with a lute in his hands, for he had taken to the instrument as soon as he was able to pluck the strings. And though he had had formal tuition for a while, his tutor had announced that the boy had brought the gift with him into the world and there was little more he could teach him. Yet the need to support his mother and her other impoverished children when their father had died, had ended any thoughts Nicholas might have had of taking up music. Instead he had entered the Customs Service and been appointed a Riding Officer, a force originally intended to counter owling but now used to fight smugglers generally.

The music grew in intensity and Nicholas allowed his mind to wander over the events of the last few days. It was strange that finding Jacob Challice bruised and bleeding should have decided him to call in extra help to smash the Mayfield gang. For though he had no love for the man, that assault, together with the information that a shadowy figure was the gang's true leader, had forced Nicholas to admit he needed assistance. He must combine forces with John Rogers and Lieutenant Jekyll, the most dedicated smuggler hunters in Sussex, other than the Jarretts, who were already hunting the gang down.

Yet now that he had done it, now that he had cast the die that must inevitably lead to the destruction of Kit Jarvis and his minions, and no doubt of Jacob Challice as well, Nicholas was not happy. He took himself to task as the music changed course, sighing out a melancholy air that spoke of meetings and partings, greetings and farewells.

'I know I have done the right thing,' he thought. 'I am a conscientious Riding Officer, sworn to do my duty, and that is the code by which I have abided.'

Yet in a strange sort of way, Nicholas had a grudging admiration for Kit and Edward, who had the audacity to live outside the law while possessing a certain reckless charm. In fact, Nicholas thought grimly, if he had to choose between spending his life with the law-abiding John Rogers and Lieutenant Jekyll or the villainous Challice and Jarvis, he would choose the rogues.

He had not taken to Rogers at all when he had met him on the previous day, feeling there was something cruel about the hop-grower turned Revenue man. But Jekyll, who had arrived some time later, had been a different matter. In him, Nicholas had sensed fanaticism, and one look at the piercing eyes had confirmed his suspicion. The lieutenant was conducting a personal campaign against wrong-doers and was filled with something approaching religious fervour when it came to the matter of smugglers.

Hugging his lute even closer, Nicholas recalled the conversation of the evening before.

The three men had met in Rogers's house in Horsham, served supper by a sulky looking Mrs Rogers who had banged the plates down in front of them as if she resented their very presence. As soon as she had gone, Rogers had turned to Grey, his mouth full, and said, 'There is a reward out for the Mayfield gang, you know. But that is not the only reason Jekyll and I will join forces with you. The men are a scourge and must be made an example of. They have been running amok for over five years now and all attempts to bring them to justice have failed.'

'They have been very successful,' Nicholas had answered carefully.

'They are evil,' Jekyll had put in coldly. 'They are a drain on our society and obviously have allies in high places to have gone on so long and so well.'

'Obviously,' Rogers had echoed. 'But that is not the point at issue. With Grey's help I now think we have the best chance of all. He has studied their movements and hideouts and through him we might catch them on a run.'

'That is precisely what we must do,' Jekyll answered. 'Otherwise we can never get the evidence to convict. All of them have been arrested yet each one has slipped through the net. What we want is a case so watertight that even a bribed magistrate has no choice but to send them down.' Jekyll turned his cool gaze on Nicholas. 'I hear there's a highway robber working the London road in Mayfield. What about him?'

'What do you mean?' answered Nicholas, feeling himself grow uncomfortable, yet not understanding why.

'Surely Kit Jarvis has declared war on him. Might the highwayman not lead us to the smugglers?'

Nicholas feigned a blank expression. 'I don't follow, Lieutenant Jekyll.'

A look of impatience crossed Jekyll's face but he continued in an even tone, 'Let dog eat dog. Let the robber tell us when and where there is to be a run.'

'It's too far-fetched,' answered Grey, standing up but not having the nerve to look the lieutenant full in the eye. 'How would he know?'

'Because the criminal classes know everything. They pick up information as the rest of us pick up food.'

'I don't think this man is typically criminal class,' answered Nicholas, regretting it immediately.

Jekyll's eyes were beads of light as he said smoothly, 'So you know his identity?'

Nicholas felt he was being dragged before a headmaster, a commanding officer, an elder brother. 'No,' he stuttered, 'I base my surmise on reports I have heard of his robberies.'

'Such as?'

'That he lets some ladies keep their jewels.'

Lieutenant Jekyll gave a snort of indignation. 'Lieutenant Grey, you cannot be so naive! A pretty face might turn a man's head for a moment but you can take it from me that he is as low as the rest. The gentlemen of the road, as they so picturesquely term themselves, are nothing short of vermin and they should be destroyed similarly.'

Raising his wineglass to his lips, Nicholas realised that his hand was shaking. He put the vessel down again and said, 'What do you suggest?'

'That we bribe the highwayman to give us details of the next run. You can surely track him down, Grey. Then when you do so offer him a pardon if he will work with us.'

'But I have no authority to do that.'

'That is beside the point. What matters is that the Mayfield gang are finished for good. Tricking a highwayman is of little consequence in comparison with the welfare of the majority.'

Nicholas Grey did not know what to say, fixed as he was with that glassy stare.

'You make no reply?'

'I find it difficult to do so, Lieutenant Jekyll. You are right of course but it goes against the grain with me to lie to anyone on an issue so vital.'

Now he sat with his lute, wishing that the clock could go back and he had stuck to his original plan to tackle the Mayfield gang single-handed. But it was too late for that now. Rogers and Jekyll were on the trail and would never leave it. He, Nicholas Grey, had betrayed them all and could not comprehend why the thought of this should so profoundly upset him.

'But my dear,' said Lucy Baker. 'I am afraid I do not fully understand. Tell me again what happened.'

She was sitting in John Langham's salon, looking out over the distant hills and at the colour of the early evening sky. The place was as delicate as the inside of a seashell and, in fact, the whole house with its gracious staircase and beautifully proportioned

359

rooms at the front, and quaintly beamed Tudor farmhouse beyond, enclosed her with such loving warmth that her tender heart longed for the day – heaven alone knew how distant – when she and John would live there together in harmonious and contented married life.

Her dear friend made no answer but merely shook his head, an expression of bewilderment and anxiety on his face.

'That is the point, Lucy,' he said. 'I do not know what happened myself. All I can tell you is that Challice died for a moment or two. His heart actually stopped beating. Or at least that is how it seemed to me.'

'And this happened in the dream state?'

'Yes. I know it was wrong of me but I was experimenting with him. I have told you that twice I have made grown men adopt the position of a foetus. I could not help but think it would be amusing to see such a hatchet-face as Challice do likewise.'

'And then he died?'

'Yes. I said to him, "I want you to go back before your birth. I want you to remember how you were," and at that instruction he started to choke.'

Lucy stood up and crossed to the window, her back turned to John. 'But that would mean he died before he was born. It would mean that he had known death before this life.'

Langham stood up and went to stand beside her, slipping a loving arm about her shoulder. 'What are you saying?'

Lucy turned to look at him, her eyes suddenly abrim with wonder. 'That perhaps this life is not the only one we experience. That perhaps you took Challice back to the death he had before his present birth.'

John shook his head, looking frightened. 'But that goes against the teaching of our Lord.'

'Does it? Did He not say, "In my Father's house are many mansions." Could the mansions not be lives?'

Langham looked totally perplexed. 'I cannot credit it, Lucy. It is utterly beyond belief.'

Miss Baker tilted her chin, something of the look about her that had once been on the face of an eleven-year-old girl suddenly faced with sole control of an enormous family. 'There is only one way to find out.'

'What do you mean?'

'You must do it to me, John. You must take me back before my birth.'

He shook his head violently. 'I would not risk it. Supposing ...'

'Suppose nothing. You know what caused that. You told Challice to go back and remember how he was just before his birth. Do not use those words with me. Tell me to go back many years. Tell me not to relive my death. Oh John you must! It is in the interests of science.'

Langham wrestled with himself. His fascination with the dream state was so great that he was tempted. Yet if anything should happen to Lucy ...

She guessed what he was thinking, saying, 'But, dearest, Challice did *not* die. You told me yourself he walked out of here unaided. John, we will never know the answer if we don't try.'

He gave in, more than half willing to do so. 'Then we *shall* try, but be assured that if you are in any danger I will bring you back to the present immediately.'

As Lucy settled herself, her hooped dress as she lay down turning her into the shape of a swan, John Langham pulled the heavy curtains across the windows. Then he sat in a small chair by her side.

'Close your eyes, Lucy. There is no need for you to look at my watch. Now I am going to count from one to ten and as I do so you will begin to get heavier. Each part of your body so heavy that you feel you would like to sink into a deep sleep.'

He looked at her, seeing her only as a patient and noticing how already her hands had gone limp and her breathing become measured. With her willingness not to resist the dream state she was an ideal subject for any experiment he cared to conduct.

'Now Lucy, I want you to go back. Back and back and back again. Beyond your birth but much further back than that. Not to anything remotely like death. Back to —' John hesitated, the un-Christian words sticking in his throat, 'a life, perhaps before this one.' How could he dare utter such blasphemy? And yet he must go on. 'Back, my sweetheart, back to a much earlier time.'

John sat still, watching Lucy's face over which a radiant smile was now slowly beginning to spread.

'Are you there, Lucy?'

In the dream state she nodded her head.

'Where are you, darling? And —' He was almost too afraid to say it but he forced himself, 'who are you?'

She laughed aloud, but instead of answering his question said, 'He's chosen me! He's chosen me!'

'Who has chosen you?' asked John, shaking his head in disbelief.

'Robert. His father gave him free choice between two and he has decided to marry me.' In her dream Lucy laughed again, and it was the happy sound of a young girl.

John Langham could not believe what was happening. Surely, if ever such a thing were possible, here was proof of more lives than one.

'And are you going to marry him?'

'Oh yes. I love him, and besides I will one day be mistress of Sharndene.'

'Sharnden?' exclaimed John, his calm manner vanishing and his voice taking on a note of utter amazement. 'Then who are you, Lucy? Who are you?'

'Why, I'm Margaret of Ewhurst,' she said with a smile. 'Future bride of Robert de Sharndene, heir to the Lord of the Manor who lives in a great moated house in the valley of Byvelham. They call that valley magic, did you know?'

'Yes,' answered John slowly, hardly able to credit that this was actually taking place. 'Yes, I am beginning to believe they might be right.'

THIRTY-NINE

His mother kept running away from him and when Jacob
finally caught her up, it was to see that she had subtly changed,
that the dark eyes which had stared at him for such a long time
after she had died, had changed to long green ones with flecks of
gold in their centre. She laughed at him a little and then pinned
a ring to his hat. 'That will keep you safe, my son,' she said, and
then she began to walk away. Terrified, Jacob started after her
and woke to find that he had crossed to the window in his sleep.
Shaking his head to wake himself, he leaned on the sill and
looked out.

From the tall London house, Challice had a view that was
dominated by St Paul's Cathedral, for he was in the City,
disposing of his latest haul to his fence. It had been a rich picking
because two nights before he had been lucky enough to chance
on the coach of Thomas Pelham, Duke of Newcastle. The
duchess's jewels alone had been worth a fortune and Jacob had
quickly rid himself of those with the exception of one piece, an
emerald necklace that reminded him of Henrietta's eyes. It had
sparkled green fire when he had turned it in his fingers in the
safety of the cottage at Coggins Mill, and though he had known
it was damning evidence against him, had decided to keep it.

He crossed back to the bed and lay down upon it, trying to
sleep but unable to put Henrietta from his mind. He had not
seen her for three weeks, though twice he had ridden through
the night to Glynde and stayed concealed amongst the trees,
looking at the house where she lay asleep.

Jacob got up again, hot with passion and wild imaginings.
Then the unpredictable streak in him flared and, despite the fact
it was the middle of the night, he drew on his breeches, boots and
riding coat. He would go to Henrietta now, make some excuse to
see her, pose as a gentleman, anything! Anything at all, as long
as he could see those funny dimples warm into a smile and clasp
the duchess's necklace round the curve of that delicate throat.

*   *   *

'Another letter from Miss Baker,' said Mrs Trevor, looking over her tea-cup, which she held in one hand, the letter in the other. 'Why, Henrietta, she has asked if you may stay again. She says that her household are clamouring for your presence because you make them so gay and lighthearted.'

'But she does that here,' said Arabella, who at seven years old was the youngest of the nine Miss Trevors and an ardent admirer of her eldest sister.

'And besides we need her to help with our embroidery,' said Elizabeth, nearest to Henrietta in age and forced to take on her duties when her sister was absent.

'But Mother could do that,' answered Henrietta serenely.

'Oh no she couldn't. This is to be a coverlet and cushions worked by the nine Miss Trevors and them alone. It would spoil it if anyone else did a stitch.'

'Elizabeth, please,' put in their mother, 'it is not seemly to raise your voice in that manner. And in any case your opinion has not been sought. I and I alone will decide whether Henrietta may go on a visit.'

There was a brief silence during which Elizabeth addressed herself sulkily to the taking of tea, while Henrietta and her mother studied one another.

'She's growing so beautiful,' thought Mrs Trevor. 'I must give a ball. It is high time she was married and with her generous dowry I know she can attract a title.'

She sighed a little. The complex business of arranging a marriage and treading a delicate path through the maze of dowry, jointure, pin-money, portions, trusts and remainders with the bridegroom's father, was not one that Lucy Trevor relished. But it was a necessary evil – and something that she would have to repeat eight times more if she were to see her girls successfully wed. She gazed fondly at her little boy, who sat beside her silently eating a cake. No such problems with him. As Squire of Glynde he could be assured of a good match with any heiress of his choice.

Henrietta's voice brought her back to the present. 'May I go, Mother?'

Mrs Trevor hesitated. It occurred to her that one of the Baker bachelors might be behind these constant invitations and the thought did not please her. Wealthy though the family might be, she felt certain that Henrietta could do better.

'I – I'm not sure. You have only just come back from Mayfield.'

'Yes, but then I had to go and identify that man. This would be a proper visit.'

'Umm. I hope it is not that you are bored here at Glynde.'

'No, Mother, it is not that,' said Henrietta, her eyes steadfast. 'It is just that at the palace I can be myself without interruption. Do you understand?'

Looking at the nine other children sitting round the room, Mrs Trevor understood at once.

'Very well, my darling, you may go this time. But I shall expect you to be home for a while after that. We have preparations to make.'

'Preparations?' Henrietta looked blank.

'A year from now I would like to see you married, Grace. When you return from Mayfield it is my intention that we set the wheels in motion by giving a grand dance.'

'But, Mother . . .'

Lucy Trevor smiled. 'Be assured you will not have anyone displeasing forced upon you, dearest. Though wealth and position are important they will not be allowed to take over-riding preference. Within social limitations you may marry the man of your choice.'

'Oh dear,' said Henrietta.

Jacob Challice only stopped once on his journey from London to Glynde, resting himself and his horse for a few hours before he plunged on through the heat of the day until he came to Mayfield, where he turned off towards the Downs just as the shadows of the trees began to lengthen.

He had formed no definite plan, only aware of such a burning desire to see Henrietta again that it brought in its train a sense of elation. Jacob felt as he rode that nothing could stop him, that he was master of the situation, that obstacles would crumble in the path of such fervour. And so it was that when he saw a coach bearing the Trevor coat of arms rumbling towards him on the evilly bad road from Blackboys to London, he thought for a moment that it was an image that his extraordinary state of mind had conjured up. Nonetheless, he took the precaution of disappearing into a clump of trees and watching narrowly.

It was her! His longing for Henrietta had actually wrested

round circumstance and sent her to him. Throwing caution to the winds, Jacob pulled his neckerchief up over his face and with only the dusk as protection, lurched across the coach's oncoming wake, a cocked pistol in either hand.

'Stand fast,' he shouted, and as the coachman's hand went for his gun, growled, 'Don't – or by God I'll kill you.'

A scream from within told Jacob that Sarah the maid was aboard and a second later her terrified face appeared at the window.

'Oh God's wounds,' she shrieked. 'It's the same one, Miss. The one who held us up at Pennybridge.'

'It can't be,' said Henrietta impatiently, and the maid's head leaning out was replaced by that of the mistress. Jacob swept off his hat, forgetful of the fact that in his haste to leave London he had omitted to put on his wig. He saw Henrietta's eyes go straight to the mass of red hair which grew in thick and luxuriant curls about his head.

'As red as a fox,' she said. 'So it *is* you.'

He leant forward in the saddle, lowering his voice to the merest whisper. 'Yes, and I must talk to you. I am going to tie these two up, Henrietta, but I promise I will not harm them.'

'And what of me?'

In an even lower tone, Jacob said, 'I would not lay a finger upon you unless you wanted it.' Out loud he shouted, 'You, get down from the box. And you —' He waved his pistol in the direction of Sarah. 'Get out.'

She burst into tears. 'I can't bear it, Miss. Twice in a month. What will become of me?'

'Just do what he says, Sarah, and no harm will result. Go along.'

The weeping girl reluctantly stepped down and was joined a moment later by the glowering coachman. Henrietta bit her lip anxiously as she watched the two of them marched into the trees at pistol point. But before she could call out, Challice was back and had got up into the coach beside her, his hard face softened by emotion, as he gently bent his mouth to hers. Unable to help herself, Henrietta opened her lips and all the longing between them flowed.

He kissed her again but this time lightly, gently, his lips running over her eyes and nose and finally her dimples. 'Dearest Henrietta,' he said.

'You must go,' she answered. 'Go before some traveller comes along. Jacob, I do not want you caught.'

'I'll leave on one condition.'

'And that is?'

'That you meet me in the woods above Bainden tomorrow morning.'

'I cannot do that. I will only get to the palace this evening. And, in any event, how did you know I was bound for there?'

Challice laughed. 'I guessed. But if you won't meet me in the morning will you come in the evening, after you have dined? I will wait for you until it gets dark.'

'When you will go off and rob some innocent traveller.'

Challice would have stopped her with a kiss had not the distant sound of horses sent him jumping from the coach and rapidly on to his own mount.

'Farewell until tomorrow. You will find your servants tied to the oak tree a hundred yards to the right of here.'

And with that he swept off his hat and was gone into the woods before Henrietta had had time to draw breath.

It could not have been a nicer homecoming. Nicholas Grey had returned to Mayfield and his lodging at Sharnden, after an absence of over a week, to find an invitation to dine awaiting him from Miss Lucy Baker, and for that very day. A postscript had been added that Miss Trevor would also be present.

The occasion warranted a bath and a good rub with a flesh-brush, and as Nicholas sat in the scented water he deliberately kept his mind off the unpleasant prospect of what lay before him after this intriguing social diversion was over.

He had left Rogers and Jekyll that morning, once again meeting them in Rogers's home and once again finding both of them, in their differing ways, formidable. It was Jekyll who had suggested that Nicholas should set a trap for the highwayman of Pennybridge, using himself as bait.

'Once you know who he is we have won half the battle. He'll do anything for a pardon. Anyway you say he already has a grudge against Jarvis. An argument over a woman, wasn't it?'

Nicholas muttered something inaudible wishing, yet again, that he had not gone to them for help.

Rogers had stood up at that, his thickset frame looming,

dwarfing the little room by the mere breadth of his shoulders. 'I intend a surprise move,' he said.

'Of what nature?' Nicholas had asked.

'I can only say that it will involve the Jarretts.'

And with that Lieutenant Grey had to be content.

Determinedly putting the bounty hunters from his mind, Nicholas concentrated on finishing his bath and dressing in his best clothes – grey breeches buckled over fine quality stockings, a rose-coloured waistcoat embroidered with silver threads, and a cinnamon-coloured velvet coat – hoping that he would do justice to the grand surroundings of the archbishops' palace.

The family awaited him in Lucy's little saloon, the room seeming crowded with people, for not only were every one of the Bakers present but also the delectable Miss Trevor, wearing a blue open robe and much frilled petticoat, together with John Langham.

Nicholas bowed politely to the assembled company, wishing that he could spend the entire evening with Henrietta and forget the others. To cover up his thoughts he engaged the surgeon in conversation.

'Were you able to do anything for Jacob Challice, Sir?'

Much to Nicholas's surprise a look that he could only describe as furtive crossed Langham's face. 'Yes ... yes. His wounds have healed.'

'An extraordinary business,' Nicholas went on, hoping to glean information. 'He is obviously not the highwayman of Pennybridge because Miss Trevor says so. And yet Kit Jarvis has such a grievance against him. I wonder why.'

John Langham looked even more uncomfortable. 'Who knows? Probably a woman.'

Nicholas nodded his head slowly. 'Probably.'

The scent of flowers told him that Henrietta had come to join them and Nicholas, eyes shining, turned to her. In that moment he realised that he could never again be quite the same person, for love had finally come to him. Not for him the slow building up, the gradual turning of affection into something more. For Lieutenant Nicholas Grey it was to be grand passion, enormous yearning, the consuming flame of utter commitment to the life of another.

'Miss Trevor,' he said, hardly trusting himself to speak.

She curtsied. 'Lieutenant Grey. How have you been since I was last in Mayfield?'

'Well, madam, but hardly here either.'

'Oh?'

'I have been away on business. And you?'

'At home with my mother and sisters and brother. I have worked on my embroidery and walked in the park.' The dimples were showing.

'It sounds very peaceful.'

Henrietta sighed. 'Indeed it was. But I often ask myself, Lieutenant Grey, if peace is everything. Sometimes I think it would be fun to be a man and live a thoroughly adventurous life. I often dream I am a man, you know.'

He smiled, more than a little amused. 'It is very difficult to imagine you as male, Miss Trevor.'

She looked at him seriously. 'Nonetheless, it does recur.'

'And what sort of man are you in your dreams?'

Henrietta frowned. 'That's just the point. Nobody brave or interesting. Just an ordinary creature with an aptitude for carpentry.'

Nicholas put his head back and laughed so loudly that all conversation ceased and everyone turned to look at him.

'What's the joke?' said Thomas, flourishing a lace handkerchief and dabbing it at one of his nostrils.

'Miss Trevor said something amusing,' answered Nicholas, a little embarrassed.

'Obviously,' came the reply, not kindly, and Grey thought angrily that the man was a caricature, a middle-aged fop dressed for a court ball, instead of a younger son of a local squire, living in a remote part of Sussex.

Noticing the atmosphere, Lucy called everyone to dine and the family and guests progressed in pairs down the grand staircase and into the great hall, arranged with a long table down its centre. As he escorted Henrietta to her place, Lieutenant Grey felt himself swept up in the past, looking at the decaying magnificence of what had once been the dining place of the archbishops of Canterbury, and feeling again an inexplicable sense of familiarity.

They took their seats, old Squire Baker at the head of the table with Henrietta on his right and Philadelphia on his left. At the foot sat Lucy with Nicholas and John Langham.

Interspersed between them were George, Thomas and Nizel, the last of whom sat on the other side of Henrietta and blushed unceasingly, his face a peony in full bloom. If his presence had not placed so much distance between Nicholas and the object of his affections that they were unable to converse, the Lieutenant would have been amused.

Hungry after his ride, Nicholas was glad when good solid English food – and plenty of it – was served. Obviously not for Lucy Baker the doubtful delights of French cuisine, as was the growing fashion in so many prosperous houses: the first course was heartily native, consisting of a whole tench boiled in ale, dressed with lemon and rosemary; soup with vermicelli (an exotic touch Nicholas thought); a chine of mutton and some chicken pie.

But when this was cleared away the meal proper was finally begun and Nicholas was able to partake heartily of pigeons and asparagus; a fillet of veal with mushrooms and high sauce; roasted sweetbreads and a hot buttered lobster. Delicacies followed in the form of a vast apricot tart with a pyramid of syllabubs and jellies in its centre. Fresh fruit came last of all.

It was as the white port was being served that Lucy said, 'What a pity we have no musicians.'

Old Squire Baker, flushed from gorging, answered, 'What do you mean, child? Musicians aren't for eating to.'

'But they used to be. Look at that gallery up there. Once that would have been filled with minstrels.'

Nicholas never knew why he said, 'I will play for you,' but the fact remained that he did, rising from his feet under some sort of compulsion.

Though some of the others looked a little stunned, Henrietta clapped her hands together and said, 'Lieutenant Grey, could you really? What do you play?'

Spurred on, Nicholas said boldly, 'I could play the lute – if Miss Baker wishes it.'

'Of course I wish it,' answered Lucy firmly and beckoning to one of the servants directed them to fetch the lute that lay in the withdrawing room.

'And shall I go into the gallery?' asked Nicholas, half joking.

'Oh yes! What fun. Do you object, Father?'

'It's all the same to me,' answered the old squire. 'Every

damned note of it sounds the same. All a lot of caterwauling. Go ahead, Grey, if it amuses the ladies.'

Nicholas bowed, took the lute from the servant, and mounted the spindly staircase to the gallery above. Two small chairs still stood there and Nicholas sat down, only the top of his head visible to those who watched from below. He put his hand to the strings but the tune he had intended to play did not come out. Instead there sounded an air from another age entirely, an air so lively that the feet in the hall below began to tap and Lucy whispered down the length of the table, 'He's very good.'

And while they applauded, Nicholas played on and on, beautiful melodies and plaintive love songs combining in one overwhelmingly disturbing sound. Even the old Squire stopped spluttering and closed his eyes, though not in sleep. And Henrietta, listening to the glorious cadences, suddenly realised that Nicholas Grey was in love with her, that every note he played was for her. She realised too that she had feelings for him, but whether those feelings were of love or affection – or a combination of both – she was not sure.

Suddenly there was silence and the family and guests looked at one another, stunned. It was over! Nicholas appeared from the gallery, exhausted, and as they all burst into wild applause he stared straight over the heads of everyone and directly into Henrietta's eyes.

The words were on his lips before he could stop himself, and there in the great hall of the old palace, the couple exchanged a silent greeting as he whispered, 'I love you.'

It was dark when the dinner party, which had begun just after two in the afternoon, finally ended. And as the Bakers and Henrietta stood at the palace door and waved off the two guests, she suddenly realised that she had forgotten all about Challice, alone and waiting in the woods above Bainden. Guiltily she turned to go inside but then wheeled once more to look at Lieutenant Grey who by now, his face quite expressionless, had mounted his horse to go. His eyes briefly met hers and they gave each other a half smile which, in both their cases, masked different but equally profound emotions. Then they turned away again and he was gone, trotting down the drive beside John Langham's coach and off in the direction of Sharnden.

It was as he parted company with the surgeon and headed

down the track leading to Coggins Mill, that Nicholas heard the tramp of feet and a general hullabaloo, and, as he hurried towards the sound, saw in the light of flickering torches what looked like an arresting party. He drew nearer and realised that was just what it was, recognising to his amazement the leathery face of John Jarrett, a member of the family recently cheated of Francis Hammond's arrest by the decision of a local magistrate. But not thwarted for long it appeared now, for once again Hammond walked in their midst, his hands manacled and his face a picture of misery.

'What's going on?' said Nicholas, as they drew level.

'Oh, Lieutenant Grey, it's you,' answered Jarrett, startled and obviously a fraction embarrassed. 'We've got the bastard again – and he's to go to a different justice this time, not one whose pockets are weighted down with bribes.'

'Did you catch him thieving?'

'No, Sir, fornicating – if you'll forgive my frankness. He was under a tree with a village girl going at it hammer and tongs. We caught him with his breeches down all right.' Jarrett burst into a bellow of laughter and rubbed his hands together. 'Wretched little ram,' he added in an undertone.

Nicholas could not resist a smile. 'Where are you taking him?'

'To the cellar of the Star for the night. We daren't risk the Oak. We'll have him before the beak first thing tomorrow.'

'I wish you luck,' said Nicholas. 'Do you need any help?'

'No, Sir. We can manage the little prat-mopper. If it's all the same to you, Lieutenant.'

Nicholas sighed. 'It's all the same to me,' he answered, adding under his breath. 'I've been told to search for bigger fish.'

'Then goodnight, Sir.'

'Goodnight.'

The Lieutenant turned his horse away, wishing that he lived in different times and had chosen a job which did not involve the hunting down of his fellow creatures, an occupation with which he found himself growing less and less in sympathy.

FORTY

A light rain was falling in the valley of Bivelham, blessing the earth and bringing with it a fine soft mist. At the head of the dale the mist was heavier, hiding Stream Farm almost completely, so that the people therein felt even more protected than usual. Despite the weather the kitchen door was open and from within came the sound of laughter. Francis Hammond's voice, as light and naughty as he was, dominated all.

'What a night!' he laughed. 'First that bastard Jarrett catches me having a buttock jig, and then I'm locked up in the cellar of the Star. And then you, Ted.'

Edward grinned. 'You should have seen their faces, Kit, when we burst in. Do you know the landlord screamed in fright and Jarrett looked as if he would burst his bladder.'

'Did he?' asked Emily.

'No, he hung on but it was a close thing.'

'They looked horrific,' Francis went on. 'All three had their faces painted black and were in their shirts, brandishing pistols.'

'So Jarrett released you?' asked Kit.

'He had little choice with a gun in his back. God's wounds, but the man cursed some oaths.'

'It was well done,' the smuggler said to his half-brother. 'I wish I had been there.' He changed the subject. 'I hear that Challice has been lying low these last few days. What's up with him?'

'My mother says he's in a mood,' said Emily. 'Has been ever since he got back from London.'

'I've got to shift the bastard,' came from Kit. 'I swore to get him off my patch and by God I will. How he survived that beating I'll never know.'

'I can't understand how he got off free,' Edward put in. 'Miss Trevor couldn't have had a good look at him after all.'

'Or too good a look,' said Francis, his preoccupation with women as ever coming to the fore. 'Perhaps she fancied him.'

Emily found herself blushing as she said, 'I shouldn't think so, he's too rough for her.'

373

'It takes all sorts,' Francis persisted. 'Perhaps the thought of a night with a gentleman of the pad excites her.'

Feeling Kit looking at her, Emmy did not reply and it was left to Edward to say, 'I should think he could be attractive enough if he wanted to be. Those rugged men often are.'

Francis suppressed a giggle, grateful for the fact that Edward had saved him from a dangerous situation. 'May I lie low here for a few days, Kit?' he said straight-faced.

'I think that would be wise. Lieutenant Grey will be in a frenzy over your escape, and unfortunately I don't think he's the type to accept a bribe. I believe threats might be more to the point.'

'Well we've got to do something. He's turning into a nuisance.'

'What with him and Challice,' sighed Kit. 'Life is growing daily more difficult.'

'What does Dash say?'

'That he thinks Grey is soft on Miss Trevor.'

'Another one!' exclaimed Emily. 'What is so special about her?'

'Pretty eyes,' answered Kit, only to be treated to a jealous black look as Emily turned on her heel and silently left the room.

Despite the showers, Henrietta Trevor rose early that same morning and, putting on a riding habit which consisted of a long skirt with a panel of embroidery at the base, a thigh-length buttoned waistcoat with a longer open coat above it, a Steinkirk cravat, gloves and a tricorne hat, set off alone from the palace. She was heading for Bainden, wondering if Jacob Challice might be there and she could keep the rendezvous which she had missed the previous evening.

As she rode, Henrietta felt her mind to be in a whirl, amazed that two men – either of whom her mother would deem thoroughly unsuitable – had declared a fondness for her in the same day. And wondering, too, why she felt attracted to both of them at the same time.

As she climbed the hill leading to the wood she saw that Challice did indeed await her and as she approached heard him call, 'I thought you might come. I waited for you last night.'

'I'm sorry,' she answered stiffly, suddenly nervous. 'I was delayed at dinner and could not get away.'

'Flirting with Thomas – or was it Nizel?'

'Neither,' she answered, adding 'What concern is it of yours?'

'Every concern.' He pulled her close to him so that she could feel the hardness of his body even through the thickness of her clothing.

'Why?'

'Because I'm falling in love. I lay awake all last night because I hadn't seen you, and because you don't approve I have not been out on the pad.'

She was silent and Jacob went on, 'Now I have made you angry. Here, let me bring back your pretty smile.'

He bent his mouth to hers and kissed her, then moved his lips and kissed her eyes and nose, and the place where her funny dimples sprang.

'Oh Jacob,' she said pushing him away, unable to think.

Challice released her, his hands trembling. 'Henrietta, do I dare hope ...?'

'No,' she answered, turning away. 'There can be no future for us. When I return to Glynde Place my mother intends to launch me onto the marriage market. She will give an elegant dance packed with possible suitors. And though she would never force me to marry anyone repellent to me, she will make sure that the place is filled with young, rich, handsome men, who will turn my head.'

'Perhaps I should attend, dressed as a gentleman. I have plenty of money.'

'Yes, gained at the expense of others.'

Once again Jacob caught her to him roughly. 'Henrietta, stop it. There is something between us despite everything. An attraction that draws us close regardless of the barriers created by our backgrounds. If that is not so, why did you deny I was the highwayman? You said yourself that the words of betrayal would not come out.'

It was true, everything he uttered, and as he bent to kiss her yet again, Henrietta felt an overpowering sense of oneness with him. 'You're right,' she whispered. 'I, too, am falling in love.'

The night was ebony streaked with silver, for a thousand stars danced in a sky dark as a rook, while a slim crescent moon sailed through the heavens like a schooner with hoisted sails. Despite the glory of the scene, nothing stirred; the whole of Mayfield lying asleep beneath the brilliance. Only a black-cloaked horseman stood motionless in the trees beside the road known as Pennybridge, listening to the sound of a coach starting its perilous descent of the steep and twisting road. In the starlight, Jacob Challice smiled.

He already had his kerchief over his face because of the moonshine, and his hat was pulled so well down that only his eyes were visible. In this way he felt safe to step out at the moment when the coach slowed for the steep bend and call to the passengers to 'Stand fast.' For now he robbed with a purpose, truly believing that he and Henrietta Trevor had been brought together by fate and were destined to spend their lives as one. If he had to, Jacob would go out every night, widening his net, until he had sold enough jewels to allow him to make investments or buy a trading ship. Anything to acquire the veneer of respectability that would leave him free to court the eldest daughter of the late Squire of Glynde.

The awaited sound came and Jacob heard the coachman call, 'Whoa,' and the horses' feet begin to slip. He moved forward through the trees and was out on the road in a second, his pistols cocked and pointing, one at the coach box, the other at the window.

'Stand fast,' he shouted hoarsely and looked up to see if the coachman was armed. To his astonishment there was nobody there and no head appeared at the window in the door, which bore the Baker insignia. 'Stand fast,' Jacob called again, and the next second was knocked from his horse, which reared in fright, as something flew through the air and landed hard on top of him.

The highwayman hit the ground with such a crunch that his breath flew from his lungs and he lay helpless and gasping, unable to protect himself, as his disguise was ripped from his face.

'So it *is* you,' said a voice. 'I knew it all along.'

He looked up, fighting to get air, to see Nicholas Grey leaning over him, pointing a pistol right at his heart. 'One move, you bastard, and you're a dead man. You've deceived me long enough.'

As the Riding Officer stood up slowly, never wavering the direction of his aim and watching Challice through narrowed eyes, the highwayman regained his normal breathing and got to his feet.

'I'm tired of you,' Grey went on. 'You have terrorised this road during the last few weeks and got away with it. Well, that's at an end now. You will remain under arrest until you are taken for trial. You're going to dance on the end of a rope, Challice.'

Jacob broke into a drenching sweat, the very thought of such an end filling him with terror.

'Oh Christ,' he exclaimed involuntarily.

'Indeed!' said Grey. 'Now get into the coach. I'm taking you straight into custody.'

As Challice turned his back to clamber aboard, Nicholas's face changed. Much as the robber had been a thorn in his flesh, his strange grudging admiration of the man was only just hidden beneath the surface. He hated doing this and wished that Edward Jarvis had not rescued Francis Hammond, making it more essential than ever that somebody peached against the smugglers and that dragoons could be sent to catch them in the very act of loading their goods. Cursing his job, Lieutenant Grey stepped aboard, dropping his eyes just for a second to see the step.

Now it was his turn to go flying as a fist like a hammer knocked the pistol from his hand and crashed onto his jaw in the same swing. Nicholas fell backwards onto the ground, to see Challice darting away across the road.

'Stop or I'll shoot,' he yelled, but Jacob ignored him and went sprinting on. Reaching in the pocket of his cloak for the other pistol, Nicholas fired towards the retreating figure. There was no sound and it had vanished into the darkness by the time Grey struggled upright.

'Curse the bastard,' said Nicholas furiously. 'I swear I'll arrest him and enjoy it next time.'

But he knew that Jacob had to act fast. Now that Lieutenant Grey had seen his face there were only two things left for Challice to do: get away from Mayfield as quickly as he could – or kill the Riding Officer before he could talk.

The banging on his front door in the middle of the night woke John Langham so abruptly that he had leapt out of bed and crossed to the window before he had fully recovered his senses. But once there, and having opened the casement, he woke up properly and leaned out, his nightcap slipping forward rakishly as he did so.

A shadowy figure stood in the shaded porch, his face concealed by a large feathered hat. On hearing the window open the figure looked up and called out hoarsely, 'Mr Langham?'

'Yes,' said John nervously. 'Who is it?'

'Challice, Sir. Jacob Challice. I wonder if you might help me. I've been shot.'

'Shot?' John leaned forward further and, sure enough, could see that Challice was clutching his shoulder and a trickle of blood was running through his fingers and onto the paving stones below. 'Wait a moment, I'll come down.'

He opened the front door to see Challice, white-faced, standing there swaying as he grasped his gushing wound.

'Good God,' said John, 'who has done this to you?'

'A smuggler,' answered Challice tersely. 'Can you help me, Sir?'

'Of course. Come in and go through to my private room. I'll send a servant to you with a drink.'

Five minutes later John, fully dressed but minus his wig and wearing a linen cap on his head, came into his sanctum to find Challice lying on the couch, his eyes closed in pain and the blood seeping profusely through his coat. Much as the surgeon thought, the bullet was lodged firmly in the top of Jacob's arm.

'I'll have to get that out, Challice. Unless I do so the wound will continue to bleed and you'll be done for.' Knowing what had happened previously, the surgeon hesitated before saying, 'I have a method whereby you will feel no pain during the operation. No more than as if I was tapping you on the arm.'

'Then use it,' answered Challice a trifle impatiently, his granite face creasing as he pressed his lips together to stop himself from crying out.

'Look at my watch as I swing it to and fro and listen only to my voice. Soon your eyes will grow tired and you will close them and after that you will feel me touching your shoulder. That is all you will feel, Jacob. I see that your eyes have closed. I will count slowly to twenty and when I reach that number you will be deeply relaxed but still able to hear me. Do you understand?'

'I understand,' answered Challice disjointedly.

'Good.' John took his knife and passed it again and again through a naked flame, finally plunging it deep into the flesh at the top of Jacob's arm.

'Do you feel me touching you, Jacob?'

378

'I do.'

'A gentle touch, is it not?'

'Very gentle,' came the answer in that flat, slightly unearthly, voice.

Saying no more, John Langham concentrated on drawing forth the bullet and draining the wound, which he smothered in a paste made from healing herbs before fixing a dressing in place. Then, stopping to wipe his brow, he considered his patient who still lay in the dream state, oblivious of all that had been done to him.

'Jacob,' said John, 'are you comfortable?'

'Yes,' came the whispered reply.

'Then I want you to go back to long before you were in your mother's womb. But not back to death itself. Go back, Jacob, to twenty years before you were born. Where are you?'

'Nowhere. Floating in darkness. Nowhere at all.'

John hesitated, with such an excellent subject as Jacob, was he risking the re-enactment of something as awful as the hanging? He chose his next words very carefully.

'Jacob, I want you to go back four hundred years. Go back to that time. Are you still floating in darkness?'

'No. I am in the woods, watching my friend.'

'What is your name?'

'Marcus de Flaviel, squire of Gascony.'

At those words John had a most curious sensation. Something in his memory made a connection and he knew that he had heard the name before.

'Tell me what is happening.'

'I am sitting on a tree-trunk and my charge Colin . . .'

'Your charge?'

'It is my duty to look after him because he is a simpleton with the mind of a boy. He is playing the gittern now. He plays like a god.'

'Strange,' thought John, 'the very words I used to Lucy to describe the talent of Lieutenant Grey.'

'Go on.'

'He is playing and I am listening and I am thinking that I both love and hate him.'

'Why is that?'

'Only because of Oriel his wife. We are lovers, she and I.'

'Does this not worry Colin?'

379

'He does not know. He is an innocent in every way.'

'What will you do when he has finished playing?'

'We will go home to the palace and have soup before the fire. And Oriel will laugh and listen to our adventures. She loves us both in entirely different ways.'

'What is the name of the palace?' asked John, feeling that the ultimate coincidence surely could not be possible.

'The archbishops'.'

'And where is it?'

'In England, in Sussex. A place called Maghefeld.'

'Is it the palace of the Archbishops of Canterbury?'

'Yes. It is the archbishop who has employed me to look after Colin who is his brother.'

'And how did you come to England?'

'With my foster father, Sir Paul d'Estrange, knight of Gascony.'

John Langham felt himself break out in a sweat. He knew the name. But Challice was continuing to speak.

'But he is not just a knight, he is also a herbalist. He studied Arab medicine with a priest. He has also made beautifying preparations for Oriel's mother, Margaret de Sharndene.'

'Margaret de Sharndene,' repeated John wonderingly. 'So you knew her then?'

'Oh yes,' answered Jacob. 'I know her well.'

FORTY-ONE

The showers that had visited the valley and village for over a
week had finally turned into rain. And a downpour at that. The
central track that ran through the heart of Mayfield had
become a sea of mud through which carts and carriages bumped
with difficulty as their wheels squelched into the quagmire
below. Frequently they got stuck, and then would come a
general heaving and shoving as brawny men put their shoulders
to the problem and lifted the conveyances out bodily, sending
them on their way amidst a chorus of cheers. It was May time, it
was England, and everyone accepted without grumbling that it
was pouring with rain.

In the midst of all the driving water the palace was an island
of security. Because the old squire felt the cold so badly these
days, fires had been lit in most of the living-rooms and Lucy
fussed about making sure that everyone was comfortable and
had enough to eat and drink, meanwhile piling the old man
with so many rugs and shawls that all that could be seen of him
was an angry old face peering out from its various wrappings,
rather as a tortoise from its shell. He was in the seventy-ninth
year of his life and quite as horrid and pernickety as everybody
expected him to be.

Because of the inclement day, most of the Bakers had gathered in the great withdrawing-room to play games, chatter and
– in the case of Nizel – make soft pencil sketches of the assembled
company. In tune with the national mania the other Bakers, in
company with Henrietta, were gambling small amounts on
cards; the old squire, Lucy, George and Philadelphia involved
in a session of ombre, at which he appeared to be cheating,
secreting the cards beneath his layers of wrapping. Philadelphia,
quite pink in the face, obviously wanted to remonstrate but was
constantly hushed by George who, today, wore a new wig of
even vaster proportions.

Thomas, declaring that country folk really should keep up
with London fashions, was attempting to explain the intricacies

of quadrille to Henrietta, loudly proclaiming that it would soon be the universal employment of life in fashionable circles, while his pupil, trying desperately hard to concentrate, thought about Jacob Challice.

The serving of tea into this scene of domestic country life called for a break in activity and it was during this interlude, filled with the sound of the old squire chewing gummily upon a cake and noisily gulping his drink, that a servant entered discreetly and murmured something to him.

'Speak up,' shouted the old man, cocking his ear with his hand.

'Lieutenant Grey has called to see you, Sir. He says it is a matter of some urgency and asks whether he may speak with you in private in the saloon.'

'Damn the fellow! Just when I was winning at cards, too. Oh very well, show him up. I'll come when I've finished.'

Old Squire Baker swallowed the remains of his cake, reached for another, and gurgled down his cup of tea.

'What can he want,' he grumbled. 'Lucy, what does he want?'

'I don't know, Father. Perhaps he has news of the smugglers – or the highwayman.'

'The highwayman!' said Henrietta, half rising. 'Surely they cannot have caught him.'

'Why not?' answered Thomas, eyeing her narrowly. 'He cannot terrorise the same route indefinitely and expect to get away with it. The fool should have moved on.'

Her reply was drowned by the sound of the old man getting to his feet, scattering shawls to the four winds – or in this case the anxious hands of Lucy and Philadelphia – and taking George's arm, at the same time calling for his stick. Nizel hurried up with it, dropping his sketchpad and pencils as he did so, and there ensued a few moments of total pandemonium, which hid the fact that Henrietta had dramatically lost colour and been forced to sit down again.

With the disappearance of her father, Lucy attempted to restore order by insisting that everyone had more tea and Henrietta suddenly found herself with a cup in her hand, seated, unexpectedly, next to Nizel who was turning the colour of a peony at her very presence.

In a frantic effort to cover her distress, Henrietta decided to engage him in conversation. 'Nizel, we have scarcely spoken since I arrived. How are you getting on with your painting? I should so enjoy to see some of your watercolours.'

'Th... they're not very good,' he stammered, going puce and looking, for one ridiculous moment, the image of his father.

'But nonetheless I should like to do so.'

'Well... er... I keep them in Charity's old room. If you would like to...' He stopped abruptly as it occurred to him that it was not the done thing at all to invite a young lady into a bedroom and went such a ghastly shade as a result that Henrietta wondered if he was going to have a fit.

'Perhaps you could bring some of them down...' she started, but her sentence was never completed for from the saloon leading off the withdrawing-room came a roar like a bull.

'What!' the old man was shouting. 'You let him get away! God's wounds and zoonters, Grey, what is the world coming to?'

There was a murmured reply and the conversation subsided once more. Henrietta's heart began to thud with relief. Whoever it was that Grey had apprehended had managed to escape. Her eyes filled with tears, which were just beginning to brim over the edge, when the same servant re-entered and said, 'Lieutenant Grey would like to see you, Miss Trevor.'

'Me?'

'Yes, ma'am. The Squire says he'd be obliged if you would step this way.'

As she left the withdrawing-room with everyone watching, Henrietta felt fear replace every other emotion. She convinced herself during the few moments that it took to walk to the saloon, that she and Jacob had been observed meeting, that she would be taken back to Glynde covered in shame, that her family would be so shocked that the only course open to her would be to go abroad and take the veil.

As she raised her hand to knock on the door it opened, and the old squire appeared, hobbling out on the arm of a servant.

'He wants to speak to you on your own, my dear,' he whispered. 'Don't let him bully you. He's got some notion about Challice.'

'Has he been caught?' she whispered back.

'He's escaped but he's wounded. It will only be a matter of

hours now before he's recaptured. You've nothing to fear from a common highwayman.'

He burbled something else but Henrietta was beyond listening, beyond hearing, as, with not a moment to recover herself, she swept her hoops through the door and stood for the second time in three days, looking into the pewter-coloured eyes of Nicholas Grey.

Much to her amazement they were twinkling as he said, 'Do sit down, Miss Trevor. I won't keep you a moment.'

Very stiffly she answered, 'You wanted to see me, Lieutenant?'

'Yes.' He perched on the edge of the writing desk, one booted leg swinging. 'Yes, it is about the man you identified – or rather did not identify – here at the palace. I recently set a trap for the highwayman, and he walked right into it. It was the same man, Miss Trevor. You must have made a mistake.'

Unable to think of a thing to say, Henrietta fought for time by answering. 'I am afraid I don't understand you.'

'The highwayman of Pennybridge is Jacob Challice, Henrietta. Your lie to protect him has failed.'

'How dare you,' she answered, rising to her feet and turning a furious face towards him. 'I simply was mistaken, that is all. Anyway I don't believe you. Did you catch him red-handed?'

'In the very act of robbing a coach in which I was travelling on the roof.'

Despite everything, Henrietta repeated in astonishment, 'On the roof?'

Nicholas grinned. 'A trick I taught myself some years ago. Drive the horses from above and then launch yourself at your quarry. It usually works – unless I miss.'

In normal circumstances Miss Trevor would have laughed but now she was too upset. 'And where is Challice now?'

'Gone to earth. I shot him while he escaped.'

The room circled unpleasantly and Henrietta put her hand to her head. 'Oh merciful God,' she said.

Nicholas left the desk and crossed over to her, holding both her arms with his hands. 'Henrietta,' he said earnestly. 'You don't have to say anything in reply but there is something that I most urgently have to say to *you*. It is my belief – please keep silent – that you *did* recognise Challice and for some reason denied the fact. I don't know how much the man means to you, if anything, but I must warn you that he is doomed. Forces are massing against him – forces far stronger than I – and he will end on the gallows. That is beyond a shadow of a doubt. I beg you, for your own sake, not to become any further involved with him.'

His dark grey eyes regarded her very seriously as he spoke again. 'This could not be a worse moment to declare myself, Miss Trevor, but so be it. I have more than a fondness for you as you have probably guessed already. In fact the other night, inspired by music and wine, I said that I loved you.'

'I know,' Henrietta whispered.

'I am glad of that, because it is true. I think, looking back, that I probably fell in love with you at our first meeting. I realise, of course, that there is no future for us. I am a humble Riding Officer and far down the social scale from the daughter of the Squire of Glynde. But that does not mean that I do not want to protect you and see you happy. Therefore, dearest, darling, beautiful Henrietta, I implore you to be careful. Danger lies ahead for Challice – and for you too if you go on consorting with him.'

She could not make an answer, in fact she could do nothing but burst into a storm of weeping, flying into Nicholas's arms and resting her head against his beating heart.

'Nicholas, is Jacob really in danger?' she said.

'Terribly. The old squire is posting a reward for his capture, dead or alive, and every bounty hunter in Sussex will be after it. To make the situation even worse two professionals are on their way here. And they will not stop until they have Challice in their clutches.'

'Then he must leave the area?'

'It is the only way.'

There was a momentary silence during which the Lieutenant and the young woman stared at one another. Then she said, 'You have told me this so that I can warn him, haven't you?'

'Henrietta,' came the measured reply, 'I think if you ever see him again you are implicating yourself in a highly dangerous situation. But, knowing you, I am sure that you will persist. The kindest thing you can do for Challice is to warn him off and make sure he goes. I have already told you the likely consequences if he does not.' Nicholas paused and then went on, 'I tell you this not because I am his rival for your affections, but because it will hurt you if anything happens to him. I am doing my best to be fair.'

She hugged him close to her again. 'You are being more than that, you are being the soul of honesty. It shines out of your eyes.'

Nicholas caught her to him hard. 'But don't think that makes me any less the man. I love you and want you and would go to the ends of the earth if I thought there was any chance of winning you.'

Her reply never came because, throwing caution aside, he bent to kiss her, there in the Bakers' household with the family in the very next room. Now she knew him to be a true rival to Jacob, for his kiss was hungry, demanding, telling her that he wanted her as much as did the highwayman. Yet, within herself, Henrietta knew that the flame that Jacob had lit in her, the flame that had affected both her heart and body, was missing. The kiss was deep, satisfying, but lacked that one divine spark that separated love from friendship.

They drew apart and Nicholas said, 'My dear love, go and wash your face. I shall bid Miss Baker adieu and take my leave. I promise you I shall not enquire about Challice further, provided you give your word that you tell him quite clearly of the danger he is in.'

'But if he has been shot, where is he?'

Nicholas gave a wry smile. 'I should try the house of Mr Langham the surgeon if I were you.'

She smiled. 'If he is there, why don't you arrest him?'

'And lose my only chance of you loving me? Never! I may be a Riding Officer but I am no fool. No Henrietta, let Challice and I be on equal terms in your eyes.'

This time it was Miss Trevor who stood on tiptoe to kiss the Lieutenant.

That evening the rain stopped early, so that when the Bakers had finished dining they were able to go out and take some fresh air. Both Thomas and Lucy ordered carriages; she obviously – or so Henrietta thought – making her way to see John Langham; he, appearing in immensely grand dress, going off mysteriously in the direction of Tunbridge Wells, no doubt to sample the delights of the new season at the spa. Nizel, on the other hand, clapped an even more battered straw hat on his head than usual and, grabbing his easel and paints, vanished into the country-side.

With only George and Philadelphia left for company, Henrietta decided to take a short walk to try and make some sense of her many and confused thoughts, before she retired early for the night. She put a light mantle over her dress, pulled the hood around her head, and made her way on foot through the palace gates and out into Mayfield.

As Henrietta walked down the eastern track she saw that the fields and hills to her right glowed gold as the sun began its descent from the high point in the heavens. Soon pinks and mauves, violets and yellows, together with red, would fire the sky but now the evening was as sharp and sweet as a cool pale peppermint.

Breathing in the delights of such splendour, Henrietta proceeded on, passing on her left a cottage that reminded her of a ship and various other old and interesting properties that by their very timbered presence seemed to speak of Mayfield in another age. Only the problem of Jacob and Nicholas and her overwhelming emotions stopped her from feeling harmoniously at one with her surroundings.

With her mind going over the problem, Henrietta stepped on down the track only to have to jump back hastily as a horseman came riding by at some speed. He reined in hard as he saw her and called, 'My apologies, Madam. I was preoccupied and did not notice you. Forgive my rudeness, please.'

Henrietta smiled an acknowledgement, only to find herself looking at a tall, thin young man dressed in the uniform of a lieutenant in Brigadier Groves's regiment. He dismounted as soon as he had calmed his mount and bowed before her, military style.

'I do hope you were in no way injured, Miss...?'

'Trevor. Henrietta Trevor. No, I am perfectly all right thank you.'

'Then praise be.' He smiled winningly and she noticed that though his mouth curved upward to show a set of firm white teeth, his eyes remained unlit, taking in every detail of her appearance with a look that was both cool and appraising.

'Jekyll, ma'am,' he said, bowing again neatly. 'Lieutenant Jekyll, at your service.'

Henrietta dropped a polite curtsey. 'You are visiting May-field, Lieutenant?'

'In a way. I shall be staying at the Barracks for a while.'

'The Barracks?'

'At Fir Toll. Where the dragoons were stationed during the recent arrest of a highwayman.'

'Oh! So you are here on army business, Lieutenant Jekyll?'

He laughed, again displaying his dazzling teeth. 'Nothing that need worry your head, dear lady. Just keeping an eye on things.' As before, his gaze remained detached.

Henrietta's heart sank with alarm. Could this be one of the bounty hunters that Nicholas had mentioned earlier in the day? Desperately she tried to probe without appearing to do so.

'So you are going to round up the smugglers, Lieutenant?'

'That would be telling, Miss Trevor. Why for all I know you might be one of them.' He laughed uproariously at that while Henrietta smiled feebly in return. 'No,' he went on, his face becoming serious, 'I am here merely to see that law and order are maintained. Not easy in these ruthless times, I'm sure you'll agree.'

Henrietta murmured something suitable and the Lieutenant said, 'May I escort you home, Miss Trevor, or do you have further to walk?'

'I thought I might take the air a little longer, thank you Lieutenant. I am staying at the palace by the way, a guest of Squire Baker and his family.'

'Then hopefully I shall have the pleasure of renewing our acquaintance, as I intend to call on the squire and present my compliments tomorrow.'

'Perhaps I shall see you then,' answered Henrietta, by now thoroughly alarmed and wishing only to be alone that she might plan how best to warn Jacob of this new threat to his safety.

Once again Lieutenant Jekyll bowed. 'Until then, Miss Trevor. May I wish you a pleasant evening.'

'And to you also.'

He remounted, still watching her, and Henrietta was aware of those cold light eyes following her as she turned to continue her journey down the eastern track, away from the village.

In the same evening, Lucy Baker made her way by coach to John Langham's house, wanting only to pour out her account of

388

the day's happenings to her dearest friend. But for once she found the surgeon, usually so calm and comforting, in a frenzy, even having gone so far as to forget his well-curled wig and have his house-cap upon his head when she arrived. There was an inner excitement about him and he almost forgot to kiss her when the last of the servants had departed, leaving them alone together in his gracious saloon, filled with the warm glow of the setting sun.

'What is it?' she said at once. 'John, what has happened?'

'An unbelievable thing,' he said. 'Lucy, I have had further evidence of your life as Margaret of Sharnden.'

Now it was her turn to feel excitement. 'What do you mean? How could you have done?'

Pulling her almost roughly to sit down beside him, John whispered, 'Through Jacob Challice who lies upstairs at this very moment.'

'He is here! John Langham, have you taken leave of your senses? You, a respected surgeon, harbouring a criminal. What is the matter with you?'

Looking abashed, John said, 'It is part of my research, Lucy. Pray do not be angry. I sent Challice back in time, and he spoke of Margaret of Sharnden and of Paul d'Estrange. He said that Paul was interested in medicine and herbalism. A strange feeling gripped me when he said those words. Perhaps I, too, was part of your past.'

She smiled a little sadly. 'Perhaps you were, but will you ever be part of my future?'

He patted her hand. 'One day the way will be clear for us.'

'Oh I do hope so,' answered Lucy, as with her eyelids already dropping, she tucked her feet neatly onto the graceful sofa and began to watch the swinging pendulum in Langham's hand, listening to his voice taking her back on a journey through time.

A casual observer watching Lieutenant Jekyll enter the Barracks – the old and beautiful house in Fir Toll that had, for the moment, been requisitioned by the military – would have seen a tall thin officer go in. But had he waited an hour he would not have recognised the strange creature that emerged, a creature wearing a shepherd's smock, great straw hat, to say nothing of dirty old boots and a rough-spun pair of breeches. He would have been even further surprised to see the Lieutenant climb into a battered cart, hitched to a sturdy horse in blinkers, which he drove towards the south east of the village, climbing the tortuous track upwards until he had vanished into the trees at the top of the slope.

Once out of sight of prying eyes, Lieutenant Jekyll urged his conveyance on so that the enormous sweep he was taking through woods and farmlands, enabling him to reach Coggins Mill without passing through the village, could be accomplished while there was still enough light to see. Finally, threading through a dense coppice, the cart began to go downhill and Jekyll, unobserved, crossed the main London coaching road and, passing between the cottages, found what he was looking for. Before him stretched a sunken track almost hidden from view. He had found Kit Jarvis's own personal route out of the village.

Driving the cart along it for a certain distance, Lieutenant Jekyll finally drew off into the shadow of some thickly growing trees and, lighting a pipe, settled down to wait.

The sky darkened and a new-born moon appeared fitfully between clouds of frosted milk. As the heat of the evening vanished, the road seethed with mist, and Jekyll hugged his arms round himself to keep out the sudden cold. He was just lighting another pipe when he heard it, the approach of muffled hooves and the quiet march of men. His luck and his intelligent guess had held; with only a tiny moon, a run was taking place. The smugglers were on their way.

Jekyll braced himself, dousing his pipe. Timing was essential now. He peered into the mist and had the eerie experience of hearing men and horses passing below but seeing nothing – just as if a ghostly army was on the move. From the volume of sound the Lieutenant guessed that a convoy of eighty, including horses and carts, was making its way to the coast this night.

He waited his moment and as he heard the last of the carts rumble beneath him, hurried his conveyance down the slope and joined the convoy, saying, 'I thought I would never see you. A wheel broke loose just as I was setting forth,' to the driver in front. There was a grunt of greeting and then silence, and in the misty darkness Jekyll grinned.

The secret road went steadily along the side of a wood, near to the land of Merryweather Farm and watermill, and then began to climb, running directly beneath a curious house, half Tudor, half modern, which Jekyll believed belonged to a surgeon. Now they were in the heart of valley country and the road plunged into thick woods, once the hunting lands of the Lords of Glynde. Jekyll, less experienced a cart driver than the others, found it hard to negotiate the rough terrain and was glad when the convoy suddenly pulled to a halt.

From his position at the back the Lieutenant had no idea why they had stopped but took the opportunity to jump down and quickly relieve himself, making this his excuse to take note of what was happening.

The procession had come to rest in a glade and Jekyll was astonished to see that in the heart of it lay a large ruin, surrounded by a moat. An entrance bridge crossed the water and, straining his eyes in the darkness, Jekyll observed that the stones and slates of the ancient pile were being systematically plundered for building purposes elsewhere. But this, or so it would appear, was not the only function of the deserted house. Beneath piles of brushwood stacks of barrels could be seen, standing in what must have once been a spacious courtyard.

Jekyll's curiosity overcame him and throwing discretion to the winds he said to the man nearest him, 'Who owned this place?'

The smuggler gave him an odd stare and answered, 'The Lords of Glynde. It was the hunting lodge of one of them. Probably John Waleis who fought at Crécy.'

'Of course,' said Jekyll quickly. 'My memory isn't what it was.'

Any doubts that the other man might have had, however, were quietened by a call from the head of the train, presumably from one of the Jarvis brothers. The procession moved on, climbing up, through heavy woods, and then down again, passing close to a farm called Gillhope, and at last coming to the banks of the Rother. Here, Jekyll noticed, the smugglers had sown a crop – their term for sinking a raft of tubs to await later collection – brought up by river from the Romney Marshes.

The convoy of men began to follow the course of the river, going in the direction of Burwash, and then to the coast. Under his breath Lieutenant Jekyll began to whistle cheerfully. He had the feeling that a long night lay ahead.

* * *

It had not been as easy to slip away from the smugglers' train as the lieutenant had envisaged. Much to his horror when they had finally left the Rother he had been joined at the back of the convoy by Edward Jarvis, heavily armed with hanger and bat, and they had ridden almost side by side for the rest of the journey. Though Jekyll, for obvious reasons, would by far have preferred to remain silent, Edward had said in a businesslike voice, 'I want you to handle Dash's personal consignment. He is very short of brandy and has asked that it might be taken straight to him. Can you see to that?'

Jekyll took a calculated risk. 'I'm not sure of Dash's identity, Master Jarvis. I don't help out very often.'

Edward's face went blank. 'Oh no, of course you don't,' he said, and had cantered off.

Jekyll, wondering whether he had said the right thing, knew that this was the moment to leave, but the smell of salt was in the air, together with the wild, sad song of the ocean, and he saw that from the clifftops flashing lights were signalling out to sea. An answering flash brought forth a cry of triumph and the landing party began the perilous descent to the beach below, to conceal themselves amongst the caves and rocks until the crucial moment.

'Get that cart down there, Tom,' said a voice by Jekyll's ear and he saw that Edward had returned and was riding close beside him.

'Yes, Master Jarvis,' he answered gruffly and, pulling the reins tightly in, launched the wretched horse on to the steep and twisting path.

'Easy there, whoa,' he called, aware that Edward was watching everything he did.

Anger possessed the lieutenant; anger that he had been foolish enough to get himself into this position; anger that Edward Jarvis had probably seen through his masquerade and at any moment would set upon him. Then he thought of his credo, that provided the majority benefited in the end it mattered little how the ends were achieved. Pulling a pistol from somewhere deep in his disguise, he put it to Edward's head and hissed, 'Count yourself dead if you so much as sneeze. As far as I'm concerned you can keep quiet for the rest of this journey.' Then he brought the butt of the gun down on the hapless man's skull and watched as Edward silently fell from his horse onto the cliff path. Looking hastily round, Jekyll saw that he had been unobserved and without even pausing continued his journey downwards to the beach.

The galleys were coming in from the offshore lugger and the lieutenant saw the men break cover and begin to run into the shallows to grab the long rope. He realised that the other carts were beginning to rumble forward and he followed suit, wondering how long it would be before somebody found the unconscious Edward.

The sea was washing round the cart's wheels and the sound of men heaving barrels out of the surf drowned every other noise, so that when a pair of hands abruptly dragged Jekyll down from the cart and onto the sand he was totally taken by surprise. He looked up to see Edward, blood streaming down his face, raising his bat aloft.

'I don't know who you are,' the smuggler said savagely, 'but nobody does that to me. When you wake up, my friend, you'll be with Davy Jones.'

The lieutenant knew no more as Edward's bat crashed down onto his head, knocking the sea and the sky and the stars into one great whirring mass of oblivion.

FORTY-TWO

Suddenly high summer came to the village and valley. In the early mornings fingers of mist lay over the land telling of the great heat to come later in the day and, as the sun rose in splendour, the landscape was bathed in a sharp, brilliant light in which, by afternoon, it was almost too fierce to venture forth. The dark woods were drenched in sunlight and larks rose high in the summer air above the hot cornfields. Only the clear-flowing river, dappling coolly over stones and moss, retained its sharp, fresh currents and chill little ripples.

The residents of the palace remained in the shade. Philadelphia, wearing muslin and a straw hat, swung gently to and fro in the arbour, George, sweating profusely beneath his wig, pushing the swing in a somewhat bored and distracted manner. Lucy sat in the shadow of the trees, reading aloud to her father who slept with his mouth wide open. Beneath the great oak, Nizel could be spied painting more slowly than usual, while Thomas, clad, for him, in the total disarray of a short coat, breeches and cap, played tennis half-heartedly with his brother the Vicar of Mayfield, who had come to call.

Pleading that she must get more air, Henrietta requested a carriage be brought round and, kissing Lucy firmly on the cheek, said that she really did not need anyone to accompany her and stepped inside, telling the coachman that she would like to catch the breeze that blew on the high ground above Sharnden. Once out of sight of the palace gates, however, Henrietta announced that she had changed her mind and that she would pay a call on Mr Langham. And there she proceeded in what she hoped was reasonable secrecy.

The footman who answered the door directed her to wait in an ante-room and it was from the elegant silence of this chamber that Henrietta distinctly heard a murmured conversation in the saloon, followed by feet hurrying up the curving staircase, and then a door opening and closing upstairs. She smiled to herself. It would seem that Nicholas was right and that Jacob Challice was hiding out at Luckhurst Hall.

A few moments later the door opened and John Langham hurried in, apologising for not receiving her at once. With a great show of innocence, Henrietta replied that she hoped it was not inconvenient as he obviously had other callers and, when he protested that he was alone, looked surprised.

They then proceeded into the saloon and awaited the arrival of the tea tray, and it was not until this ceremony had been enacted that Henrietta finally said, 'Mr Langham, I have come to hold you to a promise you made.'

He looked slightly puzzled. 'What promise was that, Miss Trevor?'

'You once told me of a technique in which your patients entered a dream state, and agreed that one day you would conduct the experiment on me. I am wondering if, as we are all staying indoors to get out of the heat, this afternoon might be possible?'

John Langham hesitated, then said, 'Miss Trevor, before I consent to do so I think I should warn you that, since we spoke last, there has been a new development involving this technique. A development that I do not consider completely without risk.'

Henrietta looked puzzled. 'I'm afraid I don't understand, Mr Langham.'

'I do not understand completely myself.'

'Can you describe the development to me?'

John Langham proceeded to tell her about his experiments, omitting to say who the subjects had been. Henrietta's face grew more and more incredulous as he spoke, until she finally burst out, 'But that is against all the teachings of the Church, Mr Langham. How could such a thing be possible?'

'I have thought about that too, my dear, and I think there is a solution.'

'Which is?'

'That if it *is* so, if a human soul really does experience more lives than one, then perhaps each life is an effort to draw nearer to perfection.'

'And if that fails, if only a meaningless life is led, the soul must come back and learn everything all over again?'

'I don't know,' answered John Langham, leaning back in his chair. 'But it would make an enormous kind of sense.'

There was a long pause during which Henrietta stared out of the window at the golden afternoon, wondering if she had ever seen such a sight before with eyes that had once belonged in a different face. Finally she said, 'Have you experienced this phenomenon yourself, Mr Langham?'

'Alas not.'

Henrietta stared at him. 'But you say it is likely we meet the same people again? That they are our companions throughout the entire journey?'

'Certain indications lead me to believe this, yes. It is possible that promises made, oaths sworn a thousand years ago, might yet be kept.'

Henrietta stood up, a look of determination about her. 'Mr Langham, I am so intrigued that I implore you to try the technique with me. If there is an element of risk, then I can only say that every time one journeys forth in a carriage after dark one hazards.'

Both thought of Challice at these words and Henrietta wondered if he sat upstairs, hidden from the world, but knowing she was there and longing to see her; while the surgeon hoped that the highwayman would not be so foolish as to show himself.

Langham stood up too. 'Miss Trevor, we will conduct the experiment. I am afraid that I am very easily persuaded.'

She smiled as they went through to his private room and he drew the curtains against the brilliant day. At once the place became like a mysterious cool cavern, one shaft of light, full of whirling specks, throwing a splash of gold onto the Turkey carpet. John's writing desk suddenly seemed to loom large and heavy in the gloom and it was almost a relief for Henrietta to lie prone upon the sofa and close her eyes, wondering as she did so what strange journey she was about to make.

The surgeon's voice, with its vibrant, insistent quality, began to penetrate her consciousness and Henrietta frowned to herself. The experiment was not going to work. For some reason she was going to find it impossible to participate in the extraordinary sequence of events which John Langham had described to her.

She heard him give instructions and vaguely tried to follow them, thinking there was little point in saying it was no use until he had finished speaking. She thought, too, that there seemed no purpose in moving when it was so much easier and more practical to remain lying down. In fact the warmth and comfort of staying still began to sweep over her until she no longer had any wish to get up.

From a long distance away, Henrietta heard Mr Langham ask her where she was. She concentrated hard and saw, rather to her astonishment, that she stood in the doorway of a little cottage built beside a pond, which she recognised as the ruin beneath Bainden. Turning away from the door, Henrietta realised that a tall, dark-haired girl with slanting green eyes stood in the room, watching her with a strange expression on her face.

She gasped and heard John say, 'What is it, Henrietta? What can you see?'

From Miss Trevor's mouth a gruff voice answered.

'I can see Jenna. I am seeing her as if for the very first time. I always thought her a beanpole but I was wrong. She is beautiful, glorious. I realise now that I love her.'

'Who are you?'

'Benjamin Mist, carpenter of Maighfield. And she is Jenna Casselowe. I must marry her, I have to marry her. She is my soulmate and at last I know it.'

John Langham watched in disbelief as over Henrietta Trevor's well-brought-up features came an expression that combined not only love and adoration but also the dawning of desire.

'Is such a thing possible?' he murmured to himself as Benjamin Mist, talking through the girl, spoke the first hesitant words of village courtship.

Henrietta recognised the writing on the letter at once. She also recognised the same dirty urchin, who this time came to the door of the palace and for his trouble was rewarded with food from the kitchens, there being leftovers of the evening snack – some game pie, a pudding with a suet crust containing pigeons and liver, and a dish of kidneys and oysters.

The child, having washed this down with ale and finished off with apple tart and cheese, left the palace with his stomach bulging, while the note was taken up to Henrietta on a silver salver, where she sat playing backgammon with the Baker family.

Lucy, ever observant, noticed that Miss Trevor – who had returned late from her afternoon drive looking somewhat pale –

did not break the seal but kept the letter intact to read in private. At that Miss Baker leapt to the conclusion that Nicholas Grey was corresponding with her young guest, and hoped fervently that no unsuitable love affair was about to take place.

But Henrietta gave no hint as to the identity of her mysterious correspondent, despite several bright-eyed glances from Lucy, and when the company finally made for their various rooms at eleven o'clock, Miss Baker had to content herself with being enormously intrigued. A situation made even worse when next day she swept into the breakfast room, full of morning sunshine and the smell of toast, to discover that Henrietta had not yet returned from her early ride.

In a rare moment of annoyance, Lucy turned to her sister-in-law and said, 'I cannot think what possesses Henrietta sometimes. Why, she seems hardly to enjoy our company, she is out and about so much.'

'I envy her,' answered Philadelphia, sighing. 'If I did not suffer so with nervous attacks I should spend far more time out of doors. Wouldn't I George?'

He patted her head without looking up from his newspaper. 'Yes, my dear. Certainly. Of course.'

Furious, Lucy answered, 'But Henrietta is a guest here. You might think she would spend a certain amount of time with her hosts.'

'She does,' said Thomas, coming into the room yawning. 'She beat me at backgammon last night. You can't blame the girl if she wants to get out on her own sometimes. It must be fairly repressive at Glynde with nine younger children and a widowed mother for company.'

'Far less repressive,' answered Lucy sharply, 'than being stuck in Mayfield with a family of eight to bring up.'

They all looked at her astonished, except for George who still had not emerged from behind his paper.

'It's a good thing Father can't hear you,' said Nizel eventually, breaking his customary silence.

'And why is that?' His sister's chin was dangerously high.

'Because he would be bound to remind you of your duty.'

'Duty be damned,' shouted Lucy, rising to her feet and throwing her napkin on to the floor in disgust. 'I have given all of you the best years of my life. I have sacrificed everything only to see two sisters marry before me and two brothers not bother to marry at all, so comfortable is it for them to be waited on hand and foot by that maid-of-all-work, that drudge, that less than the dust creature. – Lucy Baker. Now get on with it, all of you. I am ordering the carriage and going out for the day. Philadelphia, you are in charge of running the house. Good-morning.'

And with that she swept out leaving behind her a sea of astonished faces. George lowered his paper, aware of the sudden silence. 'Anything wrong?' he said, and was more than mortified when Philadelphia, in a noisy flood of tears, threw her spoon at him before slipping slowly beneath the table in a dead faint.

Challice was waiting for her as Henrietta had known he would. There, in the midst of that tidal wave of blue, his black-coated figure stood beside his horse, looking anxiously about him. When he saw her, he ran forward, his arms outstretched. They kissed eagerly and Challice drew Henrietta down to sit beside him in a little glade by a quiet dew-pond.

'Are you hurt?' she said. 'I have been so worried ever since I heard you were shot.'

'I've recovered,' he answered. 'It was bad at the time but Mr Langham took the bullet out for me. Though say nothing of that or a good man might be in trouble.'

'I shall say nothing,' Henrietta answered, and then laughed. 'But I knew you were there anyway.'

'How?'

'Nicholas Grey told me. And beside I called at Luckhurst Hall yesterday and sensed your presence in the house.'

Jacob sat up straight, looking puzzled. '*Grey* told you. How the Devil did he know?'

'He did not say. He simply asked me to give you a message and said I would find you at John Langham's house.'

'So he knows you see me? What game does that cunning bastard play that he sends messages to me through you and yet does not come to arrest me? I don't trust him at all.'

'I do,' answered Henrietta roundly, moving away slightly. 'I think he is one of the best people ever born. He told me he wanted you to have a chance of escape, yet said to warn you that forces he could not control were massing against you. I think he is the most honest man in the world.'

A look of amused annoyance crossed Challice's hard features.

'I see that you have a very soft spot for him indeed. Am I to take it that my attentions are no longer welcome?'

Henrietta blushed furiously. 'Of course not. I like Nicholas Grey as a friend, that is all.'

'And what of me? Am I just a friend to you? If so, you must tell me now and save me future pain.'

'How can you speak of the future when you know we have none?'

'I know nothing of the kind,' Challice answered. 'One day we will be together always, not enduring secret meetings like this.'

'Please,' she said, 'don't make the little time we have together unhappy. Can we not be joyful?'

For answer he drew her into his arms again, kissing her gently and holding her so close to him that she could feel every beat of his heart. The kisses grew in strength until they became almost frantic and it was then that Henrietta realised if she did not draw away from him she would have no choice but to go on, to become his, to unite her body with Challice's and yield up all that was girlish and childish about her.

Not quite sure of herself she half pushed him away, but he ignored her, holding her all the harder, kissing her all the more. Suddenly she ceased to care what happened, wanting him to take her to womanhood, forgetting who they were and that their love could never be sealed by marriage. She slipped beneath him, then opened her eyes wide in shock as he roughly pushed his way into her. The pain was agonising, ruthless, and in the strangest way, glorious.

Henrietta bit her lip as Challice moved rhythmically and steadily, consummating his love with strength and passion. Then after a few moments she began to feel pleasure herself and it was then that she started to move with him, curving her back upwards and holding him close to her. Far away, she was aware of something like an explosion that drew ever nearer until it finally burst within her, leaving her gasping and crying and trembling with awareness, taken over the brink with a sensation she would never have believed possible.

When it was all over, when every exquisite feeling had finally died away, they sat up, leaning against the trunk of a tree. Jacob smoked his pipe quietly, while Henrietta entwined her fingers with his, listening to his heart and loving him.

'Is it always like this?' she said eventually. 'For everyone?'

'No,' he answered, looking at her seriously. 'It can be the most miserable experience in the world.'

'I can hardly believe it.'

Jacob turned her face to his, his fingers gentle beneath her chin. 'I'm afraid it's true. But we'll speak no more of that. Tell me Grey's warning. Is it that I should move to another patch?'

'Yes. He believes that you are in danger as long as you stay here.' She turned on him a curious face. 'Jacob, while you were in Mr Langham's care did he put you in a dream state?'

Challice looked guarded. 'He told me not to speak of it.'

'You may talk frankly with me because he tried the same experiment. Only in my case it failed. Nothing happened at all.'

'Nothing?'

'I simply lay on his couch, felt drowsy, then got up again. Did anything happen to you?'

'Oh yes,' answered Jacob slowly. 'A great deal.'

'Will you tell me of it?'

'One day,' he said quietly. 'But this is not the time. Rather let me ask you if you hate me for what has taken place?'

'How could I?' she answered. 'I felt when you took me that it was something I had been waiting for all my life.'

Challice looked at her with a very strange expression on his face as he said, 'And so did I.'

Beneath Lieutenant Jekyll's piercing stare, Nicholas Grey dropped his gaze, wishing for the thousandth time that he had never become involved with the bounty hunters.

'I simply can't understand how Challice can have vanished,' Jekyll was saying, while Rogers stood in the background muttering. 'You say you wounded him?'

'I believe so. I shot in the darkness but I really don't see that I could have missed.'

'Then where *is* the bastard? You have checked with the local physician?'

'Yes, Lieutenant Jekyll,' said Nicholas, a sudden edge beginning to creep into his voice. 'I have.'

Rogers rumbled from the back of the room. 'Then he must have left Mayfield. God knows where he's hiding out by now.'

'Christ's blood,' swore Jekyll violently. 'I am getting tired of this. These confounded villains seem to be getting the upper hand all the way along the line. I swear to God I'll shoot to kill if I so much as see one of them.'

'And get accused of unlawful shooting,' said Rogers, moving forward so that his large frame blocked out the light. 'You'll have to be more subtle than that, Lieutenant.'

The three men stared at each other moodily, until Nicholas, determined to end this uncomfortable meeting, said in a businesslike voice, 'Well gentlemen, with Challice gone to earth, how do you propose to put your plan into action?'

For once in his life Jekyll looked perplexed. 'To be honest I am not sure how to proceed,' he said. 'It is imperative that we know when a run is to take place and summon the militia well in advance.'

'Then I suggest,' answered Nicholas, 'that you bribe someone else to peach.'

Both Rogers and the lieutenant turned to him simultaneously. 'Who?'

He shook his head. 'I have no idea. As far as I can see the whole village is either loyal or frightened. I have come across no one who talks out of turn.'

Jekyll sat down, resting his arms on the table and sinking his head into his hands. 'There's got to be a way,' he said.

Nicholas remained silent wondering, yet again, why the lieutenant made him so nervous. What was it about the man that gave him such authority?

'If you can think of a plan I will do my best to put it into action,' he said finally. 'It is perfectly true that Kit Jarvis and his brother cannot go on having things their way for ever.'

Jekyll shuddered exquisitely, his thin shoulders twitching. 'Do not remind me of him, please. He bound me to a rock that submerges at high tide. He can be prey to no human compassion whatsoever. If it had not been for a passing fisherman . . .'

'Strange,' answered Nicholas, without thinking. 'I have heard that he is a flip-flap. Or at least has tendencies of that nature.'

Jekyll's head slowly rose and once more he turned his unnerving gaze on Nicholas. 'Do you mean that he is a sodomite?'

'I think he might like to be. I do not believe that he actually is.'

'Then there's our answer,' said Jekyll, flashing his cold smile at his two companions.

Rogers gave a raucous laugh. 'Send in another one to draw him out you mean?'

'Precisely. And I know the very man – or should I say creature? – for the job.' Jekyll stood up, rubbing his hands together in sudden excitement. 'One door closes, another opens. Thank you for that information, Lieutenant Grey.'

'I did not think it would be so useful, Lieutenant Jekyll. Though I should have realised that to trap a man by exploiting his weaknesses is a fairly obvious choice.'

'You balk at it? It has been done since history began.'

He smiled thinly and Nicholas's thoughts turned once more to Henrietta, wondering where she was at this precise moment and what she was doing.

'. . . is that agreeable?'

He realised that Jekyll had ended with a question and said hastily, 'Er . . . yes. Of course.'

'Then you will return to Mayfield and concentrate on tracking down Challice and leave the Jarvis brothers to us?'

'Yes. I'll do that. Though I suspect he has returned to London long since.'

'Probably,' said Jekyll, looking gloomy for a second. He brightened again and added, 'But if we can haul in the other fish it won't matter if one slips through the net.'

'No,' said Nicholas thankfully. 'We can settle for one of them getting away.'

As Henrietta and Jacob kissed for the last time, Lucy Baker's coach turned into the circular drive of Luckhurst Hall and pulled up before the graceful pillars of its entrance. She descended and went to the front door, which was opened by a footman who said, 'Mr Langham has gone out visiting patients, Miss Baker, and we are not expecting him back until later. Would you care to wait?'

Still furious with her family, she answered roundly, 'I most certainly would,' and swept into the saloon, removing her mantle and handing it to another servant.

After a moment, looking about her, Lucy sat down and stared

out of the window, wondering how long she would have to wait before John's return, and deciding that she was so cross she would remain all day if necessary.

Her thoughts were broken by the arrival of the steward and, having been served with refreshment, Lucy walked through to John's consulting room to take a book from its overflowing library. But even before she could put her hand up to take one, a sheaf of papers entitled, 'Notes on the return to the past of Lucy Baker, Jacob Challice and Henrietta Trevor', caught her eye and drew her, open-mouthed, to stand beside the desk on which they lay.

She was astonished. So Henrietta had also been experimented upon. Knowing what she was doing was utterly wrong and that if John ever discovered the truth it might put an end to their friendship, Lucy nonetheless put out a furtive hand, grabbed the papers and hurried back into the saloon. She sat once more upon the window seat – shaded from outside by a flowing tree – and started to read.

John had written his notes in a matter-of-fact medical style and the beginning, which recounted how he had actually discovered that patients could be sent into the past, was full of details that Lucy already knew. But it was as she read on that she found her jaw beginning to drop with astonishment, and had to put a hand to her head to stop herself growing faint.

'On the second occasion that I returned Jacob Challice,' she read, 'he found himself in blackness thirty years before his death, which led me to the conclusion that the death by hanging had occurred to someone who was relatively youthful. I have so far been afraid to attempt a discovery of the identity of the hanged man for fear of Challice once more re-enacting his death, with fatal consequences. However, when I asked Challice to go back four hundred years he promptly named himself as Marcus de Flaviel, a squire of Gascony, and said that he lived in the palace at Mayfield, where it was his function to care for the then archbishop's – named by Challice as de Stratford – half-wit brother.'

Lucy laid down the pages in growing excitement, then read on. 'The most amazing part of this return was that Challice (as Flaviel) claimed knowledge of Margaret de Sharndene (see notes on return of Lucy Baker), Margaret's daughter Oriel (whose child he claimed to have fathered), and Paul d'Estrange, knight. If this is so it would appear that Lucy Baker and Challice were acquainted in a previous life, which would seem almost irrefutable evidence that such lives do exist.'

She turned over the page and read, 'Lucy Baker, when returned, adopted the identity of Margaret de Sharndene, wife of Robert de Sharndene. Questioning while in the dream state revealed that he had picked her out of two possible brides and she was greatly flattered by this attention. On a second occasion I moved her forward in time to when she was Robert's wife and it seemed that she had several children by him, three of whom survived – namely Hamon, Piers and Oriel (see notes on Jacob Challice). Subsequent research amongst historical records shows me that not only did Margaret exist but that she outlived her husband, a victim of the Black Death, and in later years married a Paul d'Estrange, mentioned by Challice. Further evidence that the stories recounted by patients while in a dream state are not just figments of their subconscious imagination.'

Lucy looked up again, shaking her head in bewilderment. So she and Jacob Challice had been acquainted in her life as Margaret de Sharndene. It was almost beyond the limits of human capability to believe it. She turned over another page.

'By far the most shocking return was that experienced by Henrietta Trevor. In fact so extraordinary was it that I instructed her, while still in the dream state, to remember nothing of it and to believe that I had failed in my experiment with her. Miss Trevor returned to a previous life in which she had been a man!!' John had underlined this and put two exclamation marks. 'Even more incredible she was on the brink of falling in love with a young woman named Jenna Casselowe and as Henrietta's previous self (named as Benjamin Mist, carpenter of Mayfield) spoke words of great tenderness and endearment, yet of a rustic kind that someone as delicately raised as Miss Trevor would have been unlikely to know. For this reason I am forced to conclude of the three returns this surely provides the strongest evidence of a previous life, being so entirely different from the one at present enjoyed.'

Lucy dabbed at her forehead with a fine handkerchief. So Henrietta had been male. Would that explain a certain wilfulness about her?

'Oh gracious,' thought Lucy. 'I almost wish I had not seen this.'

She looked down once more to re-read the last few words and thus did not hear the door of the saloon open. It was not until footsteps had half entered the room that she looked up and saw Jacob Challice – a horrified expression on his face – standing in front of her.

'Miss Baker!' he said. 'I had no idea that you were here.'

She gave him a confident smile. 'But *I* knew that you were in residence, Mr Challice. Mr Langham has confided in me but, despite that, there is no need for you to be afraid. I have no intention of betraying you.'

He looked relieved. 'I thank you most sincerely.' He added more calmly, 'Have you been waiting long? I do not believe Mr Langham will be back until late.'

'I have been here long enough to read this,' she answered, holding the sheaf of papers aloft.

'What is it?'

'Notes on your return to a former life – and also on mine.'

'Mr Langham has been experimenting on you?'

'Jacob, before we say any more I think you should read it. I believe that it will help you to understand why, putting aside moral issues, I could never break faith with you. We have known one another before, it would seem.'

She handed him the papers omitting to give him the one dealing with Henrietta. But he saw it and asked, 'Is that confidential?'

'It deals with the return to the past of someone other than our two selves.'

'May I not see it?'

Not knowing quite why she did so, Lucy handed it to him, saying, 'I shall leave the room while you read it. It deals with matters that are most strange and disconcerting.'

'But whom does it concern?'

'Why, the person who saved your life, Mr Challice. None other than Miss Henrietta Trevor herself.'

Long after dinner had been cleared away, John Langham, Lucy and Challice sat over the port and spoke of the miracle that had been discovered.

'May we speak of Henrietta?' said Lucy eventually.

'I am not allowed to discuss a patient. It is against my professional oath,' came the cautious reply.

'Then I shall talk of her to Jacob,' answered Lucy, who had had enough wine to make her brave. 'Do you think she was Oriel?'

'It is possible I suppose but we will never know, will we, Mr Langham?'

'I shall never experiment with her again, if that is what you mean,' answered John slowly. 'It is not fair to hear these things come from her mouth without her knowledge.'

'Send me back to before I was hanged,' said Jacob suddenly. 'I *have* to know the answer to that riddle. I have the strongest feeling that it could shed light on Miss Trevor's experience.'

John and Lucy looked from one to the other and she, by now firmly feeling the effects of port, said, 'Oh please do so, John. This is surely the night when the truth must come out.'

'But supposing it contains material not fit for your ears, my dear?'

'I shall put my hands over them,' she answered, laughing.

It took John no further persuading and Jacob went at once to the dining-room's most comfortable chair and sat in it, crossing one booted foot over the other, looking almost excited. Lucy watched in growing astonishment as Challice closed his eyes and appeared to slip quite easily into a peaceful sleep, despite the fact that he was still speaking to John.

'Now I want you to go back to the life which ended in your death by hanging, do you understand me?'

Jacob nodded and said, 'Yes.'

'Good.' John, who had grown more confident in what he needed to do, now said, 'I do not want you to relive that hanging. I do not want that at all. I would like you to go back three months before and tell me where you are.'

There was silence and John repeated again, 'Three months before your death, Challice. Where are you?'

Again there was no response and then Jacob suddenly let out a slow agonised moan.

'Merciful heaven,' said Lucy, starting violently. 'What is the matter with him?'

'I don't know,' answered John quietly. 'I'll try to find out.' In a louder voice he said, 'Jacob, what is it? Are you ill?'

In a higher tone than he normally used, Challice answered, 'I wish Benjamin would come. What can be keeping him. Oh!' He cried out again, obviously in distress.

John and Lucy stared at each other and both said 'Benjamin!' with one voice, Lucy adding, 'So he was right. He *did* know Henrietta.'

But their conversation was halted by another moan from Challice. 'Oh God, he must come soon.' Then a look of determination crossed his face and he said, 'I'll cry out no more, no matter what. I shall ride this sea alone if I have to.'

'What is happening to him?' said Lucy. 'What sea is he talking about?'

'I do believe,' answered John wonderingly, 'that Jacob is experiencing labour.'

They stared at each other in disbelief as Challice, his expression one of total concentration, obviously began to feel a contraction.

'Oh God's life, I want my husband,' he said, between gritted teeth.

'It's all right, Jenna,' said John. 'He's here. He's just arrived. Everything is going to be all right. You *are* Jenna, aren't you?'

'Yes,' gasped Jacob, 'that is my name – Jenna Mist. He won't go away again, will he?'

'Oh no,' said John, very seriously indeed. 'It is my belief that Benjamin will never go away from you, not until the end of time.'

FORTY-THREE

The heat at noon on that blazing day in late July, 1721, was indescribable, and most sensible people sat within their houses with the blinds drawn, or else took refuge in the cool and cavernous welcome of an ale house. It seemed that only labourers and fools were abroad and Nicholas Grey, riding fast towards Glynde and wearing an entirely new outfit of clothes, wondered with a wry grin into which category he fell.

Ruefully, Nicholas looked back over the last few weeks – weeks in which Henrietta had returned home to her family, Jacob had vanished from Mayfield, and the Baker family had resumed their normal way of life – and wondered if there was any purpose left in his remaining a Riding Officer, or even staying in that small, smuggler-plagued Sussex village. For what good could he do? Jekyll and Rogers had their own schemes to bring Kit Jarvis to justice, and the highwayman had gone. At that moment, on his way to see the girl with whom he was hopelessly in love, Nicholas felt like giving everything up and starting life again, as a musician perhaps, or even a strolling player.

How he had received an invitation to dine at Glynde Place, he could not be sure. Nicholas had written to Mrs Trevor – so desperate to see Henrietta that he would have dared anything – and requested that he might be permitted to call. To his astonishment an invitation had followed almost at once. Then, Nicholas thought, the true fool had shown himself.

He had rushed to Hastings to a good but reasonably priced tailor – nothing like as stylish as his counterpart in London, of course, but Riding Officers hardly earned a fortune – and had ordered a new suit made of embroidered satin, comprising a collarless close-fitted coat, waisted and flared to the knee; a glorious waistcoat, left open to reveal a frilled shirt-front with ruffles at the wrist; and knee-breeches with long, fine stockings, together with buckled shoes.

But even as he had put it on, Nicholas had felt himself

somewhat pathetic, an ordinary young man dressed as a fop. Then his fighting spirit had returned. Jacob Challice had vanished and he, Nicholas, had as much right to call on Miss Trevor as the next man, had he but had the social position and fortune necessary to ask her mother for her hand. Yet fate had many strange quirks and twists before situations were resolved, and comforting himself with the thought that Mrs Trevor might like him so well she would make history and welcome one of the lower orders as a son-in-law, Nicholas proceeded on through the gruelling heat.

By the time he reached the village of Glynde he was in a lather of sweat and, ignoring two maidens who watched him, giggling all the while, removed all clothes but his breeches and doused himself beneath the pump. Then he rubbed himself with some scented water kept in his saddle bag, and dressed again, sedately entering the grounds of the big house and passing through the cherry garden, and the arch, before finally going into the quadrangle, to dismount at the front door.

They were all waiting for him in the long gallery above and, as Nicholas climbed the magnificent staircase, he felt this to be the most nerve-wracking moment of his life. But once inside the room so many impressions swamped him that he was no longer able to think of himself seeing, instead, the glorious panelling of the gallery walls, the solemn face of the little boy who was now the squire, the dark beauty of Mrs Trevor, and the fact that Henrietta had lost her sparkle and stood up to welcome him a pale shadow of the girl with whom he had fallen in love at first sight.

'My dear Lieutenant Grey,' Lucy Trevor was saying, extending a hand in Nicholas's direction, 'how very good of you to call. I believe that Grace misses all her friends from Mayfield.' At Nicholas's puzzled look, Mrs Trevor laughed and added, 'You will know her as Henrietta, of course. She does not think her first name suits her.'

'But it does now,' thought Nicholas, seeing his dear one so pale and quiet.

'I like both names,' he answered tactfully, and kissed Mrs Trevor's outstretched hand with a certain warmth. He saw her shoot an appraising look at him from eyes which, though very different from her daughter's, were equally brilliant.

'Come and sit next to me, Lieutenant,' she said, smiling.

'Henrietta tells me that you are a very adventurous young man and I should so like to hear about some of your exploits, that is if you are permitted to speak of them.' He nodded assent and Lucy Trevor went on, 'My daughter also says that you are an outstanding musician. Will you play for me and the elder girls after we have dined? I shall send the younger ones out that we may listen in peace.'

'I should be pleased to do so, ma'am.'

'And have you brought your lute?'

'It is in my saddle-bag. I rarely travel without it.'

'If I had half your gift,' said Henrietta, speaking for the first time, 'I would never be separated from a lute either.'

Obviously something of his feelings for her must have shown in Nicholas's expression just then, because, as he smiled his thanks at her, Henrietta lost colour and looked at the ground. After that she did not address another word to him, even though the meal took well over two hours to consume. Nor did she do anything more than clap when, finished at last, she, her mother, Elizabeth, young Lucy Trevor, Mary and Anne took their places in the gallery to hear Nicholas play; while from below came the sounds of Margaret, Ruth, Gertrude, Arabella and little John being led away for a game of ninepins under the lime-trees.

As always, Nicholas was transformed when he struck the strings and Mrs Trevor, looking at the mobile features, found herself wishing that this young man who obviously cared for her daughter so desperately, came from a different station in life and that it would be possible for her to welcome him into the family.

But such thoughts were swept from her as she leant back in her chair, closed her eyes, and heard the lyric notes of a love song steal through the room. It brought back so many memories that Lucy Trevor found herself weeping silently, mourning more than she had done for months the loss of her own dear love who had gone from her when he had been not yet forty years. As the music ended, Mrs Trevor opened her eyes again to see that Henrietta, too, was crying silently into her handkerchief.

'Thank you, thank you, Lieutenant Grey,' the hostess called, beating her hands together. 'Now I will tax you no further. I am sure that you would like Henrietta to show you the park. It is very beautiful in the late afternoon and I feel certain you could do with a little air after your exertions.'

Bowing to Mrs Trevor, Nicholas offered Henrietta his arm and, without saying a word, the couple descended the great staircase, went out through the quadrangle and crossing the path that ran over the ha-ha, found themselves alone at last.

Now, with something approaching determination, Nicholas made for a sheltering clump of trees and it was only then, when he was quite sure that they were hidden from prying eyes, that he turned Henrietta to look at him and said, 'What is the matter? You have not yet said a word to me, and you are as pale as death. Henrietta, what is troubling you?'

She did not answer, merely shaking her head from side to side, the tears beginning to course down her cheeks again.

'Is it Challice? Has he deserted you? Is that it?'

'No, no,' she sobbed. 'He has not deserted me. He has had to go away to save his life. He is hiding . . . No, I must not tell *you*, of all people . . . But he will return, when he has enough money to invest, and take his place as a gentleman.'

Nicholas laughed aloud. 'Sweetheart, Challice could never be a gentleman if the moon turned blue. What you mean is he will give up highway robbery and settle down. That is a very different matter.'

Henrietta looked annoyed. 'It is cruel of you to laugh, Lieutenant Grey. Jacob loves me and wants to marry me.'

'And your mother will give her consent, I suppose?'

'If he has reformed and calls himself a merchant, perhaps.'

Nicholas shook his head. 'Then if that is the case, why are you so miserable?'

His tone was bitingly sarcastic and he knew it. But he was past caring. He loved Henrietta boundlessly, endlessly, and now he had to stand and listen to her weep for another man. But worse was yet to come.

'It is not just the parting, Nicholas. It is that I am so afraid.'

His tone became more gentle. 'Of what, sweetheart? Nothing can hurt you while I am here to protect you.'

Her voice dropped to a whisper and she clutched his arm. 'Can you keep your own counsel? If I tell you something, do you promise you will pass it on to no other?'

'I swear it on my life.'

'Then I believe that I am with child.'

The world spun and the stars went out and Nicholas Grey realised that it only took a second for a heart to break. 'I see. It is

Challice's obviously.' She nodded and a ray of hope came back. 'Did he take advantage of you, was that it? Did he force his attentions on you? If so I'll kill him for it.'

'No, no,' she said, starting to weep again. 'I gave myself to him – not once but many, many times – before we parted company. It is my fault just as much as his.'

Nicholas made no answer, fighting off hot, furious tears.

'I see that I have shocked you. Oh dearest Nicholas, I couldn't help myself. One day you will meet a woman who means everything to you and then you will know what it is like to be in love.'

He pulled her to him roughly. 'I have already met her and it is you, as well you know. Why, I would give my life – and willingly – to change places with that bastard. Oh, God damn it, Henrietta, you have broken my heart.'

He pushed her away and turned his back on her to hide the fact that he openly wept. She came and stood beside him and said, 'If Challice did not exist then I would love you for ever, Nicholas. You see, I *do* love you. But not in the way you want me to. That's the tragedy of it. But that does not stop the feeling nonetheless. It is there and always will be. I care for you deeply, Nicholas Grey.'

They were in each other's arms, their tears mingling as they both wept for the sadness of the situation, and then they exchanged one great and powerful kiss. In that kiss was everything they had always meant to one another, all their past love and friendship fused in a moment that transcended passion, and became something rare.

'I will love you to death,' he whispered.

'And I you. Nicholas, my own dear friend.'

They said no more, walking hand in hand now, perfectly in harmony.

'How can I help you?' he said after a while. 'Do you want me to take a message to Challice? I swear that I will not betray him. I presume he does not yet know about the child.'

'No.' Henrietta stopped walking and turned to look at Nicholas, her eyes very serious. 'Nicholas, you may not believe this, but I think I was fated to bear Challice a baby.'

'Why do you say that?'

'You must not laugh at what I am going to tell you. Do you promise?'

413

He nodded, and she went on, 'Mr Langham, the surgeon, has discovered a technique by which he can send patients into a day-dream and in that state their minds go back to the past. You look incredulous but it is true.'

'Did Mr Langham experiment on you?'

'He tried to but it failed, and though I begged him to do so again he refused. But Challice is convinced we have been lovers at least once before. If so I may have borne him a child in another life.'

Nicholas sat down on a tree trunk. 'I don't believe this. Not a word of it. When you die you go to heaven, not on to other lives.'

'How do you know?' asked Henrietta, sitting down beside him.

He could not answer that. A memory was coming back to him; a memory of his music-teacher shaking his head at Nicholas's parents and saying, 'I can teach him nothing further. He has brought the gift into the world with him.' And of his wondering at the time what it could possibly mean.

'You are right,' he said slowly. 'Nobody has probed death's secret. It was narrow-minded of me to answer as I did.'

'Then you do not scoff?'

'On the contrary,' answered Nicholas with determination. 'I shall ask Mr Langham if he will conduct the experiment on me.'

Seeing the shadows begin to lengthen, they stood up and began to walk slowly back to Glynde Place.

'What do you want me to tell Challice?' said Nicholas.

'That I must join him if what I suspect is true. That I would rather my good mother was faced with a runaway daughter than the shame of a bastard birth.'

'And will he stand by you?' asked Nicholas, not to denigrate his rival but to reassure himself.

'He will. He believes that we are meant to be together. Nothing will make him go against that.'

'Then whisper to me where he is and I promise that I will find him for you.'

Henrietta stood on tip-toe and there, in the early evening sunshine, she and Nicholas Grey gave each other one long last kiss of farewell, before she began to murmur in his ear.

Knowing that there was a price on his head, Edward Jarvis rarely ventured forth without the protection of either his brother or another member of the Mayfield gang. But this night, at the end of a blisteringly hot day and with both Kit and Emmy in London, he craved not only a deep draught of ale but also a little human companionship. Knowing that he would be safest of all in the Royal Oak in Mayfield, Edward saddled up one of the nags that they kept at Stream Farm for local errands, and set off.

It was an evening of crystal clarity, the trees of Snape Wood etched like fingers against a sky which was a bowl of light, splintered here and there with silver clouds. Birds swooped everywhere and in the distance a cuckoo sang his song of summer above the roses of Wenbans.

The Oak was very full, all the labourers coming in to slake their thirst after the exhaustions of the day. But though he was recognised, Edward knew he was safe. There was no one there who could not be trusted – either by reason of bribes or threats – and he sat down in a dark corner and set about getting a little drunk.

Much to Jarvis's horror as his eyes got used to the dim light he saw that someone else sat in the corner, someone who was gazing at him with velvety eyes – the deep mauvish shade of a flower, and full of admiration. Embarrassed, Edward quaffed his jug in one and called to the pot boy to give him a refill.

A soft, educated voice spoke from the gloom, 'It would give me great honour, Sir, if you would allow me to make the purchase for you. I have long been an admirer of yours – and of your brother also, of course. I do have the pleasure of addressing Mr Edward Tomkins, alias Jarvis, do I not?'

Edward's hand shot out and grabbed the speaker's wrist like a vice. 'Keep your voice down, you fool. Nobody speaks my name in public. Show yourself if you want to live. Lean forward into the light.'

The man did so and Edward could not help an involuntary gasp, so handsome a creature sat before him. 'Allow me to introduce myself,' the man said, smiling. 'John Dinnage – known to my friends as Dido. I have recently left university and have no settled future so am here to throw myself on your mercy, Mr Jarvis.'

These last words were said with such a winning look that Edward felt the dreaded lurch of his heart which he always thrust down so ruthlessly.

'What do you want me to do?'

'Introduce me to your brother that I may beg to join your organisation.'

Edward frowned. Much as he found the young man captivating, something about the story did not ring true.

'Why should life as a free-trader appeal to a university graduate?'

Dido leant forward, his knee accidentally pressing against Edward's. 'For two reasons,' he whispered, 'one that I support our true king, James; and the other that I am amoral.'

Jarvis stared at him. 'What do you mean?'

'Just that. I want to know the thrill of smuggling because it is against the law; I want to take risks and cheat. I was born for sensation, Mr Jarvis. Any sensation. I cannot help myself. Wickedness excites me.'

Edward – only too aware that Kit would be furious if he found out – said, 'We can't talk here. It is dangerous. Where are you lodging?'

'Here at the Oak. Shall we speak further in my room – or would that give rise to comment?' He gave an engaging grin.

'Yes,' answered Edward shortly. 'We'd better go to Stream Farm.'

'Where is that?'

'Near Wadhurst. It is where we lie low.'

'So I can actually see the place where the great Jarvis brothers plan their runs – and take their women?'

Edward did not answer, merely saying, 'I shall leave the Oak now. Follow me in five minutes time,' and was rewarded by Dido giving him a smile that spoke not only of gratitude but also of unimaginable delights to come.

The meal had been excellent and, now that the ladies had withdrawn, an elegant sideboard decorated with scrolls and rams' heads was opened to reveal a row of chamberpots. These were passed round with the port and the gentlemen relieved themselves. Then, very comfortable, they settled back to smoke pipes, drink and converse until they rejoined the ladies, Nicholas Grey thinking how very different from his recent dinner at Glynde Place when he had been the sole adult male.

John Langham was entertaining the Bakers and one or two others and, rather to his surprise, Nicholas had found himself included amongst the guests. Yet the mystery was made clear when Mr Langham, ever the considerate host, had said, 'I wondered if you might play for us, Grey. The ladies enjoyed it so much at the palace and I know they would like another opportunity of hearing you.'

Nicholas had bowed and brought his lute, which now lay awaiting the moment when the surgeon would signify they were ready. But at present the gentlemen were in full flood of conversation and the subject under discussion was the sudden disappearance of the highwayman of Pennybridge.

'Do you know where the villain went, Lieutenant?' asked George loudly.

'No, Sir,' answered Nicholas unblushingly.

'I reckon he's dead in a ditch somewhere,' put in a bluff country-spoken man. 'I'll wager a guinea Kit Jarvis put him out of the way. They don't like intruders on their territory, you know.'

'Do any of us?' asked Thomas, flapping the air with a lace handkerchief. 'Damme, I take it amiss if anyone should occupy my place at the gaming tables, so I do.'

Nizel, going very red, said, 'I think fights over territory are ridiculous, particularly at the level you have just mentioned.'

'Fights over territory stem from the animal kingdom,' John put in urbanely.

'But we are not animals,' Nizel answered, 'we are meant to be civilised human beings.'

'Well, there is nothing civilised about smugglers and high-waymen,' said the bluff man crossly. 'They are vermin and deserve to be put down. But if they kill one another, all to the good say I. Saves us the trouble, what? Though I must say I enjoy a good hanging.'

Listening to it all, Nicholas's thoughts went racing, wondering what he could do to get Henrietta away from such a dangerous life, yet knowing that – unless the highwayman deserted her – she was bound to marry the man. If only he had fathered the child, Nicholas thought grimly. What a different future he could have made for her.

His thoughts were interrupted by John Langham rising with the customary words, 'Gentlemen, shall we join the ladies?' adding, 'I am sorry to hurry you but I know how anxious they are to hear Lieutenant Grey play.'

The bluff man said forthrightly, 'I think I'll stay here if you've no objection, Langham. No offence, Lieutenant, but I never did have an ear for music.'

John smilingly nodded consent and the rest trooped into the saloon where Lucy, Philadelphia and the bluff man's wife – a small birdlike woman with darting brown eyes – had arranged themselves prettily about. Philadelphia, Nicholas noted with alarm, was already dabbing at her eyes and as she saw him she started to sniff, saying chokingly, 'Music always makes me cry so, particularly that of dear Lieutenant Grey.'

'I will try to be merry,' he answered, hoping he was in good enough spirits.

The summer sun was still high as the young man sat down, his back to the light so that the features of his face were cast into shadow. And today as Nicholas began to play it became almost impossible, with the slant of the sun's rays, to look at him clearly. Despite his promise to Philadelphia, the airs he chose all had an underlying note of melancholy, of a longing for love that could never be fulfilled, of a searching and seeking for a soulmate that could never be his. And it was just as he had finished a serenade that Nicholas, looking up, saw Lucy gazing at him with a strange expression on her face, almost as if she was seeing him properly for the very first time. Her lips formed a word but he could not read what it was and Nicholas bent once more to the lute.

By the time he had ended his recital not only Philadelphia wept. He saw to his astonishment that both Lucy and Thomas, of all people, were suspiciously red about the eyes, and John Langham was blowing his nose loudly. He assumed from this that he had performed well but tonight Nicholas's thoughts were so far away that he could not recall a note.

'My dear Sir,' said the surgeon, holding out his hand. 'What can I say? You played superbly. I will admit frankly that I was moved to tears.'

'Very nice,' said the birdlike woman. 'Ever so pretty. Well, I must go and fetch Roger before he falls asleep amongst the pisspots.' She laughed uproariously and went out. And it was in the slight murmur after her departure that Nicholas took the opportunity of saying quietly to his host, 'Mr Langham, I wonder if I might have a word with you in private. Would it be possible for me to stay on for a while after the other visitors have gone?'

John looked mildy surprised but nevertheless answered, 'Of course, of course, Lieutenant. After your outstanding music nothing could be too much trouble.'

Thanking him, Nicholas waited in the saloon as his host waved off the guests, calling out cheerily until all the carriages had swept round the circular drive and disappeared through the wrought-iron gates. Then a few moments elapsed before Mr Langham appeared in the doorway with a decanter of port and two glasses, saying, 'Now, Lieutenant Grey, in what way may I help you?'

Nicholas decided to come straight to the point. 'Sir, I believe that you conduct experiments whereby it is possible for you to take a patient back to what appears to be a life before this one.'

Langham looked rather cross and said, 'Who told you that?'

'I dined with Mrs Trevor at Glynde a few days ago. It was Henrietta who spoke of your work. But pray do not be angry with her. We were speaking of another matter and she was in some distress. It was then that she told me of it.'

'I see,' answered John, but said nothing further.

'I will confess,' Nicholas went on, 'that I was extremely sceptical – except for one thing.'

'And that is?'

'My music-teacher once said that I had brought the gift of playing the lute into the world with me. I have always puzzled as to what he meant by that – now I am wondering if you might hold the key, Mr Langham.'

'You want me to try and find your past, Lieutenant?'

'Indeed I do, Sir. On one condition.'

'And that is?'

'That you let me remember it all, holding back nothing.'

'But you could learn things that might shock you, Lieutenant Grey.'

'Oh no,' said Nicholas. 'I am past shocking, Mr Langham. Too much has happened recently to allow me to ever be shocked again.'

'There they go,' said John Rogers. 'Look!'

He pointed with a finger that trembled slightly and Lieutenant Jekyll following the line of it, gave a muted shout of triumph.

'So that little bawd has managed it! Jarvis has succumbed.

419

Dinnage said he would ride past with him tonight if the plan succeeded.'

John Rogers gave a large-mouthed grin. 'Well done, Jekyll. What's the next move?'

'We call up a group and follow them to West Chiltington, and in the darkness surround the house. Tomorrow morning when the bastard has got his breeches down ...' Jekyll cracked with laughter and slapped his thigh, the cold eyes for once looking amused. 'We call on him to surrender. What do you think?'

'It's foolproof. Can you imagine Kit Jarvis's face when he hears his brother has been caught in a pretty boy's bed?'

Jekyll wiped his eyes with the back of his sleeve. 'He'll come to rescue him and that will be the end of him as well.'

'Not if we don't hurry,' said Rogers nervously. 'I'll go and get the others.'

'Don't forget the constables.'

'No.' Rogers looked through the window at the descending sun. 'I'll meet you in an hour on the Storrington Road.'

'Excellent,' answered Jekyll, his face composed once more. 'This night sees the beginning of the end of the Mayfield gang.'

Beyond the window of John Langham's study the sun was beginning to lower itself in a splendour of scarlet ribbons and, as the surgeon turned away from the casement to look at Nicholas Grey – who lay on the couch in what appeared to be a calm and dreamless sleep – a splash of colour lit his face making it rubicund and kind. It fell on the face of the sleeper, too, smoothing out his anxious expression and giving him a boyish, untroubled air. John Langham sighed. The moment had arrived and, if he kept his promise, Nicholas would be left to carry the burden of what he remembered for the rest of his life. Small wonder indeed that John hesitated before saying, 'Nicholas, can you hear me?'

'Yes.' The flatness of the reply told Langham everything. He was in the presence of another excellent subject, one just as good as Jacob Challice had been.

'Nicholas, I want you to go back in time. Back before you lay in your mother's womb. Back before you swirled in darkness. Back to the last time you were alive. Back to when you were fifty years old in that life. Where are you?' There was a pause. 'Where are you?' John repeated.

'In London with my husband,' said a remote voice.

'Your *husband*?' John exclaimed.

'Yes – but no one knows of it because we are married secretly. All the world believes I am his housekeeper.'

'And why is that?'

'Because he is famous and highborn and educated – and he also likes men as well as women.'

Breaking his promise without hesitation, John said, 'Nicholas, you will remember none of this when you wake. Do you understand?'

'I understand.'

'Then tell me your name. Who are you?'

'I am Agnes May,' answered Nicholas. 'Known as Agnes Casselowe because of my husband's deceit. When I was a girl I dreamed of marrying him but I was so ugly and simple I knew I had no hope. But when my sister was hanged for witchcraft . . .'

A million trumpets sounded in John Langham's brain as all the pieces of the puzzle began to fit into place.

' . . . he took pity on me because I was left to bring up my little nephew. He told me that if I could accept him as he was, he would marry me.'

'What is his name?' asked John.

'Tom May, the poet. He was a favourite of King Charles but has turned against him and joined the Parliamentarians.'

So Nicholas had been alive at the time of the Civil War. John would have asked another question but the Lieutenant was continuing to speak.

'We have two sons – he always pretended to the other servants that they were bastards.'

Nicholas smiled and just for a fraction of a second his features seemed to melt away, and John caught a glimpse of Agnes May, fat and jolly and comfortable, and just the sort of wife for a poet of doubtful sexual inclination.

'I want you to go back to the life before that of Agnes May, born Casselowe. I want you to go back to, shall we say, the summer of 1335 . . .' He had picked that date because of the notes taken on Lucy Baker and Jacob. 'Were you alive then?'

'Oh yes,' came the eager reply, and the surgeon saw that Nicholas's face had changed again, looking now both vulnerable and pathetic.

'Then who are you?'

'Colin. Colin de Stratford. My brother is the Archbishop of Canterbury. He is very kind to me and brings me sweetmeats. And he finds people for me to play with. First there was Wevere and now I have Marcus. And soon I am to marry Oriel who loves me so much.'

'Thank you, Colin. Now I will say goodbye to you for good. Nicholas, I am going to count from one to twenty. When I reach twenty you will wake up feeling refreshed and well. You will remember nothing of your life as Agnes whatsoever. You will remember everything about Colin. Do you understand?'

'I do.'

'Good. I will begin to count now. One, two, three, four, five . . .'

The surgeon's voice droned on as darkness finally fell over Luckhurst Hall and those within its walls who had, at last, learned the final truth.

A long night that night; a night in which Nicholas Grey, after talking most earnestly with John Langham, left the surgeon's house and headed straight for a village near Blackheath, and to the poor and seedy cottage in which Henrietta Trevor had told him Jacob Challice could be found. A night in which John Rogers and his men – Lieutenant Jekyll having unexpectedly been called to duty elsewhere – surrounded Dido's house in West Chiltington and lay in wait. A night in which Henrietta Trevor wept into her pillow knowing that no further flux had visited her body, and that there could now be no doubt left that Challice's child dwelt within her.

Edward woke early to see John Dinnage's golden head beside him on the pillow, and at last recognized what had always been in his nature. In many ways, it was an enormous relief to be able to admit that he was not born as others.

He sat up, looking at the sea of clothes that lay upon the floor and remembering last night with a delirious happiness. Very slowly and lazily he rose, stretched, looked down at his nakedness and, still smiling, pulled on a pair of rough old breeks. Then he went downstairs.

It was unnervingly quiet, not even a bird seeming to sing. Slightly suspicious, Edward opened the door that led into the garden and looked outside. A voice that appeared to come from nowhere said, 'All right, Jarvis. This is it. I call on you to surrender.'

'Christ!' shouted Edward, bolting back up the stairs.

Dido was stretching enticingly as he fled back into the bedroom. Seeing his expression the younger man called in alarm, 'God's head, what is it?'

But Edward did not stop to reply. Grabbing his sword and pistol he hurled back downstairs and went out running, screaming an oath at the top of his voice, and heading straight for the human cordon that surrounded the house. There was the sound of a groan as he cut his way through and headed, barefoot and naked from the waist up, to the open countryside beyond. Then a shot rang out and Edward went down in a spurt of raw red blood.

'I've got him,' shouted Rogers in triumph. 'I've got the bastard. Now Kit Jarvis, it's your turn to go.'

He reached Blackheath at dawning, full of awareness and knowledge, and stood for a long time looking at the humble house in which Jacob Challice was lying asleep.

Then, taking his lute from his saddle-bag, Nicholas sat upon the dew drenched ground and played a tune from England's past.

Much as he had expected, within ten minutes the bolts on the door were shot back and Challice appeared, wearing a shirt and breeches thrown on to cover his nudity.

On seeing Nicholas, his hand flew to his pistol and he shouted, 'Grey! What the Devil are you doing here?'

Ignoring the barrel pointing straight at him, Nicholas ran forward. 'Shoot if you will, Challice,' he called. 'But realise one thing if you do. There is no threat to you. Knowing what I do it would be impossible to kill you.'

Jacob turned on him a look of doubt. 'Colin?' he asked uncertainly.

Nicholas nodded his head. 'I've come to find you at last,' he said.

FORTY-FOUR

The last days of August continued as hot and fierce as the rest of that extraordinary summer and Lucy Baker, sitting in the shade of the oak-tree planted by Tom May and wearing a large-brimmed hat, wondered if her family's minds were beginning to be affected by the heat: Philadelphia did nothing all day but sigh, George spoke to no one, Nizel vanished for hours on end, while Thomas spent most of his time wearing far too many clothes and looking thoroughly miserable as a result. Furthermore, there was a strange atmosphere in the village itself, as if the attacks against the smuggling gang had thrown the local people into an ill humour.

Yet what had caused Lucy most consternation was a letter from Henrietta, mysteriously worded and begging Miss Baker to come to Glynde and see her. Lucy had duly arrived and had been quite shocked by what she found. A pale-faced Henrietta had whispered that her entire future relied on Miss Baker inviting her to stay at the palace for one final occasion before the grand ball, planned for September, which was to place Henrietta firmly on the marriage market. Lucy had been thoroughly embarrassed by the whole situation, especially as Mrs Trevor had looked far from pleased at the idea.

'But Miss Baker,' she had said, 'that would be Grace's fourth visit to Mayfield this year.'

Lucy had smiled, hoping that her consternation did not show. 'But two of the occasions were not planned, Mrs Trevor. One was when Henrietta stayed after the robbery, if you remember, and the other was to identify the villain. Before the summer is over and travelling becomes bad, it would give us all so much pleasure if you could agree to one more visit.'

Mrs Trevor had handed Lucy tea in a bone china cup. 'But I need her here to plan the ball, Miss Baker. I do not wish to be unhelpful nor, indeed, churlish, but I do rely on Henrietta so much since the death of my husband.'

Lucy had sighed. 'Yes, I sympathise. I became mother to my family before I had even entered my teens.'

Mrs Trevor's face had softened. 'And you are still at their head, Miss Baker, or so my daughter tells me.'

Lucy had sighed again. 'Yes. I do believe that there will be no chance to pursue my personal happiness until my father has died and my sister-in-law expects a child. She is very young for her age, you know, and between ourselves, Mrs Trevor, often behaves like a spoiled little girl.'

'Then the sooner she has a baby, the better.'

'I agree with you, but at the moment there seems absolutely no sign of it. I do believe she has a fear of the whole procedure.'

Mrs Trevor, who had given birth to Henrietta when she had been only nineteen, had made a disapproving noise. Then she had said, 'Miss Baker, I can see that you *do* lack amusing female company, and I have all my other daughters. I am being very selfish. If it would give pleasure to both you and Henrietta for her to stay, then I agree to a short visit.'

The victory had been won and two days later one of the Trevor coaches, followed by another full of luggage, had set off for Mayfield, and for the first time in weeks Henrietta had smiled. A secret message from Nicholas Grey had told her that Challice had returned and was once more lodging with Lizzie Pearce at Coggins Mill. At last she would be able to discuss the future with the father of her child.

Now she sat reading aloud to old Squire Baker who was, as usual, fast asleep, wishing that the hours would pass until it was dark, when it was the plan that she would slip quietly out after pretending to retire early, and go at once to where Challice lodged. She stopped reading at her thoughts and the old man promptly woke up, poking his neck forward like a tortoise in the sun.

'Go on, gel, go on,' he said.

'I'm sorry, Squire Baker. I thought you were asleep.'

'And so I was. But I can't sleep unless you read. That makes sense, don't it?'

'Perfect sense,' answered Henrietta, and gallantly continued to drone on until at last the call came to dine and she could go into the palace and change her gown before the repast.

Fortunately for such a hot day, Lucy had chosen lighter

foods, concentrating on locally caught fish and the more delicate meats and fowl. But even though the dishes were tempting, Henrietta found herself hardly able to eat, longing for the moment when the meal would be over and she could be reunited with Challice.

When finally she rose from the table, her plan to go in secret was thwarted by Thomas, who challenged her to a game of backgammon, declaring that she owed him the opportunity of getting his revenge and refusing to be denied. Reluctantly, Henrietta started to play, though it struck her that Thomas was more interested in conversing because he said, almost at once, 'Has it reached your ears at Glynde that one of the Jarvis brothers was caught?'

'No,' she answered, 'we are rather sheltered from the news there. What happened?'

'He was badly wounded and then captured. But when he was brought before the Horsham justice, Mr Lindfield, the magistrate found that John Rogers – the bounty hunter who arrested him – had no right to do so and promptly put Rogers in prison for making an unlawful arrest. Jarvis was placed in the charge of the constable but escaped, my dear Henrietta, disguised as a woman. La la la!'

He waved his lace handkerchief in the air while Henrietta looked astounded. 'But how is it they manage to get off so lightly?'

Thomas looked wise and laid his finger alongside his nose. 'Ah? Who knows?'

'Do you think the magistrates are being bribed by someone?'

Thomas looked noncommittal and raised one shoulder. He went on, 'But that is not all. Eight days later Rogers made another attempt, this time backed up by Lieutenant Jekyll and a party of Grenadiers. They surrounded an inn at West Chiltington – quite a haunt of Edward Jarvis these days – and captured five smugglers and thirty-four horses on their way to make a run.'

'And were they imprisoned this time?'

'On the contrary, my dear. It happened again. One man was committed but the Horsham magistrate released the rest for want of evidence. Want of evidence with the horses already equipped for carrying tubs!'

'It is beyond belief,' said Henrietta. She paused then added,

'Somebody in a very high place must be behind the Mayfield smugglers. Don't you think so, Thomas?'

'Indubitably. All gangs must have their financier – and their brains. I expect there is some rascal nearby laughing at us all.'

'Yes,' answered Henrietta slowly. 'I wouldn't be surprised if you are right.'

Dash left the palace by way of his personal tunnel and, walking swiftly though somewhat crouched, within a few minutes had emerged into the cellar of the Royal Oak. There, in the stables, his horse awaited him and, just as dusk fell on that late August day, he headed off through the woods on the long way round to Stream Farm.

It was a glorious evening, the sky the colour of wine and the air as warm and sweet as the taste of it. The jewel tones of the valley of Bivelham struck Dash afresh and, even though his business was urgent, he stopped for a moment to look at the purple hills, where they swept down to clover fields, and up again to the bright harsh emerald of the trees. The thread of the river was ruby in that dying light and soon, Dash thought, skeins of silver would lie over all, as darkness brought peace and silence to the sleeping landscape.

The candles of Stream Farm were already lit when he arrived, and the door was opened to him by Emmy, looking suspiciously as if she might be expecting a child. She smiled nervously and bobbed a curtsey, a little timid in the presence of Dash himself. He smiled at her.

'And how are you, my dear?'

'Well, Sir. Thank you, Sir. I'll call Kit.'

'Is Edward here?'

'Yes, Sir.'

'Then I would like to see him too.'

In response to Emily's shout, the brothers came in together and the strange likeness between them, some times more visible than others, struck Dash quite forcibly. Yet, he thought, Edward had changed in some intangible manner and wondered whether his recent wounding and capture had affected him. There was something softer about him, a sleepiness about his eyes that had not been there before. Dash noticed that he was wearing a diamond in one of his ears.

'Well,' he said without preamble, 'tell me everything.'

The brothers began to speak together and Dash motioned Edward to start first. It was perfectly obvious to all present, from that one gesture alone, who was the real leader of the Mayfield gang of free-traders.

'I went to stay at West Chiltington with friends and Rogers must have got on to it somehow, for during the night he surrounded the house and the next morning shot and arrested me.'

'And Mr Lindfield played his part?'

'As you made sure he would, Dash.'

The leader smiled and said, 'I hear you made your escape disguised as a woman, Edward.'

The smuggler coloured a little. 'My friend's sister Mary, who lives nearby, lent me some clothes.'

'And she also testified that Rogers had agreed to drop charges in return for a bribe?'

Kit spoke. 'Your plan to discredit Rogers and Jekyll is working superbly. You have excelled yourself, Dash.'

Dash cleared his throat and crossed one silk-clad knee over the other. 'But that won't last indefinitely, gentlemen. Mr Lindfield has already been reprimanded for letting you go free, Edward; he has also had a warning about releasing Francis Hammond and his cronies. Despite everything, I believe that if either of you are caught again you will be sent for trial.'

Kit said, 'Well, that hasn't happened yet,' but there was a note of uncertainty in his voice.

'You must be very careful,' Dash went on severely. 'I don't want either of you to do a run for a month, is that clear? Don't make the mistake – as I have told you so many times before – of underestimating Jekyll and Rogers, or the Jarretts either. It has become a matter of personal pride with all of them now to see you both dead or transported. So lie low, d'you hear?'

Shuffling their feet and looking gloomy, the Jarvises muttered agreement.

'And by the way, Edward,' said Dash, as he stood up to take his leave. 'No more visits to your little friend in West Chiltington for a while.'

Kit grinned. 'Oh come now, Dash. If Edward wants to visit Mary Dinnage secretly surely you won't stop him.'

'I am not referring to Mary,' said Dash coldly, framed in the doorway. 'I am speaking about her brother John. Good evening, gentlemen.'

He stepped outside but not before he had caught a glimpse of Kit turning to Edward with an expression like thunder upon his face.

As Dash left the palace by his own secret exit so Henrietta, too, stole out into the lengthening shadows and made her way on foot, not daring to attract attention by taking a horse, to the gates. Here she passed rapidly through and turning left hurried to the track known as Fletching Street. Nicholas had told her to wait for him in the private room of the alehouse called the Carpenter's Arms. Feeling both conspicuous and embarrassed beneath the landlord's knowing gaze, Henrietta hurried up the small back staircase and into the dingy room, where her relief on seeing Lieutenant Grey was so great that she hurried straight into his open arms.

Eventually Henrietta said, 'Is Challice coming here?' and Nicholas answered, 'No, he daren't risk being seen. There's a price on his head. I am to take you to him at Coggins Mill.'

'Is he lodging with Lizzie Pearce?'

Nicholas looked a little grim. 'Yes, but only because he cannot hazard going anywhere else.'

'I thought she was treacherous.'

'She is, but he has bribed her well enough to hold her tongue.'

'The sooner he is away from there the better.'

'And you are still certain you want to go with him, sweetheart?' said Nicholas, taking Henrietta in his arms again.

'How can you ask? You know I love him. Surely you would not come between us?'

Nicholas held her away from him. 'I could not do that. You see I love him too.'

In the stuffy little room beneath the eaves, Jacob Challice sat in the moonlight with Henrietta Trevor, and realised at last why they could never part, what it was that had drawn them together from the very start.

'Fate has been too strong for us,' he said. 'We can never escape each other.'

'Do you want to escape?' she answered quietly. 'Now that I am to bear your child?'

He drew her to him closely. 'I used the wrong word. I meant that our lives, our souls, are inextricably woven. We will always be together.'

'But what of Nicholas? He has also been with us. Are we to leave him now?'

'No, he is to stay with us. There will be no future for him now that he has helped a criminal to escape.'

'But where shall we go? What can we do?'

'We must make for Deal and pick up a ship bound for the American Colonies. They are anxious for settlers. We can start a new life there and the child can be born in peace and safety.'

Henrietta was silent and Challice kissed her gently. 'The idea frightens you, doesn't it?'

'No, I am not afraid. It is just the thought of saying goodbye to this forever. Of giving up Glynde Place and Sussex and lovely England for an unknown country.'

'But I will be with you – and Nicholas.'

'As you always have.'

They looked at each other and smiled and just for a moment seemed to see three boys laughing on the sands as their horses raced towards the sun.

'To the past,' said Henrietta, 'and all its wonderment.'

'To the future,' answered Jacob, 'and everything that lies ahead.'

The hammering on the door of Stream Farm during the hour before dawn sent a thrill of unease through Kit Jarvis as he lurched awake. There was something about this persistant banging that seemed to bode no good. Jumping out of bed and pulling on his breeches, he went downstairs. Then, as he snatched open the door, Kit realised what a fanciful fool he had been, for the figure that stood there was only that of a small boy, barefoot and ragged, and panting with exhaustion.

'What is it child?' he said. 'Where are you from?'

'Burwash, Sir,' gasped the urchin. 'I live in the cottage next to your mother. She's very ill, Mr Jarvis. You must come at once.'

'Christ's blood, I *knew* something was wrong.' He opened the door properly. 'You'd better come in while I dress and fetch my brother. What's the matter with her?'

'I don't know, Sir. But my Ma be afeared she might be dying.'

'God's wounds!' said Kit, shouting up the stairs, 'Emmy,

Ted, get up. Mother's ill and we must go to her now.' There was no response and he bellowed even louder, 'Wake up for the love of Heaven.'

There was the sound of plodding footsteps and a moment or two later Emily appeared, clad in her shift and yawning. 'What's amiss, Kit?'

'This boy has just ridden from Burwash. He says that Mother's dying. Get dressed, Emmy. I'll wake Ted.'

'He isn't there,' Emily answered flatly. 'I looked in his room on my way downstairs. His bed hasn't been slept in.'

'God's teeth,' swore Kit violently. 'So the little bastard's crept out. Can't keep away from his pretty flip-flap I suppose. I'll string him up.'

'Kit!' Emily shouted. 'Remember the child. Go and get dressed.'

She hurried up the stairs with Jarvis close behind her and ten minutes later they were mounted, the boy sitting in front of the smuggler, leaving the poor old nag who had carried him from Burwash to rest her bones.

The little convoy climbed the track beneath Wenbans and went on the high ridge towards Mayfield, passing through dense trees in order to do so. But no sooner had they emerged than the copse seemed to come to life. Branches were parted as narrowed eyes peered out, there was a glimpse of uniform and the jangle of spurs.

'Right lads,' said Lieutenant Jekyll. 'The bastard's going to walk right into it. The other route to Burwash – and quickly. If any lag behind, we'll meet in the wood behind old Mother Thomkins' house. Understood?'

There was a murmur of assent and Jekyll turned to Rogers with a grin. 'I think this time we've got him,' he said.

'By God, I hope you're right,' answered the other, as the cavalcade started off.

Nicholas Grey was ashamed of himself. He had been so utterly, totally, hopelessly inebriated that he had fallen down in the roadway and then vomited like a child, over and over again with no control. Then he had crawled away and slept beneath a tree until morning, his head spinning as he closed his eyes.

He had been reasonably drunk when he had escorted Henrietta back to the palace and helped her climb in through a downstairs window. But having left her and knowing that he had no further responsibilities that night, Nicholas had returned to the Carpenter's Arms and gone a little mad, pouring ale down his throat as if it were going out of supply.

He had never been more miserable in his life, loving two people so much that he could never bear to be parted from them, yet dreading the prospect that lay before him. He could just imagine his future as the permanent bachelor friend of their growing family, being called 'Uncle' by Henrietta's children, living close by, yet breaking his heart with loneliness every time he returned to the solitude of an empty house. Then, of course, would come the added torment of Henrietta trying to persuade him to marry some worthy young woman and start a family of his own, when all he would want would be to take his friend's wife into his arms, into his bed, into his life, and love her till he died.

The easy answer was, very simply, that he should let the lovers go and stay in England to face the consequences. For Nicholas felt quite convinced that Lieutenant Jekyll's cold crystal gaze would soon see through the fact that Lieutenant Grey had assisted a wanted criminal to escape, and place the miscreant on a charge. Then would come a trial, and imprisonment, or even transportation. Whatever decision he made, Nicholas had thought, gulping yet another pint of ale, the future looked bleak.

The drink had helped a little, blurring everything, making him jolly for half an hour. But then had come the shambling gait, the slurring words, the sickness, and finally the cramped and uncomfortable sleep beneath a tree, only to wake with a pounding head and fireballs for eyes. Watching the sky suddenly drench pink, Nicholas felt ready to weep again at a new day's dawning, wishing that he had been born as Henrietta's brother and that this cruel jealous situation had never arisen.

Suddenly tired of thinking about it all, Nicholas stood up and went to where his horse stood tethered outside the alehouse, its eyes closed in sleep.

'Come on, old friend,' he said. 'I must go back to Sharnden and tidy myself up. Will you take me?'

The horse woke up and whinnied knowingly, or so it seemed to its owner. Then moving very carefully so as not to strain his aching head, Nicholas mounted and set off at walking pace.

As always when a fine day was in store, the valley lay like a lake of mist, the tops of trees islands, the isolated branches spars of long-drowned ships. As Nicholas plunged down towards the hamlet of Coggins Mill, wondering if Jacob was up and about, the vapour closed all around him and, suddenly, he could see little more than a yard or two in front of him.

The smithy, when he came to it, gave him a shock, for he had not realised that he had wandered off the track. Yet he must have done so, for even though he was not native to the village he knew that there was no forge at the place he imagined himself to be. A smith was working within too, an odd-looking fellow dressed like a monk of long ago.

Nicholas hesitated, wondering whether to call a greeting or pass quietly by in the fog. But, as if he sensed a presence behind him, the smith turned abruptly and looked straight over to where the lieutenant stood. Nicholas saw brilliant, gleaming eyes that blazed a great wild anthem of light.

With a cry of terror, Nicholas hid his face in his hands, not daring to gaze any more at something so immense. When he lowered them again the forge had gone, vanished into the mist from whence it came. The lieutenant could not help himself- he wept. Not only with fear but also with the impact of the extraordinary vision at which he had been allowed for a moment to gaze.

The mists cleared, the sun came up, and through the burning heat of an afternoon in a dusty Sussex village, a raggle-taggle procession came riding. At its head, like conquering heroes returned from the war, came Lieutenant Jekyll and Revenue Man Rogers, behind them a troop of Grenadiers, in their midst a cart bearing one solitary prisoner, heavily manacled. Kit Jarvis was being brought back to his patch in the full shame of public humiliation.

As the cavalcade started the climb up Fletching Street and then down Mayfield's central course, windows opened and people ran out of their houses, dogs barked and babies cried and a great shout went up. 'It's Kit Jarvis, they've got Kit Jarvis.' But he just stood there with his head bowed, his wild blue eyes bent to the floor of the cart. The lawless hero of the people would not look at his subjects on the day he was brought back humbled.

They took him to the Barracks, the old house in Fir Toll

where the soldiers were stationed, gave him bread and water for his meal, and locked him in a room with Lieutenant Jekyll and three Grenadiers, who changed watch every hour. Kit was given straw to sleep on and a chamberpot for his relief, but he had to be assisted with that for, on Lieutenant Jekyll's strict instructions, not for one moment were the chains to be struck from his wrists.

It was a terrible kind of triumph and, hearing the commotion from the street just as the Baker family sat down to dine, the old squire sent a servant to find out what was afoot. The man returned with the extraordinary news that Kit was taken and the curmudgeon let out a bellow of triumph.

'So they've got him at last! Let's hope that this time those crooked Horsham magistrates will send him down.'

'Hush, Father...' started Lucy, only to be drowned by the old man letting out a series of prolonged war-whoops.

After that there was a moment of pandemonium, during which Thomas raised his glass and said in a loud voice, 'Here's to justice and the downfall of those who evade it. What say you all?'

George cried, 'Hear, hear,' and raised his glass, and Philadelphia giggled alarmingly as Nizel, better dressed than Henrietta had ever seen him before, downed his wine in a gulp. Lucy on the other hand did not drink, being too busy fussing over her father who had turned an extraordinary shade of purple. Henrietta, thinking she would be toasting the downfall of Jacob Challice, pretended to sip but really took no wine at all.

The meal subsided into more regular behaviour, George saying, 'Lindfield won't let Jarvis go this time. He was reprimanded over the last incident, you know.'

To this, Thomas answered, 'Lindfield is a law unto himself. He'll do what he thinks best.'

Going very red, Nizel put in, 'You mean what he's *told* best, surely?'

Violently nodding agreement to this last remark, old Squire Baker attempted to speak but choked on his mouthful of food and went an even more vivid shade.

'I do believe,' said Lucy, standing up, 'that Father should lie down and the ladies withdraw. Henrietta, Philadelphia, will you join me?'

So with the aid of two footmen she gallantly steered the

protesting old man away and there was a sudden silence. Into it George said firmly to the remaining servant, 'Port and chamberpots, please. I feel an urgent need of both.'

Mopping their brows almost simultaneously, his two brothers emphatically added their sentiments to his.

As soon as he decently could, Dash left the palace by his private route and took the horse that always awaited him at the Royal Oak. As he rode through the dusk in the direction of Snape Wood he muttered, 'If that bastard Ted Jarvis is not about I shall make it my personal business to shoot him. Kit has got to escape trial. There is too much at stake should he stand. The trouble with our free-trading friend is that he knows too much.'

His face took on a look of grim determination as he forded the stream that ran almost at the farm's foot, dismounted, and began banging upon the door in one movement, his fist crunching onto the wood as if the Devil himself were calling up one of his disciples.

'Jarvis, you bastard,' he shrieked. 'Where are you? Show yourself. Your brother's as good as hanged and I cannot get him free on my own. Unless you help me he is a dead man.'

The voice behind him made Dash wheel in fright. 'I'm here,' it said quietly.

Dash turned to see Edward standing by the stream, absolutely miserable. Tears ran down his cheeks and his shoulders heaved with sobbing.

'Christ's body, man,' Dash said impatiently. 'There's no need for that yet. Kit may be in danger but he's a long way from his box.'

'It's not that, it's not that,' answered the smuggler in muffled tones.

'Then I'll take a guess. You've been betrayed by your lover.'

'How did you know?'

'Because he's in the pay of Jekyll. I checked up on Dido after you were captured in his house. How much have you told him, Edward?'

'Nothing, nothing.'

A wiry hand shot out and grabbed Edward's wrist in a vice as Dash said, 'Know one thing Jarvis, if the Mayfield gang survives this catastrophe you will never work with them again. You are finished. We cannot afford those whose foolish talk between the sheets could endanger the lives of others. Now go to and let me in. There's work to be done if your brother is to fight another day.'

With a sob, Edward opened the door of Stream Farm and the two men went inside.

Lieutenant Jekyll sat at table in the Barracks, eating a late but excellent supper. Before he had left his post locked in with Kit Jarvis, he had seen to it personally that the smuggler was tied by ropes to a heavy oaken chair, and it had been first Jekyll, and then Rogers, who had personally checked that the great bolts on the door were all shot home. Only then did they feel safe in leaving their prisoner, to eat their first meal of the day.

To start with conversation had been sparse, as they fell like wolves upon ham, black pudding, sausages, pies and pickles. But now, generously imbibing a vintage port, Rogers said, 'And where is Mayfield's gallant Riding Officer, I ask? There has been no sign of him since the prisoner was brought in. What can the fellow be doing?'

Jekyll, in an unusually expansive and generous mood, answered urbanely, 'Be fair, Rogers. He was given the task of tracking down Jacob Challice. We specifically told him to leave the smugglers to us.'

'Nonetheless,' said Rogers truculently, 'on hearing that we had brought Jarvis in, the least he could do was call and offer congratulations.'

'Perhaps he is not in the village. He has probably followed Challice's trail to London.'

'Well I don't like it,' Rogers mumbled on, 'I think the fellow is lacking in devotion to duty, so I do.'

It was at this point that a corporal entered the room and said, 'Lieutenant Grey to see you, Sir,' and even before Jekyll's cry of 'Come in, come in,' had left his lips, Nicholas was standing in the doorway.

'So you're here!' said Rogers abruptly.

'Yes, as soon as I heard,' answered Grey, taking the seat to which Jekyll had waved him. 'Well done. He must have been a difficult fish to land.'

'And you,' Rogers went on unpleasantly. 'Was your quest concluded? Do you have Challice under arrest?'

'I'm afraid not, Sir. I followed him as far as the City and there his trail grew cold. It is my opinion that Challice has returned to Norfolk.'

'Really?' said Rogers caustically. 'How interesting!'

Grey lost colour and Jekyll thought how ill he looked, strained and not at all the handsome sensitive man he had been when first they met.

'You seem exhausted,' he said, half wondering at himself that he was being so kind. 'I suggest you go home and have a good night's sleep, for tomorrow we shall need your help.'

'Tomorrow?' Grey repeated blankly.

'We are taking Jarvis to Horsham under armed guard. We must have every outrider we can get. It is my opinion that the smugglers, under the leadership of young Edward, will try to rescue him.'

'What do you want me to do?'

'Be here at daybreak. We shall ride then.' Jekyll's tone altered and, briefly, Nicholas had a sense of sympathy with him. 'We *must* get him this time. He has cocked a snoot at all of us for so long. Surely it is the time for the tide to turn.'

'I will do all I can to help,' said Grey, his mobile features haggard. 'Would you prefer that I spent the night here in order to be on call?'

Jekyll paused – and fate hung in the balance for a moment. Then he said, 'No, there's little room and you look as if you need some rest. But be here early. I want Jarvis safely behind bars before the heat of the day comes up.'

Lieutenant Grey stood up, and once again Jekyll thought he looked fit to drop. 'Go on, lad. Go on,' he said gruffly. 'We'll see you at first light. Don't be late.'

Nicholas gave a fleeting smile and left the room, pausing only to put on his cloak before he stepped out into a night that had, at last, grown mercifully cool.

'How much more,' he thought, 'must I endure of this charade?'

The sudden sound of cartwheels coming towards him, faint yet somehow persistent, sent Nicholas scurrying into the shadow of a vast horsechestnut-tree. Afterwards he knew that it was providence that made him hide there like a conspirator, watching as the cart halted before the door of the Barracks and a woman slowly climbed out.

The light from the lantern hanging outside the door fell fully on her face, and Nicholas gasped silently. It was Lizzie Pearce, in her hand one of the posters offering a reward for information leading to the capture of Jacob Challice, dead or alive.

The highwayman lay half awake, lying on his back, his hands beneath his head, looking at all the countless stars beyond the thatch above him.

'On the day after tomorrow,' he thought, 'all this unendurable waiting will be over and it will be safe to leave. If only it could be tonight – and Henrietta and Nicholas were with me.'

He slept a little, dreaming that he wandered in the ruined cottage by the pond beneath Bainden, finding a ring there that had once belonged to Marcus Flaviel. Then a distant thudding brought Jacob back to consciousness, and hurrying down through the heart of Lizzie's silent and empty home, he realised the banging was on her front door and cautiously went to stand behind it.

'Who's there?' he called softly, only to hear Nicholas say, 'Jacob, for God's sake let me in. There isn't a moment to lose. Lizzie has been to see Jekyll.'

Challice heaved at the locks, shooting them fast again as his friend, gasping and perspiring, stepped inside.

'What has happened? Tell me of it.'

'I was leaving the Barracks and saw Lizzie Pearce as she arrived. She had a reward poster in her hand. She will betray both of us, Jacob – and probably Henrietta as well. You must leave here immediately.' He paused, and then added a little more slowly, 'I will bring Henrietta to you tomorrow. Then you must both make at once for Deal.'

'But what about you?' said Jacob, taking his friend by the arm. 'What do you intend to do?'

'Lie low somewhere near here. Jekyll and Rogers are bound to come looking for you. It is my intention to draw them away, set a false trail. You and Henrietta must have time at least to get to Rye. Then you can pick up a boat – any boat, fisherman's, smuggler's – and go round the coast.'

'But when will you join us?'

'As soon as I can. You can be assured of that, Jacob.'

They embraced each other silently, kissing one another upon the cheek. Then they proceeded to more mundane things, hurriedly packing up Jacob's few clothes, hiding his worldly goods and money within his saddlebags, and checking that no clues as to his being there were left in that hot and stifling little room.

'Where shall I hide tonight?' said Jacob, as at last they left the cottage and rode through a vast and enigmatical night.

'In that ruined cottage beneath Bainden. Do you know it?'

'Know it? I've just dreamed of it.'

'Then perhaps it is an omen. Go there, Jacob, and tomorrow I will bring Henrietta to you.'

The highwayman wheeled his horse to look at his friend beneath the canopy of stars. 'Come to us soon, Nicholas,' he said. 'None of us will ever get very far without the other two.'

Nicholas smiled in the starlight. 'I'll come to you whatever happens.' Then he wheeled his horse. 'Till death – and beyond,' he said, and then galloped away into the darkness.

Jekyll started his journey to Horsham as soon as it was light enough for the men to see their way. There was no question of waiting for Grey to join them now that Lizzie Pearce had told him the truth; in fact the great dilemma that he and John Rogers faced was what to do next. Should they get their prisoner to Horsham and return to arrest Challice and the lieutenant, or should they keep Jarvis in the Barracks and make sure of capturing the other two? In the end, with the fear of a rescue bid at hand, they decided to get Jarvis into the county gaol as quickly as possible and return for the others immediately Kit was under lock and key.

It was a misty morning, yet in the pale light blue of the sky a milky moon could still be glimpsed, while its brother sun was already a fierce golden ball proclaiming yet another glorious day.

The procession rode as before, the cart bearing the manacled Kit still in its midst. This morning, however, Jekyll had taken the precaution of placing two extra men in with him, heavily armed and with orders to shoot the smuggler if they came under fierce attack. And to boost the contingent to full strength, the Jarretts, carrying with them warrants issued by Justices of the Peace, rode beside Rogers at the head.

The party passed easily through Mayfield and out on to the Horsham road, but it was as they were nearing Cross in Hand that Jekyll suddenly stiffened. He was certain that behind them, muffled by the sound of their own horses' feet, had come the pounding of hooves.

'Halt, and prepare to defend yourselves,' he called.

They closed ranks tightly just as four men – a pitiful little number ranged against that large and well-armed party – came out of the trees. Despite their masks, Edward Jarvis was immediately recognisable by his diamond earring. He seemed almost hell-bent on suicide for he headed straight for Jarrett, shouting wildly as he came.

'Open fire,' shouted Jekyll, drawing his own weapon and taking aim at a heavily masked man wearing a dark cloak. There was a return burst but the lieutenant saw that he had drawn blood, for the man gave a cry of pain and dropped his pistol.

From the cart, Kit had started to shout. 'It's hopeless Ted. You're outnumbered. Withdraw. There's no point in us all getting killed.'

'I can't leave you,' came the frantic reply.

For a second there was something of the old gleam in the smuggler's wild blue eyes. 'I'm not done for yet. There's a long way to go before I dance on the rope. Now be off, while you've still the chance.'

'After 'em lads,' shouted Jekyll as the four rescuers wheeled round and headed back into the protection of the trees. 'Let's catch all the bastards if we can.'

Kit laughed disconcertingly. 'That you'll never do, Lieutenant Jekyll. The day won't come when the Jarvis brothers give in. You'll be hearing a great deal more about us, mark what I say.'

'Fine words from a cock sparrow,' answered the lieutenant, starting his party on the move again. 'Let's hear your song when you nest in Horsham Gaol.'

'Aye, you'll hear it,' said Kit. 'You'll hear it well – until the bird finally decides to fly.'

At ten o'clock the breakfast gong sounded in the palace and the various members of the family appeared to congregate in the breakfast room, with its small tables and posies of freshly picked flowers and golden early sun. George and Philadelphia, who had taken a leisurely stroll in the grounds, were the first to arrive, followed by Thomas, superbly dressed and wearing the very latest style of cravat. Lucy bustled in from interviewing a new housekeeper, and old Squire Baker came in on the arm of a servant, ready for another day of argument.

They took their seats, and coffee and tea with thick rich cream were brought in. Noticing that there were two people absent – Henrietta and Nizel – Lucy delayed the serving of food, only permitting the toast to be fetched.

'Henrietta has gone riding, I take it?' she said.

Philadelphia giggled wildly. 'I think she is having an affair of the heart, Lucy.' Despite George's efforts to hush her, she persisted. 'As George and I took a turn round the lake this morning we saw her meet Lieutenant Grey. They went off together. It is very romantic, isn't it?'

'No,' said Lucy, 'it is very unsuitable. Oh dear, oh dear.'

All their heads turned hopefully as the door opened but it was only Nizel, badly out of breath and sweating profusely. Mumbling an apology he took his place at the table.

Lucy turned to him rather crossly. 'Where have you been to get into such a state? You are not fit to sit at table with civilised folk.'

He went crimson. 'I was miles away painting when I heard the gong. I had to run to get here in time.'

He went to pick up his knife and Lucy saw him wince in pain.

'What is the matter with you, Nizel?' she went on. 'You are not entirely yourself this morning.'

'I cut my hand while I was out.'

'Well, I shall dress it for you after breakfast. Unless it is very bad, in which case I shall see to it now.'

'Oh no,' said Nizel. 'It's only a flesh wound. It can wait.'

He picked up his cup with shaking fingers and all the family watched in horror as drops of red blood spilled onto the crisp white tablecloth.

'Oh Nizel!' said Lucy. 'Whatever have you been up to?'

He smiled embarrassedly. 'Nothing out of the ordinary,' he answered. 'I can truly say it was nothing out of the ordinary at all.'

As they came to the track that led down from Bainden to the little lake with the ruined cottage beside it, Nicholas drew to a halt, and Henrietta reined in as well.

441

'Why are you stopping?' she said.

'Because I'm going to leave you here.'

'You're not coming down to say farewell to Jacob?'

'I took my leave of him last night. And beside, dearest Henrietta, I would rather say goodbye to you while we are alone. Will you dismount for a moment?'

'Of course.'

He slipped from the saddle and held his arms up for her and she slid into them and remained there, putting her hands behind his neck and drawing him close.

'Why don't you come with us now?' she said. 'I am sure it is dangerous for you to remain.'

'Not really. I shall lead Jekyll and Rogers off on a wild goose chase and then, when I have lost them, make straight for Deal. It will give you the head start you need, Henrietta.'

'But you might miss the ship.'

'Then I shall follow on the next. I'll find you wherever you are.'

'But the American Colonies are vast.'

'Jacob said he would make for Virginia, so I shall also.'

'I don't like it, my darling. I do not think the three of us should separate.'

'I love you so much that I could never leave you, you must believe that.'

They embraced, exchanging a kiss that said everything, letting the other know how deeply they felt.

'If only I had been your lover,' said Nicholas, as they drew apart.

Henrietta smiled. 'Perhaps you once were but we can no longer remember.'

'Perhaps. Now go to Jacob. I shall watch to see you meet him safely.'

He lifted her into the saddle again and once more Henrietta bent to kiss him. 'You will never leave us, will you?' she said.

'Never,' came the whispered reply, as she galloped away.

At the time when they would normally have sat down to dine, Lieutenant Jekyll and John Rogers had the enormous satisfaction of seeing the gates of Horsham Gaol swing to behind the departing figure of Kit Jarvis.

'Got 'im,' said Rogers, rubbing his hands.

'Got him indeed. But there's more work ahead. I suggest we leave at once for Mayfield.'

'Perhaps the birds have already flown the nest.'

'I doubt it. With a price on his head Challice would be very wary of travelling by daylight. I think they'll make a run for it by night.'

Rogers pulled at his bottom lip reflectively. 'What do you reckon to that story of Mother Pearce's that they've got a woman with them?'

'I don't know. She seemed emphatic that a doxie called on Challice a night or two ago, and that Grey knew her. Rum, isn't it?'

'Rum as hell,' answered Rogers. 'But I'll say one thing.'

'What's that?'

'If they've got a woman in tow it will slow them down.'

Grinning at one another, the bounty hunters mounted their horses. 'Straight to Coggins Mill?' asked Rogers. 'Or do we go to the Barracks first?'

'Straight to Coggins Mill. We'll surround the house as we did with young Jarvis – but this time we shoot to kill.'

'You think we should finish Challice off?'

'The reward said dead or alive, my dear John. No further comment is necessary I would have thought.'

Jekyll turned to the weary troop of Grenadiers. 'All right lads, this is the final push. Two more villains to get into the net – and then it's leave for the lot of you.'

There was a feeble cheer as the little cavalcade took off.

'And what about Grey?' asked Rogers, as he rode. 'You're not going to kill him as well?'

'And get myself into trouble? Indeed no. No, it will be far more fun to see him sent for court martial and transportation.'

The relentlessly burnished day reached its peak, and by the time the party reached Five Ashes was past its best, the fading light seeming overblown and rather inclined to dust.

It was then that Jekyll announced that he had changed his mind, that they would go to the Barracks and pick up reinforcements to hide on the banks above the smugglers' road. Accordingly the group broke left to Fir Toll and, by the time the other dragoons had joined them, the day grew cold and dull as the light began finally to die.

It was a very strange evening, Jekyll thought, for, as if the villagers knew there was something afoot, nobody stirred along the central thoroughfare. He had never seen Mayfield quite so quiet or quite so deserted and, as the posse turned down Fletching Street, the feeling was endorsed. Not a soul moved anywhere.

They turned left to Coggins Mill and Jekyll saw his first glimpse of life. A pure white cat with eyes of vivid blue sat in the middle of the track, washing its face with a long skinny paw. It turned to look at them as the group approached, then got up and walked disdainfully away.

Going down the hill, Jekyll raised his hand to bring his party to a halt.

'This is where we split up,' he said. 'I shall go down the smugglers' road with Mr Rogers. I want six of you lads to surround the house, and the rest of you fan out along the track and the smugglers' way. Keep yourselves well hidden. If Challice fires at any of you, shoot to kill. If Lieutenant Grey does likewise, only wound. Jenkins, you can call them out.'

The Grenadier saluted. 'Very good, Sir.'

'Now into your positions – and quietly.'

As he headed up the free traders' secret pathway, Jekyll found that his heart had begun to quicken with excitement. He was sure that tonight would see Challice finished, that evil would be stamped out. Much to his astonishment he found that he had started to pray that all would go well and that his fervent attention to duty would be rewarded. Still in this strangely elated mood, he crouched amongst the trees that lined the road.

There was a massive silence, not a breath of wind stirring the trees and the night creatures quiet in their lairs. It was almost frightening when Rogers gave a muffled cough and Jekyll furiously whispered, 'Shush.'

Then they heard it. The pounding of hooves in the distance.

'He's coming!' said Jekyll, cocking his pistol in readiness.

He saw Challice from a long way off, recognised his dark coat and feathered hat as the highwayman approached, lying low in the saddle to avoid the trees. From his position on the slope above him, Jekyll took aim and put his finger to the trigger. A million thoughts raced in his brain: that right would be done; that the sacrifice of a life in order to bring safety to others was more than justified; that he, Jekyll, was an instrument of the Lord.

He fired and Challice fell like a stone, his horse careering on in fright up the hill. With a wild shout, Jekyll and Rogers ran down the slope to where the body lay, face down.

'Turn him over,' said Rogers. 'He may not be dead.'

Jekyll paused, a curious sensation coming over him, a feeling that something had gone terribly wrong. He moved the body over and looked down at the corpse which lay, dead as a dog, in a pool of blood. He saw Nicholas Grey's mobile features look up at him, the pewter-coloured eyes still wide and staring, the mouth open to release a small trickle of blood. Then that face seemed to vanish and for a second Jekyll thought a little simpleton lay dead, a half-wit that once he had loved and cherished.

'May God forgive me,' he said. 'I have killed my brother.'

Rogers looked at him astounded. 'What?'

Jekyll shook his head, collecting himself. 'I'm sorry. It was the shock. I lost my wits for a moment. We've killed Grey not Challice.'

'No,' said Rogers firmly. '*We* did not kill him, *you* did, Lieutenant Jekyll. And so I shall bear witness when it comes to the enquiry.'

With the corpse still gazing up at him, the lieutenant found that he could do nothing but make the sign of the cross.

EPILOGUE

They stood at the ship's rail and watched the coast of England become a mere fine line in that leaping, rolling, luminous ocean that was all that lay between Henrietta and Jacob and the rest of their lives together.

They had sailed with the tide and seen the sweet, clean wind pick up the sails and billow them out to greet the white clouds that escorted the little ship from the harbour. They had laughed at that and then they had cried because Nicholas had not come running up the gangplank at the very last minute as they had thought he would.

'He didn't come,' Henrietta had said. 'Oh Jacob, he didn't come.'

'But he will, my darling. He gave us his promise. Do you remember?'

'But suppose something has happened to him?'

'He will still come to us,' Jacob had answered firmly.

Now England was rapidly vanishing and there was nothing but the mighty ocean and the thought of the bustling American Colonies that lay on the other side to cheer the couple, who suddenly seemed small and vulnerable as they stood side by side, watching their homeland disappear for ever.

But then, without warning, Henrietta gave a cry and put her hand to her body. 'It moved, Jacob. I felt my baby move. It is alive.'

He looked at her questioningly. 'I wonder what makes it do that? What it is that suddenly breathes life, so that the child is nothing one minute and a person the next.'

'Perhaps a soul has just entered in.'

'Perhaps.'

They turned to go below, out of the wind that was now blowing fresh and cold about them.

'Will we ever see Nicholas again?' said Henrietta sadly.

'He gave a promise and it is one that he will not break. We will see him.'

'I hope so,' answered Henrietta – and in her womb the baby danced for joy.

447

HISTORICAL NOTE

This book is a combination of fact and fiction but the principal events are mainly true. John de Stratford certainly spent time at Mayfield Palace and died there and his involvement in the abdication of Edward II and subsequent raising up of the boy king, Edward III, are matters of recorded fact. However, the existence of his half-wit younger brother is a matter of speculation.

Robert Morley's affair with Debora Weston is imaginary but what *is* true is that Robert married late – in 1614 when he was thirty-seven. His bride was Susanna, daughter and heiress of Thomas Hodgson of Framfield. Robert became an MP, sitting in the Parliaments of 1620 and 1623–4 as member for Bramber and in 1627–8 as member for Shoreham. Before his death in 1632 he was appointed Sheriff for both Surrey and Sussex. He had six children by Susanna and his heir Harbert, aged sixteen at the time of his father's death, became a royal ward but later joined the Parliamentarians during the Civil War.

Tom May also joined the Parliamentarians after his disappointment at not being named Poet Laureate on the death of Ben Johnson. Tom was strangled to death by the strings of his own nightcap after 'going well to bed'. There is recorded evidence of his keeping 'beastly company' but none of his ever having married. His secret liaison with Agnes is, therefore, a matter of conjecture.

The two indictments against Alice Casselowe, Witch of Mayfield, read as follows: 'Alice Casselowe of Mayfilde, spinster, on 6 June, 18 Elizabeth, at Mayfilde, bewitched to death 1 ox valued at £4 of the goods and chattels of Magin Fowle, gentleman. Endorsed. *Billa vera.*' And 'On 1 June, 18 Elizabeth, at Mayfilde, bewitched to death 2 pigs valued at 10s. of the goods and chattels of Richard Roose. Endorsed. *Billa vera.*'

That Alice Casselowe died in Horsham Gaol before her sentence was served is recorded as follows: 'Memoranda. She died in prison as appears by Coroner's inquisition taken in Easter term, 19 Elizabeth.'

That her great-niece followed Alice into the pursuit of the black arts is supposition only.

The career of Gabriel Tomkins, alias Kit Jarvis, is so extraordinary that he merits a book to himself. In comparison with Kit, Dick Turpin pales into insignificance. Though his arrest by Rogers and Jekyll in 1721 led to the end of the Mayfield gang, Kit himself was a long way from finished. He escaped from Horsham Gaol by bribing the gaoler but was recaptured and transferred to London to avoid both a rescue attempt and an acquittal by a Sussex jury. He stood trial in the Court of Kings Bench on 27th October 1721, and was sentenced to seven years transportation for assault on officers of the Customs. However, Kit bargained, and in return for information his sentence of transportation was postponed. Edward, too, was caught and sentenced but managed to get himself transferred back to gaol in Sussex from the Fleet Prison. By 1724 both brothers were free again.

By 1729 Kit was once more involved in smuggling in Sussex and continued to operate until the 1730s when he was captured. Those returning from transportation before serving their full sentence – though there is considerable doubt that Kit was ever transported at all! – risked hanging. The resourceful Jarvis therefore gave evidence to the Parliamentary Select Committee on smuggling and as a reward was appointed a Riding Officer! In 1736 he was promoted to the rank of Surveyor at Dartford and was also taken on as a bailiff by the Sheriff of Sussex.

However, Kit found it almost impossible to remain law-abiding and after innumerable adventures was dismissed from the Customs service in 1740. He went to live in St Giles in the Field, in London, stealing away from Dartford in the still of the night.

The next sighting of Kit was as a highwayman when he held up the Chester stage in 1746 but soon he was back at Rye working once more with the Hawkhurst gang. But it was as a highwayman that this extraordinary character finally met his end. Caught at last, he was sent to Bedford and was tried at the assizes for highway robbery. It was there that he kept his final appointment with the hangman.

The involvement of a member of the Baker family with the Mayfield gang is pure surmise based on one or two historical clues. Firstly, the odd positioning of the blocked-up tunnel entrances in the cellars of the Middle House and the Royal Oak, all seeming to lead to the palace; secondly, the fact that the Horsham magistrate was obviously bribed by someone of power; thirdly, that it would have been impossible for Mayfield's leading family to, at the very least, have been unaware of all that went on during the dark hours in that amazing Sussex village.

The love affair of Lucy Baker and John Langham finally drew to a happy conclusion. In 1723 old Squire Baker finally died at the age of eighty, leaving the lovers free to marry at last. This they did in 1725 when Philadelphia was expecting her first child and Lucy could finally consider that her duty had been done. Philadelphia had six children in all and died comparatively young in 1741. George, older than she, outlived her by fifteen years.

Grace Henrietta, eldest of the nine Miss Trevors, is still something of a mystery, though her death is recorded in 1797, which means that she would have reached the amazing age of ninety-four. Whether she sailed for the American Colonies is a matter of surmise and even her descendants do not know the full truth.

Of all the people in this story there is one who is still to be seen in Mayfield. Jacob Challice – or is it Nicholas Grey? – haunts Pennybridge to this day and was sighted as recently as 1986. The ghost is known as the Highwayman of Pennybridge and has become part of Mayfield's folklore.

BIBLIOGRAPHY

Mayfield, the Story of an Old Wealden Village, E.M. Bell-Irving;
Edward II, Caroline Bingham;
Witch Hunting and Witch Trials, C. l'Estrange Ewen;
Medicine – An International History, Paul Hastings;
The Later Middle Ages, George Holmes;
Edward III, Paul Johnson;
English Landed Society in the 18th Century, G.E. Mingay;
Gabriel Tomkins, Paul Muskett;
Smuggling in Kent and Sussex 1700–1840, Mary Waugh.